BLOWOUT!

THOMAS N. SCORTIA
FRANK M. ROBINSON

BLOWOUT!

Franklin Watts 1987 New York Toronto

Library of Congress Cataloging-in-Publication Data

Scortia, Thomas N., 1926–
Blowout!
I. Robinson, Frank M.   II. Title.
PS3569.C587B5   1987   813'.54   86-28970
ISBN 0-531-15030-5

Few books are written without the aid and assistance of those kind enough to contribute their knowledge, their physical help, and most of all, their patience. The authors are indebted to the following for all of the above:

Nicholas J. J. Scortia
Professor Sidney Coleman, Harvard University
Professor Paul Horowitz, Harvard University
Dennis and Vivian Callanan

And especially Maude Curry Kirk, who turned out, to our surprise and delight, to be one of the best line editors in the business.

As always, our errors are our own and do not reflect upon the wisdom and knowledge of those from whom we sought help.

Thomas N. Scortia, Frank M. Robinson

PROLOGUE

He paused before the entrance to the man cage that would carry him down two hundred feet into the depths of the cut and the long tunnel that stretched under the East River. He shivered and took a firmer grip on the clipboard with the maintenance check-off, feeling a fresh sense of foreboding. Fat snowflakes settled slowly onto the collar of his mackinaw and crept into the warm place between the back of his neck and the thick fur. He ignored the wet chill of the melting snow and once again went over the check-off list in his mind.

Why hadn't somebody caught it before now? And why had the report been hidden in the first place? It was a matter of dollars and cents—and lives. So many of the first to guarantee the safety of so many of the second. . . .

From far below he could hear the refrains of a Christmas carol on the intercom of the dig along with the occasional shouts of workmen. The shift had been pared to a holding group, but there were still sixty men in the cut. Merry Christmas, he thought, momentarily forgetting his fears. It was Christmas Eve—just three days past his birthday. Their birthday.

He tugged the mackinaw tighter around his neck. The day before, a cold front had moved in from the northwest, leaving a heavy deposit of snow and sleet along its icy border. The TV news said Rochester had been hit with two feet of snow and Watertown, first deluged with sleet and then smothered with snow, had declared an emergency. Now the front had arrived at the city, and temperatures had plummeted. New Yorkers, usually phlegmatic to the end, were scurrying from one brightly lit shop to another, ringing up season-end totals of dizzying proportions.

He shrugged at the thought of the last-minute shopping confusion. Ever since the orphanage, each Christmas he had given

(1

Brad something special. This year, he had saved for months for Brad's gift. But then, they were more than just brothers, had been for many years. They never talked about it, and he was quite sure nobody questioned two brothers living together.

He smiled, anticipating the look on Brad's face when he saw the new VCR and camera Christmas morning. Brad would try and top it, of course. He always did. His smile widened, then faded when he remembered what he had discovered in the office that morning.

He pulled the wooden gate of the cage down behind him and hit the switch. The platform moved slowly into the depths of the cut, the winch above muttering with a well-oiled smoothness. He watched the raw walls of the vertical shaft move past, their pitted surfaces highlighted by the unshaded bulbs strung along them. He was getting more nervous now, afraid his inspection would only confirm what he already suspected.

A distant mechanical murmur grew in intensity as he descended. He knew the sound—the growl of the electric motor that drove the huge pumps delivering compressed air to the head of the cut. Sealed by an elaborate pressure head, air at three atmospheres braced the forward end of the cut and held back the tons of water overhead while the digging crew pushed steadily forward.

He caught his breath. Had he detected a dragging hesitation as the compressor recycled?

The cage bottomed roughly. The gate squeaked as it rose, sticking at one point. He swore to himself, remembering the Project Office had shifted four men from the maintenance crew just this past week. Foolish move. The cut was behind schedule and moving into the penalty period. They had to have enough men to fill the shifts during the holidays. But instead of hiring more, the company had taken them from maintenance. . . .

He stepped from the cage and walked rapidly toward the nearby motor corral that held the little electric cars, each scarcely more than a stripped-down golf cart. He chose one, grasped its tiller, and started at full speed toward the sound of the laboring compressor. He was acutely aware of the massive cast-iron shields, welded together to form the main support of the tunnel.

(2

They curved over his path like so many red-tinged ribs, turning the tunnel into what looked like the gullet of some prehistoric beast. The image came to him then—Jonah and the whale.

Not all of it looked like that. The masonry crews had been at work and in places moisture-discolored cement cloaked the rusting ribs of the monster. A few more days, and it would all be gray concrete.

He hadn't gone more than fifty feet before he cut the motor to listen. Had there been a change in the sound of the compressor motor? Like most high-ballers, he had developed a sensitivity to the sounds of the equipment around him and the faint groans and trills from the earth above.

He shivered again, as if somebody were scraping a piece of chalk across a blackboard. The sound was high-pitched, almost beyond audibility, but he could sense it in the mastoid bone behind his ear. Was it the hundreds of tons of rock and mud shifting, sliding past each other and generating an inaudible shriek? Or did it come from some friction point in an engine rotor? He listened intently, feeling a growing sense of unease.

He started the car again, steering parallel to the narrow gauge rails that ran the length of the tunnel. He pulled aside once as the muck train labored past him, its engine pulling a string of cars, each loaded with rock, mud, and sand from the forward head of the cut.

His little electric car moved quickly over the smooth section of the floor, which had been poured and cured only four days before. He drove from one bright pool of light to another, darting through the menacing shadows between. All the while his sense of dread increased as he thought about the maintenance clipboard tucked under his arm. What was the old poem? For want of a nail?

The noise of the compressor grew as he approached. It was a large double-cylinder machine, its grease-encrusted surface lit by unshaded bulbs swinging in the stream of air from a nearby ventilation duct. He cut the engine of his car and listened carefully for any irregularity in the sound of the compressor motor. Nothing, just a solid, steady hum. But something was wrong, he could sense it. . . .

"Hi, Chief—Merry Christmas."

He squinted at the man who had appeared from around the far side of the compressor. Probably sneaking a drink from a pint he had smuggled into the cut. He ignored the greeting.

"Anything wrong with the compressor, Simmons?"

"Not that I know of—sounds smooth as silk to me."

"I thought I heard a bearing noise as I drove up."

Simmons looked blank. "Probably the bearings of your car—they don't do a good job of maintaining these bugs. Compressor sounds okay, though."

"Hell it does," he grunted. He started the car again and then, a hundred feet farther into the cut, killed the electric motor once again to listen. He wiped his face as a drop of condensation from one of the ribs above spattered on his hard hat and ran down the brim to drip on his cheek. There wasn't anything obviously wrong, yet the sense of foreboding wouldn't go away.

He glanced up, studying the shadowy metal plates with their enormous ribs that arched above him. Just beyond were tons of rock and mud and finally the river itself, more tons of black, dirty water surging toward the ocean.

He started the car again, moments later arriving at the massive dam and airlock that blocked the head of the cut. Two cast-iron shields had recently been hauled into place, but they hadn't yet been riveted together. Water and wet sand slowly oozed from their seams. The dam itself was a great, braced metal structure that filled the cut from edge to edge. The narrow gauge rails for the muck trains ran through a materials airlock in the face of the dam, entering the dig area where muck crews loaded the trains with mud and rock spoil.

Progress was slow and dangerous because of the pressure overhead and the unexpected pockets of sand. Past the dam, the tunnel walls were supported by compressed air as well as being buttressed with wood and metal. A personnel airlock in the face of the dam held six men and opened in turn to a decompression chamber that seated twelve. The nitrogen dissolved in a man's blood had to be released slowly and pass through their lungs. Reduce the pressure suddenly, and the nitrogen reappeared as bubbles in the blood, resulting in the deadly bloody froth of "the bends."

From behind him now came the sound of voices, mingled with the soft whine of several electric cars. The new shift. He glanced at his watch—ten minutes to midnight, ten minutes to Christmas. The voices of the men echoed in the hollow depths of the cut, ringing metallically from the arched shields overhead. He suspected most of the men were a little drunk and considered sending back the worst offenders.

Then he shrugged again. The men realized how dangerous it was to be drunk under three atmospheres. And if he sent back those who'd had a drink or two, he'd probably be relieving the whole shift. But he couldn't help being concerned about them; it was something that was built in. He adjusted the position of the clipboard under his arm. Too bad everybody hadn't been just as concerned. But even the chief engineer would have to back him up once he saw what junk the company had been buying to protect their men. Once he told—

He didn't finish the thought. The screaming, whooping sound of a Klaxon suddenly filled the cut. The disaster alarm! Its whooping continued and climbed in pitch as it echoed from the walls farther down the tunnel. Then, behind it, he heard the rushing sound of mud and water falling from a height. He knew instantly what it meant.

"Blowout!"

A dozen men took up the cry, and he leaped from the seat of the electric car and ran toward the airlock in the dam. He shoved the operator on duty aside and hit the keys that would open the outer door.

"Hey, Chief, stop!"

The operator grabbed him by the arms and pulled him back. Through the thick glass ports of the airlock, he saw a boiling mass of water, frothy with sand and mud, cascading down over the ports on the far side of the lock, blotting out his vision.

"The men!" he screamed, and knocked the operator away again, clutching at the outer door of the lock. Two more workmen grabbed his arms and pulled him back. He struggled, dimly conscious of the Klaxon and the distant roar of voices. He broke *free and aimed a wild punch at one of the men, felt his fist connect and saw the man sprawl backward. He turned back to the door and hit the "open" key. The massive outer door moved inward on silent electric motors. He darted through, leaping for the wall that separated the lock from the raging torrent in the cut.*

He pressed his face to the glass of the inner port. Through the water pouring from the blowout in the roof of the cut, he saw the dark bodies of men struggling against the torrent. He watched in horror as the deluge knocked one man to his knees. His body disappeared under the rising water. Other men in the digging crew struggled against the flood, desperately trying to reach the airlock.

His hand jerked for the electric switch that would open the inner door. Maybe he could get the men through the door before the cut completely filled with water. . . .

Before he could push the switch, somebody yanked his hand away. Men jammed into the airlock behind him, trying to pull him back to safety behind the dam. He broke free and struggled back to the port.

The head of the cut was filled with a raging spume of water and earth and sand. The men were no longer visible. He pressed his face against the cold glass of the port, trying vainly to make out details in the tumbling water. He could see struggling black masses, and once again he tried frantically to open the locked door. It never occurred to him what might happen if he succeeded.

Before the men pulled him back for the last time, he managed once again to jam his face against the port. A dark shape drifted toward the glass, its limbs lax and lifeless. He started screaming as he was pulled back through the outer lock. He managed to turn for a final look just before the electric motors closed the lock forever.

The last thing he saw was a white, wide-eyed face looking out at him through the port. In spite of the dirty water swirling about it, every detail of the face etched itself in his memory.

The distorted face of the dead man staring at him through the port was his own.

CHAPTER 1

The terminal was almost deserted, most of the ticket counters and baggage check-ins abandoned. The restaurant had been closed long ago, though a small, mobile coffee bar was in operation by the one United counter still in service. The rows of plastic chairs in the boarding lounge were empty, facing huge, rain-streaked windows that looked out on a landing pad with three old 767's sitting on it and an ancient 747 parked outside a distant hangar. An Army troop carrier was deployed nearby, and Nordlund guessed that security guards were going over the plane with bomb detectors and dogs to sniff out plastic explosives.

Washington National Airport was almost closed down, and Dulles might as well be. Air traffic within the country had slowed to a trickle, and overseas flights were practically nonexistent. Nordlund squinted through the gusts of rain swirling about the tarmac. That was it—four planes, count 'em, four. A few years ago, there would have been dozens.

He shivered inside his raincoat. For all practical purposes, the terminal was unheated. How long now since the second oil embargo? Two, two and a half years? And they had another week to go before the official start of winter. This season, it was really going to hurt.

He walked over to one of the plastic chairs, set his briefcase down, and picked up a newspaper somebody had left behind. He read the headlines—the usual terrorist incidents—frowned, and checked the date. It was three days old. Cleaning ladies apparently were an endangered species, along with ticket counter personnel.

"Hey, mister, security line's right over there."

He hadn't heard the soldier walk up, and he automatically felt chilled. He had read about the new airport security guards who shot first and examined your luggage later.

"I've already been through the security check," he explained patiently. "I'm ready to board."

The young soldier was sweaty with suspicion, his right hand resting a shade too firmly on his sidearm.

"No, you're not, mister—no such thing as a single check anymore. Get in line over there and hope they don't pull you out for a full body search."

Nordlund couldn't tell whether that was just a gratuitous piece of information or a threat. He shrugged and walked over to the line forming up by the tables alongside the walk-through metal detector. Where the hell was Kaltmeyer? He glanced around the cavernous terminal again. It reminded him of deserted railroad stations when he had been a boy, before the Twentieth Century Limited and other trains had faded into oblivion in the face of five-hour flights coast-to-coast.

Maybe it was time for the trains to come back. And maybe Kaltmeyer and he would do it. The bullet train would be half as fast but far less vulnerable. And trains always did have a certain mystique. . . .

He shifted his briefcase to his other hand and wondered why the delay. The line waiting for the final security check before boarding United Flight 23 to Chicago was now at least fifty deep. Then he noticed a fat man by the metal detector complaining loudly about the wait. Suddenly, guards took him by the arms and dragged him struggling through a side door by the boarding gate. Nordlund guessed the pudgy man would be subjected to all the indignities of a full body search and probably be held long enough so that he'd have to stay in Washington overnight.

He glanced around the terminal again. There was no line for any other flight, but that didn't surprise him. Nobody traveled anymore, not unless they absolutely had to.

"Dane?"

For a big man, Franklin Kaltmeyer was certainly light on his feet—probably a remnant of the days when he had been a high baller doing deep tunnel work. He was sixty now, graying at the temples, but in damned good shape, everything considered. The men working the cut said he stayed fit by being mean, and maybe they were right.

"Mr. Kaltmeyer."

A quick handshake. "How long's the line been like this?"

"Ten minutes, not long." Nordlund hesitated. "You could probably walk right on through—you're a VIP."

Kaltmeyer looked sour. "Somebody would yell favoritism, and we've got a bad enough press without fighting that."

"How do you think the committee hearings went?"

They had both been witnesses before Senator Bergman's Subcommittee on Transportation—one week lost out of a schedule so tight it squeaked, just to trade barbs with a bunch of hostile senators. They hadn't even had time to compare notes.

"As bad as it looked. But they'll forgive us everything if we make hole-through on time."

Kaltmeyer took out a small notebook and started checking figures. Nordlund fell silent, edging forward a step or two every time the line moved up. He consciously started people-watching; then he realized he wasn't looking at people in general as much as he was staring at the same woman about ten paces ahead of him. Not as attractive as Diana but enough to catch a man's eye. He guessed she was in her midthirties, ten years older than Diana and five pounds overweight, but definitely a handsome woman in her dark blue cashmere business suit. Her face was solid enough to be Irish, but high cheekbones gave it a touch of the exotic. Light brown hair, medium length. . . .

He frowned. Good features, and she knew how to use makeup. But once you broke it down, there was nothing really outstanding about her. It was probably the entire package, her attitude, the way she carried herself.

He kicked his bag forward again, still engrossed in studying her, and nearly stumbled over the person in front of him. He refocused his eyes, an apology already forming on his lips.

There were half a dozen school kids ahead of him in line, giggling among themselves. Judging by their uniforms, they were probably from some exclusive and very expensive private school—one-way to Chicago cost a thousand dollars, and usually only businessmen flew it.

"Sorry, son."

A sulky " 'Sall right."

The boy was eight, maybe ten—small for his age, neatly dressed, reddish hair and freckles. He'd be cute if he weren't so sullen, a kid right off the new Mickey Mouse Club on the tube.

"Going home for the holidays?"

The boy glanced up, then back down at the school bag by his feet. Unlike the others, he seemed shy and nervous. "Yeah."

So go ahead and be shy, Nordlund thought, feeling a twinge of hurt. He had a soft spot for kids, probably because children were among the many things Diana hadn't wanted to give him. The line started to move again but the boy seemed glued to the spot. Nordlund nudged him, and he whirled, grabbing up his bag.

"Line's moving," Nordlund said, mildly surprised.

The boy was sweating. "I think I've got the wrong flight," he stuttered.

Nordlund pointed at the boarding pass in the boy's pocket. "No, you've got the right one." He smiled. "It's the only one."

He never remembered exactly what happened after that, but it began when two security guards walked into the boarding lounge, spotted the boy, and started running toward him.

"Hold it, son—we want to talk to you!"

The frightened boy grabbed his bag and ran toward an exit.

"Somebody stop him!"

The boy and the guards disappeared through the lounge doors. There was dead silence. Nordlund and the others in line stared at the corner where the boy had disappeared. Then a guard said in a loud voice, "Everything's all right, folks, everything's all right. Boarding in five minutes."

Kaltmeyer murmured, "Christ, they really train them young, don't they?"

"You think he was one?"

Kaltmeyer shrugged. "Why else would the guards have gone after him?"

The line was moving rapidly now, the guards wanting to clear the terminal.

"Okay, folks, let's move ahead, let's move it. You all got a plane to catch."

It wasn't until Nordlund was through the gate and walking onto the plane that he remembered the woman in the blue cashmere suit. She had disappeared.

"What'll you have, Danc?"

"Scotch, straight up."

"Make that four," Kaltmeyer said to the stewardess. He glanced at Nordlund, grim-faced. "I don't think one will do it, and my guess is they're going to run out pretty soon."

"The poor kid," Nordlund said. "I never would have figured him . . ." His voice trailed off.

"Neither would anybody else. That's the point. They've used grandmothers as mules, they've used pregnant women as mules—kids were the next logical candidates. Con them into bringing something on board for good old Uncle Al, I suppose. Poor little bastard probably had no idea what was going on."

"That's hard to believe," Nordlund protested.

"Not so hard—probably happens every day, but we don't hear about it."

Like a lot of people, Kaltmeyer was paranoid on the subject, Nordlund thought. But then again, why had the boy been so nervous, and why had he run when the guards headed for him?

Kaltmeyer was right about one thing—the stewardesses did a land-office business peddling booze, and in less than half an hour they had sold out. After they had picked up the empties, Nordlund placed his attaché case on the fold-down table and took out a portable design computer with a large LED screen. He punched in a code and a moment later was looking at a line drawing on the screen.

Kaltmeyer glanced over, curious. "What's that?"

"Concrete barge—new way of positioning caissons in deep water so we can use shaped charges to drill through to underwater tunnels. It should save us weeks on future projects." He paused, recalling an argument he'd had at the Field Station three weeks before. "Metcalf doesn't think it will work."

(11

Kaltmeyer looked sour. "You still want him for your assistant? Orencho was going to can him."

"Orencho was wrong—Metcalf's a good man. He's young and he doesn't get along with the men, but he knows his engineering. The rest of it is seasoning."

Kaltmeyer began thumbing through the schedule book he had opened. "He was in my office bucking for your job the day after Orencho disappeared. Or didn't you know?"

Nordlund shrugged it off. "Sure he wants it. But his only chance of getting it is to prove he's better than I am. By trying, he's good for the company, and he keeps me on my toes."

"Just be careful he doesn't keep you off balance as well as on your toes." Kaltmeyer went back to the schedule, Metcalf forgotten. "Once we get back, we've got a lot to do—either we make hole-through before the end of the year, or Congress will nail us to the wall." He looked up. "We going to make it? You're chief engineer—you're the authority."

He had been chief engineer for all of two weeks, Nordlund thought—enough to appreciate the job's responsibilities but damned few of its privileges.

"Yes, sir, I think we'll make it."

"I'm not paying you to make guesses, Dane."

Nordlund felt sweat gather in his armpits. "We're making as much speed as we can without endangering the men."

"Nobody asked you to endanger the men." Kaltmeyer ran a stubby finger down his appointment sheet. "For me, Dane, the Lake Michigan tunnel is just another project. For you, it's your baby. I wouldn't have it any other way. Just don't miss the deadline for hole-through." He glanced up. "And don't forget the demonstration tomorrow afternoon at McCormick Place. I don't know how many will be in the Japanese delegation. About six, so I hear."

"Japanese delegation?" Nordlund asked politely.

"Last-minute arrangements. They're representatives of a government consortium, thinking of joining with us when we bid for the western leg."

"Housing," Nordlund said, thinking out loud. "We'll need to put them up for the better part of a week, right?"

"No problem—half the hotels in Chicago are empty."

"What about Steve Phillips and Major Richards? Not much time for security clearance—"

"Dane." Kaltmeyer folded his glasses and stuck them in his pocket, then turned to Nordlund with mild exasperation. "Look, you're my right-hand man, and right-hand men have to take care of some of the petty stuff along with the important things. I don't travel with secretaries, I don't make reservations. Tell Janice to take care of it, or tell Metcalf to do it—that's your job, telling other people what to do. Steve's nose will be out of joint because we didn't give him advance warning. He's the Administration point man, and if he had his way, we'd have to clear it with him before going to the john. So butter him up. Richards is no problem—have Janice give him the names, he'll make a call to Tokyo, and in ten minutes he'll know everything he needs to know. All right?"

"Yes sir, boss," Nordlund said, faintly sarcastic.

"I say 'Jump,' you ask 'How high?' Simple, isn't it?" Kaltmeyer said it with a smile, but to Nordlund he looked like an amiable wolf.

Nordlund laughed and put the computer back in his attaché case. "If you say so. Anything new on Orencho?"

The smile died. "Your predecessor's probably in Brazil spending the million bucks he got away with. Which reminds me, the GAO will be sending in a team of auditors, thanks to good old Max. Not your worry this time. Mine."

Nordlund felt uneasy. "There was a lot of truth in the Senate committee's criticism. Max could never have gotten past a good internal audit from national headquarters." He never did know why there hadn't been one.

"The hell with the goddamned committee! Orencho got the headlines, and now they want some of the press. They haven't the foggiest idea of the real magnitude of the project. Neither do you, for that matter. Running an audit on the project would be like auditing World War Two—there's a quarter of a million men involved, and more subcontractors than I can count."

For one of the few times since he had known him, Kaltmeyer sounded old to Nordlund. He had touched a sore spot.

Before the committee that morning, Kaltmeyer had twice lost his temper when questioned about internal audit safeguards. He hadn't been a good witness, and Nordlund felt relieved when Kaltmeyer had finally been excused.

"It's the biggest damned engineering project the world has ever seen," Kaltmeyer mused, the fire suddenly out. "The bullet train will link the coasts and the major corridors from Boston to D.C. and L.A. to San Diego. And the cut's one of the biggest parts of it. Compared to the tunnel under Lake Michigan, the one under the Channel is child's play. Even the Seikan tunnel between Hokkaido and Honshu is strictly bush league."

He looked at Nordlund, his expression calculating. "You've got a part of it, Dane, you want the rest? You're up for chief engineer for the western leg if we get the contract, you know that."

"Yeah, I want it," Nordlund said slowly. "I don't know if I'd kill for it, but I might be willing to maim."

"All you have to do is prove yourself. Make hole-through on time, and if Kaltmeyer/DeFolge gets the contract, you're a shoo-in. But don't tell your friend Metcalf—he'll start looking for a new job tomorrow. He's probably got the loyalty of a bitch in heat."

Troy Metcalf was more reliable than that, Nordlund thought. Or was he?

Kaltmeyer yawned and put away the schedule book. "You'll want to take a vacation after the ceremonies, Dane. Ask Diana to go along with you, and see if you can mend your fences. You're never going to do any better, you know—she doesn't really want the divorce."

He meant well, Nordlund thought, resenting every word of it. And when it came to the former Diana DeFolge, he might be right. But even if Diana was the daughter of his partner, it still wasn't any of Kaltmeyer's business, and he knew it.

So why was he pushing it?

Half an hour later, Nordlund unbuckled his seat belt, muttered something about the john, and headed for the rear of the plane. Most of the passengers on the red-eye were now asleep, lulled by a smooth flight and too many drinks. Inside the lavatory he got rid of five dollars worth of cheap airline liquor, then ran cold water into the basin and used a paper towel to dampen his face and hands and another to dry them. He was too big for the tiny room—apparently its designer never thought somebody who weighed two and a quarter and stood six two would ever use it—and felt mildly claustrophobic.

Kaltmeyer may have been right about Diana. There was another aspect he hadn't mentioned but only because he probably hadn't thought of it. Nordlund crouched so he could get a better view of his face over the tiny plastic sink.

You're thirty-seven, old boy, and you're not getting any younger. Engineering and tunneling are your life, but a hard hat is a poor bed partner, and you're never going to father a family by sleeping alone.

And then the old bitterness came back. Diana didn't want children. Under any circumstances. She had never been that definite before marriage, but afterward she had made no bones about the fact that children weren't part of her game plan.

He had opened the door and started back up the aisle when he saw the woman in blue again. She had the overhead light on to read, the glow highlighting her face.

He paused by her seat, and when she glanced up, he said, "Don't mean to disturb you—I saw you in line, but I thought you had missed the flight."

She put the book aside and smiled. "I barely made it." She pointed to the empty row across the aisle. "Have a seat? If you want to talk for a while, I'm willing. Still too shaken up to sleep, I guess."

He smiled back and sat down. She was direct, he'd give her that. And her voice was as attractive as her figure, throaty without being husky and with the inflections that implied sincere interest. He guessed she would be extraordinarily easy to talk to. He slid into the seat and held out his hand. "Dane Nordlund."

Her grip was more firm than polite. "You're in construction, aren't you?" He showed his surprise, and she smiled and said, "Just a guess, really. You look like you started working construction when you got out of high school. You put yourself through—engineering school, right?—worked construction during the summers and stuck with it afterward. Either that, or you're a CPA who jogs three times a week and plays racquetball on the weekend." The smile faded. "Besides, you're flying, and the only ones who fly these days are politicians, businessmen, and construction engineers who have to travel from job site to job site."

"Which are you?" he asked.

She laughed. "None of the above. Now what do you do, Dane?—really."

He told her about the project and the bullet trains and the deep cut, the tunnel beneath Lake Michigan.

"I've read that it's a lot of money," she said. "Is it worth it?"

It shouldn't have surprised him—that had been the tone of the committee hearings all week long. The largest engineering project in the world was all well and good—but was it worth it?

"I think so, but I'm prejudiced. I suppose for the short term, we can't afford it. For the long term, we can't survive without it. Bullet trains aren't as fast as planes, but they're still fast. They're safe, and for all practical purposes, we don't have planes anymore."

"Safe," she mused. "I wonder if anybody will be safe anymore."

"Because of the boy at the terminal? He probably had no idea what he was bringing on the plane. If he was bringing anything at all."

She shook her head. "He wasn't, but he could have been. His school bag was full of books and pens plus a clay dinosaur. The guard who went through the bag had children of his own and later got to thinking the dinosaur was too sophisticated for a ten-year-old. So he went looking for him. The boy had been frightened by the first check, and when he saw the guard again, he panicked and ran."

Nordlund stared at her, disbelieving. "You're going to tell me the clay dinosaur could have been plastique and one of the pens a detonator, right?"

She nodded. "It's possible. They weren't, but the guard was nervous and decided to do a follow-up. Can't blame him, really."

"What happened to the boy?" he asked.

"Detained for checking with his school and his parents. He'll be released for the next flight home tomorrow."

"Who told you all this?"

She hesitated. "One of the guards."

"And if it had turned out the boy was some sort of subteen terrorist, I supposed a guard might have shot him."

She was more thoughtful now, puzzled by his response. "I suppose so. If the guard was nervous."

"And you would approve?"

"I might, depending on the circumstances." She looked at him gravely. "And you would not."

"Sorry if I bothered you," Nordlund muttered, standing up. "I have to go over some reports." Frightened people were willing to believe anything, but he hadn't thought she was the type. She had no compassion for the boy at all.

Back at his seat, there was a small bottle and a plastic glass full of ice. Kaltmeyer opened one eye when he sat down.

"I bribed a steward. These days you can always depend on one of them having a private stock."

"Thanks, I can use it." Nordlund emptied half the bottle over the ice and swallowed a huge gulp. He hadn't even gotten her name; she had manipulated the conversation so she never had to give it.

Which was no great loss, except to his ego.

Despite himself, he suddenly felt wistful. Since separating from Diana, it seemed as if he had been on a constant search for someone as lonely as he was. For a brief moment, he thought he had found one.

A dozen seats behind him, the woman in blue opened her bag and took out two file folders. Both were marked "Confidential," and each had a four-by-five glossy stapled to the front cover. The second file was the one for Dane G. Nordlund. The G stood for Geoffrey. Except for a slight tinge of gray at the temples, his hair was black—the type of black usually found only among Indians and Orientals. You'd probably have to go back to his grandparents to account for it.

He was very attractive. The file folder said he was married, but he hadn't been wearing a ring, and he had come on to her—at least at first. Which meant he was married and had taken his ring off because he was on the prowl; but that didn't seem likely—he wasn't the type. Or he was widowed. Or divorced. Or separated. Whichever he was, it didn't matter anymore. And that was really too bad.

The other file was for one Franklin Kaltmeyer, probably his seat companion. She'd go over that one later. Then she thought of the boy again.

What would she have done if she had become suspicious of him once on board and he had turned out to be the real thing? She was glad it hadn't happened that way. The boy had been a dead ringer for one of her nephews.

She glanced at Nordlund's photograph once more, then slipped the file folders into her bag and zipped it shut. She nestled it comfortably in her lap and closed her eyes for a short nap.

Dane Geoffrey Nordlund—what a nice name. He was going to be one surprised engineer when she ran into him again. But then, she'd be willing to bet her world was filled with far more unpleasant coincidences than his.

CHAPTER 2

The wind whipped the snow past the front of the Airport Marriott while Nordlund waited for the shuttle to the O'Hare parking garage. The flight had gotten in at two in the morning, delayed by a blizzard over Ohio and Indiana, and he was still groggy from five hours of sleep. He pulled his coat tighter around him. It felt colder than D.C., probably no more than twenty degrees. And Chicago cold was a damp cold that could chill you clear through to your bones. Great Christmas weather.

The image of the red-headed boy at Washington National flashed into his mind, and he shivered, this time not from the frigid air. The boy had been an innocent kid, going home for the holidays. Could he have been something else? The woman in blue had thought so, but he still couldn't believe it.

The shuttle arrived, and five minutes later he was driving his Volvo down the Kennedy Expressway toward Chicago. There was too much snow on the ground, and he decided not to turn control of the car over to its built-in navigation computer; he didn't trust it to react quickly enough if he should start to skid. Besides, he had his own favorite route to the Field Station. It might be slower, but it was a lot more scenic.

It was seven in the morning, and the streets were deserted, though heavy traffic at any time was a thing of the past. The city looked seedier with every passing year, or maybe he was just tired from the flight. But seedy or not, it was a city he loved, the city where he had been born—the most underrated city in the United States.

He took the exit ramp at Foster and drove over to Lake Shore Drive. The wind was blowing freezing scud off the lake and the Drive was slick, but it was still one of the world's great highways. There were waves of ice-blue water on his left, and blocks of elegant apartment buildings fronting the Drive on his right. Unfortunately, the swirling snow hid the new two-mile extension of the Navy Pier that jutted out into the lake. There was a fifty-acre artificial island at its end, the future Chicago terminus for the project and the current home for the Lake Michigan Tunnel Field Station, but to his disappointment the snow whited that out as well.

He took the curve around the Drake Hotel, fighting for control on the icy pavement, and a few blocks later he turned onto the access road to the pier.

"ID please."

The new guards at the checkpoint were formal and serious, and even the ones who knew him as well as they knew Major Richards had yet to smile. He rolled down the window and handed over his holographic ID card, waiting impatiently while they fed it into the thumbprint computer.

"You're cleared, sir. Watch out for patches of ice on the pier."

He passed another checkpoint just before the exit to the island, then parked in the executive lot. It was difficult keeping his footing on the slippery steps to the wooden Administration Building.

He ran into Metcalf in the second-floor hall.

"How's the barge coming, Troy?"

"A lot of bugs—I think it's a toss-up."

You would, Nordlund thought. "We'll talk about it later."

"You did good at the hearings, fella."

Nordlund turned just before entering his office, watching Metcalf as he disappeared around the corner. He was a small man, about five eight, with black hair, an Irish swagger and the enviable store of energy that so many small men seemed to have. He had probably been working for hours, yet somehow he still looked fresh. That was one reason to resent him, Nordlund thought. Metcalf was just twenty-eight and made him feel old. Kaltmeyer's warning flashed into his mind but he dismissed it.

Metcalf was a crackerjack engineer. He was also too young, too clean-cut, too smart, and too upscale. An image like that could kill you in this business. Metcalf wouldn't be competition until he drank too much, had a troubled marriage, grime under his fingernails, picked fights, and talked dirty. The high-ballers might respect him then.

He took the side entrance to his office rather than entering through the glass double doors bearing the gold legend KALT-MEYER/DEFOLGE CONSTRUCTION. He dropped his attaché case on a chair, hung up his coat, and unwound the scarf from his neck. He dabbed at his dripping nose with a handkerchief—he sure as hell was coming down with something—and thumbed quickly through the messages tucked in a corner of his desk blotter. There was nothing that wouldn't wait.

He yawned and walked over to the automatic coffee machine in the corner. He twirled the pressure knobs to brew his favorite Colombia-French Roast mix with a half-portion of cream, waited twenty seconds while the hot water worked its way through the filter tapes, then took out the steaming cup. The first sip made him wince. Six months of experimentation, and he'd yet to make a cup of decent coffee. Maybe more chicory, drop the brewing temperature—

"Welcome back, boss." Janice was in the doorway. "You receiving yet?"

He desperately wanted five minutes alone with his coffee. "Anything that's really important?"

"Del Styron's hot to see you. And Steve Phillips says he has to set the details of the hole-through ceremony, that it can't wait."

Nordlund gave up. "Come on in, see if you can do better with the unholy machine than I did." Janice was the one person without whom Kaltmeyer/DeFolge would crumble into dust. A wise-cracking, middle-aged, matronly type who had never married, she wasted her maternal instincts on everybody who worked the cut and somehow made the day easier to get through. She was, he thought, one of God's blessings.

"Rumor is that a half-dozen Japanese observers are going to show up for this afternoon's demo. They'll need a place to stay, preferably some hotel that will make them feel at home."

She flipped open her notebook, looking at him over the top of her gold-rimmed glasses. "I've heard the rumor. It's for real?"

"Kaltmeyer told me on the way in. Apparently it had slipped his mind."

"We'll make reservations for eight—just in case—at the Executive House. They've got a sushi bar I've heard is great."

"How antsy is Phillips?"

She looked serious. "He's under a lot of pressure from Washington. He also doesn't like you, and that's a bad combination."

"Kaltmeyer doesn't like *him,* so that makes us even." He smiled. "But thanks for the warning. Send him in when you hear him coming."

She made a face.

"I'll smell him—his after-shave precedes him."

Nordlund was just starting his second cup when Janice held the door open for Steven Phillips. He glanced up and pointed at the coffee machine. "Help yourself, Steve."

Phillips look annoyed, and Janice hurried over to brew him a cup. "Cream and sugar, Mr. Phillips?"

Nordlund hid a smile. You had to know her to catch the sarcasm.

Phillips sat down, taking pains to arrange the crease in his trousers before crossing his knees. He was in his early thirties, with thinning sandy hair and a narrow face, a bachelor who followed *GQ* slavishly when it came to his clothing and regularly paid fifty dollars to have his hair styled, though Nordlund thought he could have done better with a bowl. But Phillips was dangerous. The columnists usually referred to him as "a political animal," which meant he could slit your throat so fast you wouldn't know it until you tried to turn your head. Politics was Phillips's first and only love. He had started organizing student groups for the president when he was in college and the president was still a senator. Phillips was close to the throne, and if he bulled the cut through to completion—or could claim that he did—he'd be a lot closer.

Phillips plucked at a piece of lint on his coat sleeve. "I watched the telecasts of the hearings, Dane. I thought you did very well." His voice had just enough of a nasal Beacon Hill accent to be annoying.

"Thanks." What Phillips wanted to say was that he had done all right but that he, Phillips, could have done much better. "I didn't want to go, Steve—there was too damned much to do here."

Phillips nodded distant acknowledgment—he hated to be called Steve—then got right down to business. "So when do you plan on hole-through?"

"Sometime around the first of the year—I can't pin it down exactly. Depends on the strata we encounter in the last quarter-mile. There shouldn't be any surprises, but you never know."

The real trouble with talking to Phillips was that you couldn't read the man's face, you couldn't tell what Phillips was thinking. But then, you never had to wait long to find out.

"Not good enough, Dane. You're six months behind schedule, and the Administration can't afford any more delays. I need a commitment."

Only Kaltmeyer could really make him sweat, but Phillips came close. "You don't understand my position—"

Phillips held up a thin hand, his voice ugly.

"You don't understand mine. If we don't have hole-through before Congress reconvenes, there's not a chance in hell of pushing through appropriations for the western leg. We're not allowed deficit spending anymore, which means we've had to gut half our social programs to get the money for the project. This country won't sit still if we can't show real progress soon, and by that I mean something we can flash on the six o'clock news so a hundred million voters can see it."

"What'd you have in mind?" Nordlund asked dryly.

Phillips edged forward in his chair, his eyes bright.

"Hole-through before Christmas. Have a little celebration with the locals, the people here, and then a major one after the holidays. The governor and the mayor, maybe a gaggle of senators and representatives—I'm sure I could get the president to

(23

say something via satellite hook-up. Lay enough track so we can push a car or two through the cut to make it worthwhile mediawise.''

Nordlund heard his own voice turn chilly. "I'm not in the business of issuing guarantees."

Phillips stood up, gripping the edge of the desk so hard, the veins in his hands stood out.

"You better be, Mr. Nordlund. You don't make hole-through by the end of the year, congressional opposition will clip the purse strings when it comes to the western leg, and without the western leg, the deficits of the project will be more than this country can stand. The Administration will lose the Congress in the next election and the presidency after that."

Phillips was perspiring, his hair damp on his forehead. "You understand me? I'm not going to let that happen."

He might ask "How high?" when Kaltmeyer told him to jump, Nordlund thought, but he wasn't about to do the same for Phillips. "Maybe you better talk to God and not to me, Steve. I don't know what's in that rock—nobody does. We'll do the best we can, and that's all I can promise you. If I push the men any harder, then I'm risking not only the tunnel but their lives."

Phillips brushed at his face with a handkerchief, then jammed it back into his breast pocket. He was silent for a long moment. When he started talking again, his voice squeaked with anger.

"It isn't politic to say this, Nordlund, but I'll spell it out for you anyway. I don't like you. I didn't think you were the man for this job, and I told Kaltmeyer that. I don't like your assistant, Metcalf, either—he's too goddamned young, and he's what my grandfather would call a wisenheimer. And I don't like old bastards like Beardsley stirring up trouble all the time. You think I can't see it? The Lake Michigan tunnel has taken longer than any other part of the project, and it's sopped up money like a sponge sops up water. Well, this month is delivery month and you're going to deliver. You fail, and I promise you the Administration's not going to take the heat—you people are. We'll have you and your friends testifying before committees in Washington until next Inauguration Day."

He turned on his heel and headed for the door.

Just before he got there, Nordlund said, "You forgot your coffee, Steve."

He took his own cup and walked out onto the small balcony overlooking the entrance to the cut. His breath came out as fog in the chill morning air. He stared over at the bank of cages that rose from the access shaft protected by the huge cofferdam holding back the waters of the lake. It was a long way down, four hundred feet from the surface to the floor of the tunnel.

Three of the cages were at the surface discharging the night shift, a mass of anonymous faces under varicolored hard hats. The yellow ones were worn by the men in the forward part of the cut, the ones who did the actual digging. One of the yellow hats broke away from the group and lumbered toward the Administration Building. Beardsley. Nordlund could spot him a hundred yards away—the man was almost sixty and weighed close to three hundred pounds; in Beardsley's case, it was all muscle. Then he noticed the thick sheaf of papers clutched in Beardsley's right hand. *Oh Christ, not again.* Beardsley was the night shift supervisor and secretary for the local union. He was usually easy to get along with, but when he showed up between shifts, it was always a sign of trouble.

"Looks like you're in for it, Dane."

Metcalf had followed him out onto the balcony, a cup of coffee in his hand. Janice must have let him into the office, and he had brewed the cup before stepping out.

Nordlund sniffed. "Hey, let me try that." He took the cup from Metcalf's hand and sipped. Perfect. "How'd you do it?"

Metcalf looked blank. "I don't know, just twirled the knobs and waited a minute."

Nordlund was starting to feel the chill and stepped back inside. Metcalf trailed after him. "The president's errand boy was just in here. He wanted me to guarantee hole-through by Christmas."

"That's because he's an asshole." Metcalf considered for a moment. "But we'll probably make it."

Nordlund half-smiled. "He said he doesn't like me."

"Some people don't."

"He said he doesn't like you, either."

"The man has no taste."

Nordlund laughed. "So let's give him a chance to develop some. Phillips is all yours. Keep him out of my hair—I don't care how you do it."

"That's not exactly an engineering problem," Metcalf said slowly.

"You're my right-hand man, Troy. And sometimes right-hand men have to handle petty stuff along with the important things." He'd have to thank Kaltmeyer for the line next time he saw him. Except, of course, Phillips wasn't petty stuff.

Metcalf thought about it for a moment, then said cautiously, "Anything else Phillips was unhappy about?"

"Yeah. He thinks Beardsley and the union are slowing progress." Maybe handling Beardsley should become Metcalf's problem, too. If he could learn to get along with the shift foreman, the other high ballers would be a snap.

"That one's easy."

Nordlund leaned back in his chair. "I'm listening."

"I'll tell him that Beardsley's political, that he'll take his case to the newspapers and TV and tell the whole country the Administration's canning all the old-timers who really know how. You know how many people are over sixty in this country? How many senators and congressmen? The Administration has enough problems with Congress as is." He cocked his head. "How'm I doin'?"

"It's always nice to know when I've made the right decision. What'd you want to see me about?"

"I've checked with Dietz at the east team headquarters in Benton Harbor. The new cutters arrived for the mole, and the team's making great progress. They're into limestone strata, so hole-through by Christmas should be a cinch."

Maybe he should have given Phillips a guarantee after all, Nordlund thought; then he was glad he hadn't. Whatever date he might have given Phillips, he would have been pushed to cut it in half.

"What's the downside?"

"No downside." Metcalf hesitated. "Unless Styron has one. He's beefing about the program again."

"With less than a quarter-mile to go?" Nordlund felt annoyed. What surprises could be left in the strata? They were so near completion, the computer program for the rock strata under the lake was almost irrelevant. "Is he serious?"

Metcalf nodded. "He's been complaining about the program as long as I can remember, but he's really upset about it now."

Nordlund drained his coffee. "Let's go to Operations and take a look."

The Operations Room took up more than half of the third floor of the Administration Building. In spite of using movable partitions to give individual engineers a sense of privacy, it was still essentially an engineering bullpen—too crowded, too noisy, too cold in the winter, and too hot in the summer. The wall opposite the huge picture windows overlooking the access shaft held a large holographic projection of a strata map of the lower part of Lake Michigan and the land along the shore. The map had developed slowly over the last two years from radar, sonar, and spark soundings and was a triumph of computer graphics. It was also a first; Nordlund was sure it would become the standard for all future tunneling projects.

Within the three-dimensional projection, two thick lines snaked toward each other from opposite shores of Lake Michigan. One originated from Benton Harbor, Michigan, where the bullet train entered the eastern portal of the tunnel, while the other started just west of Chicago, in the forest preserves outside Cicero. The space separating the two tunnels beneath the lake now looked no wider than the thickness of Nordlund's thumb.

He spotted Styron by the computer terminal tied into the mainframe at the University of Chicago. The geological data were fed into the mainframe, which did the stress analysis as well as compute charge composition and placement for the most efficient blasting pattern. It was a technique Nordlund had developed himself, one he knew Metcalf admired, even though he had never said so.

Nordlund almost put a hand on Styron's shoulder, then drew

back. Styron was a pudgy, fussy man, perpetually bundled in sweaters, who perspired as much in winter as he did in summer. Touching him was like touching a damp, slightly mildewed washcloth. Nordlund shifted his hand to Styron's chair and leaned over to inspect the graphic on the screen, a cross-section of the ground beneath the lake.

"What's wrong, Del?"

Styron glanced up. "It's Mr. Lammont's program again, Mr. Nordlund. Look at the data from his spark soundings last year." He touched the keyboard before him, and several successive cross-sections appeared. "These sections go into the path of the cut. You can see the granite we're into now fading into layers of medium-soft limestone."

Nordlund pointed at the screen. "What's the haze on these layers?"

"Porosity. But I can't tell how much." Styron sounded as if he wanted to wring his hands. "These cross-sections are generated when the computer rotates the data ninety degrees, and sometimes details are lost. But the data from the spark soundings seem inconsistent in this area."

Nordlund could sense Metcalf at his side, staring at the screen with him. "If it's porous limestone, we may be running into trouble, Dane."

Nordlund traced the hazy area with a fingertip. "What do you mean by inconsistent data?"

"What we're finding and what was predicted by the program don't agree. I'll admit I don't fully understand Mr. Lammont's program and its limitations, but it seems to me a high percentage of agreement should be essential."

"You satisfied with the data in our local memory banks?"

Styron squirmed, and Nordlund guessed that Styron was afraid his job would be on the line if he hollered wolf when there wasn't any.

"Not really, Mr. Nordlund." He hesitated, uncomfortable. "You understand, this is the first time I've had access to the complete program. Mr. Orencho only allowed me to work with sections of it before."

"Then you better bring all the raw data down from the

mainframe and start going through it. Have Zumwalt give you a hand."

"I won't need help," Styron said, a trace of acid in his voice. He mopped at his face. "I don't mean to imply that Mr. Lammont's program—"

"You're working for Kaltmeyer/DeFolge, not Lammont," Nordlund said curtly. The trouble with Styron was, he didn't know whose ass to kiss first.

"I guess I would feel a lot more comfortable if I could play with the raw data," Styron admitted.

"Then do it," Nordlund ordered.

Out in the hallway, Metcalf said, "You realize how often he's complained about Lammont's program?"

For just a moment Nordlund felt nostalgic about the time when all he had to worry about was his own job and Max Orencho worried about everybody else's. "Styron's not happy unless he's complaining."

"You're not concerned?"

Nordlund stopped before his office door. "Yeah, I am," he said slowly. "Lammont's program has been faulty—how often? Half the time? I don't know where the hell the bugs are in it. But I don't think it matters a damn, either. Ten days from now, the program will be history."

Metcalf shrugged. "Okay, Dane, you don't worry, I won't worry."

Nordlund patted Metcalf on the shoulder. "Right, I'm not going to worry—I didn't say you shouldn't worry." He turned the knob, then paused. "We're due at McCormick Place at two, but I'd like to check out the fabrication site before then. See you on the helicopter pad in fifteen minutes."

"Yes sir, boss."

Nordlund wondered where he'd heard the same words spoken with the same amount of suppressed anger before. Then he remembered.

He'd said exactly the same thing to Kaltmeyer on the plane.

Beardsley was standing at the window, slump-shouldered, staring out at the drifting snow. Nordlund liked the big man, which didn't mean it was easy to put up with him. Beardsley knew the history of tunneling backward and forward . . . hell, he *was* the history of tunneling. Although he had been with Kaltmeyer/DeFolge only a few months, his résumé had been a Baedeker of the underground construction industry.

Beardsley had looked him up when he was inspecting a tunnel job in the Bay Area, and Nordlund had brought him in six months ago. It had been a happy decision. The union local at the Lake Michigan tunnel was in horrible shape, and since Beardsley had been secretary of the union at his last job, the national union had seized upon him as a troubleshooter, forcing an election in which Beardsley had become secretary of the local.

It had been a stroke of luck for the union; Beardsley had quickly straightened out the local. But in some respects it hadn't made Nordlund's job any easier. Getting Beardsley to accept something new was like force-feeding spinach to a baby.

"What's up, Art?"

The big man straightened and turned around, startled out of his brief reverie. He waved the roll of printouts he was carrying. "I got to talk to you about this Mickey Mouse charge placement, Dane. This is one time it's not going to work." He sounded hoarse, prepared for an argument.

Nordlund felt old. Five hours of sleep, and he had all afternoon to go through yet.

"Can't it wait, Art? I'm late for the demonstration at McCormick Place."

Beardsley acted as if he hadn't heard him. "It's these placement patterns from your gee-whiz computer boys. And the charges. Who thought up the idea of using two different kinds of charges? I was placing charges before you were in diapers, and I can't see any sense to it. You're not only using two different kinds, but the charge holes vary from shot to shot."

Nordlund started to lose patience.

"God*damn*it, Art, what's your problem? We get maximum penetration with this technique, you know that. The computer figures the charge placement based on the soundings from the drill heads at the cut. For the charges themselves, we're using seventy-five percent dynamite around the center while we use ammonium nitrate-oil charges on the periphery. The dynamite's faster detonation wave clears the central debris, which lowers the resistance to the slower detonation wave of the nitrate charges. It's damned efficient.''

''I don't like it,'' Beardsley muttered, shaking his head. ''The standard charge placcment always works pretty well.''

Nordlund glanced at his watch. He was running out of time. ''Tell you what, Art. We'll do one your way and one mine. Then we'll weigh the spoil from the two shots. I'll bet you ten bucks the new way is better. Fair enough?''

Beardsley grinned. ''Make it a hundred.''

''You're on. Now get the hell out of here, I'm late.''

''Sucker,'' Beardsley said under his breath. Nordlund heard it but waited until his office door had closed before smiling to himself. His hundred couldn't be safer.

He packed up his briefcase, then remembered something that had been in the back of his head all morning. He punched the intercom. ''Janice, has anybody heard anything more about Orencho?''

''Not a word, boss. The police are watching the bus stations and airports, and the highway patrol is checking for him on the freeways, but nobody's reported anything yet.''

Max couldn't have vanished into thin air, Nordlund thought. Traffic in and out of Chicago had fallen to the point where you could seal off the city fairly easily. If Max had tried to leave, the authorities would have picked him up.

How the hell did Max think he could get away with it? And why had he done it in the first place? Orencho had been a mystery to him from the very start—a tall, handsome man of fifty with a pencil-thin moustache and a head of thick brown hair hidden under a slouch hat he seldom removed, even in restaurants. If anybody had wanted to film his biography, Orencho was good-looking enough to play himself. Divorced, a wife and two sons in Denver, a variety of stunning womcn friends he took to social functions around the city, a town house on the Near North Side. . . .

But as the poem said, was he happy? Nordlund sure as hell

(31

didn't know, and he doubted that anybody else did, either. Orencho was charming when he had to be, but he was the type who discouraged friendships off the job and seldom discussed anything but work on the job. A top-notch engineer, but nobody on the project seemed to know much about him beyond that. Kaltmeyer must, but Kaltmeyer had little to say about Max Orencho except to swear that he would break his neck if he ever found him.

Then Nordlund had another thought. Ten to one Max wasn't in Brazil. Smart money would bet that Max hadn't even left Chicago, that he was still somewhere in the city waiting until the heat died down before trying to sneak out.

And there was always the possibility that somebody else had found Max first and that Max was now in no position to leave at all.

But who would have been looking for Max?

CHAPTER 3

It was a five-minute ride by helicopter from the Field Station to the shield fabrication shed at the West Portal. The pilot passed low over the cleared area in the forest preserve, and Nordlund counted six shields outside. Two were finished and three were in various stages of completion, their stressed-steel frames partly covered by polyester-impregnated fiberglass cloth. The sixth was hidden by a large electric curing blanket. It would take a day for the polyester to set before the hollow structure could be pressurized. Then, bowing slightly under three atmospheres, the shield with its multiple prestressed steel rods would be loaded onto a truck and driven through the portal to the head of the cut, where it would be cemented into place.

The 'copter hovered for a moment, gradually settling onto the pad a hundred yards away from the shields. Nordlund climbed out, followed by Metcalf. It was a little after noon, and the temperature had dropped even more. Nordlund cursed himself for having forgotten his muffler back at the station; if his cold turned into the flu, he had only himself to blame.

They walked over to the shields. Nordlund noted that Evan Grimsley, the morning shift supervisor, was overseeing the loading of one of the shields onto a truck. He frowned. Where the devil was Swede? He usually took care of this.

"Think we'll make hole-through in time, Mr. Nordlund?"

Grimsley's words came out as tiny puffs of vapor, freezing in the chill air. He was a squat little man, twenty-five years younger than Beardsley and without Beardsley's thin coating of polish. A man who showed up every Monday morning with a raging hangover, blew his nose on his sleeve, and kept his men in line through threats, an occasional free beer at the local tavern, and a weekly brawl that he always won. Grimsley was irreplaceable.

"We'll make it when we make it, Evan." Nordlund ran his hand over the edge of one of the forms. Amazing how much weight it could support—and how much time was saved when you could fabricate it on the spot.

"Rumor says it's going to be before the first of the year."

Nordlund walked over to check the next shield. "Hope so, Evan."

"The men are getting up a pool. You wouldn't be good for a hint, would you?"

"Leave it alone, Grimsley," Metcalf snapped, annoyed. "Like the man says, we'll make it when we make it."

"Thanks for the information, Mr. Nordlund," Grimsley said, glaring at Metcalf.

Nordlund glanced at the two of them, then said quietly, "Isn't this shield overdue to be trucked into the hole, Evan?"

Grimsley touched his hard hat. "I'll get on it right away, Mr. Nordlund." He shot Metcalf one last look, then turned and walked back to the men by the truck, all of whom had been watching and whispering among themselves.

When he had gone, Nordlund motioned Metcalf to follow him over to a far shield, out of earshot of the men. "You could try a little more tact with the crew, Troy." He was tired, and it was a struggle to keep his temper in check.

"You could try backing me up," Metcalf said hotly. "You don't do that very often."

"I back you up when it's important and when you're right." Nordlund shoved his hands deep into his pockets, trying to warm them against his body. "That was a small thing to sound off about back there." He cocked his head. "What's between you and Grimsley?"

"He's been on my case—he's been on it for a year now."

"He baits you and you rise to the bait, is that it? That's real dumb. What happens when I'm not around, Troy?"

"Why the grilling? I get along with the rest just fine."

They were facing each other now, their breath condensing in a small cloud between them.

"I don't think you do. Beardsley has complained about you;

so have some of the others. They think you're a good engineer, but they don't respect you.''

"Because I say what I think?"

"Because you don't stop to think before you say something. Because *you* don't respect *them.*"

Metcalf stood spread-legged, teetering slightly on the balls of his feet.

"Let's have it, Dane. You don't much like me, do you?"

Nordlund felt his control start to slip. "I think you're a damned good engineer. I also think your nose has been out of joint ever since Kaltmeyer picked me to fill Orencho's spot."

Metcalf's eyes were angry slits. "I was here from the day they first turned dirt, four years ago. You're a late bloomer on this job."

Nordlund fought to keep his voice down. "You're right, you've been here since the tunnel started. But Kaltmeyer thinks you need seasoning. So do I. You've been a desk man, you haven't spent that much time actually working with the crews in the cut." He paused. "And you've got a lousy attitude. Orencho wanted to can you because you didn't get along with the high-ballers."

A few more years, and Metcalf would understand why he wasn't qualified. He didn't now, but maybe that was standard for young men on the way up.

"It really doesn't matter a damn whether the high-ballers love me or not," Metcalf said in a brittle voice, "as long as the boss's daughter loves you."

Nordlund felt his face go red. "That's enough, Metcalf." He started slogging through the snow toward the 'copter. "We're late."

Once on board the Bell, they stared in silence out opposite windows. Just before landing on the pad at McCormick Place, a sullen Metcalf said, "We sounded like a couple of kids back there, didn't we?"

"Forget it, Troy."

Metcalf had meant it as an apology. What made it difficult to accept was that Metcalf had a point—how much of one, he didn't know.

But what was worse was that Kaltmeyer had been right on the plane. Metcalf was a knife at his back.

There was military security and metal detectors at the entrance to the huge meeting room. Nordlund and Metcalf waited for their ID thumbprints to be verified, then Metcalf headed for the bar while Nordlund worked his way through the crowds to the buffet table. That was something else he had forgotten back at the Field Station—his lunch. He made himself a thick sandwich from the cold cuts, glancing around the room to see who was there.

Off to the right, a dozen yards from the buffet table, was a platform with a huge relief map of the bullet train project. In the rear of the room was a raised dais, where a trio of chamber musicians played light classical music. Most of those in the crowd he didn't recognize—a handful of people from Kaltmeyer/DeFolge Construction mingling with a tight little group of men with Oriental features, the Japanese team that Kaltmeyer had mentioned. He guessed the rest were politicians and media people. The men who seemed ill at ease and out of place, who never visited the buffet or the bar, were undoubtedly security. There were a lot of them.

The stewards at the bar were offering coffee—with few takers—and champagne and premixed Ramos Fizzes to everybody else. Nordlund noted that Metcalf was nursing a small glass, and he guessed they were also serving whiskey on the rocks and straight up for those who wanted it.

"You're a little late, Dane." He turned to see Kaltmeyer striding toward him, a glass of champagne in his hand, trailed by his twelve-year-old son, Derrick, and one of the Japanese. Kaltmeyer looked unhappy.

"Sorry, Frank, I wanted to do a quick tour of the fabrication site before coming over. They've been slow delivering the shields."

"I was hoping you'd do the briefing for the visiting engineers," Kaltmeyer said more gently. "However, I managed a short talk, and we filled in with the tape." He turned to the

Japanese, "Hideo, I want you to meet our chief engineer on the Lake Michigan tunnel project, Dane Nordlund. Dane, Hideo Nakamura from Nippon Engineering."

"My pleasure," Nakamura said, extending his hand. He was about fifty, taller than Nordlund might have expected, with clear, almost olive skin, thick black hair, and deep brown eyes. He wore glasses, but his face was full without the flatness usually found in Orientals; the Mongolian fold in his upper eyelid was barely noticeable. Nordlund guessed he had some Caucasian blood and would have bet money his father had been an American serviceman during the American Occupation. His respect for Nakamura went up; mixed bloods had a difficult time in Japan. They had to be twice as aggressive and twice as bright as others in their peer group to get anywhere.

Then the name suddenly clicked, and he flashed a smile. "The pleasure's mine, Mr. Nakamura. I've read several of your papers on charge placement."

Nakamura looked somber. "Written in the folly of my youth when I knew everything. I have forgotten much since then."

"Don't say that," Nordlund said, grinning. "They were of great use in my own work and some of the articles I've written—please don't shoot down my footnotes."

Kaltmeyer finally acknowledged the nudging of the boy at his side. "Ricky, it's been all of two weeks since you've seen Dane."

Nordlund held out his hand for a solemn shake. "There's another Blackhawks home game in ten days, Derrick, I'll get the tickets."

Derrick turned to his father. "Can I watch while Mr. Nordlund explains the project? I won't get in the way?"

"He won't be any bother," Nordlund cut in.

Kaltmeyer shoved the boy forward and nodded at Nakamura. "Then I leave you both in very capable hands—I've got some catching up to do with the others." He waved at another Japanese engineer and started threading his way over to him.

"I take it this is your young assistant?" Nakamura said, smiling at Derrick.

Nordlund laughed. "He will be someday—more probably my boss." Derrick reddened and studied the pattern in the parquet flooring. He was a good kid, Nordlund thought, a boy who was quiet and studious and remarkably easy to like. A wiry build, but Nordlund had a feeling he'd really have to be provoked before he got involved in a fight.

"Have you seen the map of the project, Mr. Nakamura?"

"Hideo, please—I have had no explanation of it."

Nordlund guided both of them over to the broad relief map. It took up most of the end of the room, measured thirty by forty feet, and included the entire United States. To the left was a small table holding a transparent relief map of the lower part of Lake Michigan and the surrounding areas of Illinois and Indiana. It was more elaborate than the holographic projection in his Operations office, though it didn't display the earth strata. What it emphasized was the thin vein of the completed tunnel system—the twin bullet train tunnels connected by a smaller service tunnel—running beneath the bottom of the lake.

"Very impressive," Nakamura murmured. He pointed to a number of large tanks, located at intervals of half a mile. "And these?"

He must know, Nordlund thought. Nakamura wouldn't have come ten thousand miles for the demonstration without knowing details of the bullet train down to the last rivet.

"Reservoirs of liquid nitrogen. They cool the superconducting magnets that ring the train cage. The magnets raise the train a fraction of an inch off the rails and pull it forward at speeds approaching three hundred miles an hour."

Nakamura tugged at his lower lip. "Is three hundred the limiting speed?"

"Far from it. Theoretically we could approach Mach One, but we've settled on three hundred until we know the system better."

"If you enclosed the system in a shell holding a soft vacuum, you might be able to achieve Mach One." Nakamura was studying him very carefully, sizing him up, and Nordlund felt vaguely embarrassed.

"I understand you're building such a system in Japan."

"Planning it," Nakamura corrected. "We believe speeds above Mach One are possible."

"That's easier in Japan with the shorter distances. Here, we're talking over nine hundred miles just to link Chicago and New York."

"Show him the whole system," Derrick said proudly, already halfway over to the next table.

Nordlund and Nakamura followed, easing through the crowd gathered around the huge map. The almost-completed leg from Chicago to New York was a thick black line, the tunnel under Lake Michigan a red stripe.

Nordlund cleared his throat, conscious that others around the table would be listening, too. "This next year the eastern leg should be finished—Chicago to New York via Toledo and Cleveland. The eastern corridor, 440 miles from Washington, D.C., to Boston and linking Baltimore, Philadelphia, and New York, was finished last year. Prototype trains are already making test runs in these sections."

He pointed out a ghostly line that ran from Chicago westward to Los Angeles. "The proposed route for the western leg connects Chicago, St. Louis, and Los Angeles by way of Dallas and Phoenix. More than two thousand miles."

"An enormous cost for one country," Nakamura said softly, studying the map.

Nordlund shrugged, guessing what Nakamura really wanted to discuss. But finance was Kaltmeyer's department, not his.

"Expensive but necessary. Airlines carry less than ten percent of the traffic they did five years ago. The bullet train is fast—and secure. Limited access in populated areas, laser beam security on the exposed routes. Nobody could get close without breaking the beams and alerting security forces."

Nakamura pointed a stubby finger at the Lake Michigan tunnel. "Why, Mr. Nordlund? Why underneath the city as well as the lake?"

Nordlund shrugged. "Buying up the right-of-way would have taken too long and cost too much. With the new moles, it's cheaper and faster to tunnel under urban areas rather than go through the courts and fight a thousand eminent domain cases

(39

and have to pay through the nose for the property anyway. And security's far easier when you can control access. No way it could be controlled if the train ran right through the city.''

Nakamura moved his finger slightly. "Why not an immersed tube tunnel on the lake bottom? It would have been quicker and cheaper.''

"Not necessarily. And not as secure in any event. With the tunnel sitting on the lake bottom, it could be sabotaged from above—look what happened to the BART tunnel from San Francisco to Oakland, the loss of life and commercial disruption there. It's a little more difficult to destroy a tunnel with a hundred feet of rock protecting it.''

Nakamura reluctantly took his finger away. "And the total cost?''

"Eighty million dollars a mile for the western route in present-day dollars. Total cost of the Chicago-New York route will probably top out at 160 billion.''

Nakamura sucked in his breath. "Expensive, but as you say, necessary." His eyes spanned the map from Chicago to Los Angeles, and he looked up at Nordlund with a small smile. "You *will* need help.''

Nordlund managed a small smile back. "We'll have to take the long view. Projected freight revenues alone should retire the construction debt and the interest payments in a few decades. Not a bad investment, considering the alternatives.''

"In some circumstances, perhaps optimism is the wiser course." Nakamura changed the subject. "I understand the dedication ceremony will be the day before Christmas Eve.''

Nordlund felt himself turn livid. Phillips had issued his own timetable and was going to try to force Kaltmeyer/DeFolge to meet it.

Derrick was enthused. "Boy, that'll be great! Will you be there, Mr. Nakamura?''

"Of course," Nakamura murmured. He waved a hand at the map. "Such an important project, Mr. Nordlund. I imagine the pressure for haste on the part of your government is very great.''

Nordlund grimaced, remembering his earlier conversation with Phillips. "There's a lot depending on whether we make hole-through on time."

Nakamura's expression was now one of sorrow. "In Japan, the men who dig the tunnels set the deadlines. We tried it the other way with tragic results."

He paused, seeing something in his mind's eye that Nordlund could only guess at.

"I lost my son in the second Seikan tunnel under the Tsugara Strait between Honshu and Hokkaido. There, haste made for a very personal kind of waste."

CHAPTER 4

"I always thought you should be on the lecture circuit, Dane." The voice was a deep contralto and a very familiar one. He turned. Diana had been standing behind him, for how long he couldn't guess. He introduced her, and Nakamura nodded, taking in the situation at a glance. He looked down at Derrick.

"Perhaps Mr. Nordlund's young assistant could show me the room with the model of the train?" He bowed slightly to Diana, then to Nordlund. "I think we should talk again later."

Derrick tugged at Nakamura. "It's right over here—it's the biggest train set I've ever seen."

Nordlund watched them go. Like the boy at the airport, Derrick could have modeled for the son he would like to have had. At twelve, you could already see the shadow of the man he would become.

They disappeared into the other room, and Diana said, "I meant that, Dane. You're really very good when it comes to lecturing."

Diana looked as young and beautiful as ever, Nordlund thought. She was twenty-six now; they had married when she was twenty-two. He had been ten years older, but it wouldn't have helped if he had been a hundred. She had known too much about men, and he had known too little about women—bouncing around the world on various engineering jobs had limited his experience and preserved an almost adolescent naïveté. When he had met Diana, she had been his dream of female perfection come true. It had been a hasty match; he was poor but had a family name and had attended the right schools. Senator De-Folge was rich and had a daughter whom he thought ought to be safely married for reputation's sake—both hers and his. All three had gotten what they thought they wanted, and in one way or another, all three had been disappointed.

Diana always dressed elegantly and for the demonstration had chosen a black sheath with a small choker of pearls and a bright pink jacket. The effect was startling; Diana always kept one step ahead of what most women wore so she always looked daring and trendy. He could hear her friends now: *Diana can wear those clothes—Lord knows I couldn't.* She was aware of the effect, and he knew she gloried in it.

"Thank you, Diana," he said curtly, "if you mean it."

"Of course I mean it. I seldom say anything I don't mean."

She was tall with tight, hard breasts and well-muscled legs. Maybe a shade too lean. She had been an anorexic in high school and still had little interest in food—going out for dinner and drinks with Diana had always meant drinks and conversation. Her ash-blond hair was arranged in a perfect coiffure, not a strand out of place. And she was impeccably made up. After four years of marriage, he knew the amount of work she put into her dress and makeup—and the cost. She had insisted on paying for her clothes and cosmetics out of her own money, which meant her private allowance from her father. He had understood it—sometimes engineering hadn't paid very well—but he had also resented it. She had always been much more her father's spoiled little girl than a wife.

And then, like the marriage itself, he had gotten over her.

"You can at least look pleasant," she said in a low voice, still smiling. "Right now you look the perfect picture of the unhappy ex-husband."

"That's the first time you thought I was perfect at anything."

"Not true and you know it—I thought you were perfect at a lot of things, if not always the important things."

Nordlund felt his face stiffen. "You're still good with the one-liners."

She faked a pout. "There was a time when you appreciated that." She laid a finger on his lips. "Let's call a truce. You've got work to do here, and so do I."

"Truce," he agreed. He had never enjoyed fencing with her but had tolerated it. That had been one of the many things that had gone wrong. She could never resist a clever line, even when it was directed at him.

"You haven't returned any of my calls," she said, glancing around the room to see who was there.

"I've been busy."

"Dane, a phone call doesn't take more than a minute."

"With you there's no such thing as a phone call that lasts only a minute."

She turned back to him, small red circles of anger in her cheeks. "I thought we had a truce."

"All right," Nordlund said. "I didn't call because I didn't think we had anything to talk about."

"I don't believe that," she said in a flat voice. "Our marriage wasn't all bad. Not for me, and certainly not for you."

Nordlund looked around, embarrassed that somebody might have overheard. It wasn't the time and it wasn't the place. But time and place seldom meant anything to Diana; half their arguments had been in crowded restaurants.

"I didn't marry you for your money, Diana."

"I didn't try and buy you with it, either."

"I wasn't thinking of you."

"Father? He didn't hire you, Kaltmeyer did. And he hired you because you were a good engineer. Or so he's told me, more times than I care to remember."

She was winning this one, Nordlund thought. She was hitting above the belt and making the blows count.

"You're getting warm," he said, angry in self-defense. "I was an engineer, and you had no interest in that world."

"I sure tried, Dane. I even went deep-sea fishing with you when you were assigned to that project in Florida. I still have the scars to prove it." She held up her right hand so he could see the jagged red scar on her thumb.

He frowned. "You should get a skin graft and have that removed."

"I keep it to remind me of Florida."

"You hated Florida."

"Not really. It was just that you were seldom home, and when that job was finished, you went right off to Lima."

"And you hated Peru."

She rolled her eyes. "God, how I hated Peru."

"That was my career," he said. "You knew it when you married me."

"I thought you were going to be an engineer at home. I didn't know you were going to make the whole world your oyster."

"Diana," he said slowly, "I really wanted to be independent. I didn't want to work for Kaltmeyer/DeFolge. Ever. I hired on a year ago because the project was too big and too glamorous for me to resist. The marriage didn't fall apart overseas, it fell apart right here. Remember? Six months ago it finally went to hell, but it had been headed there for four straight years."

Suddenly there it was, the thing they no longer talked about. It wasn't his job, and it wasn't the DeFolge money. They were two different, completely independent people, and the one thing that might have held their marriage together was impossible for them. Diana was too self-absorbed to give him children, and he didn't want a marriage without them.

She was checking out the room again, and something she had said earlier came back to him.

"What did you mean, you had work to do here?"

"You used to say I led a protected life." She couldn't keep the resentment out of her voice. "Not anymore. Since the separation, I've become very active in the senator's business affairs."

Nordlund stared. "I don't follow you."

"I've become an executive vice president for Interlock."

"Your father's holding company?" He hadn't heard anything about it, but then, people had learned never to talk to him about Diana. "That's hard to believe."

"Believe it," she said in a low voice. "It's new and it's exciting and I'm damned good at it."

It was a side of her that he had never seen, a self-assurance that was considerably different from the arrogance of a wealthy man's daughter. She had made the switch from the perfect hostess to the poised businesswoman without missing a beat. He looked impressed, and she took immediate advantage of it.

(45

"Dinner with me next week, Dane? For old times' sake—no commitments."

She didn't mean that, and he knew she knew it. But he was curious how deep the changes went.

"I'll call you."

"No, Dane, I'll call you."

"Next week," he promised.

Then he caught her private little smile of triumph and realized it had been her scene from start to finish. She had played it to the hilt—and very well. She really hadn't changed at all. It wasn't a matter of love or lust—it was a matter of possession. He was something her daddy had bought her, and she wanted it back.

"Fine. Now for God's sake, Dane, get me a drink."

He ran into Kaltmeyer and Nakamura at the bar making polite conversation, though it was obvious they had been watching him. Kaltmeyer nodded in the direction of Diana.

"What was that all about?"

Nordlund shrugged. "I'm not sure. Women have a way of appearing to change just when you think you know them. And then you discover they haven't changed at all."

"A woman has a secret soul," Nakamura said, "and we see only a shadow of it, mirrored in her eyes. But the shadow changes as the light changes."

"Very pretty sentiments," Kaltmeyer said, motioning for the bartender to bring them another drink. "But I'm not sure I understand them."

Nakamura smiled. "To be understood is to forever lose the essence of what is woman."

Kaltmeyer stared. "You're quoting, aren't you?"

"Of course."

Kaltmeyer picked up his drink and looked relieved. "Thank God; for a moment I was afraid you had made that up." He motioned to a man in the crowd, and when he came over he said, "Murray, you remember Dane? Dane, Murray Lammont." He pushed away from the bar, motioning Nakamura to follow him. "See you at the demonstration, Dane. Don't be late this time—public speaking's not my strong point."

He had been on the project a year, Nordlund thought, and he'd met Murray Lammont perhaps twice. Lammont was rail thin, graying, with a thick salt-and-pepper moustache. The bottom edge was slightly stained from the pipe he constantly smoked. Formerly a geology professor from a small college in Wisconsin and an expert on soils and geological strata, he'd made a fortune by breaking geological surveys down into computer programs that were then sold to various engineering companies. Rumor had it that Kaltmeyer/DeFolge and Lammont went back decades, that K and D had been one of Lammont's first clients.

Nordlund shook a hand that felt like crumpled tissue paper. "It's a pleasure, Mr. Lammont. Buy you a drink?"

"If it's on Frank and the senator, certainly."

The drinks arrived, and Nordlund said, "Del Styron has been having trouble with the program. He's been complaining about the sounding data from your survey."

Lammont looked thoughtful and made a show of tamping tobacco into his pipe. "What's wrong?"

"He says there are a number of anomalies in the data."

"I'll call him tomorrow. There's nothing wrong with the program, though, if that's what worries you."

"That's what worries me. We've had trouble with the program ever since I've been on the project."

Lammont's face was expressionless. "Really? I never heard any complaints from Max." He slipped the tobacco pouch into his pocket. "I guess the demonstration will be starting soon. Thanks for the drink, Mr. Nordlund."

The bastard. Nordlund stared after him. Orencho had never complained? That was hard to believe; Max had bitched about it constantly. He picked up Diana's drink from the bar and went back to the buffet table where they had been standing. She wasn't around.

"I'll take that, Dane—Diana's in the little girls' room."

Senator Alan DeFolge was the last person he wanted to meet and the one person he had known in advance he couldn't avoid.

"I couldn't help but watch you talking to Diana. It was good to see you two together again. She misses you, you know."

Like Beardsley, the senator was a big man, but very little of it was muscle. Pudgy, cynical, and balding, what little hair he still had was plastered tightly against his pink scalp. He drank too much, but Nordlund couldn't remember ever seeing him drunk.

"We've been separated for six months, Senator, and the marriage was down the tubes long before that."

He didn't bother hiding the bitterness in his voice, and DeFolge nodded sympathetically. "The truth is she doesn't want to lose you, Dane. She's got too much of an investment in you."

"And you do, too, don't you, Senator?"

DeFolge rolled the liquor in his glass, studying it for a moment before answering. "Her investment's emotional, of course. As for mine, I think you're being a little hard on me. If you want to call me a conniving old man, that's your right. I love my daughter, I'd do anything for her. But to give a qualified man a crack at a job he's more than capable of doing doesn't sound like a lot to me. Frank's got veto power anyway; if you were no damned good, it wouldn't matter what I wanted."

Nordlund glanced at his watch. Five minutes to three—time he started the demonstration.

"I'm having dinner with Diana next week, Senator. But I wouldn't make anything of that if I were you."

DeFolge looked pleased. "I'm sure you'll enjoy each other's company, Dane." Then, almost as an afterthought: "Nippon Engineering's thinking of making a bid for the western leg, along with us. The chief engineer's spot will be wide open."

Nordlund didn't dare look back for fear DeFolge would see the rage on his face. The son of a bitch had been manipulating people for so long, it was automatic. DeFolge was convinced that every man had his price and that being appointed chief engineer on the western leg was his. Kaltmeyer had thought that, too, had as much as said so on the plane coming in. If he wanted it, all he had to do was kiss and make up with Diana. DeFolge's talk about giving a "qualified" man a chance was so much bullshit. All things being equal, there were a lot of qualified men. But when it came to him, all things were far from equal.

The meeting room was almost empty now, most of the guests having left for the demonstration next door. Nordlund was half-way across the room when somebody cried "Dane!"

He turned to see Janice hurrying across the floor toward him, her gold-rimmed glasses, secured by a thin chain around her neck, bouncing against her breasts. "The demonstration hasn't started yet, has it?"

"It can't start without me, Janice." He took her by the arm, glad for once to see a face without guile. Just before they entered the demonstration room, she paused and said, "You know a Cyd Lederley?"

He looked blank. "I don't think so. What'd he want?"

"She—she said it was Cyd with a C. She'll be dropping by the office tomorrow, said you met in Washington."

It hadn't been all committee hearings during the week in D.C.; there had been the usual parties where the hostess made sure he met the best if not the brightest of the available young women in town. But he didn't remember anybody named Cyd.

For that matter, he didn't remember anybody named Susan or Jennifer or MaryAnn either, and he was sure he had met several.

She would take up valuable time—time he really couldn't afford—but that might not be all bad. Maybe she could take his mind off Diana.

The demonstration room was as large as the room with the buffet, but it was bare except for what looked like a toy train landscape that took up most of the floor, complete with miniature mountains and tunnels and a little western town. A wormlike cage of silver mesh threaded its way through the Styrofoam countryside and made, in effect, a complete circuit of the room. The mesh was supported at intervals by a solid ring from which a complex of small cables ran to a juncture box. A technician carrying a Dewar bottle of liquid nitrogen moved quickly around the landscape, filling small reservoirs with the liquified gas.

The guests were seated in folding chairs behind a thick Plexiglas screen facing the model, to one side of which was a small podium. Nordlund tapped the microphone on top and said, "Make yourselves comfortable, folks. It will be a minute or so before the system stabilizes."

The technician seemed to be having trouble with one of the reservoirs, and Nordlund caught his breath. *Please, God, don't let anything go wrong now. . . .*

"Dane, can we begin?" Kaltmeyer was standing with the chief technician by the control board for the model rail system, fidgeting with the various knobs.

Nordlund glanced again at the man with the bottle of liquid nitrogen. He held up a circled thumb and forefinger. Everything was set.

"As you can see," Nordlund began, "the rail system is a continuous cage of magnetized rails that levitate the cars." He waved a pointer at the motionless model train in front, which consisted of a control car and head-to-foot linking of six other cars. It was about the size of the old-time Lionel trains that Nordlund could remember begging for when he was a kid.

"The motive power is provided by the rings, spaced along the tracks. These are actually liquid nitrogen-cooled solenoids— magnets that develop an unusually strong magnetic flux. They literally suck the train along, each ring becoming inert as the train passes. The momentum of the train carries it toward the next ring solenoid, which is then energized and pulls the train forward once again."

He paused, studying the faces of the audience to be sure they understood. The engineers already knew how it worked, the media could ask questions afterward, and the security men couldn't care less. He spotted Diana in the audience; she looked bored. Janice, on the other hand, was fascinated; her mouth was slightly open as she concentrated on every word he was saying.

"The sequencing is controlled by a computerized device in master switching stations every ten miles. These receive radio signals from the train, and they control velocity and braking, as well as other functions. Since there is no friction of wheels on rails, we can achieve some phenomenal velocities."

"I understand that the Boston-to-Washington test line has achieved three hundred miles an hour," somebody said from the crowd.

Nordlund hid a smile. Nakamura was acting as his shill. "That's true, sir. We believe we can operate consistently at this speed for long stretches—perhaps at even greater speeds." There was a murmur from the crowd. Nordlund leaned over to the technician by his side and said in a low voice, "It's all yours."

The technician signaled his counterpart at Kaltmeyer's control board, and a moment later the train began to move, slowly at first but with increasing acceleration. The model had a safety governor that limited speed to sixty miles an hour, still an impressive speed for a small model.

The train reached the first curve, banking on its side as it went in. It sped through the short leg of the landscape, still accelerating. Nordlund felt the hair on the nape of his neck stiffen. The train should have slowed for the curve. Now it was traveling along the return leg, hitting at least forty miles an hour and still building up speed.

The model's movement had become a blur. Nordlund flashed a quick glance at Kaltmeyer. He was looking smug, obviously proud of the model's performance. The train hit its second lap at a good fifty miles an hour and came out of the first curve doing sixty. Then Nordlund realized the train was still accelerating. He left the podium and ran over to the control board and the technician operating it. "Cut the sequence, Jeff, we've seen enough."

The man was sweating. "I can't—there's a malfunction in the control box." He jiggled the lever in front of him. "Jesus, Dane, it won't obey commands."

The train was now literally screaming around the track, and the people in the first row of seats had nervously edged their chairs back. As the model returned to its starting point for the third lap, it seemed to gain new speed. It hit the long stretch of the landscape at well over a hundred miles an hour. The train was now impossible for the eye to follow.

Nordlund sensed rather than saw the train when it went into the first curve again. This time the silver mesh cage buckled as

(51

centrifugal force drove the model against its side. The mesh suddenly tore, and the train, now a free missile, sped directly toward the far wall. It hit with the sound of an explosion, along with the crash of falling plaster.

Nordlund stared at the wall, ignoring the guests who sat dazed in their chairs, not quite sure what had happened. The runaway model had blasted a six-foot-diameter hole through the plaster wall and part of the brickwork beyond, coming to rest half in and half out of the building, a twisted piece of silver junk.

Kaltmeyer and Nakamura were at his side now, both talking at once, though it was only Nakamura whom he clearly heard.

"Too much haste, Mr. Nordlund," the Japanese was saying, shaking his head sadly. "Too much haste."

CHAPTER 5

He stood by the big picture window in the living room, watching the snow swirl past the streetlights outside. It was the Christmas season again, but all it would bring him would be pain and remembrance. He had vivid memories of the first Christmas after the blowout—how many years ago now?—and they were almost as painful as the blowout itself.

He had been alone for months in a room with a white-sheeted bed and antiseptic walls that constantly seemed to be closing in on him. Through the barred window he could see the broad stretch of snow-covered ground that surrounded the building and the stand of weathered oaks through which a family of squirrels had scampered and chattered during the summer. He had liked to watch the squirrels, with their nervous movements and the quick flick of their tails. There were few animals that struck him as being so much . . . alive.

He was feeling better, he had told himself. For a long time— had it been a year?—he had found himself breaking down and sobbing unexpectedly. The anguish would well up and overcome him, flooding him with such emotional pain, he was incapable of thinking.

That had been especially true when he looked into the mirror and once again saw . . . his face. It would trigger such a violent reaction, they had to remove all reflective surfaces from his room, including any metal or highly polished trays.

He had finally progressed to the point where they allowed him a small shaving mirror, though they hadn't yet removed the paint from the large mirror in the bathroom. They told him that with time he could leave and go back to the outside world. Back to cold nights and silent rooms . . . and hatred.

He hadn't told them about the hatred. When he felt it well up within him, he'd go to the bathroom and turn on the shower before he started screaming, or he would throw himself onto the bed and muffle his voice in the pillow.

He had become an expert on hatred. And he knew who he hated. He had made a list with four names on it, the ones most responsible. Someday he would make them pay; it was just a matter of time. But before then, he knew he had to learn how to control his hatred, to direct it. To become . . . just sane enough.

He wasn't prepared for the entrance of Dr. Merrimac and two of his orderlies. He sat patiently while frail, white-haired Dr. Merrimac explained they weren't really satisfied with his progress, that his mood swings and fits of depression, his outbursts of rage, were cause for concern. What were they going to do? he asked. The doctor's recommendation was to increase his intake of tranquilizers and antipsychotic medication.

He protested. He didn't like the mood swings and the fits of depression, either. They made his life a living hell, an emotional prison far more harsh than the locked wards of the mental hospital. But he needed the rage that went with them, he needed the motivation and the edge it provided. He couldn't afford to be happy . . . to forget. He did not tell the doctor that.

During his excitement, he almost forgot the orderlies. He noticed just in time that they had become tense and watchful, too watchful.

It took a great effort to calm down, to assure the doctor that naturally he respected his clinical judgment. The orderlies relaxed. And when did the doctor propose to start the program? Why, that same afternoon, Dr. Merrimac said. The doctor went to great lengths to explain how the medication worked and to assure him there would be no pain and few side effects. He nodded, letting the doctor assume he was satisfied with the explanations. Finally, the little doctor and the two orderlies left.

He knew then that he couldn't stay. He had needed the year for rest and emotional recuperation and time to assess the blame for the terrible tragedy. Now he had done that, and it was time to leave. The increased medication would threaten his control, threaten his plans, might even dim the memories of what had

(54

happened, the memories that drove him. He couldn't allow that to happen.

It was approaching noon, and he knew that nearly everyone would be in the cafeteria. They would expect him in the dining hall, and as long as they thought that's where he was going, nobody would stop him. He pulled his robe around him and stepped into the empty corridor. The discipline among the attendants was very lax. But after all, there were few patients one might classify as dangerous, and some of them were even allowed supervised furloughs in the nearby town.

He turned into the deserted east corridor, walking away from the dining room. It was dangerous now, but the door to freedom was in sight. Then he heard noises and realized someone was coming. The nearest hiding place was a mop closet, and he ducked into it, closing the door behind him. Inside, the air was musty with the odors of sour mops and bleach and the acrid smell of human sweat. He searched for the light switch and turned it on.

The closet was large, easily four by six. There was the usual collection of mops, long-handled squeegees, and pails. An overhead shelf held boxes of detergents, bottles containing blue window-cleaning solutions, and white plastic containers of bleach. The smell of sour perspiration came from some work clothes hanging on a nearby hook. Blue jeans, a sweat shirt, and a pair of dirty sneakers. There were no socks.

He took off his bathrobe and pajamas and forced himself to put on the work clothes. Then he turned off the light, opened the door, and glanced out. There was no one in sight. He slipped out and started for the door at the end of the hallway. Nobody stopped him. Once outside, he walked rapidly away from the building, trying to ignore the snow and the cold. Then a man shoveling the walk looked up and yelled, "Hey!" He waved and continued toward the gate. Once outside, he would be free. There would be no way to trace him. They had taken his fingerprints when he entered the year before, but when he had been assigned to the records office, he had taken advantage of the opportunity and removed the prints from his file, later shredding them and flushing them down the toilet in his room.

(55

He almost made it without incident. He had only to step through the iron grillwork gate to freedom. It was a shock when Dr. Merrimac rounded the corner, a foil-wrapped sandwich in his hand. The frail, little man stopped, startled, and demanded, "Where are you going?"

"I'm leaving," he said.

The doctor shook his head. "We can't allow that, you're not ready."

He struck the doctor with his fist, catching the old man on the side of the head. The doctor dropped instantly, his neck broken.

The walls on either side of the grillwork gate were lined with bushes at least ten feet high. He pulled the dead man into them and covered him with dead leaves and snow, heaping them over the body until he was satisfied Merrimac couldn't be spotted by anybody passing by. He felt no regret, no sorrow. The doctor's death didn't strike him as tragic as much as a fact to be noted and then forgotten.

And after all, the doctor had tried to stop him, had tried to prevent him from carrying out his plan. Nobody could be allowed to do that.

An hour later he was on the main highway, thumbing his way back to the city. It was Christmas Eve. But there was no hurry—if not this Christmas, then the next one or the one after that. It might take several years, but the four would answer for his terrible loss. He felt the familiar wave of anguish sweep over him then, and for a moment he wasn't able to move, even when the Mustang stopped and the driver leaned out to wave him forward.

He hadn't thought of the dead Dr. Merrimac again. Not until tonight. The Christmas season had arrived once again, complete with snow and street-corner Santas and window displays for the kids. It had taken a number of years, but his plans were completed. It was time to start executing them.

He left the window and walked back to the table where he had been jotting down notes. It didn't take him long at all to find out where the man was hiding. There were only so many

(56

addresses to check, and at one time or another he had followed the man to all of them.

The police had been fools. But he couldn't deny they had also been thoughtful. They had left the man for him.

CHAPTER 6

Nordlund arrived at the Field Station early the next morning to discover that the disastrous model demonstration was coffee-break-conversation topic number one. When Janice brought him his morning sweet roll, she gauged his mood carefully before kidding him about it. "All the high-ballers are saying you tried to get even for Pearl Harbor."

Nordlund winced. "I'm just grateful nobody got hurt. I wanted an observers' platform above the display, but I was overruled." He took a bite out of the sweet roll. "Aside from that, Mrs. Lincoln, how'd you like the show?"

"I've got to admit, it had a smash ending. Seriously, I thought it was quite impressive, despite the accident. So did everybody sitting around me. How'd the boss take the crack-up?"

"Pretty well. Besides, the model was courtesy of United Electronics—it wasn't our gadget." He walked over to the coffee machine and jiggled the controls a moment. "You made arrangements for the visiting firemen?"

She pulled out her pad and adjusted her glasses. "I looked them up at the demo. Everything was arranged for yesterday, but they'll have to supply their own geisha girls."

Nordlund was only half-listening. If he increased the percentage of chicory, added five seconds to the brewing time, and dropped the temperature of the hot water a few degrees, that should just about do it.

It didn't. He made a face and set the coffee cup on his desk. "What's the schedule?"

"Del Styron—as soon as possible. Then Mr. Phillips and Major Richards. Phillips didn't look happy, and the major wants to talk about the Japanese."

"Did you give him their names?"

She nodded. "No problem, just protocol, I gather." A glance of curiosity. "An auditor and his crew from the GAO are due in this morning."

It took a moment before he recalled Kaltmeyer's conversation on the plane. He would bet they hadn't been expected this soon.

"Sorry, Jan, I thought the old man told you. Some of the fallout from Max's mess."

"Rumor says it's DeFolge's enemies in Congress. Any truth to that?"

"Search me. Any problems with them, check with me, and I'll tell you if you have to refer it upstairs. That it?"

She shook her head. "A Mr. Hideo Nakamura has been waiting for you. I think he was at the demonstration."

It was the first pleasant meeting she had mentioned. He hurried into the outer office and spotted Nakamura sitting patiently on the small sofa opposite Janice's desk. "Mr. Nakamura— what a pleasure!" Once back inside his own office, he pointed at the brewing machine and said, "It makes tea as well as coffee, if you'd prefer it."

Nakamura shook his head. "American coffee, black, is a treat for me." He looked apologetic. "Mr. Kaltmeyer said you would not mind if I spent the day as an observer. Perhaps one of your men could show me the tunnel later."

"Swede would be glad to. I have a wrecking crew from Washington coming in, but maybe I could join you this afternoon." He hesitated, remembering Del Styron and the program. "I have to go over some computer programs with the chief geologist. Would you be interested . . . ?"

Nakamura smiled. "I would be most grateful, if I would be no trouble."

"No problem," Nordlund murmured, embarrassed by Nakamura's excessive politeness. He buzzed Janice to get Styron, and a moment later the sweaty little geologist bustled in with a thick sheaf of printouts. Nordlund made the introductions, and Styron nodded impatiently, distracted by his armload of data. He spread the sheets on the light table.

"This thing floors me, Mr. Nordlund. I've been going over the raw data in more detail, and I must confess there are some spots that look very strange."

Nordlund peered over his shoulder. "Anything critical?"

"I'm not sure." Styron frowned. "There are data areas I don't understand." He pointed to a string of numbers on the printout. "Mr. Lammont and his crews carried out extensive soundings for a mile on either side of the tunnel route and less extensive spot-sampling ones for an additional ten miles on either side. They used spark echoes, radar, and sonar data, and then the computer generated a complete strata model covering ten miles on each side of the route and to a depth of one mile."

"Reliability?"

"Seventy-five to ninety percent. Supposedly." He circled an area on the sheet before him with a pudgy forefinger. "Take this cross-section. The machine reads it as a layer of sedimentary rock rising to a thick layer of limestone with some porosity and organic occlusions, topped finally with shale and a layer of silt—exactly what you would expect for a lakebed."

"And below the sedimentary rock?" Nakamura interrupted politely.

Styron made the connection for the first time. A visiting Japanese geologist, which meant somebody important. He was visibly impressed.

"Probably igneous, Mr. Nakamura. Very old, perhaps primordial." He turned back to Nordlund. "But here we have a similar profile half a mile from the tunnel route. Extensive limestone, like an unruffled sheet."

"So what's the problem?"

Styron took a breath. "The discontinuity with the sedimentary rock is too gradual. This area shows solid limestone—no occlusions, no porosity, just solid stone."

Nordlund looked blank. "What are you driving at?"

"The stratum looks like an isolated phenomenon. It's surrounded by other limestone of distinctly different characteristics, yet the program indicates this other stone is completely continuous with the solid area."

Styron sensed that he wasn't making himself clear. "What I mean, Mr. Nordlund, is that what the computer program predicts and what we're actually running into are two completely different things."

"What did Lammont say?"

Styron looked uncomfortable. "A flaw in the computer's ability to extrapolate from his program."

"You agree with that?"

Hesitation. "I find it difficult to believe."

"Then call Lammont and tell him to come out and work with you. If he gives you any static, refer him to me."

After Styron had left, Nakamura said sympathetically, "Your last quarter-mile is turning out to be the most difficult, I presume."

Nordlund nodded, worried. "If it's all solid rock, that's one thing. The new moles make good progress in rock, and since the tunnel's stand-up time in rock is almost indefinite, we don't need to shore up the tunnel walls or the ground arch while we cement the shields into position. Looser soil, we'll have to shotcrete the walls and the arch for support. If it gets loose enough, we'll have to grout the whole area before digging through it, maybe even work under pressure if we hit mud. We'll lose time— and considering the pressure from Washington, I don't have the time to lose."

"Mr. Lammont," Nakamura said slowly. "A good man?"

"One of the best in the business." Nordlund tried to read the future in the bottom of his cup of coffee. "So I thought, at any rate."

He had been back in the office only three days and already he could feel the pressure rising. When he had been offered the chief engineer's job, he was excited and a little afraid. It was a bigger job than he had ever held before. But it wasn't the work as much as the responsibility. Give Kaltmeyer credit, he had warned him it would be like this.

He buzzed Janice to have Swede, Beardsley's chief assistant, show Nakamura the tunnel. After the Japanese had left, Nordlund leaned back in his chair and stared at the framed photograph above the coffee machine that showed himself and Diana posing next to a large marlin, one of the souvenirs of the job in Florida.

For him, the pose had reflected the real thing; he loved deep-sea fishing. Diana, of course, didn't. It was like Diana and tennis. She hated the game, but she knew she looked good in tennis shorts and shoes with a sweater looped loosely around her neck. So she faked it. She was good at faking a lot of things.

But nobody could do it forever. Sooner or later, they found you out.

The thought hung there for a moment, as if it somehow had greater importance attached to it. Then he shook himself, realizing that in ten minutes he was scheduled for a meeting with Metcalf, Phillips, and Major Richards and that he had no idea what he was going to say.

One thing he knew for sure. He couldn't afford to tell Phillips about the possible flaws in the computer program.

"December twenty-third for the actual hole-through and local ceremony," Phillips said, not bothering to hide his enthusiasm. "Christmas Eve is out—too much competition for the evening news. That will give us time between the holidays to get the shields in place and maybe lay a single track for the major event January third. Barring a reactor meltdown or World War Three, we should have the six o'clock news and the morning papers pretty much to ourselves."

Metcalf looked curious. "Why so worried? There's no way hole-through would be ignored by the television networks or the newspapers, it's too big."

"You want to schedule it for Christmas Eve?" Phillips asked sarcastically. "You can forget it then. People will be trimming the tree, doing last-minute shopping or stuffing the Christmas turkey. We might as well be digging a ditch in Melrose Park for all the play we'd get."

Metcalf caught a warning glance from Nordlund and shrugged. "Sure, Mr. Phillips, the twenty-third makes sense."

Phillips looked slightly mollified. "Schedule it early enough so the television people can set up their cameras and get enough tape for the evening news; the networks can pick up from the affiliates half an hour later. The papers are more flexible—we'll have locals plus stringers from the *Times* and the *Post*. The big show will be ten days later. We'll get the governor and the mayor, plus half a dozen Midwest senators and the majority whip from the House. Maybe a little human interest with the actor who appeared in that tunnel picture on TV the other night. . . ."

He paused, groping for a name. Nordlund said drily, "Richard Dix in *Transatlantic Tunnel*. It's an ancient rerun, Steve. The actor's been dead for decades."

"Joke, Dane," Phillips said, deadpan. "I'll have my secretary type this up and copy you with the details. Could we get a car to run through the cut? It should be easy to lay enough track so we can push it a few feet. We could borrow one from the railroads or maybe the Chicago subway system. Anything to show the system is ready to go—or will be soon."

Nordlund felt grim. "You're getting ahead of yourself, Steve. I can't promise hole-through in nine days."

There was a moment of silence. "I thought we had decided all this the last time we talked," Phillips said in a tight voice.

"You did, Steve, I didn't."

It was Metcalf who cut the ice. "Everybody here will do their best, Mr. Phillips. I think all of us realize the importance for the Administration. From what we know, hole-through certainly won't be that far off from the twenty-third. If we hit it before, we can stall a day or so to fit it into your schedule."

Phillips shot Nordlund a small smile of triumph. At least somebody at Kaltmeyer/DeFolge was on his side.

Nordlund decided not to push it. Hole-through would happen when it happened, despite Phillips's private schedule. If Steve had to keep the champagne on ice for a day or two longer, that was his problem. But he had to admit that Metcalf had handled it just right. Be accommodating if they made hole-through ahead of time, don't emphasize that they might not. Now, if Troy could only do as well with the high-ballers . . .

"What about security, Major?"

Major Harry Richards had sat poker-faced throughout the discussion about hole-through, but then, Nordlund couldn't remember when he had ever offered an opinion about anything concerning the cut. Burly and with a brush cut, Richards was in his early forties, so obviously the military man that he didn't have to be wearing his uniform for those who met him to guess he was in the service. Affable, he nevertheless kept his distance from the "civilians" on the cut. Nordlund didn't know whether he was Phillips's creature or not, but he did know that security had been tight as a drum from the day he had started working at the cut, and Richards had kept it that way ever since.

"We can handle it, provided you don't throw me any last-minute curves like the Japanese observers." He said it with only the slightest hint of don't-do-it-again in his voice.

"Kaltmeyer's idea, not mine. Any problem with them?"

Richards smiled slightly. "I lost some sleep staying on the line to Tokyo, but then, I guess the people in Tokyo lost some, too."

"What about Steve's scenario for the first shindig?"

Richards glanced at Phillips, thoughtful. "Ask the TV people to set up pool coverage. Same thing for the papers—can't have everybody and their kid brother down in the cut. And keep the foreign dignitaries away; they bring their own security people, and it's hell's half acre trying to clear all of them." He paused. "That's not just a suggestion, Steve. If there's any quarter where trouble would come from, that would be it. Nobody gets on the island without a pass signed by me, and that goes for the media as well as the politicians. No personal articles go in or out without being checked, and if in doubt, I'll refer them back to you."

Nordlund felt surprised. "You expecting something?"

Richards shrugged. "Not especially. It's just that the situation itself is a setup. Important people, cameras at the ready, crucial event for the country . . . I don't know how many thrillers they've written about moles in the CIA and God knows where else, but I keep wondering why it couldn't happen on something like this. We've got a thousand people working on both ends of the cut, and how much do we really know about them? The number of traffic violations they've logged, their social security number, and if they own their own house, and that's about it."

He suddenly smiled. "I'm not asking you guys to worry, that's my job. But don't forget that some people might think it would be the perfect time to blow up the tunnel."

The light on the intercom was winking at him, and Nordlund flicked the switch. "What's up, Jan?"

"A Mr. Samuel Wilcox from the General Accounting Office, Dane. And his assistant, Cyd Lederley." He caught a smile in her voice and wondered why. He looked up at the others in the office.

"Before you leave, you might as well meet these people— you'll have to check them out anyway, Harry. And they'll probably be spending as much time with you as they will with me, Steve." He flicked the switch again. "Okay, send them in."

Samuel Wilcox was closer to seventy than sixty, frail, with graying hair and the impatient air of a workaholic. Nordlund could picture him going through the books late at night, a small computer on the desk in front of him, and his faded blue eyes picking through the numbers on the screen.

But the woman in blue who followed Wilcox really caught his eye. They had met in Washington, she had told Jan.

At Washington National Airport, to be precise.

For one of the few occasions in Nordlund's life, time seemed to run in slow motion. Phillips was on his feet and holding out his hand, but his voice was antagonistic. "I'm surprised to see you here, Wilcox."

The old man pumped his hand exactly twice. A bland expression masked any emotions he might have felt toward Phillips. "I go where they send me, Steven. And they never send me anyplace without good reason."

"I'll tell that to Michael next time I visit him at Terminal Island."

His hostility didn't seem to bother Wilcox at all. "I'm sorry about your friend, I always have been—he showed a lot of promise. But he was caught with his hand in the cookie jar, and that was nobody's fault but his own.''

Richards was shaking Cyd Lederley's hand with a good deal more enthusiasm than Phillips was showing Wilcox. "It's good seeing you again, Cyd.''

"Harry, what a pleasant surprise—nobody warned me.''

He grinned. "And they say there are no secrets in Washington.'' He turned back to Nordlund. "Dane, Cyd Lederley, a friend of mine from old Foggy Bottom.''

"We've met,'' Nordlund said curtly.

"On the red-eye coming in,'' Cyd added with a forced smile. "Mr. Nordlund and I had a long talk.''

Richards picked up on the tension in her voice, raised his eyebrows, and said, "Save me a luncheon, Cyd,'' then nodded to Nordlund. "I'll get back to you later about their IDs, Dane.''

And then the others had left as well. Metcalf took Wilcox up to introduce him to Kaltmeyer and the chief accountant, Henry Leaver, a man as old and bloodless as Wilcox himself. Leaver, Nordlund mused. If he had buried any bodies on behalf of Kaltmeyer/DeFolge and it was up to Wilcox to find them, it would be a dead heat. Leaver had been with K and D since time began; the bodies would certainly be buried deep.

"You could offer me a chair, Mr. Nordlund.''

He pointed to the couch. "I'm stunned by the coincidence.''

"I meant to tell you on the plane. You didn't give me much of a chance.''

"You had all the chances in the world, Miss Lederley.'' He let the conversation hang there and felt only mildly guilty when she looked uncomfortable.

"The boy,'' she said quietly. "You were angry because you obviously felt something for him and thought I didn't. That's a pretty harsh judgment to pass, considering how little we know of each other.''

She had a point, though he hated to admit it. He was a bleeding heart, and she kept her feelings to herself. It didn't mean she didn't have any.

(66

"So let's try and get to know each other better." He walked over to the coffee machine. "I can make you a cup of coffee, or you can have tea if you prefer." She was a tea-type person, he knew it. "We have Earl Grey, English Breakfast, Oolong, Orange Pekoe—you name it."

"English Breakfast, if it's no bother. You like deep-sea fishing?"

He couldn't help smiling. "That's my wife in the photograph—we're separated. I love deep-sea fishing, but she never did." He brewed himself a cup of coffee and was shocked to find it was perfect. Then he cursed quietly to himself; he'd been in a hurry and couldn't remember how he had done it.

As she crossed her legs and leaned back on the couch, he was reminded of when he had first seen her at the airport. She was the type of woman they called handsome rather than beautiful. Striking in her way, though she couldn't compare with Diana. Then the disquieting thought occurred to him that if she couldn't compare, why did he keep comparing her?

Back behind his desk, he said, "I really don't know what you and Mr. Wilcox are looking for, but you can depend on the cooperation of me and my staff. It may be a little hectic around here for the next ten days or so. We're trying to complete hole-through by then."

"Hole-through?"

"When the two ends of the tunnel meet—about four miles out in the lake from the access shaft outside." He cocked his head. "Mr. Kaltmeyer said I should offer you complete cooperation, but I really don't know why you're here." He tried to put it on a friendly basis and failed. "Just why *are* you here?"

For a moment she looked blank, then recovered. "The bullet train project has taken an enormous amount of money, Mr. Nordlund, and the Lake Michigan tunnel more than its share."

"It's been money well spent," he said defensively.

"Some members of Congress think Max Orencho was compensated a bit too well for his services."

"Max was a thief. That doesn't mean everybody is, that the project's being looted."

She put down her cup of tea on his desk blotter. She had been trying to keep it friendly, too, but it wasn't working.

"There weren't many safeguards to prevent it in his case. GAO's curious what they were, if any, and what there is now."

Now wasn't the time to argue it. "How many in your group?"

"Twelve, including myself and Mr. Wilcox. We've been given space in the K and D Building downtown, but Mr. Wilcox and I will also be keeping offices on the third floor here."

That was Steve Phillips's section; well, they could fight it out with each other for the space—and it ought to be some fight.

She looked offended. "Did I say something funny?"

"No, it's just that that's where Steve Phillips has his offices. I'd appreciate it if you'd try to make arrangements with him before asking me to intercede." He could imagine the argument and stifled a smile. "I assume Phillips and Wilcox knew each other in Washington?"

"Mr. Wilcox sent a friend of his to jail for five years. Kickbacks in the Department of Defense."

Nordlund felt chilled. Wilcox apparently always got his man, and considering the strings that Phillips must have pulled, the old man couldn't be bought off or intimidated.

"So what will your procedure be here?"

She studied him with slate-gray eyes. "Conduct a financial investigation of everybody of importance connected with the Lake Michigan tunnel. We'll need access to bank records; we'll subpoena them if we have to. We'll try to pin down every false entry, every misappropriation, any kickbacks or sweetheart deals traceable to Max Orencho."

He had a vague memory of the Rickover scandals a decade or so before, when the father of the nuclear navy had been pilloried for accepting a rug and some silverware from defense contractors, if he remembered correctly. He felt vaguely uneasy. There was something personal about this, and then the obvious hit him.

"You'll be investigating me, won't you?"

She nodded.

"Why?"

"For one thing, you're Max Orencho's replacement. For

another, you were elevated above a number of other senior engineers.''

"I was the best-qualified for the job," he said coldly. "The others didn't have as much experience in the field.''

She started rummaging in her bag, not meeting his eyes. "I don't mean this in any personal sense. But you're also married to Senator DeFolge's daughter, and Senator DeFolge is more than half of Kaltmeyer/DeFolge. The senator's business dealings are complex; his holding company controls a number of firms that function as subcontractors on various phases of the project. In some circles there's a natural concern about a possible conflict of interests.''

"I earned my job," Nordlund said, trying to keep back his anger. "I didn't get it because I married Diana DeFolge.''

"I'm not accusing you of anything, Mr. Nordlund. I'm just trying to explain why you'll be included in the investigation. The reason is because you can't possibly be left out.'' She took a business card out of her bag and wrote quickly on the back. "I meant to give this to your secretary. Both Mr. Wilcox and I have rooms at the Marriott. Those are the numbers.''

She stood up and walked to the door, then turned. "You're very proud of the job you do here, aren't you, Mr. Nordlund?''

"I think I do a good one.''

"I'm sure you do," she said quietly. "I'm also sure that at times it's a difficult, frustrating, and dirty job. I do a good job, too, and it can be just as difficult and frustrating and dirty as yours.''

He stared at the door for a good five minutes after she walked out. Two weeks before, he had been appointed to fill Max Orencho's shoes, and he had been on top of the world. In two days the world had turned brown before his eyes, and now he felt trapped. Neither Kaltmeyer nor DeFolge had done him any favors. He was qualified for the job—he knew better than they just how well-qualified he was—but apparently he was also a pawn on their chessboard. He didn't know if they had any strings on him other than Diana, but he would bet money they did. And of course, Cyd Lederley would find out what they were.

He slid open his desk drawer to drop her card into it, then

reached in and pulled out a pair of dice that he had once taken away from a compressor man in the cut. He rolled them on the desktop. Seven. He tossed them again. Another seven. He reached for his letter-opener and scraped at one of the dots. A tiny bead of mercury oozed onto the desk blotter.

The dice were loaded.

But then, so was life, his marriage, and the job he had signed on for without reading the fine print.

Max, where the hell are you when we really need you?

CHAPTER 7

His anguish and his anger built with the holiday season, and with them the disorientation and distortion that he recognized as growing symptoms of the insanity that always hit him then. When he walked down the street, everything looked distant and somehow twisted out of shape, as if seen through the wrong end of a telescope. But he was used to it now, and he could maneuver easily enough through the holiday crowds or the stores jammed with Christmas displays. More and more, it seemed as if he were a tiny little man trapped inside the prison of his head, busily working the miniature levers and buttons that moved his arms and legs.

The streetlights had winked on an hour before, and now it began to snow. It was dinnertime, which meant the man's girlfriend would be at the piano bar where she sang. The man would be alone, probably preparing himself an evening meal. He never went out anymore, he was afraid he would be recognized. But he would have to move soon, probably Christmas Eve, one of the few times during the year when the airports would be crowded and security thin.

Which meant there was no room for delay.

He passed a woman in a blue Salvation Army uniform, her high-cheekboned face flushed with the cold, her eyes red and watering. She was tinkling a bell above an iron pot dangling by a chain from a tripod. The sign said Merry Christmas and was decorated with a few leaves of holly—real ones, not painted. She deserved something, at least, for originality. He dug into the pocket of his mackinaw and pulled out three coins, which he dropped into the pot. She flashed a smile. He stared blankly back, but something was written on his face that made her look quickly away.

The man's girlfriend lived in a ten-story brick apartment house. Its front door was shielded by a gold-bordered blue canopy that stretched out to the curb. He glanced up and was acutely aware of every detail of the aluminum piping that supported the canopy, every stitch in the stretched canvas. It took an effort not to lose himself in the complexity of it, to just stand there and stare at the canopy all night. He pushed through the glass doors into the apartment house lobby. It was fancy, almost opulent, and he wondered how long the man had been supporting the café singer and how much it cost. But then, the man could afford it.

He avoided the carpet that ran the length of the lobby, stepping carefully on the terrazzo flooring to one side. He knew that if he used the carpet, the deep pile would swallow him up, that he would sink into it until it closed over his head as the sandy waters of the river had closed over him—had it really been him? Hadn't it been someone else?—so many years before, draining away his life until he had become an automaton that ate and slept and worked until someday it could get revenge.

The glass-enclosed directory was on the wall next to the elevator. He switched his briefcase to his left hand and ran a forefinger down the listings until he found the café singer's name. Opposite the directory was a speaker grill with a row of numbered buttons. The man would be smart enough not to answer, so he chose one at random, mumbled something about a delivery, and waited. There would be no questioning—there were always deliveries this time of year.

There was a buzzing, and the elevator doors slid quietly open. He entered and pressed the button for the sixth floor, trying to ignore the sound of "Adeste Fideles" from the speaker in the ceiling of the elevator cage. Some of the workmen had been singing that in the tunnel when . . . when . . .

The door closed with a soft rush of air, and the elevator began to rise. Deep in the prison of his skull, he felt a sudden surge of anger that smoothed out to a sense of anticipation. The elevator came to a stop, the doors opened, and he walked down the hall to apartment 603. There was nobody in the hallway,

(72

and he put his ear to the door and listened for a moment. The evening news was on the television. Of course the man would be listening to that, waiting for a mention of his own name. He quickly slid a plastic card between the door and the lock. A moment of resistance, and then he turned the knob and walked in. The man had felt secure enough not to throw the deadbolt. Nobody would think of looking for him here. The café singer was one of many women friends the police hadn't known about, that nobody had known about. But nobody had followed the man as long and as patiently as he had.

The man was sitting on the couch in the living room, his back to the door. He had heard nothing; he hadn't been expecting to hear anything.

"Hello, Max."

The man jerked around, his face suddenly white. He looked different. He had shaved his moustache and dyed his hair.

"I brought you some things you left at the office."

The man didn't know what to think, except that he apparently represented no immediate threat. The police hadn't followed him in; neither had anybody from the company. The man was suddenly sly, offering him a drink. Why the visit, what did he want?

"I knew you weren't coming back, and I thought you would be interested in looking something over."

It seemed perfectly logical that of course the man would believe him. But even if he didn't, the only alternatives were to call the police, which the man could hardly afford to do. Or kill him. But with what? He looked around. If the man kept a pistol, it would be in the bed table or perhaps in the desk in the study nook just off the living room. He walked over to it. The man followed him, too close, too eager. He was right. It was a safe bet there was a gun in the desk, probably in the middle drawer. He stood close enough to it so there was no way the man could pull it open.

He took a folder out of his briefcase.

"I thought you ought to see these, Max."

The man opened the file folder and then leaned closer when he saw the yellowed clippings with the headlines screaming of the disaster beneath the East River.

The man was off guard now, absorbed in the clippings from the past. The man didn't see him take a short metal rod, covered with layers of black friction tape, from his pocket. When the man suddenly glanced up, frightened and suspicious, it was too late. He brought the rod down, hard, just behind the man's right ear. He crumpled without a sound. Only a faint trickle of blood above the ear marked where the metal rod had landed. He felt for the man's neck and took his pulse by pressing up just beneath the jawbone. He was still alive.

He ignored the body and walked quickly through the apartment, pausing in the kitchen to lift the lid of a simmering pot and sniff. Inside were several unpeeled potatoes, carrots, onions, and some cubes of stew meat simmering in a broth that smelled faintly of garlic and marsala wine. It would be ready by the time the woman came home. A candlelit dinner for two.

The bathroom was tiled in pastel blue, the top tiles decorated with a scroll pattern in a deeper blue. The tub was the same deep color, with a chromed showerhead jutting from the tile above the tub. A bottle of after-shave and a tube of toothpaste lay on the pale blue cultured marble counter that held the two circular wash basins. He opened the medicine cabinet. It was a woman's bathroom; the man was obviously a temporary guest.

He located what he was looking for next to the tub: an electric shaver in a black plastic cradle, its cord plugged into a wall receptacle, the red light indicating that its battery was charging. He moved the cradle with the shaver to the top of the commode, next to the tub, without unplugging it. The outlet switch was just below the mirror, and he turned it off. The red shaver light abruptly went out.

He went back to the living room and stripped all the clothing off the unconscious man, carrying the various articles into the bedroom and arranging them on a silent valet, placing the shoes stuffed with the man's socks directly beneath. He smiled to himself. What the well-dressed man will wear. Then he re-

turned to the bathroom and drew a medium-hot bath, testing the water with his hand.

Back in the living room, he picked up the nude body of the man and carried it into the bathroom. The man groaned weakly but did not regain consciousness. He gently slid the man into the tub, his head turned toward the faucet. Before he let him sink all the way into the water, he rubbed his fingers in the blood oozing from the scalp and wiped a smear on the faucet. Finally he entangled the razor and its cord in the man's fingers. Only then did he let the man slip all the way into the tub, making sure that the shaver was also immersed in the warm water.

"Good-bye, Max."

He reached over to the outlet switch and flicked it on. Fire flashed from the body of the razor, and the lights in the washroom abruptly went out; somewhere a circuit breaker had thrown a switch. He sensed, rather than saw, the man's body convulse briefly and then lie still.

He walked back into the living room, where the lights still burned, and slipped the file folder with its clippings back into his briefcase. He took one last look around, thought momentarily of turning out the fire under the stew, then shrugged. The woman might be hungry. He let himself out quietly. There was no way of throwing the deadbolt, but then, it hadn't been thrown in the first place.

Max had been clever but careless. But that was in keeping with Max—he had always been careless. Unfortunately, other men had paid for his carelessness. And of course, for his greed.

In the hall, he took off the gloves he had worn and dropped them into an incinerator chute. When the elevator doors closed behind him, he leaned back against the rear wall of the cage and closed his eyes. He no longer felt trapped, he no longer felt that he had to consciously move every single muscle if he wanted to walk or climb a flight of stairs or just ease his way through the crowded aisles of a supermarket. The sound of "God Rest Ye Merry Gentlemen" from the elevator speaker was warm and soothing.

He knew he would probably sleep for at least a day when

he got home. And then, once again, the pressure would start to build, and he would find himself retreating into the prison of his mind.

There were three more to go, and he had promised himself it would all be over by Christmas Eve.

Brad had always insisted they keep Christmas Day completely free.

CHAPTER 8

By Monday morning, Nordlund was beat; he had spent most of the weekend in the cut, overseeing the shifts and inspecting the spoil from the boreholes they had drilled to check out the ground that lay ahead. Styron's complaints about Lammont's program had spooked him. The program had never been right. They could have done just as well checking through geology texts and reading up on the last of the Ice Ages—the Wisconsin Glaciation and the lakes and strata it left behind as the ice sheets retreated northward ten thousand years before.

So far, at least, they were still running into solid limestone. There were no indications of "heavy ground," weak strata that might require grouting or extra support. They might even make hole-through ahead of time; there were only a thousand feet of rock left, and the moles were chewing it up at a record pace. The only negative aspect was that it would make Phillips a hero back in Washington.

He took his cup of coffee and walked through Janice's office. Then he opened the outer door so he could watch the men working in the engineering bullpen. Max Orencho might have been a thief, but Nordlund felt a growing sympathy for the man. How often had Max stood there, staring, wondering not only what was being done and how well, but who was doing it?

From the doorway he could see Styron huddled over the printouts, occasionally turning to punch more numbers into his desktop computer. Styron was a good geologist, but he had never been able to warm up to the man. Oddly enough, Orencho had always gotten along with him; there were times when Max and Styron had even seemed to be friends.

He had never been able to figure it out; Styron was such an obvious sleaze. Harry Richards had a dossier on him—he had a dossier on everybody—but Richards never gossiped. It wasn't hard to guess what he thought of Styron, though. The major was casually friendly with almost everybody working the cut, but he drew the line at the pudgy geologist. Their relationship, what there was of it, had always been frosty.

Janice walked up behind him and said in a low voice, "You stare like that, Dane, people will talk." Some of the men in the bullpen had already glanced up, obviously wondering why he was looking at them. Then, more concerned: "What's wrong?"

"Nothing—just tired." He turned back to go inside the office. "Bring the Christmas bonus list in, will you?"

Passing her desk, he stopped for a moment. Her out basket was filled with origami peace cranes made from brightly colored squares of tissue paper. He picked one up and pulled on the tail, smiling as the paper wings flapped in response.

"I made them for St. Catherine's. We're decorating a tree for a Christmas party with the little kids at Cabrini Green tomorrow night." Cabrini Green was the heart of the West Side ghetto; the tree and the party would probably be all the Christmas some of the kids would have.

"You should've gotten married and had kids of your own. You would have made a great mother." Then, embarrassed: "Sorry, Jan—just my way of saying you're one sweet lady." He'd deserve it if she said he would have made a great father.

She laughed. "Maybe next time around."

Five minutes later, she walked in with the personnel list and caught him staring out the window at the skyline of Chicago, half-hidden by swirling snow. She sat down on the end of the couch, adjusted her gold-rimmed glasses, and coughed discreetly. "Care to talk about it?"

"Nope." During the past year, Jan had had a ringside seat at his faltering marriage with Diana; she had to be bored with it by now. He blinked and focused on the list she had given him. The men were well paid for dangerous work, but fortune sometimes dealt a losing hand. He knew who deserved, and Jan knew who needed, and between them they might be able to balance things out.

When he got down to Metcalf's name, he suddenly realized he hadn't seen him all day. "Where's Troy?"

"Down in the cut with Beardsley's shift. Some argument about charge placement."

He had forgotten that he had a hundred on the line. God help him if Beardsley were a bad loser.

Innocently: "The woman with Wilcox—what's her name, Lederley?—I haven't seen her around, either."

"Attractive, isn't she?" Nordlund didn't reply, and Jan shrugged and checked off another name, writing a few words after it. "She called this morning, said she couldn't make it in until late this afternoon."

"She didn't strike me as the type who would miss her first day of work. Not unless she broke a leg or her cat got sick. And she'd get a neighbor to take care of the cat."

"Diana called, too."

Nordlund looked up. "When?"

"About twenty minutes ago; you were up with Kaltmeyer. She said to remind you that you owed her a dinner and that she's free tomorrow night."

"Where?" He usually hated it when Diana picked the spot.

"She suggested Andy's on East Hubbard, claimed you liked the jazz."

This time he couldn't complain. Andy's was one of the first places he had taken her when they were dating, and she was right, he liked the jazz. It also smelled like a setup.

"When you get a chance, call her back—make it for seven." He suddenly put the list aside, frowning. "Jan, what'd you think of Max?"

She looked at him over the top of her glasses. "Lonely man after his divorce. He handled it differently than you have."

"What do you mean?"

"Too much booze, for one thing. Too many one-night stands for another. Sort of the hair of the dog that bit him."

"You know it for sure, or just rumors?"

"I got a lot of calls for him when he wasn't in. They never left a name."

"Why do you think he took the money?"

"Because it was there." She grimaced. "Sorry, that's too serious to be funny about. After the marriage broke up, he seemed to lose interest in everything, even the tunnel. I suppose he just wanted to go away and walk on a beach someplace, and the fancier the beach, the better.''

There was a time when he wouldn't have understood that, but he did now. He went back to the list of names. Jan had made little comments after each one, some of them notations on a man's ability, reminding him of something he might have said and then forgotten. She must have remembered every comment he had ever made, then he reflected that she knew the men as well as he did, maybe better because she had made a point of getting to know the families as well.

''You going to work all night, Dane? I was hoping you'd have dinner with me. Thought you could use some relaxation.'' Kaltmeyer was standing in the doorway, his coat and muffler on, ready to leave for the day.

Nordlund put the list aside. What made Kaltmeyer think that having dinner with him constituted relaxation? ''Working on the Christmas bonuses. It's not the same if you hand them out the day after rather than the day before.''

Kaltmeyer looked sour. ''Don't be too generous. Give away the store, and some congressional committee will insist we go back to Washington and explain why we're robbing the taxpayers blind. We'll talk about them tomorrow.''

''Don't worry, I'll be reasonable.'' It was then that he caught sight of Cyd Lederley standing behind Kaltmeyer in the doorway.

Kaltmeyer noticed his glance. ''I thought Miss Lederley might join us, cheer us both up.''

It was the last thing she'd do, Nordlund thought. At least for him. ''Sorry, Frank, I've got plans, I—''

Kaltmeyer's smile faded at the corners. ''I really think you should come along, Dane.''

It was going to be business after all. The line about relaxation had been bullshit.

''Someplace with local color?''

Magnanimously: ''You pick it out.''

''Jimmy's.'' Nordlund walked over to the coatrack and

shrugged into his mackinaw. "Lots of local color, a real high-baller's hangout."

Kaltmeyer stared. "For Christ's sake, Dane, all they serve is hamburgers; we can't take Miss Lederley there."

Behind him, Cyd laughed. "I'd love it."

What hurt, Nordlund thought glumly, was that she sounded as if she really meant it.

Jimmy's was on lower Wacker Drive, close to the loading docks for the *Chicago Tribune*. Dimly lit, with a bar of polished mahogany, tables with red-checked cloths in the middle, and a row of semiprivate wooden booths opposite the bar, it had long been a hangout for pressmen. The tunnel project had changed that, Nordlund thought. Now as many high-ballers as pressmen hung out there, and sometimes it was an uneasy mix.

"Shaw's Crab House or the Cape Cod Room would have been more appropriate," Kaltmeyer grumbled. He hung his coat on a rack by the booths and helped Cyd slide in next to the wall. Nordlund followed.

Kaltmeyer slid the menu across the table without looking at it. "Order anything besides beer and burgers, and they'll throw us out."

Cyd smiled. "You've been here before?"

"Not very damned often. The crews seem to like it, why I don't know."

"Because they've got the best selection of import beers in the city, and they serve half-pound burgers," Nordlund said. "And they're cheap."

"Low overhead—take a look around." Kaltmeyer was still annoyed but beginning to thaw.

"Why import beers?" Cyd turned slightly to look at Nordlund. "I'd think this would be strictly a Bud, Miller's, and Stroh's place."

Nordlund motioned to a waiter in a white apron. "That's because high-ballers come from all over the world. German, Italian, Swedish, Japanese—you name it. They're stateless. Their world begins with the portal of a cut and ends with the hole-through, when they meet the crew drilling from the other side. After that, they're off to a new cut somewhere else.''

He ordered a Beck's and a half-pounder; Cyd had the same. Kaltmeyer ordered two whiskey and sodas. ''I'll need them when I try the food.''

Cyd casually inspected the room, taking special notice of the men at the bar and around the 3-D video machine at the rear.

''Why do you call them high-ballers? Isn't that railroad slang?''

Maybe she had a thing for working-class types, Nordlund thought, dismayed to note that he was jealous. ''Same basic idea. It refers to the elite group of tunnelers and the speed with which they can sink a shaft.''

Damn, what made her so easy to talk to? He had to remind himself that she was probably a chip off the Wilcox block, that she would be perfectly willing to send him to jail if she thought he had his hand in the till.

Then he realized Kaltmeyer had asked her to dinner in the first place to butter her up or at least to sound her out. He knew instinctively that Kaltmeyer would be out of his depth with her.

''Did you ever actually work as a high-baller?'' she asked Nordlund.

She might have thought that from their conversation on the plane. He shook his head. ''No, I'm basically a degree man, an engineer, though I've worked with them and I can talk with them. But I don't really belong. It's a very select brotherhood.''

She looked across the table. ''And you, Mr. Kaltmeyer?''

He nodded. ''I started out as a high-baller, Miss Lederley, but I'm strictly front-office now. The tunnel men are Dane's bailiwick.''

Kaltmeyer's journey from the tunnels to the boardroom would have made Horatio Alger proud. But he never talked much about his early days, and Nordlund wondered how he had ever met DeFolge.

The hamburgers arrived, and Nordlund took a bite of his, then watched as Cyd took off the top part of her bun to cut the meat with a fork. ''Too messy?''

"Partly. Also, I'm five pounds over, I can skip the bread."

That was something Diana might say. "You worry about your weight?"

"I might if I put on another five."

That was another Diana comparison, Nordlund realized, but a comparison that Cyd won.

"What drives a man to become a high-baller, Dane? Really, I'm not just making conversation."

He mulled it over for a minute, trying to put it into words. "I suppose because it's something of a glamor job. It appeals to a young man's macho self-image. And I imagine there's a special in-group feeling—it's certainly a more important identification than nationality or race."

"It also pays damned well," Kaltmeyer grunted.

Cyd was preoccupied with her hamburger for a moment, then glanced back at Nordlund. "You make it sound profound."

He took offense before he realized she didn't mean any.

"How would you like to spend your working day underground with tons of water and earth pressing down on you, sometimes breathing compressed air so thick you could almost cut it? You're driving a wedge through mud or rock, and you take your life in your hands every minute you do it." He paused, fumbling for words. "There's a mystique to being a high-baller, just as there is to being a race car driver or a rodeo rider or an airline pilot."

"I once read an article about tunnels where the author described the crews building them as raping Mother Earth, trying to impregnate her." There was a hint of laughter in her eyes.

Nordlund waved at the men standing by the bar. "You can say that to me, just don't say that to *them*."

Kaltmeyer looked up from his hamburger. "How long do you think you'll be in town, Miss Lederley?"

Kaltmeyer was getting down to business.

"As long as we have to." There was a slight emphasis on the *we*—Samuel Wilcox was there in spirit if not in person.

"You want to do a thorough job, of course."

"Of course."

" 'A thorough job,' " Kaltmeyer mused, swirling the liquor in his glass. "Sometimes trying to define *thorough* is like trying to define *up*. How thorough a job is usually depends on how much time and money is available."

Nordlund felt uncomfortable. Kaltmeyer had once again turned into the amiable wolf. How deep was the government willing to dig, how much time and money was it willing to spend? And above all, was it just a ploy by Senator DeFolge's enemies in Congress to embarrass him? If that were the case, Kaltmeyer/DeFolge might have something to worry about—but not much.

Cyd took a sip of beer and studied Kaltmeyer for a moment. "That's a question you should ask Mr. Wilcox," she said slowly. "But then, we're talking off the record, aren't we?"

Kaltmeyer nodded. "I'm not trying to compromise you, Miss Lederley, but I'd be less than human if I didn't try to find out as much as I could about your intentions—yours as well as Mr. Wilcox's."

She toyed with a last bite of hamburger. "Fair enough. The Lake Michigan tunnel has exceeded its projected budget by half a billion dollars. Mr. Orencho's disappearance has spotlighted your lack of auditing safeguards. The government is worried not only about the ultimate cost but about where the money has gone so far."

She was choosing her words with care, and Kaltmeyer listened to her impatiently. He waved a hand of dismissal.

"It's a huge project, Miss Lederley. There have been thousands of subcontractors. Some money has undoubtedly leaked through a hole here and there. But believe me, the project isn't overrun with thieves—it just happens to be a big project."

Cyd was cautious. "I'm still curious why you're talking to me and not Mr. Wilcox."

"But I will talk to him, Miss Lederley." Kaltmeyer smiled, all charm once again. "Kaltmeyer/DeFolge is a big company, but it's not an impersonal one. It doesn't have a managerial setup like IBM or General Motors. Everybody in managment here has a personal stake in the company, and I guess that's the level I'm talking to you on—a personal one."

Cyd hesitated, and Nordlund felt sorry for her. Kaltmeyer was playing the roles of good guy, bad guy like a pro.

"I'm hardly assessing blame in advance, Mr. Kaltmeyer. If the government thinks there's been overcharging on the Lake Michigan tunnel, it'll ask for a rebate." She paused. "If it's proven there's been criminal intent, there may be fines. It's possible the penalties may be harsher."

Kaltmeyer laughed. "Both the senator and I are too old to go to jail, Miss Lederley. Bottom line, what's the government's real beef?"

Cyd smiled back. "Bottom line? Kaltmeyer/DeFolge may be a big company and this may be a huge project, but this is also the age of computers. There's no justification for running the company as loosely as K and D apparently has been with the government having to pay the bill for waste and mismanagement and possibly worse. That's off the record, of course."

She said it with only the faintest hint of sarcasm. Cyd Lederley could take care of herself, Nordlund decided.

"I appreciate your candor," Kaltmeyer said dryly. He fumbled in his pocket for a pipe, filled it, lit it, and settled back in the booth, staring thoughtfully at her. There was a long silence, broken by the sounds of an argument at the bar. The argument suddenly escalated and became a scuffle. Nordlund glanced over, then scrambled to his feet.

"Jesus, it's Swede."

"Don't do something foolish," Kaltmeyer warned. "He probably got himself into it, and he's big enough to get himself out of it."

Nordlund was halfway across the floor, pushing his way through the crowd that had gathered. Swede was in his late twenties, cursed with an angelic face and blond hair. To make up for it, he was also six four and weighed two and a quarter. He was dead drunk, Nordlund noted; his right fist was clutching the ink-stained workshirt of a pressman ten years older and forty pounds heavier. The pressman was just as drunk as Swede.

Nordlund grabbed Swede by the shoulder. "Fun's over, Swede, time to go home."

"Get your . . . boy out of here, mister." The pressman swayed, held up as much by Swede's fist as by his own legs. He was bigger but he was softer, Nordlund noted. Swede could take him, but it was too late, he had already interfered.

"I'm . . . nobody's boy," Swede said. He let go of the shirt to ball his fist, and Nordlund stepped between them.

"Time to go—"

Swede launched his right from somewhere near the floor. It didn't land solidly, but it hit Nordlund just below the ear. Nordlund staggered back and felt his knees buckle. Then he was sitting on the floor, gasping for breath that wouldn't come.

"Oh, Jesus, goddamn . . ." Swede was swaying above him, his eyes desperately trying to focus on the man he had hit. "Mr. Nordlund, my God, oh, Jesus . . ."

Somebody said, "Get those assholes out of here." The pressman was pulled back into the crowd by friends. Several high-ballers materialized and dragged a blubbering Swede toward the door. "I didn't mean it, my God, I didn't know it was him. . . ."

"You all right, Dane?" Kaltmeyer was bending over him, looking genuinely concerned.

"I think I'm going to be sick," he gasped.

Kaltmeyer held up his hand. "How many fingers?"

It took a moment for his vision to clear. "Three."

Kaltmeyer helped him back to the booth. "You'll be all right. You're going to have one hell of a headache, though; he really clipped you. That's one man who'll be looking for work tomorrow morning."

"Why? Because he was drunk?" Nordlund raised a hand to his head. It felt sticky under his hair. "Christ, I'm bleeding."

"I'll get some water."

Cyd gently inspected the scalp around his ear. "It's torn, it's going to hurt for a while." She opened her handbag and found a small pack of Kleenex. She moistened them from the glass of water that Kaltmeyer brought back and began to dab at the area under his ear.

Kaltmeyer put on his coat. "We'll have to take him to

Emergency. I don't think he has a concussion, but he's going to need some stitches. Can you handle him? I'll get the car."

She nodded, and Kaltmeyer headed for the door. Nordlund stood up and had to hold on to the table for support. He felt weak and a little dizzy. "I need a drink, a double brandy," he said in a thick voice.

"I'll get it." Cyd hurried over to the bar, and Nordlund bent down to pick up the purse she had left in the booth. He lifted it by one handle, and something heavy fell out onto the wooden seat. He stared, his vision suddenly remarkably clear. A short-barreled .38, one that looked as if it had seen use. He dropped it back into the purse and a moment layer Cyd appeared with the brandy. He drained it, and she guided him toward the door.

Outside, the cold air stung the open wound in his scalp; it hurt like hell. He could see Kaltmeyer getting into his car at the end of the block; he'd drive it up in a moment. The brandy was working now, and he could feel his strength slowly returning.

"That's quite a cannon you carry," he mumbled.

She didn't look at him. "It's for personal protection."

"You're lying," he said.

CHAPTER 9

Metcalf was in a foul humor. He'd spent most of the previous day with Beardsley down in the cut, and today he'd have to play judge and jury while Beardsley set charges his way. Nordlund was going to win his bet, and everybody knew it. What only he and Nordlund knew was that he was going to be at the receiving end of Beardsley's temper when the big man lost.

This was something Nordlund should have taken care of himself, instead of pushing it off on him. Except, of course, Nordlund couldn't. Jeez, he had looked a wreck that morning. Word was that Swede had cold-cocked him at Jimmy's—what about, nobody seemed to know.

"Watch the tracks."

"I'm watching, Art."

He shifted the tiller of the electric car, avoiding the narrow gauge tracks of the muck train, and Beardsley relaxed. "You have an accident down here, you could die three times over before anybody got to you. We're four miles out from the access shaft—the guys on the other side are forty."

"Yeah, I know, Art."

Beardsley studied him a moment. "Get rid of the chip, kid. The men can see it even if you don't think they can."

He didn't need Beardsley to tell him how to get along with the men, Metcalf thought, irritated. Then again, maybe he did.

They were getting close to the end of the cut and passed several muck trains loaded high with shattered limestone from the working face. Then they were passing the end of the conveyor belt where the cars were filled with granite spoil. A hundred yards farther, and a new shield was being jockeyed into position. Metcalf inspected it as they bounced by. The fiberglass-polyester shell had yet to be filled with gunnite and was still bowed slightly from the tension of the steel reinforcing rods.

(88

Beardsley jerked a thumb at the shell. "You like those, don't you?"

"They're stronger and they're lighter, Art. And you know the time they save."

Beardsley leaned over the side of the car to spit on the tunnel floor. "Give me cast-iron shields any day. I *know* what they'll hold up. These are flimsy, and don't tell me what the computer says. By the time you find out different, it'll be too late."

Metcalf watched while a team from the gunnite truck attached hoses to either end of the shield. Moments later, high-pressure water and powdered gunnite were flowing through the hoses and liquid concrete was being squirted into the hollow spaces of the shield, displacing the pressurized air. Once it was filled and the gunnite had set, they'd have a tunnel shield of prestressed concrete that could support enormous weight.

"You tell 'em, Art."

Beardsley glanced over at him. "Wise guy." But he said it without rancor.

Metcalf moved out past the gunnite crew. He stopped the car a hundred feet from the face of the cut and checked it out. The mole had been backed off, and the screw device for removing digging spoil had been detached and hung over the conveyor belt that carried the spoil back to the loading zone for the muck train. The huge mechanical mole with its rotating digging head would be used after the rock had been loosened, but for the moment it was useless without the assistance of explosives.

He and Beardsley got out of the car and walked over to the men working at the rock face. Grimsley and a French Canadian high-baller named DuBois were operating a small box on a tripod with its spear-tipped legs firmly planted in the rocky floor. A faint reddish glow pulsed from a tube at one end.

"You're in the path of the beam, Metcalf!" Grimsley yelled.

He glanced down and saw a reddish spot the size of a quarter planted on his chest. "Sorry." He stepped aside, and the thin beam flashed down the length of the tunnel.

"Got eet!" DuBois yelled. "Bet you wan hundred bucks we close een centimeters!"

Grimsley shrugged. "Sucker bet."

The laser beam technique assured almost precise alignment of the cut, Metcalf thought. Coordinated by phone line with a similar one in the other cut, they'd hole through right on center.

"You don't like the laser guidance system either, do you, Art?"

"Not all gadgets are bad. But you gotta know which ones to trust." Beardsley studied him again, sizing him up. "I don't always get along with your boss, kid, but at least he's got experience in the hole." As an afterthought he added, "No offense."

Beardsley walked over to the face of the cut, now covered by a drilling rig set to place explosive charges. Three circles of movable bits would cut into the face, with one central bit for the burn hole, the center charge toward which all the debris would be blown when the charges were detonated. Strain gauges and other sensors on the drills fed data back to the computer in the Field Station, which in turn directed the placement of the holes and the type of charge to get maximum penetration.

Metcalf knew this was the technique Beardsley distrusted the most, the one he and Nordlund had argued about the previous Friday. He watched as Beardsley checked the charges, then turned to Hartman, the shift supervisor. "You look worried, Ed. Something wrong?"

"I'm not sure, Art. I'm waiting for the computer results from the office."

"You could wait all day for the guys in the office to get off their ass. What're you running into?"

Hartman shook his head. "Wish I could tell you. I think we're getting a discontinuity. The granite strata are tilted, and there are some softer sections above that seem to widen."

"Hell, that's nothing unusual. Crank back the rig."

Hartman looked uncertain. "Shit, Art, we'll be getting the results in a minute."

"Goddamnit, I said crank back the rig!"

Metcalf stepped forward. "Hey look, Art—"

Beardsley didn't even glance at him. "You want to run this, kid, you run it. Otherwise, watch."

Hartman turned to the crew and motioned them to pull back the rig. One of the men objected. "This is just a lot of wasted time—we'll get the blasting patterns in a few minutes."

Beardsley glanced at him, contemptuous. "Shut up, Lynch."

Chip Lynch, Metcalf noted. A new hire, and one he knew wouldn't last. He was afraid of the cut—you could smell it.

Lynch shrugged, and the crew pulled back the drilling platform, uncovering the raw face of the cut. It was a dirty white, ragged surface of sedimentary stone into which a number of test holes had been drilled as well as a large central burn hole.

Beardsley felt the surface. "Give me a mallet, somebody." DuBois brought him a hand maul with a heavy bronze head. Beardsley carefully tapped over the face of the stone, resting his free hand on the jagged outcropping. Metcalf was impressed. Beardsley was "reading" the rock with his fingers. The vibrations set up by the mallet striking the rock would be subtly different as he worked over the face of the cut, depending on what lay ahead.

Beardsley frowned, and Metcalf guessed his fingers had detected small echoes, indicating that the earth ahead might be porous. If it was, it wouldn't have the dull feel of sand or silt, but it would still be something quite different from solid granite.

"You think you can map out strata that way?" Lynch scoffed.

"Chip," Beardsley said gently, "I was sounding out cuts before your father took you to a dance and your mother took you home." He continued tapping, then turned to Hartman. "Use a conventional charge, and you'll bring down the roof. You're holing into porous limestone beyond this slab."

Hartman shook his head. "I'm going to wait for the computer reading, Art."

"We all know what the computer's going to say." Beardsley's voice was deceptively soft. "But you go ahead and do what it says, Ed. Just remember that you're the guy who will be taking the responsibility for what happens. The goddamned computer won't."

Hartman still hesitated, and Metcalf pushed forward. "Give me the phone."

Hartman unhooked the phone from his belt and handed it over. Metcalf punched in the computer department numbers, then spoke into the mouthpiece: "This is Metcalf, I'm at the working face. Check the data, we may need a soft charge here. I think we've got porous limestone ahead of us."

He listened a moment, then handed the phone back to Hartman. He looked at Beardsley. "They're going to reanalyze the sounding and strain gauge data. They'll get back to us."

Beardsley shook his head, disgusted. "When, tomorrow morning? That's what's been wrong with this goddamned cut from day one." He turned to Hartman. "You got a probe, Ed?"

Hartman walked over to the drill head and came back with a long bronze rod with a hollow center. Beardsley took it and climbed up on the apron of the drill platform, then probed the blowhole that had already been drilled. He pushed hard, meeting resistance. Suddenly the probe plunged forward a good three inches. Beardsley pulled it out and inspected the hollow in the rod. He tapped it on the side of the drill platform, and a dirty white shower of rock particles sifted from the center of the probe to the tunnel floor.

Beardsley looked down at Lynch. "Any further arguments, wise guy?" Then to Hartman: "Have a man take the dynamite and the comp B back to the bunker. We're going to do this one with nitrate and oil."

"You're taking a lot on yourself," Hartman objected.

Beardsley shrugged. "Ask Mr. Metcalf there. He'll back me up."

They were all looking at him now, and Metcalf could feel a trickle of sweat start in his armpits. He thought Beardsley had forgotten about his bet with Nordlund.

"You heard what the man said, Ed." Then, under his breath: "You owe me one, Nordlund."

It was twenty minutes before the men came back with the charges of ammonium nitrate and oil. It was a soft charge with a fairly low detonation rate, just what was needed to hole into softer limestone formations. Metcalf watched while Beardsley placed the charges and wired them into the detonation line. When he was through, Beardsley signaled the crew, and they crouched behind a portable blast shield.

Grimsley stuffed his ears with a set of ear protectors, then glanced over at Metcalf. "You got a set of these?" Metcalf shook his head, and Grimsley said, "What the hell did you think we were doing down here? Jesus, Metcalf, get smart, will ya?" He reached into his pocket and pulled out another pair. "Here, stick 'em in your ears."

Metcalf felt his face flush with anger, then forced himself to overlook it. Like the old comedian said, he wasn't getting any respect. But then, he hadn't been giving much, either.

"Thanks."

A sneer from Grimsley: "You're welcome."

Beardsley took a final moment to tie a huge blue bandanna around his nose and mouth, then flipped up the switch guard on the battery detonator and pressed the button.

The charges went off with a low roar, followed by the sound of tumbling rock. A wave of dust puffed out from the rock face, and several of the men began to cough. Metcalf's eyes stung with dust, and a light, white grit settled over his hands and clothing. Beardsley waited several minutes more, than walked around the shield toward the rock face. The other men trailed behind, their forms misty in the dust-filled air.

Metcalf followed, fumbling in his pocket for a handkerchief to cover his nose so he wouldn't breathe in any of the grit. The charges had blasted away a wedge-shaped extension of the granite outcropping, revealing a layer of porous limestone behind it. But porous was hardly the word for it. The limestone had been eroded away by an ancient water flow so that whole sections were hollow, their roofs supported by rough pillars of stone.

They'd have to get support shields in here pretty soon; they couldn't afford to gamble on the stand-up time—the rock wasn't that strong. But it looked as if Beardsley would win his bet: the blast had advanced the tunnel a good twenty feet with an enormous amount of spoil.

There was a low rumble, and Metcalf felt the hairs on the

back of his neck stiffen. Oh, Jesus, they were going to be trapped by a cave-in. . . . In front of him, Lynch turned to run, then stumbled and sprawled at Beardsley's feet.

To the left, the limestone that formed the solid wall bordering the porous area splintered and slid to the floor of the tunnel. White dust boiled about the men. The rumbling continued for a few seconds, gradually subsiding.

No one moved. Then Hartman found a flashlight and directed its beam at the haze of dust.

"Something's there." Beardsley grabbed Hartman's hand so that the beam of light probed the area where the limestone wall had been. The dust was settling out now, and in the gloom Metcalf could see the opening of a huge cave.

Beardsley lumbered into the newly opened cavern, half dragging Hartman along, the flashlight beam dancing off the walls and the rocky ceiling whenever Hartman stumbled, filling the cave with weird forms and shadows. Metcalf followed close behind, biting his lip to keep from shaking. Of all the things he was grateful for in his life, right now the one that mattered most was that he hadn't wet his pants when the wall collapsed and he had been sure the tunnel was caving in around them.

"Jesus," Lynch squeaked, "look at this."

Hartman flashed the beam on the ground, and Metcalf caught his breath. They saw two skeletons, each with bits of cloth partly covering their bones and more shreds mouldering on the ground beside them.

"How the hell do you think they got here?" Hartman asked in a shaky voice.

Metcalf knelt down by the two piles of bones. They were small men back . . . back when? Then he caught a flash of something and gently lifted an arm bone. Underneath was a doll with a porcelain head and the remains of a leather body. Close by the outstretched arm of the other skeleton were the decaying remnants of a wooden torch. The size of the skeletons suddenly made sense.

"Probably two kids," he said quietly. "They must have wandered in here years ago—maybe the cave opened in a bluff above the lake and they decided to explore it and got lost. Judging from the doll, I'd guess eighty, a hundred years ago.''

Grimsley was striking matches by a shadowy form close to one of the cavern walls. ''This one's no kid.''

Metcalf walked over. A larger skeleton, a man's. Pieces of disintegrating cloth lay beneath it, and close by a slender wooden bow whose bowstring had long since rotted away, several arrow shafts tipped with flint, and then a wooden club lined on both sides with sharp, wedge-shaped obsidian chips.

''The Indians must have been here for centuries before the European settlers arrived.'' He reached down and pulled an arrow shaft out of a clutter of chest bones. ''This one didn't die a natural death, that's for sure. He was probably chased in, killed, and left here.''

He would bet the Indian skeleton had been there far longer than the children's, and he tried to imagine their terror when they stumbled into the cavern and found the bones.

Lynch shivered in the gloom. ''Let's get the hell out of here. This is a goddamned burial ground.''

The men silently followed Beardsley back through the shattered opening into the tunnel. Just before leaving, Metcalf turned and peered into the semidarkness again. Beardsley was going to win his bet, Nordlund would be pissed, and he couldn't care less. But that wasn't the important thing.

The important thing was that they had been lucky with Lammont's program for several years, and now their luck was running out, all in the last few hundred feet. Porous limestone . . . how porous could it get? And what were they going to do with the damned cave?

He sniffed. It smelled of damp and decay and age and. . . .

And something else.

CHAPTER 10

It had been a busy Tuesday morning, and Nordlund hadn't had time to worry about his stitched-up scalp. He had sent Metcalf and Beardsley down into the cut together, suggesting that Troy use his own judgment on letting Art set the charges his way for once. Not that once would convince Beardsley of anything.

After that, he had gone over the computer program again with Styron, then asked Janice to find a Japanese caterer on the double—Kaltmeyer and the delegation from Nippon Engineering would be there at noon. Now, thank God, he had a chance to be alone with a cup of coffee and maybe spend a little time on the office sofa with his eyes closed, hoping the pain would go away. Christ, he couldn't even turn his head without it hurting.

"I put two aspirins and a carafe of ice on your desk, Dane. Didn't you find them?"

Janice. He opened his eyes a slit. "I took the damned aspirins two hours ago."

"The dispensary has some codeine if you need it."

"Don't mother me, Jan, not today."

"You got your mothering last night, right?"

"You're nosy, Jan."

"That's one of the things you pay me to be."

He sighed. "Cyd Lederley played Florence Nightingale to my walking wounded. And she was good company in the Emergency Room when I was high on Demerol. Satisfied?"

He could hear her straightening up his desk. "Just barely. Did you find her note? I put it on your desk along with the aspirins."

"Where?" He got to his feet, waved Jan away, and walked somewhat unsteadily over to his desk. A small white envelope had been tucked into a corner of his blotter. He opened it and took out the plain card. *I hope you're feeling better. Thanks for the local color.* It was signed: *Cyd.*

He crumpled it up and threw it into the wastebasket, then changed his mind and fished it out, flattened it, and slipped it into his wallet. He'd made an ass of himself at Jimmy's, but for her part, Cyd had handled the evening quite gracefully. She had even handled Kaltmeyer.

Then he remembered the gun. He had asked Cyd about it again in the Emergency Room just after they gave him the shot of Demerol, and he couldn't recall what she had said, if anything.

"Major Richards in?"

Jan raised an eyebrow. "He's always in. Want to see him?"

"Ask him to come down if he's got a minute."

Richards showed up before he had even finished his coffee. Nordlund pointed silently at the brewing machine, the signal to the major that this was official and might take awhile.

Richards made himself a cup of tea, then relaxed in the chair by his desk. "I heard about you and Swede. You should have let him fight—it would have been better than any match you'll ever see on television."

"You've seen him before?"

"We go to some of the same bars." Richards was studying him, curious why he had been called down.

Nordlund wondered how to phrase it. "What do you know about Cyd Lederley?"

A hint of wariness crept into Richards's eyes. "Lovely lady. Why do you ask?"

"She's carrying a gun. Police .38. My bet is she knows how to use it."

"Did you ask her about it?"

"She said it was for personal protection."

Richards leaned back in his chair, balancing his cup of tea on his knee. "Makes sense. She's a handsome woman; it wouldn't surprise me if she had difficulty on the street. The whole world's become a Central Park lately."

"Packing a police special is overkill, isn't it?"

Richards looked a little less friendly. "I guess the person to ask is somebody who's been mugged or raped lately."

"You've got a point." After a moment of silence: "You knew her in Washington, didn't you?"

The wariness in the major's eyes became more pronounced. "That's right."

"You dated her?"

"For a while, maybe six months. We ended up good friends."

Which meant they had been more than good friends at one time. His guess was that Richards had been in love with her once—and probably still was.

"Tell me about her."

"I can tell you that she's a very private person."

Nordlund let an angry edge creep into his voice. "You're not the only one who's worried about security around the cut, Major. I think I have a right to know a little more about Cyd Lederley than her name, rank, and serial number. I would like to know why she's authorized to carry a weapon. I could call Washington for the information, but I thought you'd be quicker."

Richards looked apologetic. "Sorry, Dane. I should have filled you in before. With the Japanese arriving, I ran out of time trying to cover all bases. Cyd has authorization to carry the pistol—she wouldn't have come out here without one. The GAO assignments concern millions of dollars. If she and Wilcox find any indication of criminal activity, it could mean huge fines and the possibility of people going to jail. People do crazy things when they're cornered, and sometimes they've tried to take it out on Cyd."

"What about Wilcox? He's kind of fragile for that sort of thing, isn't he? And if Cyd were a target, wouldn't he be even more of one?"

"She watches out for him. They're never apart during office hours."

Why hadn't Richards told him before? Cyd was Wilcox's part-time assistant and full-time bodyguard. He groaned to himself. His head was hurting again; he was going to have to ask Janice get him some codeine after all.

"So tell me about Cyd."

Richards loosened up, the tension gone. "Anything personal, you'll have to ask her yourself. She's thirty-two, from Milwaukee, earned a double degree at the University of Wisconsin in psychology and business administration. Married once, no children—the marriage lasted for three years, and she's not anxious to repeat the experience." He paused. "And I think that's all I'm going to tell you."

Nordlund took out her note and flicked it with his thumb. She had enjoyed the night. Well, with some major reservations, so had he. But Kaltmeyer certainly hadn't.

"Thanks a lot for the information, Harry. Next time, don't leave me hanging, will you?"

Jan stuck her head in the office. "Dane, Troy—"

Metcalf pushed past her. "You're going to have to come down to the cut, Dane."

"For Christ's sake, Troy—" Nordlund let the rest of it die in his throat. Metcalf looked as if he had fallen into a bin of gray flour. He remembered that Beardsley had been going to set charges, and for just a moment he felt a small knot of fear in his stomach.

"We've got problems, Dane," Metcalf said.

He dreaded riding in the little electric car; he knew that every time it hit a bump in the tunnel floor, his head would swell with pain. But by two miles in, the headache had vanished, and he could even look around without his neck hurting. The codeine was working.

Metcalf swerved past the huge mole, and then they were at the old working face of the cut, or what was left of it. The air was still hazy with rock dust, but there wasn't any difficulty making out Beardsley and the crew clustered by the mass of crumbled and splintered rock in front.

He got out of the car and walked over to Beardsley. "What's the story?"

From the smug look on his face, Beardsley was going to rub something in. "Those bright gadgets of yours didn't tell us we were holing into a porous limestone stratum."

Nordlund looked blank. "So what happened?"

It was Metcalf who answered. "Art 'read' the rock before he set the charges. He warned us that we were holing through into a very porous limestone area. And brother, was he right."

The face of the cut was a crumbling mass of white stone with a large gap in the middle. Metcalf stepped through, and Nordlund followed, trailed by Beardsley and the rest of the crew. The soft charges Beardsley had used had opened a huge space behind the working face and shattered much of the limestone structure beyond. To Nordlund's right was a large opening, the start of what appeared to be a huge cavern carved out of the limestone stratum by an ancient river. He could feel dust coating his throat and the inside of his nostrils. He sneezed, then stepped through into the cavern. The air was easier to breathe inside, but it smelled of . . . what?

Behind him, he could hear Beardsley's muffled voice: "Bring the lights in here." Hartman, the shift supervisor, stepped forward with a battery lantern in his hand and flashed it around the cave. Nordlund spotted the first two skeletons and knelt down to inspect the bones and the small doll. Metcalf was right about them being children and just as right about the ancient warrior.

"We also found this."

Hartman held out a necklace made of small red beads and what might have been feathers, the decaying remains of what looked like a bear paw dangling from it. The only artifact, besides the club and the bow plus arrows, was a spear with a long, wooden shaft and a wicked seven-inch chipped-obsidian head. The spearhead looked sharp enough to cut paper.

"Brave warrior," he mused.

"How do you know?" Beardsley grunted.

"Just a guess."

Metcalf said, "What the hell are we going to do, Dane?"

He took the light from Hartman and circled the huge cavern, almost missing the exit between two pillars of granite. He stepped through into a smaller cavern, noting the tunnel that led away into what he guessed would be still more small caverns until it led out . . . where? And how far away? The two kids had made it this far, but that didn't mean much, they'd been lost. God knows how long they had wandered around the cave system until they had gotten tired and hungry and eventually died of hunger and exposure in the damp, cold air.

In any event, wherever the exit was had probably been paved over by now.

"I don't know, Troy. What the hell would you do?"

Metcalf glanced around and shivered "Say a prayer over the bones and wall it off, I guess."

Nordlund shook his head. "First I'd talk to Kaltmeyer and Phillips. Then I'd wall it off."

As he walked back to the entrance, he kept thinking that something bothered him about the cavern.

It didn't smell right.

They had been going at it for half an hour and not getting any-place. Nordlund felt tired and beat, but unfortunately everybody else still seemed fresh.

"I think you're being too hard on the program," Kaltmeyer objected. "The best it can do is predict, and a prediction is a prediction. Most of the time it's right; occasionally it's wrong."

Nordlund turned to the pudgy geologist on his right. "What about it, Del? Within the margin of error?"

Styron hesitated, sweating, trying to guess the balance of power between Nordlund and Kaltmeyer. He took a breath and made up his mind, remembering at the last minute that he had already committed himself earlier. "Not at all, Mr. Nordlund, it never has been. It certainly isn't now."

Kaltmeyer leaned forward, resting his elbows on his knees. He had never liked Styron and didn't care if it showed. "Max never complained about it before, Del. And neither did you."

Styron looked as if he would rather be anywhere else than in Nordlund's office right then. His forehead was beaded with sweat, and he took a moment to loosen his collar. "It's true that Mr. Orencho never seemed to think it was much of a prob-lem when I complained to him. But it's only lately that I've had full access to the program."

"I think we ought to get Lammont down here and have him run it for a day." Metcalf looked over at Nordlund, his face innocent. "I'm surprised it hasn't been done before."

Nordlund smiled to himself. If Troy were trying to make points with Kaltmeyer, he was hitting on the wrong person.

"What the hell difference does it make?" Kaltmeyer disliked Metcalf almost as much as he disliked Styron. To have the two agree only infuriated him more; Nordlund could tell the symptoms. "The tunnel is almost finished; the goddamned program is ancient history. What do you think we should do, Metcalf, ask for our money back?"

"It wouldn't be a bad idea." Metcalf was losing his temper as well.

Nordlund stepped in, afraid somebody would say something they'd be sorry for. Metcalf would be fired on the spot, and that would solve one problem—except he couldn't afford to lose Metcalf, he was too good a man. "Call Lammont tomorrow morning, Troy. We'll have him go over the program with Del."

Kaltmeyer shook his head. "You can't."

Nordlund felt his face redden. One of the conditions of his taking the job had been that this type of hands-on decision would be left up to him. "Frank—"

"Lammont's out of town, on vacation," Kaltmeyer continued. "I talked with his office this morning."

That was hard to believe. Lammont leaving town when they were that close to hole-through? And when he had seen him at the demonstration, Lammont had said he would call Styron the next day.

"Did he ever get in touch with you, Del?"

"No, sir. So I called his office and couldn't get through to him. His secretary didn't say anything about his being on vacation."

That son of a bitch. "I'll have Janice track him down. He'll either come back, or I'll go after the bastard and bring him back."

Kaltmeyer looked as if he were going to object, then read the expression on his face and shut up.

Nordlund made a check mark on the note pad before him.

"All right, next item on the agenda is—what are we going to do about the cave?"

Phillips had been nervously tapping his teeth with a pencil, impatient with the discussion. Now he exploded.

"What do you mean, what are we going to do about the cave? You're going to wall it off, aren't you? Hole-through is scheduled for the twenty-third, dedication ceremonies on the third. You haven't the time to fart around with caves."

Kaltmeyer glanced at Nordlund, now more anxious than angry. "Any problem there, Dane?"

Metcalf interrupted again. "Somebody leaked it on the early shift. We're already getting calls from the newspapers and television stations. They want to know about the Indian burial ground under the lake. Also, a Dr.—I have it right here"—he pulled a scrap of paper from his shirt pocket and read it—"Coleman from Northwestern called and insists on seeing it. He claims it qualifies as an anthropological dig, that as such the state controls it and commercial interests like Kaltmeyer/DeFolge just can't walk in and do what they want with the property of the people."

"That news sure traveled fast, didn't it?" Kaltmeyer said dryly.

In his mind, Nordlund ran down the names of the men in Hartman's shift, stopping at Chip Lynch. A new man too frightened of the cut to be a good high-baller. Would he try to hold it up? Some men might do that rather than admit their fear and just quit.

There was a short silence, then Phillips cleared his throat. "I'll make it brief. If you people miss hole-through, the project will be in big trouble when it comes time for new appropriations. You'll also be running into a penalty period on the completion of the Lake Michigan tunnel, and the penalties will drive Kaltmeyer/DeFolge to the wall. When you renegotiated the contract last spring, that was one of the conditions—one that I insisted on."

He sounded calm and deliberate; only his suddenly pale face held a clue to his anger.

Metcalf insisted on rising to the occasion. "I wouldn't be

so hasty. The papers and TV will certainly play it up, and if the professor goes to court, there'll be more headlines and legal delays. It'll give the American Indian Congress time to gear up for injunctions based on the desecration of their burial grounds.''

Troy was playing devil's advocate, Nordlund thought. Not smart.

"You being funny, Metcalf?" Kaltmeyer snapped. There was a dead silence. Then: "That's what I pay our public relations firm for, to take care of that sort of thing."

Metcalf wouldn't leave it alone. "It can be trouble."

"You have a solution?"

"No, sir, I just thought I ought to point out—"

Kaltmeyer brought his fist down on the desk so hard, his coffee cup bounced off.

"Goddamnit, Metcalf, don't ever tell me what's going wrong if you don't have some idea of how to make it right!" He turned to Nordlund. "How about it, Dane? You have anything to contribute?"

Nordlund had no more desire to hold up the tunnel work than Phillips or Kaltmeyer did. But Metcalf was also right about the hazards of public opinion and the danger of legal delays. There was always the risk that the cave and its bones would turn into a cause for somebody. He glanced over at Richards, who had yet to say anything. It was just possible the ultimate solution would lie with him.

"There's something nobody's considered, and that's the Department of Defense."

Kaltmeyer looked blank. "What about the DOD?"

"The department keeps a list of all underground caves and cave systems, as I recall, for possible missile storage and silo sites. All underground construction companies are required to report such caves to the government. Right, Major?"

Richards finally came to life. "I'll check it out, but I'm sure you're right."

Kaltmeyer looked from one to the other, not quite believing what he was hearing. "They sure as hell didn't mean every little hole in the ground. And the idea's ridiculous. There's no way in the world you're going to fire off a missile from beneath Lake Michigan.''

"I can't believe it, either," Nordlund murmured. He didn't take his eyes off Richards.

Phillips got up and walked over to the window to stare at the distant skyline. "Hole-through on the twenty-third. Dedication on the third.'' He swung around, his mouth tight with anger. "You miss it, and I'll see to it that the penalties screw Kaltmeyer/DeFolge right to the wall. It won't take but one shift period to wall up the cave and get on with it.''

"I'm afraid I'm going to have to buck this up to Washington," Richards said mildly. "Then we'll have to wait for a decision from the DOD before anybody goes ahead with doing much of anything.''

Bureaucracy, Nordlund thought, he loved it. Kaltmeyer was staring at him angrily, and Nordlund knew what he was thinking: *If only he hadn't opened his big, fat mouth. . . .*

"Okay, Dane, you're the boss here. So what do we do?'' Kaltmeyer's voice was deceptively soft.

"Wall it off. We'll modify one of the shields with a thick glass viewing panel and an airlock so that people can get in to work down there. The professor can dig around for all the bones he wants; when he's through, we'll replace the one shield. It will take the heat off us from the papers and television. If anything, we'll be heroes—your PR firm will know how to handle that. And in the meantime, we'll go back to digging our tunnel.''

Phillips stared at him, his mouth slightly open. "So we end up with a tunnel with a hole in its side? How the hell's that going to look on camera?''

Nordlund sighed. "Come on, Steve, nobody's going to see it, because you're not going to let them. You're going to control the camera angles as a matter of national security and all that.''

Phillips opened his mouth several times, trying to think of something to object to. He finally gave up, his expression turning sour as he considered the possibilities. The only thing wrong with it was that it might just work.

"Everybody happy?'' Nordlund asked. "If so, then the meeting's over.''

After they had filed out, Janice came in. "How'd things go?"

"All right, I guess. Nobody was complaining at the end."

She pointed to the open intercom. "So I heard."

"Saves me the trouble of telling you all about it, doesn't it, Jan? Anybody call?"

"Thanks a lot, and yes—Diana called to remind you of your dinner date at Andy's." She looked at him, worried. "You up to an evening of haute cuisine and hot jazz?"

He wasn't and considered calling Diana back, then shrugged. What the hell, get everything over with in one night so it wouldn't be on his mind tomorrow.

"I'll suffer. And Andy's isn't all that haute—no pun intended."

Metcalf caught up with him just as he was leaving. "What the hell was that all about in the meeting, Dane? The silo idea's stupid—nobody's going to buy it."

"Nobody in their right mind, that's for sure." He tucked the ends of his scarf into his overcoat. "But before anybody makes a decision, they're going to have to think about it, and I figure that will take at least a week. Time enough for our professor friend to remove the bones and discover the cave's more of a background for a Huck Finn episode than an Indian burial plot. After that, we'll wall it up and forget about it."

Metcalf studied him, a look of admiration creeping over his face. "You had it figured out from the start, didn't you."

"Would you believe me if I said no? Thought not. Anyway, almost everybody's happy—the professor's happy, there's no bad press, and the most we lose is three or four hours of time."

"What do you mean, 'almost everybody'?"

Nordlund patted him on the shoulder. "Phillips. He's unhappy, not because he won but because we didn't lose. Can't please 'em all, I guess."

Jan was still working in the outer office, but the engineers' bullpen was empty, and all the lights were out except for one by a computer terminal. Styron was working late again, but then, Styron had been working late a lot of nights recently.

Nordlund didn't give it another thought.

(106

CHAPTER 11

Del Styron had glanced up briefly when Nordlund left, shivering in the sudden blast of cold air when he had opened the door. Inconsiderate bastard, he had stood in the open doorway for at least a minute while he searched his pockets for his car keys. Styron liked it warm—he kept his apartment around eighty and his electric blanket turned on high, and he wore thermal underwear at least half the year. At one time he had even thought of moving to Florida, but good jobs were hard to find down there and he had changed his mind at the last minute. Maybe someday.

He turned his attention back to the stack of printout sheets before him. He was finally making sense of the program, but the problem was that the program itself didn't make sense. Lammont had used too much of a fudge factor and not enough actual samplings taken in the field.

Styron worked ten minutes longer, then realized he needed more data. He turned and punched some instructions into the terminal, waiting while the laser printer spewed out blocks of thirty-two numbers on the wide, green-streaked printout paper. It was a good two minutes before the printer stopped and the screen signaled PRINTOUT COMPLETED.

He ripped the sheets from the tractor feed, folded them into an accordion pile, then ran his finger down the columns, stopping occasionally to pencil a note on the yellow pad before him. Gradually his finger slowed and his frown deepened. The data on the ground beneath the lake still showed the same discontinuities that had worried him earlier, but now there were additional inconsistencies.

Why hadn't Max ever complained? As an engineer, Orencho had been surprisingly versatile—one as completely at home with computers and programming as he was with geological surveys. He must have known that something was wrong with Lammont's program.

Styron looked again at the figures, comparing the type of strata the program had predicted for the past two years with what they had actually tunneled through. When looked at over-all, the discrepancies between the columns of figures were as-tounding. They could have done as well with a divining rod.

Maybe the method of programming. . . . He got up and walked over to the bookcase against the back wall. Let's see. . . . Lammont's thesis, *Algorithms for Strata Interpolation in Geological Soundings.* The title was intimidating. He carried the book back to his desk, leafed through it, then stopped at a page and dog-eared it to keep his place. He punched in a series of commands to the terminal, then turned back to the thesis and compared certain entries on the dog-eared page with the figures frozen on the screen.

Another minute and he leaned back. His heart was thump-ing faster now and he knew his shirt was soaked with sweat. He studied the figures on the screen for a long time without mov-ing, finally lighting a cigarette and walking over to one of the picture windows to stare out at the lake.

How the hell could he prove it? He finished the cigarette, walked back to the computer, and accessed LAMMONT in the personnel files. A short company biography flashed up on the screen, and he glanced through it. Jesus. There it was, in black and white—or black and amber, considering the color of the screen. Anybody could have found it. It was like the purloined letter. Hide it out in the open where everybody could see it, but nobody had ever *looked* at it.

It ought to be worth a raise, at least.

Except nothing was ever certain in life, and it wouldn't hurt to take out insurance. There should be something in the stock room, he remembered seeing it there once. . . . Five minutes later, he found it. A tape deck with connectors for plugging into the back of the computer terminal, headphones, and a prere-corded cassette—Beethoven's Ninth, with somebody he never heard of conducting. Maybe one of the engineers brown-bagged it and liked music when he ate his lunch back there. It didn't matter: he could cover the tab break-outs in back with tape and record right over it.

He plugged the tape deck into the terminal, loaded it with the cassette, then addressed the mainframe again from the terminal. The moment the scrolling began, he started the tape deck and leaned back in his chair, listening to the strange mixture of sounds that came through the headphones.

Three-quarters of the way through the second side of the cassette, the terminal screen blanked and the cursor spelled out END. He rewound the cassette, disconnected the tape deck, and returned it to the stock room. Back at the terminal, he studied the screen for a long moment, then made up his mind and erased the subprogram that had been his clue.

"That should do it," he murmured.

He pocketed the cassette and reached for the phone to punch in Nordlund's number. Then he hesitated. Taped to the partition just above the telephone cradle was a small wall calendar with a painting of a man fishing for marlin off the coast of Florida, the Miami skyline at his back.

A raise wasn't going to get him there. Not even a healthy one.

He snuffed out his cigarette, accessed the personnel files for the second time, and punched in another number on the telephone. It was worth a try. Who knew, he might get lucky.

He got lucky. "This is Del Styron," he said into the handset. "We talked two days ago at the demonstration, remember?" He waited for the acknowledgment, then let a hard edge creep into his voice. "I've gone over Lammont's program. I know what the problem is." Pause. "No, I don't want to talk it over with Nordlund, I want to talk it over with you. I think you know why."

There was a long silence at the other end, but he hadn't heard a click; the party was still there. The voice came back on. "Right," Styron said. "Tonight." There was a protest, and Styron smiled at the phone. "Maybe I *should* go to Nordlund." A change of mind. "Nine o'clock. Don't be late."

He eased the phone back into its cradle and smiled broadly at the marlin fisherman sailing the painted waters of the ocean.

He suddenly felt very good. Who would have thought he would ever stumble onto something like this? Tonight could be the most important in his life.

When he got home, he turned on the lights, locked and dead-bolted the door behind him, and knocked the packed snow off his boots while he was still standing on the entrance mat. The very next thing, he checked the thermostat. Sometimes the once-a-week cleaning woman lowered the temperature, despite his instructions to leave the thermostat alone. He dropped the file folders he had stolen from the office onto a nearby chair, hung up his coat, then turned to survey his apartment with its sunken living room and thick carpets and big picture windows over-looking the lakeshore fifty stories below.

Not bad for a swinging, if aging, bachelor. The one nice thing you could say about Kaltmeyer/DeFolge, they paid damned well. But not, of course, well enough.

He mixed himself a drink at the small wet bar, switched on the stereo, and relaxed on the sectional sofa. How many evenings had he sat here with Max and talked about women? Or-encho had been lonely after his divorce, picked up on some gossip around the office, and suddenly became much friendlier. But it had been a month before he had worked up enough cour-age to ask if his new-found geologist friend knew any women-about-town, women who were looking for a little fun and ex-citement without any commitments or expectations.

Max had asked the right man.

Styron took his drink and walked over to the mirror above the fireplace, self-consciously sucking in his stomach as he looked at his reflection. He could shed a few pounds, but the looks were still there; at least he still had a full head of hair. And forty wasn't really middle aged. It didn't matter anyway; women went more for money than looks these days. Anyone who thought differently was just kidding himself.

He had given Max a few names and phone numbers—later, a lot of names and phone numbers—and suggested he always make sure they had enough money for cab fare home. Max had been an innocent, but he caught on quickly. If you wanted to

(110

play, you had to pay, that was the first rule of the game. Even damned few housewives went to bed out of true love; it was strictly quid pro quo. Married men got what they paid for in food, rent, and amenities.

They used to talk a lot about different women, comparing notes. He'd bet money that Max hadn't split town, that he was shacking up in the city with one of them right now. He could probably track Orencho down if he wanted to be patient and go through his address book name by name. But what the hell, what was the point?

They had never talked much about Kaltmeyer/DeFolge. He had the impression Max had been with them since day one, and he had once accessed the personnel records to check it out. He'd been right. Then Max had disappeared, and the word was that he had absconded with millions of the company's money.

Bullshit. Max wasn't the type. A good guess was that Max had something on them, and they'd paid him to get lost. Or he had blackmailed them into paying. Well, there sure as hell was plenty to blackmail them about. Now he understood why Max had never let him see the complete program. He would have smelled a rat right away. Jesus. Kaltmeyer/DeFolge had gotten away with it.

Almost.

He glanced at his watch. Seven o'clock. Two hours to go. He walked over to the entertainment wall with the TV monitor and stereo set and turned on one of his cassette decks, the one that duplicated a cassette while it was played. He took the cassette he had recorded at work and loaded it into one side of the recorder, then loaded a blank into the other and turned it on. The massive speakers at either end of the wall promptly filled the room with the same weird chirps he had heard over the headphones earlier at work. He winced and turned down the volume.

It wouldn't take long to dub it at high speed; the program hadn't filled the entire cassette. Time to relax. He went to the kitchen, took a bottle of Stolichnaya vodka from the freezer, and poured two ounces into a chilled glass. At that temperature, the vodka was thick and syrupy, just the way he liked it. He rummaged in the back of the refrigerator, found a plastic container with five strips of lemon peel, and twisted one of them into the vodka. He was too nervous to fix a complete dinner, but the foil-wrapped drumstick left over from the night before would do just fine.

He made himself comfortable on the sofa, used the hand remote to turn on the television set, and prepared to wait. After a moment, he got up and walked into the bedroom, took the .32 out of the bed table, and returned to the living room. He placed the pistol next to the stack of computer printout sheets and file folders on the desk. It had finally occurred to him that what he was doing was dangerous, that wealthy people didn't part with large sums of money willingly. He could feel the sweat start to gather in his armpits and on the back of his neck.

When he heard the cassette deck click off, he removed the original tape, slipped it back into its plastic container, and put it down on the work ledge that jutted out a foot from the entertainment wall. The duplicate he put in the "play" slot so all he had to do was press a button and the room would be filled with the strange chirping of Lammont's computer program. He had a hunch it would be quite effective.

It was a quarter after nine, and he had begun to think he had done something very foolish when the door buzzer sounded. Where the hell was the doorman? In the garage, boozing it up again? He hurried over to the intercom by the door and told the caller to come up, at the same time pressing the entry button.

He almost ran back to the kitchen to pour himself another vodka. He mentally saw his caller open the inner door downstairs, step into the elevator, and press the button for the fiftieth floor.

The sweat was dripping off the end of his nose into his vodka, and he brushed at it with his sleeve. Jesus, how could he have been so dumb. . . .

Then the chimes sounded and he opened the door, so rattled he failed to look through the peephole to check who it was.

He froze there a moment in shocked surprise, then slowly let his breath out and relaxed.

"Well," he said, "I certainly wasn't expecting *you*. Come on in."

He turned and walked over to his desk where the .32 lay next to the stack of printout paper. On the way, he hit the "play" button of the tape deck and the weird music of Lammont's computer program filled the room.

"Come on in," he repeated, his tongue thick from the vodka. "Let's talk business."

He felt almost jovial.

CHAPTER 12

As always, Diana was late, and Nordlund took a table at the back. In its latest incarnation, Chicago's favorite jazz spot was all dark wood paneling, wooden tables, and red-checked tablecloths with a bar running down one side and a small stage at the far end. The paneling and tables had been distressed, with names and graffiti carved into the wood to go with the saw marks and nail holes. It must have cost a bundle.

He ordered a Scotch and water and settled back into his chair to wait. The group at the far end of the room was playing New Wave jazz, which wasn't his cup of tea but still superior to what passed for rock these days. Diana didn't like music of any kind; it interfered with conversation. He had found that out only after the wedding, of course. Before, she had been careful to give him the impression she loved scouting the city for out-of-the-way clubs or any new groups on the brink of hitting it big.

Nowadays, Andy's would be the last place she'd want to go. She had obviously picked it to please him—which should be some kind of warning.

He wondered how she was arranging her hours with Interlock. Knowing her temper and her conviction that the world revolved around her, he could imagine the executives who worked with her busily growing a second set of fingernails to replace the ones they'd chewed off.

It was 7:20 when she walked in the door, a light dusting of snow on her mink hat and light gray coat. A touch of the Russian, he thought. It must be the in-look for the season. She smiled, spotted him at the table, and hurried over.

"Sorry I'm late, Dane—I know how you hate it, but it really was work."

He helped her off with her coat and draped it over the back of her chair. "Don't let it bother you"—it wouldn't—"it gave me a chance to relax."

The waiter came over while she was pulling off her gloves. She glanced up. "A double Boodles martini on the rocks—Tanqueray if you're out of Boodles."

Nordlund raised an eyebrow. "Double martinis rather than a Dry Sack on the rocks? You must have had a bad day."

"Be nice, Dane. And as a matter of fact, I have had a bad day." Her eyes were shadowed, and it was the first time Nordlund could remember thinking she actually looked too thin. "I spent the afternoon with Mr. Wilcox and his assistant, Cyd what's-her-name. Both of them are cold as dry ice; I don't recommend them."

How long had it been since they used to sit and listen to the music, close their eyes, and order from the menu at random? Andy's wasn't spectacular, but it had been good enough for that, and they had gotten a huge kick out of it. At least he had.

She gulped at her drink again, and he felt a flash of concern. Diana had worked her way through a third of her martini in less than a minute of talking. Eight-to-five as an executive at Interlock apparently was a good deal more demanding than late afternoon or evening on the social circuit.

"What'd they want to talk to you about?"

She stared at him, disbelieving. "Dane, you really *are* naïve, aren't you? Do you know why Father set up Interlock in the first place?"

As always with her, Nordlund felt defensive. "So he could isolate himself from his business interests when he went into politics. It always struck me as a transparent way of avoiding any charges of conflict of interest."

"Maybe transparent to you, Dane. Actually, it worked pretty well. The operations were such that a simple blind trust wouldn't have worked at all."

He found his attention wandering to the group at the back. The pianist was doing everything but hit the keyboard with his elbows, sounding vaguely like a reincarnated Pete Johnson.

"That world's completely foreign to me," he said. He was getting hungry and wanted to order.

She set down her glass. "Dane, listen to me. I'm trying to tell you something."

She had waited all of one month into the marriage before she had insisted he be a devoted listener when she was talking. Fair enough, he thought at the time; she had dutifully listened while he had babbled on about jobs and what it was like out in the field. It was a year before he deduced that she wasn't listening at all, but was mentally phrasing what she was going to say next.

"I'm listening, Diana."

"The point I'm trying to make," she said slowly, "is that Interlock has fairly widespread real estate holdings. I'm only beginning to appreciate the full scope of them myself."

She had his attention now; when Diana slowed down, it was serious.

She signaled to the waiter for another drink. "Anyway, Ms. Cyd dug up the fact that some of the property purchased as a right-of-way by the Illinois Bullet Train Authority was owned by—"

"—Interlock," he finished. Nobody was selling lots under Lake Michigan, but there had been a lot of small farms and minor land holdings just outside the city before the bullet train hit the West Portal in the forest preserves. "Surprise."

She lit a cigarette and leaned back in her chair, supporting her right elbow with her left hand. "Dane, one of those parcels was owned by a limited partnership with Interlock as a participant. There were several other participants as well, of course."

He felt uneasy. "You're driving at something."

"You bet I am. You remember that trust Father set up in our names when we were married?"

He hadn't paid much attention to it then and had forgotten about it until now. "You mean, you and I, through the trust, have been selling real estate to the Bullet Train Authority? With your father having had more than a casual say in the route selection?"

"Dead right, Dane, I'm proud of you."

"Who else was in the trust?"

"Max."

"Nothing would have come out if Max hadn't been involved, right?"

She stubbed out her cigarette in the ashtray. "Far less likely, I should think."

The other string, he thought, angry. He wondered how long it would be before either Kaltmeyer or DeFolge would tell him that he was in it up to his neck and they could either hang together or hang separately if Kaltmeyer/DeFolge were ever hauled into court.

"I had nothing to do with it," he said in a brittle voice.

She shrugged. "I'm not the one you'll have to convince."

He leaned back and studied her through lidded eyes. He couldn't read her any better now than he could before. Self-centered, selfish, manipulative. When she had been twenty-two, it had been almost excusable. But now she was twenty-six, and he had run out of excuses.

"Why'd you ask me out tonight, Diana?"

"Honest answer? Because I want you back."

There had been a softness and an innocence about her when she was younger. It had taken him a while to discover that the softness had been strictly physical and the innocence had been faked. But there was no air of softness or innocence about her now. She had always been hard on the inside, and now she was starting to look it. The job with Interlock agreed with her.

"Why?"

She was near tears. He hated that; he had been a sucker for tears in the past. She had used them to make him feel guilty, to get the things she wanted. But they were all crocodile tears; he had never seen her cry real ones.

"Because I love you. Simple, isn't it?"

Of all the things he might have believed, that was the one thing he couldn't.

"Diana," he sighed, "the only reason you want me back is so *you* can walk out on *me*. The last time I beat you to the punch, and you never forgave me."

Little highlights of anger suddenly appeared in her eyes.

(117

She glanced at her watch, then back to him. Instead of liquor dulling the edge in her voice, the martinis had only sharpened it.

"Father introduced me to you after you came back from Saudi Arabia. You were a famous young engineer then, Dane. You were tanned and handsome and charming. I fell in love." Her voice turned acid. "You were great on the job. Off it, you were a huge disappointment. And I do mean in bed."

He felt his face go white. "You weren't that good yourself. Practice didn't make perfect after all."

"How would you know? From your vast knowledge of Florida hookers and Arab whores?" She started pulling on her gloves. "Yes, I got around. I wasn't ashamed of it, but it's not the sort of thing you tell your fiancée. Maybe I should have, but sex is the one field of American endeavor where experience is frowned upon."

Nordlund was suddenly tired of the whole conversation, and very tired of Diana.

"Why the marriage broke up is very simple, Diana—I wanted children and you didn't."

She stood up and put on her coat. "That's right, Dane. But it only makes us different—it doesn't make you any better." She picked up her purse. "Thanks for the drinks."

He stared after her, trying to figure out who had started it. Her mood had changed far too quickly, even for her. Why had she wanted dinner with him? So they could sit around and bitch at each other?

He reached for his Scotch and water, sipped at it, and noted with disapproval that the ice had melted. He looked around for the waiter, then shrugged and left a ten dollar bill on the table. He'd move to the bar; he had lost his appetite anyway. Maybe it was a night for solo drinking—his head already hurt, it couldn't get much worse.

He had just settled in at the bar when a familiar voice said, "Hello, Dane."

Cyd Lederley. Tonight just wasn't his night.

"I guess the expression is, 'Buy you a drink?' " she offered.

For the first time in his life, Nordlund really wished he could believe in coincidences.

"So you love jazz," he said sarcastically.

She was very cool. "As a matter of fact, I do. My friends in Washington said I shouldn't miss Andy's."

"What's your pleasure?" the bartender interrupted.

"Scotch and water," Nordlund grunted.

"Make that two," Cyd corrected. "And I'm paying."

First Diana, now Cyd. If anybody were watching him, they had to be envious as hell. She was dressed in a blue crepe de chine blouse and gray designer slacks with designs worked in silver threads on the pockets—chic enough, certainly for Andy's. Even Diana would have approved.

"You followed Diana, didn't you?"

"You want to believe that, then believe it. I had a very heavy interview with your ex-wife this afternoon. It's logical that I would want to see who she'd flee to for comfort."

"She's still my wife; we're only separated. And I'm afraid I wasn't much comfort."

"I noticed." The wire went out of her voice. "I'm sorry, Dane."

He shrugged. "We'll both recover. You really like jazz?"

"Both jazz and classical. They spell each other."

"You want to know about the trust?"

"Not really, and not especially now. Unless you want to talk about it."

"I'm in hot water, right?"

She nodded. "Probably some. You and your wife are recipients of a trust from her father, Senator DeFolge. Even though you've separated, that trust still exists, and the trustor has made certain investments on its behalf. The government will want to know if the trustor acted with privileged information and if the purchase in any way influenced the choice of route."

"That sounds hot enough to me," he said glumly.

She touched his hand. "If it comes down to it, I'd hire a lawyer, but I don't think I'd worry about it all that much. What's the old saying? 'The guilty flee where none pursueth'?'' She hesitated. ''I'm not so sure that Kaltmeyer and DeFolge will tell you the same thing; they might make your involvement out to be even more serious than I have. Whatever I did, I would get my own lawyer—I wouldn't let myself be represented by one of theirs.''

''They'd set me up to be the fall guy?''

''I didn't say that.''

Off duty, she sounded reasonable, he thought. Reasonable and concerned and interested, the way she'd first struck him on the plane.

She read his face and suggested, ''Why don't we order dinner? I'm starved and that's what you came here for, isn't it?''

''Where do you want to sit?''

She nodded at a booth against the far wall. ''Right there is fine.''

He led the way over and slid onto the wooden seat, facing the stage. The table between them held an ashtray and an old wine bottle with a guttering candle in its throat. The candlelight cast a soft glow over her face, emphasizing the high cheekbones and her large, dark eyes. She was a very handsome woman, he thought again—not classically beautiful or even California modern like Diana, but somehow . . . homegrown exotic. Her breasts were small but full under her blouse, and her body looked as if it were well cared for.

''You jog?''

''No—aerobics, Aikido, and modern dance.''

He managed a faint smile. ''Doesn't fit the image.''

''Of the hard-boiled businesswoman? I should hope not. Off duty, I like to cook, listen to music, read, and there are times when I'm professionally lazy—though not often.''

The waiter came and took their orders, and Nordlund said, ''All right, if we're not going to talk about your business, how about talking about mine?'' He meant it as a joke.

''I was going to.'' He looked his surprise, and she said, ''Really, I'm not putting you on. You've worked all your professional life digging tunnels. Why? What is there about tun-

nels that attracts you and the other high-ballers? To me, before
I came out here, a tunnel was just a . . . well, just another hole
in the ground.''

The Scotch had made him relaxed enough to realize, with a
shock, that he was enjoying himself. He thought of ordering
another, then decided to eat first and drink later, when he would
be more into the music. He pointed at her glass, but she placed
a hand over the top and shook her head.

"A tunnel," he said with emphasis, "is not 'just another
hole in the ground.' In purely practical terms, it's a highly sophisticated engineering undertaking. And it was never simple or
safe—the Romans and the Egyptians before them lost hundreds
of lives in building their tunnels.''

"It's that ancient a profession?''

He laughed. "Ancient? Around 2180 B.C. one of the Ba-
bylonian kings built a three-thousand-foot tunnel under the Eu-
phrates just so he could drive his chariot between the palace and
the local temple. That was a simple tunnel, a cut-and-fill job—
dig a trench, put a roof over it, then cover the roof with dirt. In
the eighth century B.C., King Hezekiah of Judah built tunnels
to bring water in during a siege, and there are water tunnels on
the island of Samos that date from the seventh century. They
only had simple hand tools back then but they were damned
good with them.''

Cyd's steak arrived, and she took a bite, then leaned back
with relief. "God, I was hungry!''

There was more of a difference between Cyd and Diana
than five pounds and six or so years, Nordlund thought. Cyd
enjoyed life, Diana bargained with it.

"You used to teach tunnel engineering, didn't you? Maybe
an introductory course?''

He looked up from his plate, surprised. "For one summer
session at Northwestern. How'd you know?''

"Because you know the history—that's what they teach in
introductory courses." She took another bite of steak. "Don't
you worry about cave-ins, that sort of thing?''

"Of course. We have occasional cave-ins, and if you're

working underwater, compressed air blowouts—like the one in the Hoboken Tunnel in the thirties when twenty men died. But there are other dangers, too. Really exotic ones.''

"Exotic? Such as?''

He cut into his own steak. Medium well, exactly the way he liked it. He should come to Andy's more often, even if he had to go alone.

"Such as the Tanna Tunnel in Japan in the late twenties, when they ran into a deposit of water under a pressure of 275 pounds per square inch. Or a similar high-pressure deposit in the Lötschberg Tunnel in the Alps, when they lost twenty-five men in the bo-gang. Or in the twelve-mile Simplon Tunnel between Switzerland and Italy around the turn of the century, where they first hit cold water and then water at 113 degrees Fahrenheit. Then there's the danger of methane gas from nearby oil or coal deposits that can be explosive as hell. That killed a lot of men when they were building the Sylmar Tunnel in California. In addition, there's carbon monoxide—ventilating a long tunnel can be a problem—and even cyanide gas. Finally, there's squeeze rock.''

"Squeeze rock?''

He paused to wipe his mouth and take a sip of Scotch. "You'll find that in the Alps and Japan—any mountainous area where the rock in the dig is under enormous pressure. It will literally flow. The rock acts like putty, and whole sections of an apparently solid floor will bulge and flow into the cut.''

"You still haven't told me why you and the other high-ballers like to dig tunnels.''

He had to think about it for a while, searching for words to express something he had always taken for granted.

"It's a lot of things, Cyd. It's the most exciting thing I can think of doing, the most rewarding way of life I know. Right now I'm stuck in an office, but I miss being down with the high-ballers and the muck crews and the bo-gangs cutting our way through the earth at fifty yards a day or even a foot a day, racing to meet the crews coming from the other direction.''

He drained the rest of the Scotch and sat there for a while in silence. Cyd watched him but didn't say anything, giving him time to collect the rest of his thoughts. Diana would have changed the subject, he thought.

"There's the camaraderie, of course. It's a tight family. You can't get high-ballers to take another job. They follow each other from California to Italy to Germany to Japan—wherever they're making a cut. High-ballers don't like open air, they hate the plains of Kansas, and they hate traveling by plane, suspended in the middle of nothing. They're happiest working underground. I am, too."

He toyed with what was left of his steak, and she sensed he didn't want to talk about it anymore, that it was a private moment of melancholy. He glanced around for the waiter. "I think I can do with a final Scotch and maybe twenty minutes of soaking up the music."

"Not a bad idea—I'll have one, too."

He wasn't at all sure she really liked jazz. But that wasn't why she was there. She'd followed Diana, but it had only been to find him.

He figured she'd make her move on the way home.

It was after midnight when he decided he'd had it for the evening. He yawned twice as a signal, and right on cue she said, "We both have to work tomorrow, right?"

He put on his coat and helped her into hers. "Give you a lift home?"

She hesitated just long enough to let him think she was debating it. "I'd appreciate it."

Once in the car, he suggested, "We could drive north along the Outer Drive for a few miles. On a night like this, the lakefront should be spectacular." He knew it sounded like a come-on, but he also knew she would take him up on it. He wasn't going to mind that at all.

"I have fond memories of the lakefront. I used to live here."

"You never mentioned that," he said, surprised.

"It was a long time ago; it didn't seem important. And we haven't talked all that much."

It *was* a nice night; it had stopped snowing and the air was now bitterly cold and crystal clear. It was the kind of night where the snapping of a twig carried for miles and walking in the snow made a sound like crunching toast. They got into his car, and a few minutes later they were on the drive. For the first few blocks, they drove in silence.

"Christmas," Cyd finally said, staring out the window. Nordlund glanced out at the trees along the parkway ablaze with tiny white lights. You might leave Chicago, but Chicago never left you, he thought; the memories of the city never faded away. You couldn't say that about many towns in the United States— New York and San Francisco maybe, Boston for sure.

She lapsed back into silence and sat staring out at the ice-choked beach on her right. Nordlund began to wonder if he had guessed wrong about her.

"Max Orencho is dead," she said at last. "The FBI called Mr. Wilcox this afternoon. They found him at three this morning—rather, his lady friend found him. She plays piano at a bar on the North Side; she didn't get home until then."

He had never known Max well—nobody had. Orencho had been a real loner. He tried to figure out why he wasn't surprised, then he realized he had been expecting it for weeks.

"How did it happen?"

"They found him in the bathtub. Apparently he hit his head on the faucet." She was quiet for a moment. "How do you get into a bathtub, Dane?"

"What?"

"I'm serious."

She was one off-the-wall lady, he thought. Except she wouldn't have asked the question unless it was important. To her. He played out the scene in his mind.

"I regulate the water, fill the tub five or six inches, then I step in."

"Position?"

"Sitting down so I can lean back." He thought he knew what she was driving at. "I'd be facing the faucet."

"Would you ever get in with your back to the faucet?"

He shook his head. "I might have when I was a kid and my mother controlled the washcloth."

"Max was found with his back to the faucet. He had been shaving, stepped into the tub with the electric shaver in his hand, fell, and gashed his head on the faucet. The shaver dropped into the water and that was that."

He thought about it. "Doesn't sound very likely, Cyd."

"I don't think so, either."

"So how do you think it really happened?"

"I think somebody hit him over the head and arranged him in the tub. Then they dropped in the razor."

He was sleepy, almost drifting off as he watched the apartment houses and the jeweled trees approach him on his left and then disappear behind him. "Not a nice way to go."

"No way is."

He hit a slick spot and was suddenly wide awake, fighting the wheel. When the car was under control again, he glanced over at Cyd, smoking calmly in the darkness.

"Which one is it, Cyd? The CIA or the Bureau?"

When she didn't answer, he got angry.

"You've made enough shrewd guesses about me, Cyd. Now let me make a few about you." He pulled off onto the shoulder, then held up his right hand and ticked off the points on his fingers.

"You don't like jazz all that much or you would have chosen a table closer to the front at Andy's. You're authorized to carry a gun, presumably for protection against rapists, muggers, and disenchanted corporate heads and other business types who might go to jail if you and Wilcox find the right evidence. But Harry Richards also implied that one of your duties was to act as Wilcox's bodyguard. That's a little far afield for a CPA, even one with a gun. Tonight I offered to talk about the trust, and you declined. Why? Because you really don't know the case that well, because you didn't have a fact sheet in front of you so you'd know what questions to ask? And—small point—Aikido is taught by police departments all over the country, and I suspect by the Company and the Bureau as well. If you'd told me you were into martial arts, I would've guessed Tai Chi; you can practice it alone, and it's the most graceful of them all. Aikido is heavy duty, you need a partner and the object is to learn how to restrain somebody as quickly as possible.''

"That's pretty circumstantial, isn't it?" she said quietly.

He had another thought. "What happened at the airport, Cyd? You were in line, and suddenly you disappeared. Where'd you go?"

Then he realized he had asked one question too many, that he really didn't want to know the answer.

She finally made up her mind. "I went after the boy. I was the one who interrogated him."

He hadn't expected her to admit it.

"Would you have shot him? If you had to?" It was what he had been holding against her these past few days; the thought that she might have been willing to shoot the boy.

"I don't know." Her voice shook. "I have a nephew who looks so much like him, at first I thought it was."

"You're Bureau, aren't you?"

"I was assigned last week."

"The audit's for real?"

She nodded. "My role in it is for real, too."

"All this because of Max?"

"Partly."

Then he had it. "The project. The Lake Michigan tunnel."

"Prime target for terrorists," she said in a flat voice. "Especially right now, with hole-through coming up."

"They'll never get down there. Nobody goes down into that tunnel without Harry Richards knowing who they are and what they're carrying." The connection was suddenly crystal clear. Richards's surprise at seeing Cyd had been a charade. "Harry asked for you to be assigned, didn't he?"

She laughed shortly. "Harry needed help. Security at the Field Station is a sieve—no way it can be otherwise, I suppose. There are a thousand men working there, and Harry really doesn't know all that much about them. How can he? Like you said, they come from all over the world. A mole could have hired on two years ago, and Harry wouldn't know."

It began to feel chilly inside the car. He started the motor and drove back onto the icy asphalt. At the next exit, he'd turn off and take her home.

"You could have bluffed me," he said.

"You want to know why I broke down and told you everything." She sounded cynical, very professional.

"That's right."

"Because my employment by the Bureau would have come out sooner or later. Because you're in top management, but you're relatively clean. Because I'm going to need your help. And because you're going to need mine."

"Back at Andy's, you were willing to let me off on the trust case," he said slowly. "Why?"

"I know a lot about your trust, Dane. And I know a lot about how the senator and his daughter operate, about how Interlock is set up. On balance, you're in trouble, but I don't think personally, and I don't think all that much. Justice is slow, but it isn't always blind. And like I said, I need you."

" 'My country needs me,' " he mocked. "Why didn't you come right out and ask me?"

"I wasn't sure of you, I didn't really know you."

He concentrated on the road, not looking at her. "Come on, Cyd, I'm not that dumb. You know everything there is to know about me."

She was staring out the window again, her cigarette a glowing ember in the darkness of the car. "There was something very important I didn't know—how you felt about tunnels, about the people you work with down there."

"You really think they're going to try and hit the tunnel?"

"I think it's more than possible. And if not the tunnel itself, maybe the personnel working there. After all, Max is dead. Somebody killed him."

"Max stole a million dollars and split. That's probably motivation enough for a lot of people."

She shrugged. "I don't know all the circumstances. Do you?" When he didn't answer, she said, "I'm serious about hitting the personnel, Dane. If they got the right people, it could really cripple the project."

"Like who?"

"Kaltmeyer, some of the department heads, shift supervisors. You."

It bothered him, but what bothered him more was Cyd herself. Every time he thought he was getting close to her, she became somebody else and something different. Cyd wasn't going to be the answer to his loneliness any more than Diana had been.

And that was too damned bad.

CHAPTER 13

"Hey, Esposito, get the lead out, willya? Grab that pick and come on up, on the double."

"Up yours, Grimsley."

It was that lousy time of year again, Evan Grimsley thought. He sniffed and wiped his nose with the back of his hand. Along with half the men working the face of the cut, he had a cold, and the mucous dripping from his nose mixed with the rock dust and built up in layers of rubber cement on his upper lip. He couldn't smell a damned thing, and he couldn't taste much, either. The only thing to be grateful about was that they weren't working under pressure.

"What do you want me to do with it?"

Esposito was in his middle twenties, not much more than five ten and one sixty, olive skinned with a broken nose, black hair, and soulful eyes that drove the women crazy. He could even hold his own when it came to drinking at Jimmy's—pretty remarkable considering his size, Grimsley thought.

"Get Felton and clear away some of that debris. How about it? We don't have all day."

Esposito grinned. "What're you going to be doin', goosin' the mole?"

"Them that knows how, does, Esposito."

They had assigned him two men to help with the mole, and for once Nordlund had used his brains. He had worked with Felton and Esposito before, and they formed one sweet team. Too much grab-ass at times, but all three of them knew when to knock it off, when it was serious time. And they got the work done, nobody could complain about that. It was Esposito's second tunnel job, but Felton was an old hand at it; Felton had worked almost as many cuts as he had.

(129

He patted the mole as he walked along its side, looking at it with the possessive eye of an operator. It was a metal beast, a huge machine that required six battery-operated motors to drive it along on its massive treads. Earlier in the shift, they had replaced the cutting heads on the circular plate in front so the mole could chew its way through the mud and dirt or soft stone of the face. They had even checked out the screw conveyor, which acted like a mechanical gut and carried the spoil from the center of the plate down the length of the mole to where it was dumped into the muck cars at the rear.

It had taken a real genius to invent it, Grimsley thought proudly. And one smart operator to run it. Only trouble was, you couldn't use it all the time. Explosives were preferred when they ran into granite, and for this reason they hadn't used the beast all that much in the past month.

"You think they're going to charge admission, Grimsley?"

Felton was pointing to the area around the cave, now boarded up with sheets of plywood and sealed by taped sheets of polyethylene—except for the door and window they'd put in so some nutty professor could work in there. So far today, they hadn't seen him; maybe he had packed up his bones and left.

"If they stuck bars in front and put you in there, they'd have one hot attraction, Felton. You could scratch your ass, and the broads could throw you peanuts."

"Up yours."

"Esposito already said that, Felton. Be original."

Grimsley held the control box in his hand and stood to one side as he guided the mole; the huge machine crushed the loose limestone under its heavy treads as it lumbered forward. Every once in a while he'd correct the angle of attack so it continued to face dead-on into the cut. They were coming up to the head of the cut now, and he slowed the machine.

"Okay, you guys, under the shield."

They ducked under the expandable metal shield that ran the length of the mole and served as protection for the men and their equipment. A few feet further, the edge of the shield brushed against the arch, and loose debris fell around them.

(130

"Hey, Grimsley, watch where you're going. You're gonna get a ticket for speedin'."

He slowed the mole still more. Up ahead, much of the limestone had powdered away and fallen in small particles to the floor of the cut. A half-dozen feet in front of them was what appeared to be a solid curtain of limestone, pocked by small indentations.

"Give it a tap, Felton, make sure it's solid. We want to know in advance if we're going to be bustin' into any more caves."

Felton crawled down in front of the mole and ran his hand over the limestone, then stepped back and struck it with his pick. The result made Grimsley catch his breath. The sheet of limestone splintered into large pieces and fell to the floor of the tunnel. One chunk from the top of the arch struck the mole's digging plate.

"You guys okay?"

Both Felton and Esposito were under the shield again; Felton had moved so fast, Grimsley hadn't even seen him.

"Maybe we ought to get Beardsley or Hartman down here." Esposito's voice was shaking.

"Because a little dirt fell on you? Don't be chicken." But just for a moment, he thought it might be a good idea. "Lemme in there." Grimsley crawled around the front of the mole and inspected the remains of the limestone sheet. Not more than an inch thick, riddled with fractures. No wonder.

"We're going to have to clean this up before we can move the mole again," Felton said. He didn't sound too sure of himself, either, Grimsley thought.

"Let's see what we got here first." Grimsley walked into the small space beyond. Another limestone face, but this one was smooth and continuous. Felton and Esposito crowded in behind him.

Felton sniffed the air. "For Christ's sake, Esposito, you let one—I can smell it."

"I don't smell a thing, asshole." And then Esposito sniffed and wrinkled his nose. "Smells like garbage," he said, contradicting himself.

(131

Grimsley's cold was so heavy, he couldn't smell anything. "Lemme check the face, then we'll get somebody down here."

"You gonna send for Metcalf?" Esposito snickered.

"Shut your mouth, spic—I wouldn't send for that bastard if he were the only one to send for. He couldn't find his ass with both hands." He took a short-handled hammer from his belt and started tapping the face. Solid.

Behind him, Felton sniffed the air again and frowned. Suddenly he shouted, "Evan, don't—"

Grimsley couldn't stop the blow in midair. The hammer hit a spot on the limestone at eye level and went right through it. A sudden rush of air struck his face, and despite his clogged nostrils, the stench of rotten eggs was almost overwhelming. He had already started to turn toward Felton and was just in time to see Esposito's eyes widen and then glaze. Felton gagged and grabbed for support that wasn't there. Grimsley instinctively held his breath.

Esposito fell to his knees, vomiting. Felton collapsed beside him, both men going into convulsions. Grimsley scrabbled over the top of the mole, desperately trying to reach the rear of the machine, his lungs aching. The raucous sound of the gas alarm filled the tunnel behind the mole, and he could hear men yelling as they ran for safety.

He slid off the rear of the beast and sprinted for a nearby electric car. He vaulted into it and goosed it for as much speed as he could get. He was dizzy, there were spots before his eyes, and finally he had to take a quick, ragged breath. Oh, Christ, it stank. . . .

He started to vomit almost immediately, then was past the gas pocket to where the air was clean. He could feel a breeze on his face, and he knew the ventilation system had automatically switched into high to clear the gas from the tunnel.

He felt sick and dizzy, and it required all his strength not to fall out of the car as it raced through the deserted tunnel. Four miles to go back to the access shaft at the Field Station, and he wasn't going to make it. . . . Then he could see half a dozen cars coming toward him. He slowed to a halt and started to tumble out onto the tunnel floor. Somebody caught him and held a mask over his face, forcing oxygen into his tortured lungs.

Metcalf.

"Where're Esposito and Felton?"

He gagged once, green bile running down his chin, and waved toward the face of the cut.

"They're dead." And then he remembered a hundred drunken nights at Jimmy's and a half-dozen fights that he always won and those times in the cut when they had been closer than brothers and worked entire shifts without saying a word because each knew what the other was thinking.

"Those poor bastards," he said, and for the first time since he was eleven, he broke down and cried in another man's arms.

CHAPTER 14

Nordlund spread the drawings out on the light table, pinning the sheets to the cork strip at top and bottom so they wouldn't roll up again. He could either drink coffee, stare out at the chill, gray skies, and think dark thoughts about Cyd Lederley, or he could keep himself busy even during his coffee break. Ten minutes with Metcalf, a quick tunnel inspection, go over the computer program once again with Styron—

Where the hell *was* Styron? He hadn't shown up for work, but he hadn't called in sick, either. It wasn't like the pudgy geologist.

He pointed to the diagram of the barge.

"The way it works, Troy, once the barge is in position, we open the sea cocks so it settles to the bottom of the lake or the river. Right here"—he pointed—"is a ring of caissons, each a foot in diameter, connected to each other by a metal skirt. The caissons are double-sleeved, with a gas charge in the upper end." He moved his hand. "See that?"

He waited while Metcalf inspected the drawing, then drew a circle in the middle of the barge diagram with his finger.

"Set off the gas charge, and the lower caisson is driven into the mud of the lakebed. We end up with a large circle of water that we can then pump out. That gives us a dry, open space ten feet in diameter for the drilling operation needed to sink a ventilator shaft."

Metcalf drummed his fingers on the table. "Good idea in theory. But I rather doubt that it will actually work."

The trouble with Troy was not what he said so much as the way he said it. He had an arrogance that he never bothered to hide when he disagreed or made suggestions. Metcalf was smart, and he knew it. He was also too good an engineer to ignore.

"Why not?"

"It's a compromise. It has to be light enough to float and heavy enough to anchor itself to the bottom once you let it sink. The model has worked on dry land, but I'm sure it wouldn't do as well under actual conditions. The walls of the barge aren't thick enough to stand up under adverse weather conditions."

"We could thicken them up, use external tanks for extra flotation. Besides, we wouldn't be drilling under rotten weather conditions anyway."

Metcalf shook his head. "Make the walls of the barge thicker and add external tanks, and it becomes too Rube Goldberg—you'd certainly have difficulty towing it."

"If you look at it in a strictly scientific sense, a bumblebee can't fly," Nordlund said, annoyed. "The real trouble is economics—the model's affordable but small, which means everything has to be scaled down. Double the size, it would have greater flotation, and then we could thicken the walls. The difficulty is cost."

"You'd have a helluva time towing it. I think—" Metcalf suddenly broke off, listening. "What the hell's that?"

The gas alarm Klaxon had begun to sound at the access shaft.

Nordlund grabbed his jacket and gloves and ran for the door. "Let's go!"

Outside, the concrete pad around the access shaft was filled with running men. At the shaft itself, Nordlund could see cages already coming to the surface filled with frightened workmen. He raced for the equipment shed, where a man was handing out gas masks to the fire-and-rescue squad. He grabbed one, then collared a high-baller who had just come to the surface, his face white with fear.

"What happened?"

"One of the crews holed into a gas pocket." The words came out in little puffs of steam.

"Which one?"

"Grimsley's—they were positioning the mole at the face of the cut."

Nordlund spotted Beardsley running toward the cage and shouted, "What about the rest of the men in the cut?"

"We're evacuating them as fast as we can—turned the ventilators on full, which should help."

"Come on!" Nordlund sprinted for the cage. He pushed in, followed by Metcalf and Beardsley and the rescue teams. The cage started down, the winch squealing in protest at the load. A dozen men had been hospitalized on the cut so far, long before he had ever been hired. What he wanted above all else was to finish the job with no fatalities.

Metcalf said to nobody in particular, "I overheard one of the men saying it smelled pretty bad, like rotten eggs."

"Hydrogen sulfide gas," Nordlund murmured.

"That crap's more toxic than hydrogen cyanide." For once, Beardsley sounded worried. "There won't be any survivors in the center of the pocket."

"You ever see anybody after they've run into one?"

"Yeah. You won't want to look at them, they're not pretty."

The cage was on rapid-descent, but to Nordlund it was taking forever. When it hit bottom and the gate opened, he dashed out and grabbed an electric car. Metcalf jumped in beside him. Beardsley followed in another car as they sped up the tunnel.

"Where does the stuff come from?" Metcalf yelled.

"Rotting vegetation with a high sulfur content," Nordlund shouted. "That pocket could have been around for a century."

Lammont's program hadn't even hinted at it.

Nordlund counted the shields as they raced by, so many to the mile. One mile, two miles . . . and then he spotted the tiny shape of another car coming toward them from the head of the cut. At least somebody had survived. The car was slowing to a halt. Nordlund braked, and Metcalf ran over to the driver, slumped behind the steering tiller.

Grimsley. Two members of the rescue squad behind them braked and ran over. Nordlund waved the others up the tunnel.

Beardsley pulled up beside him. "Leave your car for Metcalf. The rescue squad can take care of Evan."

Nordlund climbed in beside him, and Beardsley kicked the motor into high. His face was strained and grim. "I've seen this before. You get a whiff of something that smells like garbage, and then you can't smell a thing. High enough concentration, it paralyzes the sense of smell instantly. Don't know why the god-damned gas monitors didn't pick it up.''

"If they tapped into a pressurized pocket, there wouldn't have been time for an automatic monitor to sound the alarm.'' Nordlund hung on tight as Beardsley jumped the little car over the tracks for the muck train. ''We'll have to get the gas-monitoring team down here.''

"They're on their way.''

"I want to see their bodies.''

"Not much point to it.''

"I'm the guy who has to tell the families.''

"Have it your way. They're not easy to look at.''

They passed the boarded-up section by the cave, then pulled up behind the mole. The rescue squad had already parked their cars and gone around to the front of the machine. The faint odor of rotting eggs still lingered in the air, and Nordlund slipped on his mask. He followed Beardsley past the mole and into the area just before the digging head. Three men from the rescue squad were hovering over two shadowy forms huddled together on the tunnel floor, while the fourth held a lantern.

One of the men kneeling by the bodies looked up at Nordlund and said, ''There's nothing we can do. They must have died instantly.''

Both Felton and Esposito lay in grotesque positions, their eyes wide and bloodshot, their muscles still frozen after the violent spasms that had swept their bodies. Their arms and legs were locked in position, the muscles under their shirts bunched and knotted. The faces of both men were livid and distorted.

One of the rescue squad went to his car and returned with several plastic body bags. ''We'll keep them here until the coroner arrives.''

Nordlund nodded and walked back to the cars with Beardsley. He slipped off his mask. The odor was still there but fading by the minute.

Beardsley hit his open palm with his fist. ''This didn't have to happen,'' he muttered.

Nordlund felt helpless. ''It was an accident. There's no way to anticipate an accident.''

"I thought that was what your goddamned computer program was supposed to do."

"It was an isolated pocket, Art. There's no way to detect an isolated pocket." Beardsley didn't look as if he believed him. "Accidents happen," he repeated desperately. "You can't predict accidents."

"You people sure can't," Beardsley said, stony-faced.

Nordlund watched as the body bags were loaded onto the cage going up, then he and Metcalf were alone in the echoing concrete vault of what would someday be the Chicago station for the bullet train.

"Where's Beardsley?" Metcalf asked.

"He's up at the end with the gas-monitoring team."

Metcalf shook his head. "He's going to be tough to get along with; Esposito and Felton were friends of his."

"Yeah, I know."

"Any way it could have been prevented, Dane? Shouldn't the program have given us a hint?"

"At least a hint, Troy. It certainly should have given us at least a hint." When he got back to the office, he would find Lammont, no matter where he'd gone.

He walked over to the shaft and then stopped when he heard the squeaking of the cable as another car slowly descended.

"We've got company."

A minute later, the car was down and Kaltmeyer pushed the gate open, followed by Phillips and Senator Alan DeFolge. Trailing behind was the gangly form of Rob Zumwalt, Styron's chief assistant. Where the hell was Del? Why hadn't he come down? Or hadn't he shown up for work at all?

Nordlund briefed a somber Kaltmeyer on what had happened. DeFolge shook his head sympathetically whenever it seemed appropriate.

"A tragic loss, Dane, really a tragic loss. Insurance will cover the families, but the company should do something, too."

When Nordlund had finished, Kaltmeyer looked gray. "An inspector from the Bureau of Mines will be out tomorrow to look over the dig and determine if there's any company . . . culpability.''

"There won't be any culpability," DeFolge said in a soothing voice. "You can't build anything of this magnitude without a few people getting hurt. If you want to make an omelette, you've got to break eggs. How many men died of yellow fever while building the Panama Canal? How many were killed building the Golden Gate Bridge?''

"Don't worry about the inspector, Senator," Phillips said. "I'll handle him.''

"I know you will, my boy.''

Nordlund stared at Kaltmeyer. Something was going by him a little too fast, as if everybody were in on the joke but him.

"They're going to have to inspect the cut, Mr. Kaltmeyer. They'll want us to close it down when they do so. And they're going to want some changes, some kind of guarantee it won't happen again, you know—''

"I said I'd handle him," Phillips interrupted, annoyed. "We can put pressure on the Bureau of Mines. No inspector's going to give us any static.''

"I intend to give him all the help possible," Nordlund said stiffly. "We'll probably miss the deadline, but I'm not going to risk lives trying to meet it.''

The little silences were growing longer now. The six of them glanced uneasily at each other, the harsh light from the fluorescents overhead making their faces look pinched and hard.

"The . . . Administration . . . can't . . . stand . . . delay!'' Phillips was redfaced with sudden anger, his words exploding against the limestone walls. "I've gone over the reasons why a dozen times—you miss hole-through, I swear to God this Administration will break you! And I'll do my goddamnedest to help them!''

Phillips was talking directly to DeFolge, ignoring the others. But the senator was the only one who really mattered, Nordlund thought; he was the one who held the power.

"Nobody's going to miss hole-through, Steve." DeFolge turned to Nordlund. "I know how you feel, Dane—it's why we hired you. You're a crackerjack engineer, one who gets along with the men, one they trust. You know I'd do anything in the world if I could bring those men back to life, but there's no way mortal man can do that. There're only a few hundred feet more to go. Why jeopardize everything for something that couldn't be helped, something that's never going to repeat? Lightning's not going to strike twice, you know that.''

DeFolge was suggesting that the best course was to risk being sorry rather than safe, Nordlund thought. He had no idea what the inspector might find or what he would want—additional gas detectors, maybe more alarms. But whatever it was, he'd do what the inspector ordered. Granted, there was no ultimate guarantee—nobody knew that better than he did.

But two men were dead in an accident that might have been prevented. And the one man who could tell them for sure wasn't there.

"No, I don't know that, Senator. As far as I'm concerned, whatever the inspector wants, he'll get, including the temporary closing of the cut. One thing I do know is that Lammont's program needs an overhaul. We're going to have to get Lammont down here to find out just what the hell it is we're digging through.''

The senator's eyes had narrowed to slits that were almost hidden in his puffy face. "You want to close the tunnel down, is that it, Dane?''

"That's it, Senator.''

DeFolge swung around to Metcalf, his voice harsh. "You want to be chief engineer, son? It's all yours, the position just opened up. I know you want it; when Max disappeared with all that money, you hung around upstairs with your mouth hanging open, panting like a bitch in heat. Well, here's your chance, fish or cut bait. And if I were you, I'd fish.''

There was a long silence. Metcalf's eyes flicked back and forth between DeFolge and Nordlund. He was shivering, but Nordlund couldn't tell whether it was from the chill air of the tunnel or because he couldn't make up his mind.

"I . . . don't think so, sir.'' Despite the cold, Metcalf's

forehead was shiny with sweat. "You need somebody with more experience than I've had."

"There's not that much more to do, son. Tunnel's been dug for all practical purposes. Half a year to complete the twin tunnel and the service bore, oversee the finish work, and that'll be it. You'll get the credit for completing it, you'll stand beside the president at the dedication. With bonuses, it'll be the best salary you'll ever make."

Metcalf shook his head, mute, unable to reject it verbally for the second time.

DeFolge studied him a moment. "I thought I was a good judge of character, but you surprise me. You're either a fool or one of the few honest men I've met." He turned back to Nordlund, suddenly friendly again.

"I guess we'll have to strike a deal, Dane. If we're going to miss hole-through, then you're out, no matter what. We'll get some engineer outside the company to finish the job. What difference will it make? Mr. Phillips here will see to it that Kaltmeyer/DeFolge is out of business in any event. We'll do the job just as fast and as cheap as we can—anybody in our shoes would do the same. But whoever we get to replace you just isn't going to *care* that much—about the cut or about the men."

He paused, giving Nordlund time to think about it. "We'd miss you a lot. So would the high-ballers. You stick with us, you finish the cut on time, we'll make all the changes you and the inspector want—as we go along. We benefit, you benefit, and the men would be . . . let's say, healthier and happier. How about it, Dane? It's still your baby, you were actually running it even before Max ran away with the bankroll. You willing to turn your baby over to strangers?"

DeFolge sounded surprisingly sure of himself, and Nordlund hated him for it. They had him. If he left, the cut would suffer. And so would the men. Or was he just trying to convince himself he was indispensable?

He glanced at Kaltmeyer for any indication as to what he should do, then looked away. Kaltmeyer wouldn't meet his eyes,

(141

and Nordlund suddenly pitied him. DeFolge was the power behind the scenes, he always had been. Kaltmeyer had been his marionette, and now everybody could see the strings. When it had been necessary for DeFolge to step out of the shadows, he hadn't hesitated a moment in humiliating his partner.

"I want Lammont here."

DeFolge smiled in agreement. "Oh, I agree, Dane, I think all of us would like a word with Murray."

Nordlund turned to Zumwalt, looking cold and frightened in the chill air. "I'll be working with you as much as I will with Del. You can forget about eight-hour days."

Zumwalt swallowed. "Sure, Dane, I understand."

And that was it, Nordlund thought. Every man had a price, and they had found his. Nobody could run the cut like he could. Nobody would worry about the men and do as much for them as he would.

The final temptation was always to the ego rather than the appetites.

And then he desperately wanted to talk it over with somebody, somebody he could bounce his feelings off of, somebody who could confirm whether or not he had done the right thing.

Only there wasn't anybody.

CHAPTER 15

He sat in Jimmy's and listened to the noise of the men around him. He was drinking straight vodka tonight, something he almost never did. Usually he was a beer man; he was always afraid his discipline might relax under the influence of hard liquor, that drinking might become a substitute for what he wanted to do, what he knew he had to do.

Tonight his anger was so great, his desire for revenge so overwhelming, he had actually been shaking until he started drinking. And somehow it soothed him, made him calmer, more crafty as he reviewed what he was going to do later that night, a task that he had planned so carefully—oh, so very carefully.

He would have to move soon; the crimes continued. Two more men had paid for the man's greed today, and there would undoubtedly be more. He hadn't known Felton and Esposito very well, but what he did know he had liked. Esposito had been a young man with his best years before him. And Felton had spent a lifetime working in various cuts around the world. How could he have been caught in a gas pocket? And what was a pocket of hydrogen sulfide gas doing in the middle of the limestone? There was no organic material or sulfur-bearing hydrocarbons marked anywhere in the survey. And who had made the survey?

The man had his accomplices, the man had used them before and he was using them now. What should he do about them? What would Brad have done about them if Brad were in his shoes and he was the one who had drowned in the sudden rush of water behind that metal wall, his face pressed against the circle of glass, gasping for the air that had bubbled out through the riverbed?

One thing he knew for sure, Brad wouldn't be as forgiving as he had been.

(143

That was something he was going to have to think about. Who were the man's new accomplices?

He glanced at his watch. It was time to go. The people in the bar were turning misty. Once again he was starting to see the faces of men he had worked with in years past. He knew that if he started talking to them, they would report him to . . . to . . . to Dr. Merrimac.

He shivered and pulled his collar tighter around his neck. In spite of his heavy, lined leather coat and his fur hat with ear flaps, he could still feel the biting cold. It was snowing again, like it had been that holiday season so long ago, but this year there would be no Christmas to look forward to. There hadn't been, for a number of years now.

He moved back into the shadows near the tree, patiently watching the house across the street. It was late at night, but the strings of blue holiday lights outlining the doorway and the eaves were still on. The house was a large and expensive one of oak and native stone. He knew from past investigation that it was protected by an elaborate electronic security system. There was no way he could get inside without someone being warned. Besides, the man was never alone; he had a doting wife.

The man had done well for himself, he thought, and spat angrily on the sidewalk. A home in the suburbs in a little cul-de-sac that was leafy and treelined in the summertime, the entrance off the main street guarded by two brick columns and a wrought-iron gate. The man was old now, and it wouldn't be more than a year or so before he would die clutching at his chest as his heart abruptly stopped or writhing in agony as something ate him from the inside out. But he didn't want the man to pay in the natural course of living. The bill the man owed would be collected tonight.

He touched the button on the side of his digital wristwatch. It was just nine o'clock. He felt as if he had been standing there in the cold for hours, but it had been only forty minutes. His quarry would be driving in from the cut soon.

He slipped off his gloves and blew on his fingers. They had to be supple for what he had in mind. He couldn't afford to

(144

have them stiff with the cold. He blew on them again, then stopped as he heard a car coming up the street.

A shiny black Cadillac, slightly grayed by the snow, trying hard to get a purchase on the layer of ice beneath its wheels. He recognized the car from evenings past when he had watched the house. It drew up in front of the house, and the driver cut the motor and the lights.

The man must have been working late; the government accountant was probably keeping him busy disguising the truth with a storm of numbers. The man had always been very good at that.

The man got out of the car, his breath forming a cloud in the blue lights around the door. He was a tall, thin man, his white hair covered by a brown leather cap with a short visor. He reached into the car, across the driver's seat, and came out with his arms filled with red-ribboned packages wrapped in brightly colored foils. He pushed the doorbell, and somewhere inside the house, chimes rang out. A shadow peered out from the upper glass panel of the door, then a woman in her sixties opened it. She was wearing a flowered, quilted robe and huge furry slippers. She leaned forward and kissed the man, who very nearly dropped his packages. She took one of them, and they entered the house together, the door closing silently after them.

Inside the house, the woman would give him the message. But the man wouldn't leave immediately. He'd take the time to have an eggnog or a glass of hot, spiced wine. Maybe even a quick dinner. But he would be leaving soon for a rendezvous with a man he thought long dead.

There was no time to lose. This was the moment, the one he had rehearsed so often in his mind. He stepped out of the shadow of the tree and hurriedly crossed the street. He glanced around quickly—there was no one else on the street—then smashed the plastic in the rear taillight of the Cadillac with the taped head of a hammer. There was very little noise. He tapped the bulb inside, shattering the glass without disturbing the filament mount. He took a long wire from his pocket, one end of which was attached to two small alligator clips. He fastened

(145

one clip to the filament and the other to the frame of the light. He quickly payed out the wire, running it under the bumper and around the frame. It was just long enough. This end of the wire was secured to a small copper cylinder. He picked the lock of the gas cap on the side and lowered the cylinder into the tank.

It was done. The man had owed for a long time and tonight he would pay.

It was a short wait—not more than fifteen minutes—before the door opened and the white-haired man and his wife appeared. The man was carrying gloves and his leather cap. He and his wife embraced for what seemed a long time—oh, he was anxious, he wouldn't deny that—and then the man put on his cap and walked down the front steps. His wife waited in the lighted doorway. The man paused by the side of his car, waved, and then got in, slamming the heavy car door behind him. His shadowed form moved about in the driver's seat as he buckled his seat belt.

A seat belt wasn't going to help the man. God himself couldn't help the man now.

Inside the car, the man touched the starter and the motor roared to life. The woman was just closing the door as the man turned on the car's lights.

The explosion made a loud chuff *and flames spewed from the car's gas tank. Almost instantly, the Cadillac was enveloped in sheets of flame. He could see the dark figure of the man struggling with his seat belt and imagined his screams. There was no way to escape, of course. The flames were too intense, and the man was too old; his efforts to get out would be slow and feeble.*

"Good-bye, Henry," he murmured.

He watched as Henry's wife ran out into the street screaming, the quilted robe flapping about her thin shanks, the furry slippers pulling off in the soft snow. She stopped, yards away from the car, throwing up her hands to shield her face from the intense heat. She didn't see him as he casually walked away from the shadow of the tree.

He turned occasionally to watch the flames as they leaped around the car. In the doorways of the other homes in the cul-

de-sac, frightened people gathered to gape at the burning car. Nobody noticed him.

In the distance, he heard the sound of a fire engine. And much nearer, the shrieks of Henry's wife as she watched her husband burn and crisp in the front seat of the Cadillac.

It was remarkably easy to ignore her screams.

CHAPTER 16

Nordlund finished his morning cup of coffee and walked onto the balcony outside his office. There was a thaw in the air, but it wouldn't last—just long enough to turn the snow to slush so when it refroze, the streets would become hell's own highway.

He stared at the Chicago skyline and let the cold sharpen his mind. Life was a matter of choices, he thought. He'd made a bad one with his marriage, and now he was afraid he'd made another.

The warmth of the coffee suddenly wore off, and he shivered and walked back inside. What was it his grandmother used to say? *He who sups with the devil must use a long spoon.* The moral of the story was, there was no such thing as a spoon that was long enough. Not for the devil—and certainly not for Senator Alan DeFolge.

He flipped the switch on the itercom. "Del in yet, Janice?"

"Not yet, boss—you got a moment?"

"For you, of course."

Janice promptly appeared with the morning mail and dropped it in his out box, then fished it out again and went through it letter by letter, not meeting his eyes. Nordlund smiled to himself. She wanted something.

"What's up, Jan?"

"When's hole-through scheduled?"

"The way it looks now, Sunday morning. The ceremony should be around eleven. Want to go?"

She took a breath. "Dane, I've spent four years of my life working on the project. I know access will be restricted; there're probably a lot of wives who would like—"

"I just said you could go, okay? Nobody deserves to be there more than you. I'll speak to Harry about it—there shouldn't be any problem." He glanced quickly through the mail, then back to her, worried. "You got any idea where Del could be? Any sickness in the family that might have caused him to leave town suddenly, anything like that?"

It took her a moment to come down to earth and focus on Styron. "Not that I know of."

"Any personal problems?"

"Got me—but if anything's happened to him, half the hookers in town will go into mourning."

Nordlund felt uneasy. Something *had* happened to Orencho, and Del was in almost as vital a spot. Different situations, but . . .

He finished his coffee and walked into the engineers' bullpen and Styron's little cubicle. He sifted through the papers on top—unopened letters two days old, half a dozen technical journals, a scratch pad with several phone numbers on it—Janice could check those out, though he suspected what they were. Nothing else.

On a hunch, he turned to the files and started searching for the geological records of the section in which the hydrogen sulfide had been found. He went through them a second time, then realized a number of file folders were missing.

He stepped over to the next cubicle. "You got any of Del's files, Rob?"

Zumwalt looked surprised. "Something missing?"

"Don't know yet."

Fifteen minutes later, it was obvious to both of them that Styron or someone else had removed a large packet of data and printouts from the file.

"Let's try the computer."

"You got it." Zumwalt slid his lanky frame into the chair in front of the terminal and punched in several commands without success. After a moment, the screen flashed DATA DISCONTINUITY.

"Try again," Nordlund murmured.

Zumwalt edged closer to the screen, tense with concentration as the information scrolled past. He finally leaned back, baffled. "I'm sorry, no soap. There seems to be a whole section of the sounding data that's missing."

"What's it cover?"

"The area of the gas pocket and farther out north; about four square miles, I'd guess."

"Okay, let me know if you run across any of the files— immediately."

He went back to his office and found Kaltmeyer sitting on the couch, along with a stranger. Kaltmeyer looked as if he had aged five years since the day before in the tunnel.

Both of them stood up. "Dane, I'd like you to meet Neal Youngblood. He's an inspector from the Bureau of Mines."

Nordlund shook hands and did a quick sizing up. Youngblood was a younger man than he had expected the Bureau would send—maybe early forties, thick black hair, heavy frame but narrow hips, tanned, and with a grip just this side of making him wince. An on-the-spot troubleshooter, not a desk man. Hard body, high cheekbones, probably some Indian in him.

"From the Southwest?"

Youngblood smiled. "Oklahoma. My father was an oil man, so my interest in holes in the ground comes naturally."

"I thought you should show him the cut, Dane. I told him we had nothing to hide—that you'd show him everything he wanted to see." Kaltmeyer sounded preoccupied, and Nordlund wondered what he and DeFolge had talked about after they had left the tunnel yesterday. Or more accurately, what DeFolge had talked about.

"You don't want to come along?"

"I'll take a pass, something else came up." He hesitated, oddly deferential. "Unless you see some reason why I should."

Kaltmeyer was asking him, not telling him, and Nordlund felt embarrassed. DeFolge had stripped him of his rank in the tunnel and revealed Kaltmeyer as the junior partner, and neither of them had adjusted yet.

"I don't think it's necessary, Frank."

That was something else that was changed forever. It would be "Frank" from now on, not "Mr. Kaltmeyer."

Kaltmeyer glanced at Youngblood. "I have to go over some private business with Dane, Neal. Maybe you could talk to Janice for a minute—she's probably dying to know all about you anyway."

After Youngblood had closed the door behind him, Kaltmeyer settled heavily into the chair by the desk. "That wasn't very pretty yesterday, was it?" Even his voice sounded old.

"Diplomacy isn't DeFolge's strong point."

Kaltmeyer managed a wry smile. "Everybody has to take some shit from somebody, Dane. You've had to take your share from me at times." The smile faded, and he fell silent for a moment. "You know, there's a story they used to tell about General Motors. They never fired any of their top brass; buying up their contracts was too expensive. If they turned down early retirement, they'd be given a secretary and a new title—something like vice president of spare parts—and be moved into a back office at corporate headquarters. They'd spend the rest of their corporate lives going over inventories and sending letters to the other nonessential vice presidents just across the hall."

He looked out at the big picture windows where the snow had turned into a chill rain spattering against the panes.

"Once the cut is dedicated come spring, I'll retire. I'm not the type to settle for vice president in charge of paper clips." His voice developed a sudden edge. "He'll try and buy you, Dane. To Alan, everybody has a price."

Once upon a time, Kaltmeyer had had a price, Nordlund thought. Alan DeFolge had found out what it was and had paid it. And then he felt uncomfortable. He'd had a price, too.

"I probably won't be around any longer than you, Frank."

Kaltmeyer was silent, still staring at the windows, and Nordlund realized he wanted to discuss something else.

"Henry Leaver's dead." Kaltmeyer wrung his hands in silent grief. "Somebody slipped a detonator into his Caddy's gas tank last night and wired it to the lights. Left a message with his wife that an old friend had come to town and asked Henry to meet him. When Henry started the car and switched on the headlights, that was it. He was roasted alive."

Nordlund stared. "The police—"

"No leads. I've got no idea, either."

(151

First Max. Now Henry. And Styron was among the missing. He felt chilled, recalling everything that Cyd had told him about terrorists two nights before.

"I'm sorry," he said at last.

"I knew Henry a long time," Kaltmeyer said. "He never had any enemies."

Nordlund didn't have the heart to tell him that Leaver's murderer was probably somebody who had never even met him.

For the first half-hour, Youngblood was more of a sightseer than an inspector, admiring the size of the tunnel and examining the huge rings that would pull the bullet train along.

"How much farther do you have to dig?"

Nordlund slowed the car; they were coming into a relatively unfinished section of the tunnel, and the floor was getting bumpy.

"Sixty feet—we should hole through sometime Sunday morning."

"What about the twin tunnel?"

"A good two weeks longer."

"And the service tunnel?"

"About the same time."

Youngblood studied the raw walls of the shields as they passed. "That's a little unusual, isn't it? The service tunnel is usually the first completed."

"Political pressure," Nordlund said dryly. "They wanted something they could show on the six o'clock news as soon as possible."

"I've met your Steve Phillips—nasty man." Youngblood squinted at him.

"What kind of air-sampling devices do you use, Mr. Nordlund?" There was a subtle shift in his attitude; he had just gone to work.

"Continuous gas monitors are located throughout the cut. One of those kicked off the emergency Klaxons."

Youngblood pulled out a small, battered notebook from his hip pocket. "How often are they checked and calibrated?"

"Once a month. We'd had no gas problems up to this point."

They were right behind the mole now, and Nordlund braked

the car. The high-ballers clustered around the machine, curious about the inspector. Nordlund led him around to the front.

"They holed into the pocket right here." He pointed to the limestone wall. He wasn't sure if it was his imagination, but he thought he could still smell wisps of the gas, like the lingering traces of a woman's perfume after she had left the room.

Youngblood sniffed. "Still there, isn't it? Very faint now." He made a mark in his notebook. "I've checked your forward monitors, especially the Vargas models. The ionization source needs to be replaced in one of them."

Nordlund was surprised. "That's cesium 137—it shouldn't have to be replaced for five years."

"Probably an old unit, came from stock someplace." He put the notebook away and frowned. "Didn't do you much good, did they?"

Nordlund felt defensive. "They're reliable units. The gas pocket was under a lot of pressure—there just wasn't enough response time."

Youngblood leaned against the mole and studied the floor for a moment. When he looked up, his expression wasn't very friendly.

"How come that pocket didn't show on your local geological survey, Mr. Nordlund? You run a scan of the ground ahead of the rig, don't you?"

"That's standard practice—we run one every twenty-four hours."

"When you say 'we,' who handles it?"

"Del Styron. He's our resident geologist."

"I'd like to talk to him."

Here it comes, Nordlund thought. "He's not around. He didn't show up for work—"

"For two days, isn't that right?"

"I wasn't trying to hide it."

"I didn't say you were, Mr. Nordlund. What about your computer program? Who drew it up?"

"Murray Lammont and Associates."

Youngblood nodded. "Supposed to be a good man, at least he has a rep. How good's your friend Styron?"

"He's no friend, but he's one of the best."

"Go out on benders much?"

Nordlund suddenly became cautious. Youngblood had done a fast bit of research before dropping in on them. "I wouldn't know. Why?"

Youngblood walked over to the plywood that covered the cave. "If he's been gone for two days, it might be a logical explanation. Check the hospitals yet?" Nordlund shook his head. "I would, if I were you." He patted the thin sheet of wood. "I heard about this back in Washington; it must have come as a bit of a surprise."

"It did," Nordlund admitted.

"But it shouldn't have—that's the point!" Youngblood shook his head in disbelief. "You should have known, and you didn't. I think we ought to talk to your Mr. Lammont tomorrow. Maybe he's not as good as we all think."

You take the position, you also take the gaff, Nordlund thought. "We've tried to get in touch with him. He's on vacation. His office doesn't know where—or won't say."

Youngblood walked back to the car and sat down. He looked at Nordlund and slowly shook his head.

"Your resident geologist has disappeared for two days. The man who conducted the geological surveys and drew up the survey program for your computer is away, you don't know where. And a few days ago, several men died because one of those two guys fucked up. You don't run a very tight ship, do you?"

"It wasn't my job until two weeks ago," Nordlund said defensively.

"But the buck stops with you, doesn't it? At least for right now."

"You got any suggestions?" Nordlund asked, angry.

"For openers, I'd replace all the spot monitors in the twin tunnel with continuous models. And I'd suggest that all men actually working the face wear gas masks—I don't care whether it slows you down or not."

"Done," Nordlund grunted.

They rode the first mile back in silence, then Youngblood shouted over the noise, "You seem like a nice guy, Nordlund, and this is your first solo take-charge job, so this is all off the record. You guys have political influence. I'd close you down if I could, but I know I can't. With sixty feet to go, you're home free. But I'll tell you one thing. I don't care how much they offered me, I wouldn't take your job. You're not the chief engineer, you're the fall guy.''

He'd known it instinctively all along, but it had taken a stranger to tell him. Alan DeFolge hadn't wanted him for his daughter, he'd wanted him for insurance.

Diana had just been part of the bribe.

CHAPTER 17

"You going to work all night?"

Cyd was standing in the doorway, her coat over one arm. "You bought me dinner twice in a row. I thought it was my turn to buy you one."

"Considering the day, that's an offer I can't refuse." He waved her into the office. She read the expression on his face and shut the door behind her.

"That bad?"

"Afraid so."

She sat on the couch, placing her hat and coat beside her.

"You want to talk about it?"

He nodded. "You heard about Henry?"

"Early this morning. Probably as soon as Kaltmeyer heard. He doesn't know it yet, but neither he nor DeFolge will be going anyplace from now on without bodyguards and surveillance men following them."

"I thought you were blowing smoke the other night when you told me about terrorists trying to hit the tunnel."

"It's a possibility," she said thoughtfully. "It's not the only one. It may not even be the most probable."

He got up and walked over to the coffee machine. "Tea or coffee?"

"I'll wait until we get to a restaurant."

"My coffee's that bad?"

She made a face. "Your tea is. I haven't tried your coffee."

He brewed himself a quick cup, then turned the desk chair around so he was facing her. "Talk to me."

"The pattern's not right, Dane. Orencho had already left the project—for whatever reason. Killing him was irrelevant to the progress of the tunnel. Henry Leaver was vital to the economics of it all—you have no idea how vital; the IRS is going to have a field day with the K and D tax records. Styron is open. His absence is already hurting, though correct me if I'm wrong, whether he's around or not isn't going to set back hole-through.''

He nodded his head in agreement.

"And it's all . . . a little too late. Unless whatever group it is thinks they can panic the men working in the tunnel. Both Orencho's murder and Leaver's have been covered in the newspapers and on television, but so far no group has stepped forward to claim credit. Media exposure and the resulting panic are vital to their cause. Look what happened in the mideighties when a few hijackings throttled tourist travel to Europe.''

"So where does that leave us?"

She laughed. "It leaves me wanting a cup of tea after all. No cream, no sugar, just plain.'' After he brought it to her, she said, "How long have you been working for Kalt-meyer/DeFolge?''

"A little more than a year.''

"What did you know about them before you started working here?''

He laughed. "I was part of the family for three years, re-member?''

"Before you married Diana, then.''

He suddenly became cautious. "I had read about them in the trade journals for years, seen their ads for engineers in the *Wall Street Journal* and various newsletters. But I can't really say I knew that much about them. They were a stateside engineering company, and I was overseas most of the time.''

"You didn't talk to other engineers about them?''

"I may have, I don't remember. Why?''

"At one time they didn't have the best reputation.''

"How do you mean?'' he asked carefully.

"They ran a cheap shop—secondhand machinery, skimped on safety equipment, always observing the letter of the law but not the spirit. They had a habit of underbidding to get jobs, and then they found they had to cut corners to make a profit.''

He slowly shook his head. "You're trusting secondary sources, Cyd. Neither Kaltmeyer nor DeFolge would cop to that, so you must have gotten it from the competition. And they're hardly going to say anything nice."

"I didn't go to those in direct competition. It's common knowledge in the engineering field; even your suppliers agreed."

She was right, and he was being defensive. Kaltmeyer/DeFolge had never been considered princes in the business. But once he had married Diana, he had ignored the gossip—he wasn't working for them anyway.

"Maybe it was true at one time, Cyd, but they would never have gotten the contract for the project if they hadn't cleaned up their act." He hesitated. "You haven't told me the other possibilities."

"It still leaves us with the first one. A terrorist could be murdering the principals in hopes of stopping work on the tunnel. Or he might be a mole who's committed various murders but is saving his major effort for the hole-through ceremonies— either this one or the big one in January, though the president may be here then and security will be tight. If that's true, then my guess is he's somebody everybody knows, somebody with enough authority to have access to everything and everybody, who would know everybody's day-to-day routine."

He found himself mentally running down the list of those working on the cut, pausing at Metcalf, dismissing him, then coming back to him. Kaltmeyer had made him paranoid about Metcalf two weeks before, and Troy hadn't helped much since. Then he dismissed the thought. Suspecting Metcalf only meant that the job was getting to him.

"You think there're more possibilities than that?"

She sounded tentative. "It's an old-fashioned theory. But maybe it's an ex-employee, somebody who's nursed a grudge for a long time."

"That would be easy enough to check. Run back through the company history and the personnel records, see who has a motive. It'd take time, though."

"No time at all," she said slowly. "You go back ten years, and there are no records. Kaltmeyer/DeFolge kept as few as possible anyway, probably for financial reasons. And as soon as it was legal to do so, they destroyed them—all of them. If we've got a case of a disgruntled employee, then K and D just slit its own throat. There's no way of checking.''

He sat there in silence, finishing his coffee. Either possibility, they had come to a dead-end, and he didn't know where to start looking.

''I think I ought to see the cut,'' she said after a moment.

''You want to, I'll have Metcalf take you down tomorrow. He's been dying to get to know you anyway.''

''I'm flattered. What about dinner?''

He shoveled the papers on his desk into the top drawer. ''Sure. Jimmy's all right with you?''

''I thought I was taking you.''

''Another night—Jimmy's is light and quick, and afterward I thought we might drop in on Del Styron.''

''Any word on him?''

''I called half a dozen times—there's nobody home but the answering machine. Then I had Janice check with the building where he lives. High-class apartments, they don't bother their tenants without a court order. She also checked the police and the hospitals—no record of anybody answering to Styron's description. We can ask the police to look into it tomorrow if he doesn't show, but I thought we might beat them to it and pay him a visit.''

''Nice of you to ask me along.''

He grinned. ''You've got the gun.''

He got his hat and coat, then went to the stockroom, Cyd trailing after. There was Christmas gift-wrap, ribbon, and a shelf full of empty boxes. This time of year, some employees wrapped presents before taking them home so the boxes wouldn't give away the contents to the wife or kids. He wrapped an empty carton in a sheet of smiling Santa Clauses and tied it with red ribbons.

Cyd looked puzzled. ''What's that for?''

''Thought you'd never ask. It's a present for our good friend Del. If he doesn't answer the phone, chances are he won't buzz us up, either. This may get us into the building.''

(159

On the way out, he noticed DeFolge's limousine parked in the lot and the lights on in Kaltmeyer's office. Wilcox must have scared them badly. And without Henry to hide the figures, both of them were probably in deep trouble.

He suddenly wondered if DeFolge had bothered to send flowers to Henry Leaver's widow.

He drove past Styron's apartment house on Lake Shore Drive twice before parking in the underground garage. Then he and Cyd shivered outside while he worried how to get in. He doubted that the "gift" by itself would get them past the doorman. Opportunity knocked when a group of partygoers arrived for a pre-Christmas bash.

They followed the group inside, mixing with the others while waiting for the elevator. The doorman didn't question any of them.

"You two a friend of Rusty's?"

He was chubby, red-cheeked, and forty, clutching a foil-wrapped gift box of Jim Beam.

Nordlund shifted his own package so it was more obvious. "Yeah, we're from out of town. Haven't seen Rusty and the kids for years."

"Kids?"

Strike one, Nordlund thought.

"He had a couple back when we knew him."

The man stared. "He?"

"Great gal," Nordlund mumbled, tugging Cyd into the elevator after him. The party got off at the twentieth floor, but he hung back, one hand on the elevator door. Nobody looked around, and he retreated into the elevator and pressed the button for the fiftieth.

"I thought you were faster on your feet than that," Cyd said, laughing.

He grinned. "I don't get that much practice."

When the elevator doors opened on the fiftieth floor, his light-hearted mood vanished. The hallway was deserted. They walked down to apartment 5004, and Nordlund pressed the button. He could hear soft chimes inside, but there were no sounds of anyone moving about. After a minute, he pressed the button again. Somebody was home—he could see a ribbon of light under the door. Maybe Styron was avoiding someone. He pressed the button once more.

Nothing.

"I can open it," Cyd offered.

"Don't bother." The door wasn't perfectly seated. He reached for the knob, pushed, and the door swung open. He stood there for a moment, then realized he was holding his breath. He slowly let it out.

He stepped into a short hallway with a closet on his left and a small table of chrome and smoked glass at the far end with a Chinese brass lamp on top. The gray wall-to-wall carpeting felt like velvet. He quietly turned the knob on the closet door and opened it. Styron's coat was on a hook, his rubbers on the floor, his scarf and gloves thrown on a shelf at the back.

He raised his voice. "Del?"

No answer.

He walked through the hallway, Cyd right behind, and turned left into a huge, brightly-lit living room. The same gray carpeting with light, lemon-colored walls, an eight-foot leather sofa with walnut end tables on either side and a smoked glass coffee table in front, several armchairs that matched the sofa, a black pole lamp, and a walnut desk and banker's chair in a small alcove. One wall held stereo equipment and a huge built-in rear-projection television set. The adjoining wall, the one the couch faced, was almost floor-to-ceiling picture window, the lights of Chicago's North Side twinkling far below.

It was a decorator's dream, he thought. Del was living like a rich man; he must be spending every dime he made on rent alone.

"Dane."

There was urgency in Cyd's voice, and he whirled. She had walked behind the couch to go to the kitchen and was now bending over, looking at something hidden in the shadows. He hurried over.

Styron's body was sprawled on the carpeting. Near his outstretched hand was a .32-caliber pistol.

"Don't touch anything, Dane."

He didn't answer but knelt down and felt the dead man's wrist, knowing he wouldn't find a pulse but doing it out of sheer reflex. Styron's face looked pale and blotchy, his eyes sightless, the pupils dilated and fixed. His skin felt cold to the touch. Nordlund guessed he had been dead for some time, probably for the two days he had missed work. He had been shot in the chest, and judging from the frayed and scorched cloth of the shirt, it was at close range. And there had been a struggle—a brown-red smear on his shirt was the bloody imprint of a hand. Nordlund stood up and scrubbed at his hand with his handkerchief; the blood on the carpet was still faintly sticky.

Cyd used a pen to pick up the revolver by the trigger guard. She sniffed the muzzle and frowned. "There's not much odor— he must have been shot several days ago."

Nordlund watched her make the rounds of the apartment. She was very professional about it.

"No sign of forced entry. Whoever did it, he let them in."

" 'Half the hookers in town,' that's what Janice said."

She shook her head. "Bed's made up. It wasn't slept in— or on. Only one towel and washcloth were used in the bathroom."

Nordlund walked over to the desk. There was a fleck of white on the carpeting beside the chair, and he picked it up. The perforated corner of a sheet of printout paper, the same type used at the Field Station. He looked under the desk, then through the drawers. A scattering of letters, two checkbooks—neither one of them showing much of a balance, an address book, a collection of paper clips and rubber bands and business cards.

There were no missing files, no printouts. But there *had* been printouts on the desk—and maybe file folders as well. They weren't there now; Del's visitor had probably taken them.

"I'll call the police," Cyd said.

He nodded. "Sure, go ahead," he said, and closed the drawers to the desk.

He stood in the alcove and looked out at the living room while she dialed. He had noticed something when they first stepped into the apartment. . . . Then he spotted it again. The

(162

small lights glowing in the entertainment wall. He walked over. The amplifier was on, and so was the cassette deck. He studied it a moment. It was a duplicating deck, and the controls were set for making one, but both tape slots were empty; the only cassette in sight was an old one of Beethoven's Ninth that somebody had left on the work ledge.

Cyd finished talking to the police and hung up the phone. "Do you know anybody who hated Styron enough to kill him?"

"I didn't know Del that well. I have no idea who his friends or enemies were." Nordlund glanced around the apartment. "To be honest, I thought he was living in a rooming house."

"Kaltmeyer/DeFolge must have paid him a handsome salary."

"Not this handsome. If Del's rent came out of his paycheck, I can guarantee you he couldn't afford to eat out much."

"Money in the family?"

He shrugged. "Janice might know, I wouldn't." He wandered back to the entertainment wall, picked up the cassette of the Ninth, and juggled it in his hand. It felt a little rough, and he looked at it more closely. Cellophane tape had been stuck over the tab break-outs in back so it could be recorded over. On impulse, he dropped it into the left-hand slot of the tape deck and pushed the play button.

The noise from the speakers at either end of the wall was a weird mixture of whistles and chirps, at times sounding almost—but not quite—musical.

Cyd frowned. "What's that?"

He pressed the eject button and took out the cassette. "Defective tape," he lied. "You want to watch television while we're waiting for the police?"

She walked over to the window and stared at the tiny cars crawling up the Drive, their headlights reflecting off the wet streets.

"You're a news junkie, aren't you?"

"Sort of," he admitted.

When the police came, everything in the apartment would be evidence, including the cassette. He glanced at Cyd—she was still looking out the window—and slipped the cassette into his pocket, then found a news program on the tube. He watched it without actually seeing it.

He had heard that weird combination of whistles and chirps once before when a computer-buff friend had shown him a system for storing digital signals on audio tape. Unless he was mistaken, Styron had done much the same thing. And the only reason he would have gone to that much trouble would be to tape the missing data from the computer.

There had to be somebody with access to a system for playing it back so they could read the data on a screen.

"How long before the cops show? It's going to be a long day tomorrow."

She turned away from the window, stifling a yawn. "Not long, a few minutes."

He felt mildly guilty. There'd be no problems with the police. Cyd would be his cover. Because he was with her, they wouldn't search him; they wouldn't even ask many questions.

He was absolutely certain that Styron had taken the printouts and missing folders home with him. He must have taped the computer data over the Beethoven symphony while at work, then made a duplicate on the deck in the apartment. If he had, it was gone now. Luckily, whoever had taken it had overlooked the original—its label had been its protection.

Nordlund didn't know what the data concerned, but whatever it was, it had been worth killing for.

CHAPTER 18

Seven-thirty in the morning, Metcalf thought, and whoever said there was no rest for the wicked was absolutely right. Probably the same guy who said that no good deed should go unpunished. . . . He ran his finger down the morning checklist, then picked up the phone and dialed.

"Dietz? Troy here. . . . I figure there's a dozen feet remaining, but we're going to have to shave it. Kaltmeyer wants to take a sledge and crack through what's left on Sunday morning in front of God and everybody, especially the cameras."

He filled Dietz in on the details, coordinated what needed to be done on both sides, then exchanged some gossip and the latest tunnel jokes. He hung up, laughing. God had it in for him, he thought; the one high-baller he really got along with worked on the other side of the cut.

He checked his watch, then wandered into Janice's office and collapsed onto the couch. She had just come in and was hanging up her coat. She pointed to the brown bags on her desk. "One cherry sweet roll, one cheese, two bran muffins, and two large coffees, black, no sugar. I'll split it down the middle—you get the cheese roll."

"You don't trust Dane's magic machine?"

She looked at him over the top of her gold-rimmed glasses. "Sometimes I like a bad cup of coffee—takes me back to my roots in Skokie."

He wolfed down half the roll. "How's Grimsley doing?"

"Fine. He's planning on being back here for hole-through." She spread a pat of butter on a bran muffin. "I talked with a nurse at the hospital last night. She said two women had been in to see Grimsley at different times—both of them claiming to be his wife."

(165

Metcalf stared at her, his mouth open. "You're kidding."

She took her time buttering the muffin. She was doling out the gossip, teasing him. "One was Latino, couldn't speak English. The other one was Vietnamese, who also—"

"—couldn't speak English!" Metcalf roared. "Jesus, Grimsley thought of everything, didn't he? They'll never be able to compare notes." He wiped his eyes, still laughing, then gradually sobered up. "Dane said you had a list of the invited guests for hole-through."

She searched through the outbasket, then handed him a sheaf of papers. "You'll notice who's down there toward the bottom of page one."

He glanced at the list. "If Dane hadn't put you down, I would've myself." He paused, still running down the list of names. "No real celebrities are going to show, are they? Phillips couldn't even get the mayor."

"This is just a small spectacular, for the high-ballers and the engineers. The big one will be in January." Just before he reached the door, she added, "Don't forget you're supposed to show Cyd Lederley the cut later this morning."

He groaned. "Tell Nordlund thanks for nothing."

Which wasn't exactly how he felt about it, but why let Dane know? He clipped the list to his schedule board and walked into the engineering bullpen. Too early for most of the engineers, but Zumwalt was hunched over his terminal, going blind staring at the amber screen. Another time, another generation, he would've been a hippie with long hair, torn Levi's, an old lady, and two joints hidden in his wallet. At least he had the old lady—and a brand-new baby.

"What's up, Rob?"

Zumwalt leaned back in his chair, clasping his hands behind his neck. He waved at the screen. "Just going over the program again, trying to understand why what we find is so damned different from what the program says we'll find. The program should have predicted that area of porous limestone from the soundings Lammont took, but it didn't." He riffled the edges of a hundred–page printout. "This stuff is right out of the mainframe memory, but it isn't in ours."

Metcalf was puzzled. "How come?"

"Don't know. It looks like somebody erased a whole section of the data and a major subprogram from the memory."

"Who the hell would do that?" Zumwalt shrugged, and Metcalf could feel his temper start to rise. "Let me know when Styron comes in. This is as much my business as Dane's."

"Sure thing." Pause. "I got a funny feeling about Del."

Metcalf slipped into his coat. "What kind of funny feeling is that?"

"He's not the kind of guy who goes out on two-day benders. In fact, he doesn't go out much at all. If I had a place like he has, I probably wouldn't go out, either."

"When did you ever see Styron's apartment?"

"Went to a party there once. Didn't stay long—not my kind of party, I couldn't afford it. Real nice place, though."

"You walked out on a party?" Metcalf was mildly curious.

"Some guys send out for pizza, others send out for entertainment." Zumwalt gave him a knowing look. "I don't mind splitting the cost of a pizza, but that entertainment was sort of priccy."

"So Styron's stayed home two days in a row because he's screwing himself to death? Come on, Rob."

"You got a better theory?"

Metcalf snorted and didn't bother to answer. He left the building and walked across the concrete pad to the access shaft and the row of cages. It was a gray day, but the weather was warmer; the snow on the pad was melting into little puddles of slush. Why didn't Maintenance get out and shovel it off while they had the chance? Sure as hell it would freeze tonight and somebody could break a hip.

He stepped into a cage, and while it was descending he considered the logistics of getting all the guests down to the head of the cut for the ceremonies. Ten men to a cage, six if it were camera crews with equipment. If they wanted it live, they'd have to relay it from the ceremony area to the station vault and then up the shaft. Or they could just tape it and broadcast it later on the six o'clock news. Maybe they'd do both.

Lessee. . . . He got out a pencil. Five trips, five cages.

That'd take care of 250 guests. But it'd be easier to get them down than to transport them to the head of the cut. Nobody was going to walk four miles, and they didn't have that many cars for a quick shuttle; most of the guests wouldn't know how to operate one anyway. They'd have to clean up a muck train, rig it with some benches for seats. . . .

The cage bottomed with a slight jar. He climbed into an electric car and started for the tunnel head, waving at the men he passed. Some waved back; others stared, curious.

It's the new Troy Metcalf, by popular demand, he thought grimly. Appreciate it, you bastards. . . .

He passed the boarded-up area of the cave. Professor Coleman would have to be out of there during the hole-through ceremonies. Richards had probably already told him, but he'd make sure of it later.

When he was a hundred feet from the head of the cut, he killed the motor. The mole had been pulled back, and the men were working at the face to remove the last of the limestone by hand until only a thin wall would remain.

It wasn't hard to pick out Swede; he towered over the rest of the crew. Metcalf swore his shirts were worn thin over his biceps.

"How's it going?"

Swede wiped the sweat from his face with a huge dirty handkerchief. "Whose stupid idea was this?"

"Phillips's—but he cleared it with Kaltmeyer."

"I should have guessed that bastard would have something to do with it. I think it's pretty damned silly—with hand tools, this is going to take us more than twenty-four hours. With the mole, we could break through in an hour."

"Yeah, but it wouldn't look as good on TV. I understand Kaltmeyer and DeFolge are going to knock it down with a sledge."

A flat stare. "You're putting me on." Metcalf shook his head. "Okay, we'll fix it for him—maybe have Dietz hit it on the other side at the same time. I still think it's a lot of crap, though. I always thought hole-through was just for the crews."

Metcalf made a check on his schedule sheet. "Don't bitch—they're going to have a catered party down here afterward. Champagne, fancy sandwiches, cake. Everybody's invited."

Swede looked pleased. "Hey, not bad—I'll be there." He turned back to the crew. "Okay, Lynch, Buchser, Pyott, the rest of you guys, let's get your ass in gear, we only got a day, not a week."

Metcalf walked back to the car, hesitating before getting in. He looked at the rough walls of the tunnel and tried to imagine what it had been like for Felton and Esposito. What a lousy way to go. A slight breeze, a whiff of something enormously foul, and in moments they were convulsing on the rocky floor of the tunnel, dying in agony.

But there couldn't be more gas pockets, they didn't have that far to go. They only had to worry about what was ahead of them, not what might lurk along the sides. Still, he'd feel better when the shields were in place, when the rock itself was sealed off.

He glanced at his watch. Time to meet Nordlund's lady and show her the cut. She was one gorgeous woman, early thirties—a great age—and she packed enough weight so she didn't come across as fragile. From what little he had seen, she also had a head on her shoulders.

For just a moment, he thought of taking off his wedding ring and giving Nordlund a little competition, then shrugged. The trouble with smart women was that they usually checked in advance on whether or not you were married. That was one of the things that made them smart.

On the other hand, maybe she didn't care.

He laughed and started the car, heading back to the access shaft. Too bad he had to run things at the Field Station during hole-through.

It looked as if it were going to be a great party.

Cyd Lederley watched the rocky walls flow past her, then glanced up to see the circle of light that marked the top of the shaft steadily dwindle. It was an eerie, unsettling feeling, a reminder of how much empty space still yawned beneath her, and that her life depended on that one slender cable. It must be much worse when the cage was crowded.

When the circle had shrunk to the size of a dime, the cage stopped with a soft *thump*. Troy Metcalf was waiting for her, looking agreeably surprised.

"I was about to come up and get you. Riding in the cage can be pretty strange for somebody used to closed elevators."

"Strange enough," she agreed. She had met Metcalf several times in the Field Station but hadn't paid much attention to him. A small man and a handsome one. She guessed that he knew he was attractive, too.

"It was nice of you to offer to show me around, Troy."

He flashed an Irish grin—a very practiced one, Cyd decided. "Pleasure's all mine. But it wasn't an offer, Dane ordered me to. Just don't take off your hard hat anywhere along the line—against the rules."

For a moment, she was undecided how to take him, then let it pass. More than anything else, Troy reminded her of a brash kid brother.

She glanced around. "Where am I standing now?"

"This will be the Chicago boarding area right here. The terminal will be built where the Field Station is now, but down here will be the equivalent of the train shed."

She was surprised at the size of the station area that had been carved out of the rock. She figured it was three stories high and about the size of a football field.

Metcalf stretched out his arms so they were pointing toward either end where three huge holes had been drilled in the rocky walls.

"The two larger tunnels are twenty feet in diameter—they're the transport tubes. The smaller one in the middle is the service tunnel. Every thousand feet there'll be a passage connecting all three."

She noticed that the tracks were already in position, and so were several of the giant magnetic rings. Against a side wall, workers were setting up several long tables.

"Caterers," Metcalf explained. "After the hole-through

(170

ceremonies on Sunday, you'll come back here and there'll be a party." A thought occurred to him. "You going to hole-through? I didn't see your name on the list."

"I was thinking of asking Dane if it would be all right if I came. Do you think he'd object?"

Another smile, and she had to admit that his smile *was* infectious. "He'd object if you didn't."

Poor Troy, he was going to hate her when he found out that she was with the Bureau and that where she went was strictly up to her. But that was a bridge she'd cross when she came to it.

He got into one of the small electric cars and turned to her, his face serious. "Sometimes people get claustrophobic down here, especially going from the shed into the tunnel. If it happens, let me know, and we'll get you out right away."

Much to her surprise, she did feel a sudden wave of panic going from the huge artificial cavern into the relatively small tube. But a hundred feet into the tube, it had vanished.

"How far to the head of the cut?"

"Four miles. Takes about ten minutes. Pity the poor guys on the other side—they have to travel close to forty miles before hitting the head of their cut. Takes them over an hour and a half." He waved at the tunnel around them. "We do a lot of the finishing work on the tunnel as we go along. You remember in the station area, the tracks and the magnetic rings for the bullet train were already installed. As we go up the tunnel, first the rings disappear, then the tracks. Then the concrete walls will begin to look rough and unfinished. For the last thousand yards you'll see the raw faces of the shields, and the tracks for the muck train will be running on naked rock."

The closer they got to the head of the cut, the noisier and more crowded the tunnel became. Men were lining the shields with concrete, shields were being installed, tracks being laid. . . . When they passed a boarded-up area, a wooden patch in the side of the tunnel, she shouted, "What's that?"

"They hit a cave a few days back—we had no idea it was there."

"That surprises me."

(171

"It surprised us, too."

The tunnel became rocky and unfinished, and suddenly the huge metal monster that was the mole barred their way. Metcalf braked the car, and they walked around to the front. A dozen men were cutting away at the surface of dull gray stone.

"We'll back up the mole four or five hundred feet, then we'll build a little platform for Kaltmeyer to stand on when he swings the sledge. A few paces back will be several rows of VIPs, then a space for camera crews, and finally folding chairs for a hundred or so guests."

She tried to picture it and began to feel uneasy. Harry was going to have a difficult time with security.

"I don't think it's such a good idea, either," Metcalf said, watching her face.

"Not my department." For a fraction of a second, she thought he was trying to catch her off base. That was the trouble with working for the Bureau—nobody was ever above suspicion. And then she wondered if Troy Metcalf was everything he seemed to be.

She suddenly realized the men had stopped working and were staring at her. She didn't wait for Metcalf to introduce her but smiled and stepped forward, holding out her hand. "Hi, my name's Cyd Lederley."

She was right about Swede being the blond giant. Most of his hair was hidden under a yellow hard hat, but there was no mistaking his huge arms.

"I saw you at Jimmy's once," she said.

He remembered then, and his face reddened. "I was really bombed," he said apologetically. "Last thing in the world I'd do is hit Dane."

"I'm sure he'll forgive you, but I can guarantee he'll never forget you."

She met all the men and shook their hands, not worried about the dirt or stains on her dress. She felt vaguely like a celebrity. Then she and Metcalf walked back to the car. She had mentally photographed all the men working in the cut and knew she could describe every yard of the tunnel if she ever had to. She pointed to one of the small wooden sheds about five feet high hugging the tunnel wall, the doors in front secured by a padlock.

"What are those?"

"They call them jockey boxes—they're equipment lockers. You can't lug all your tools back to the access shaft every time you finish a shift, so you lock them up in one of those."

She noticed there was one by the boarded-up area of the cave and filed it away with the rest of her information.

In the car on the way back to the access shaft, she said, "You like Dane, don't you?"

"He tell you to ask me?"

"Hardly."

"Yeah, I like him. Not as much as you do."

"Not in the same way," she corrected.

He was silent for a moment. "I admire him a lot. He's a damned good engineer. But you tell him that, and I'll wring your neck."

She raised an eyebrow. "Why?"

"Nothing complicated. Just not my style. The only thing wrong with Dane is that he won't admit he's got as much to learn as he thinks I do."

Metcalf was smarter than Dane had given him credit for, she decided.

Back at the access shaft, he grinned at her and said, "You should be proud of me. I got through the whole tour without making a single pass."

She smiled. The pass that wasn't a pass. Right on time.

"You're married, Troy."

"Aren't you?"

"Not for quite a while. And in case you're curious, I don't make a habit of playing around. And neither should you." She was right—brash kid brother was the proper image for him. Then, more relaxed: "Shot in the dark?"

"Not really. You're old enough, and you're attractive enough, and somewhere along the line you've learned how to handle men." He cocked his head, grinning. "You've handled me, and

(173

you were pretty sharp in handling the men back there. For a good student, marriage is usually the best institution for teaching that sort of thing."

"It can be."

Then she realized that neither of them had mentioned Styron's death. Dane had asked her not to—he'd said he wanted to break it himself. But it must have hit the morning papers; they usually checked with the police every hour or so for homicides. They would have had it in time for the early editions. Maybe Metcalf didn't read the morning papers or had skipped today's; the high-ballers themselves probably had their news read to them by the evening anchormen.

Metcalf wasn't dissembling, she was sure of that. It wasn't a case of him hiding guilty knowledge. But it still would be interesting to watch his face when he found out. First Orencho, then Leaver, then Styron. . . . The engineers were probably just one more death away from panic.

In the cage going up, she realized she had been perspiring in the tunnel and wondered if she *was* claustrophobic. The sense of oppression she had felt all the time she was down there . . . She thought about it for a moment, trying to place the feeling. And then she had it. It wasn't claustrophobia at all. It was something quite different but just as serious.

All the time in the tunnel, she had felt as if she were being watched—*knew* she was being watched.

CHAPTER 19

Nordlund slept late and fitfully, his dreams haunted by Styron's staring eyes and gray skin. The police had been perfunctory, as he knew they would be, talking more to Cyd than to him. He had given what information he could, then driven Cyd back to the Marriott. He didn't get to bed until two-thirty and had tossed for an hour before falling asleep.

He turned off the alarm when it rang at seven, fell asleep for another hour, then finally woke up to sit on the side of the bed and hold his head in his hands. Wake up in stages, his mother used to say. Never surprise the heart. . . .

He made himself a cup of coffee and nibbled at a slice of toast, then drove slowly out to the Field Station. It had gotten warmer during the night, just enough so that the melting snow had left a thin layer of water over the harder ice beneath. It didn't take more than two skids to shock enough adrenaline into his system so that he was finally wide awake.

It was ten o'clock when he got to the station. Jan heard him enter his office and slipped in without knocking. "They just broadcast the news that Del's been murdered."

He hung up his coat, feeling as tired as if he hadn't had any sleep at all. "Yeah, I know—Cyd and I found the body."

She looked her surprise, then said hesitantly, "I called his family in Cleveland, gave them the condolences of the company. I figured you and Mr. Kaltmeyer would want me to."

"They know?"

She nodded. "The police had called them earlier this morning." Much to his surprise, her eyes were damp. "I'm sorry, Dane."

The really sorry thing was that she was probably the only one who *was* sorry. Styron had always been a cipher to him, a man with physical lusts and appetites and beyond that, a blank. If Styron had friends, he'd met them some other place than at work.

And if Jan had heard about Del's murder, others working the cut must also have heard by now. Coupled with those of Orencho and Leaver, the murders would make for one jittery crew.

"You remind Metcalf about Cyd?"

"They're down in the cut now."

Once inside his office, he took the cassette from his pocket and toyed with it a moment, then made up his mind. He might not feel much for Styron, but he felt a good deal less for whoever had murdered him—and a great curiosity as to why. He flipped the cassette one more time, then put it on his desk. He thumbed the intercom switch. "Jan, have Rob come in, will you?"

Zumwalt stumbled in a few moments later, looking half hung over from lack of sleep. A new baby will do that, Nordlund thought with envy.

"What's up?"

Nordlund shoved the cassette at him. "You remember the old sonic technique for storing computer data on audio tapes?"

Zumwalt fingered the cassette, looked surprised by the label, then noticed there was Scotch tape covering the tab breakouts, indicating that somebody had recorded over the Beethoven.

"Before my time, but I've heard about it."

Nordlund pointed at the cassette. "I think that's the kind of signal we've got there. What I want is for you to see if it can be converted back to digital form and stored on one of our laser disc memories so we can get a printout or throw the information on a computer screen."

"Who recorded it?"

"Not sure. I think Styron did."

Zumwalt gingerly put the tape back down onto the desk. "You think this is the missing data?"

"Maybe."

He touched the cassette again, wary this time, as if it might explode with hard handling.

"How come I get all the weird assignments?"

"Because you're a weird guy, Rob. And because I trust your imagination and intuition."

Zumwalt managed a sleepy smile. "Flatter me, and I'll even work late."

"When can I have it?"

"I know a guy with a recording studio over on Southport, he can do it."

Nordlund waved him out of the office. "It would be nice if we could have it by tomorrow."

"Nothing like a leisurely deadline." But Zumwalt was already halfway out the door.

"Rob." Zumwalt hesitated, his hand on the doorknob. "I don't want you blabbing this all over the office. I'm serious."

Zumwalt made an "okay" gesture with his thumb and forefinger. "I'll make a copy for safety's sake and keep them both under lock and key."

"You do that, Rob—let me know the moment you get something readable."

Once Zumwalt had closed the door behind him, Nordlund shut his eyes, trying to steal five seconds of rest. Styron's body promptly surfaced in his mind, the empty eyes already sunken in their sockets, the skin bloodless and cold to the touch. He had seen a number of dead bodies in Peru three years before, the victims of an earthquake; he had volunteered for a rescue squad to help dig them out. Within an hour, he had lost count of the dying and the dead.

But he had never gotten used to them.

It was midafternoon when Metcalf checked in, trailed by Phillips and a man who looked vaguely familiar but whom Nordlund couldn't place. Metcalf laid a sheaf of printouts on his desk.

"Less than five meters to go, and look at the boundary register—the teams will meet with an error of less than one centimeter."

Nordlund inspected the printouts showing the sounding data from both sides of the cut. Close, very close.

Phillips shook his head in admiration. "I didn't think you people would do it, Nordlund, I really didn't." He took a breath. "But I don't think a complete hole-through is what we want. What I would like is just a thin shell, something that a good pickaxe or a sledge could break through."

"As a grandstand play, that's a lousy idea, Steve."

Phillips looked annoyed. "I happen to think it's a great idea. And I'm not the only one. Kaltmeyer thinks it's terrific, and so does Troy, here. I even got Cal Briggs—"

He suddenly remembered his guest. "Sorry, Cal—Dane, I'd like you to meet a friend of mine, Cal Briggs. Cal's anchorman for the six o'clock news on WBBM-TV. He's the pool reporter who'll be covering the show. I thought I'd show him around the cut so he'll know what to expect."

Nordlund now remembered both the name and the face. Briggs was one of the better newscasters, one who wasn't afraid to look forty and who relied on an actual knowledge of the news rather than a blow-dry and a tired line of happy-talk; he even showed signs of being trained as a journalist. The only thing Nordlund couldn't understand was why Briggs was a friend of Phillips, though he suspected Steve overstated the case.

"Glad to meet you, Mr. Briggs." He shook the anchorman's hand, then turned to Metcalf. "You like the idea?"

Metcalf looked embarrassed. "It seemed like a good one at the time."

Briggs cleared his throat and cut in. "For what it's worth, I like it, too. You need a little action, Mr. Nordlund, otherwise all we'll have is talking heads."

"Washington wants it this way," Phillips added, the muscles in his jaw tightening. "I called first thing this morning."

Nordlund wondered what second-level administrative assistant constituted "Washington," then shrugged. So let Phillips win one, it was no skin off his nose.

"If you want something a couple of inches thick from the arch to the floor, it's going to take time to shave it without breaking through. And whoever's on the delivery end of the sledge is going to have to be ready to run for it. Even a thin sheet of rock weighs—pieces of it could do a lot of damage if they fell on you; they could even kill you.''

"It'll look terrific on television," Phillips insisted. "Besides, Kaltmeyer loves it—he wants to swing the sledge.''

Phillips had probably suggested to Kaltmeyer that he should be the one with the sledge. Maybe Kaltmeyer was hoping it *would* kill him—go out in a blaze of glory on the six o'clock news.

"Okay, we'll try it. What else do you have?"

"Seating." Phillips unrolled a diagram he had been carrying. "I figure a podium, maybe a few feet from the head of the cut. We'll have three or four speakers, then Kaltmeyer will say a few words before stepping up with the sledge." He looked up at Nordlund. "If you wanted to say a few words, Dane, we could probably squeeze you in, too. I could write something up—''

"You've got enough speakers, Steve. Leave me out of it.''
Phillips didn't bother to hide his relief.

"In front of the podium, there'll be a half-dozen chairs or so. I figure you and Kaltmeyer, Senator DeFolge and his daughter, two or three others." He looked apologetic. "The big show will be in January; this is sort of a dry run for that. In January we'll be loaded with celebrities.''

"Of course," Nordlund said dryly.

Phillips pointed at his drawing. "After the first row, there'll be a gap of maybe ten feet so the cameraman can maneuver for his best angles when Kaltmeyer swings the sledge and the wall comes tumbling down." He smiled at his choice of words. "From there on back, we could probably squeeze in several hundred guests—some of the engineers, the high-ballers who worked on the cut, maybe some of the office staff. There'll be interviews afterward. You can clue Cal in about who speaks English—fluently, that is.''

Nordlund had a brief fantasy of Phillips using the same line down at Jimmy's and had to suppress a smile.

Phillips looked enormously pleased with himself. "The second show will have the celebrities, but this should be pretty spectacular in its own right.''

Nordlund turned to Briggs. "I can set up tapings with the men for advance interviews if you want me to. There won't be any problem—the men will jump at the chance."

"It would be appreciated." Briggs hesitated, looking apologetic. "I didn't realize there might be any danger to knocking down the wall."

Nordlund concentrated on the diagram. "Don't let it bother you. Kaltmeyer should know what he's doing. Just don't let your cameraman get too close—our insurance wouldn't cover him. Okay, that all?" They started to file out, and he nodded at Metcalf. "Stick around for a moment, Troy."

After they had left, he said, "Be careful of Phillips, he can bite."

Metcalf reddened. "For God's sake, Dane, what do you want? You asked me to handle him, I've handled him. I don't see where we lose anything on this one. And this is what he's spent four years hanging around to see. If he had to pull every string he has in Washington, he'd get his way. You know that."

Nordlund leaned back in his chair and massaged the bridge of his nose. He was tired and depressed, and he couldn't get Styron's face out of his mind.

"You're right—sorry. You hear about Del?"

Metcalf's anger faded. "Jan told me a few minutes ago. I didn't know him very well. I was never that tight with him."

"I found the body—Cyd Lederley and myself. We had gone over to see him, find out why he hadn't shown up for work."

"That's the third one. Think somebody has it in for the cut?"

"Your guess is as good as mine. You show Cyd around?"

"Yeah. One smart woman, knows how to handle herself."

Metcalf had made his pass, and Cyd had promptly repelled all boarders.

"Cyd likes you, too." He didn't bother adding, "As a brother."

It was just before he was ready to go home, when he was tugging on his rubbers, that Cyd called him on the office phone.

"You need something, Dane."

It took him a moment to realize she was being funny. "Yeah? What could that be?"

"A home-cooked meal. A girlfriend left me her apartment until next Monday. Take my advice and don't turn it down— I'm a good cook."

A day and a night of stress and tension yet to go, and Cyd Lederley was offering him the pleasure of her company, a free meal, and an evening of rest and relaxation.

He wasn't about to turn it down.

The apartment was small and comfortable, just off LaSalle Street in Carl Sandburg Village. A single woman's home, Nordlund thought. Heavy textured curtains and a few too many floor pillows in the living room, butcher block countertops, and brown and orange Mexican tile in the kitchen. The bathroom surprised him in its neatness until he opened a cabinet door. Cyd's girlfriend had cleaned up at the last moment and swept all the beauty aids off the sink and the bathtub ledge into the cabinet. Fortunately, she'd left out a bar of soap. If he'd had to look for it, he never would have found it.

Cyd shouted from the kitchen, "It'll be steak and baked potatoes, if that's all right with you. You make the salad. I think there's fixings in the fridge." She banged through the cabinets a moment, then, "Maude has a wet bar in the living room— look and see if she left any booze. I'll take two fingers of anything, straight up."

There was a third of a liter of Jack Daniel's and an unopened bottle of Gilbey's gin in the bottom of the wet bar. He hesitated, then picked the Daniel's. It was a whiskey type of evening.

Cyd seemed at home in the kitchen, though steak was hardly a challenge. A good spaghetti sauce—now that would have been another story. He poured out two tumblers of whiskey, handed her one and said, "Here's looking at you, kid."

She took a sip and smacked her lips. "Hits the spot—don't forget the salad."

"Coming, Mother." He rummaged around in the refrigerator and found a head of lettuce and two tomatoes in the vegetable bin and half a cucumber on the shelf above. "How's Wilcox doing?"

She looked up from the counter grill. "Is that an innocent question, or are you digging?"

He held the lettuce under the water tap, shook out the excess water, and started pulling it apart, dropping small sections into the salad bowl. "Both."

"No reason why you can't ask, I guess. Sam was getting quite fond of your Henry Leaver, by the way. They might have been good friends if they hadn't been on opposite sides."

He couldn't keep the irony out of his voice. "I'm sure Henry appreciated that. Maybe Wilcox would have visited him in jail."

"I think Leaver considered Sam a worthy opponent. How do you like your steak?"

"Medium well, but I'll take it any way I can get it." The kitchen was warm, and Cyd's face was faintly flushed, strands of hair sticking to her forehead. He had vivid memories of his mother looking like that when he was a small boy and used to haunt the kitchen when she was cooking.

"I'm serious, Cyd. How's the U.S. government versus Kaltmeyer/DeFolge shaping up?"

"Better hurry with the salad; I think I'm getting ahead of you with the steak. The potatoes should be ready in about another five minutes. You might open the wine, too."

"You don't want to talk about it, that it?"

She leaned against the countertop and wiped at her forehead with the back of her hand. She didn't have to tell him anything, she knew that. But she had already let him know that he was involved.

"There's reason to believe that Max was implicated in kickbacks from some of the subcontractors and that Kaltmeyer and DeFolge knew about it."

"Anything more than that?"

She nodded. "Probably enough for indictments, and I think Sam's going to ask for some. We're interested in the property exchanges near the portal sites in both Illinois and Michigan. It sounds like someone had favored information, and I'm betting on your ex-father-in-law.''

"The conflict-of-interest laws—I'm sure the senator obeyed those to the letter, if not the spirit. He'll be pretty well shielded.''

"That's one of the things we're trying to find out.''

He finally located a wooden spoon and fork and tossed the salad with the cream garlic dressing he had found.

"Only two men would know, and one of them is dead. And Kaltmeyer will never testify against DeFolge.'' She looked noncommittal, and he said, "Okay, what makes you think he would?''

"I don't know whether he would nor not—it's more the old question of when thieves fall out.''

"Nobody could have made much money off the lots, and God knows they weren't selling any underneath the lake. I can't believe Lammont would have fudged his survey soundings to make sure the tunnel ran through property DeFolge controlled. Lammont and Associates are international authorities.''

She tested one of the steaks, making a small slit in the center and examining it for the degree of pink.

"International authorities have been bought before. But Lammont's not under suspicion.''

"What about me?''

She smiled. "There's no law against being naïve. And that's no put-down, Dane. In this day and age, it's a compliment.'' She cut into the other steak and frowned. "How'd you say you wanted yours?''

"Medium well. Why?''

"You told me medium well or any way you could get it. You shouldn't have given me a choice.''

"I'm hungry enough, it doesn't matter.''

She looked smug. "See, I told you I was a good cook. A good cook always delays the meal. When the guests are famished, anything tastes good.''

He couldn't get the image of Styron out of his mind, and he kept wondering what Max, Del, and Henry Leaver had in common. There was a tie between Styron and Orencho, and there was a tie between Orencho and Henry, but there was no connection between Del and Leaver.

"Either I'm a very good cook, or I'm a very bad one, Dane. How about letting me off the hook and telling me which it is?"

He looked up in surprise. "You fishing for compliments?"

"You haven't said a word during the entire meal."

"I've had my mouth full."

She shook her head. "Seriously. Something's bothering you."

He leaned back, staring at her. Christ, she was an attractive woman. "You're right," he confessed after a moment. "I was thinking. About three murders."

She finished the last bite of steak and reached for the pot of coffee to fill his cup. "What about the murders?"

"Whether or not they're related. The disgruntled employee trying to get even fits Leaver and Orencho—they were around since the company started. But it doesn't fit Del. He only hired on about two years ago."

"Maybe they're unrelated. From what the police had to say, Del led a pretty active social life."

He shook his head. "Can't buy that. Relationships lead to murder, one-night stands don't. Particularly when the pleasure's bought and paid for. And don't tell me a pimp had it in for him. Del didn't have the guts to stiff a call girl."

"That probably shoots the unhappy ex-employee theory, though there are solid reasons for it. Twelve years ago, Kaltmeyer/DeFolge held the contract for another tunnel under the East River in New York. There was a blowout, and almost an entire shift of workers were killed. There were a lot of bitter feelings about that, accusations of criminal negligence, but nothing was ever proved." She looked at his face. "Don't look for it in the company records, it's not there. But I've got the clips on it if you ever want to check it out."

Maybe someday, he thought.

"Del's murder wouldn't fit into that theory. What about terrorists? That's why they sent you out here—there must have been some possibilities."

"Still are, though not as great as I once thought. The cut is a tempting target, though if they're after personnel, they've made odd choices so far. Orencho had already left, Leaver wasn't essential, and Styron was strictly a third-level-engineering type. It doesn't make much sense to me—I should think the prime targets would be you or Kaltmeyer and maybe the senator."

She started clearing the table.

"How'd you ever get connected with the FBI?"

"What's a nice girl like me doing in a business like this is what you mean, right?" Her lips thinned. "It all began when I was eighteen and bouncing around Europe right after high school. The plane I was on was hijacked going from Rome to Cairo. We sat on the ground in Beirut and they shot five Americans one right after the other and threw them out the hatch. One of them was a boy I had gone to school with. At the time, I thought I was in love with Tim—we were doing Europe together."

He felt like somebody had hit him in the stomach. "I'm sorry, Cyd."

"Twelve more were killed when an American antiterrorist squad stormed the plane a day later. They were attached to the Sixth Fleet; their response time surprised everybody. They killed all the hijackers. I remember spitting on the bodies when I left the plane."

"I didn't know it was a loaded question."

She shrugged. "That was fourteen years ago, Dane. I don't think about it that often."

"You hire on with the FBI immediately afterward or what?"

She took the wineglasses and walked into the living room; he followed after with another bottle.

"Not right away. I went to Northwestern and majored in biz-ad with a minor in psychology. When I graduated, I applied to the Bureau. They hired me and sent me to Michigan State for a master's in psych. I thought it was damned generous of them; I still do."

She turned on the small stereo set, the volume on low. Pop classics, but the conversation was too serious for anything heavier. He settled onto the couch and watched her while she moved around the room. She was athletic, far more than Diana had ever been, and it showed in her movements. It was a pleasure just watching Cyd walk from one spot to another.

"You know a lot about how terrorists operate?"

She sat on the couch next to him, folding her legs beneath her. "I didn't write the book, but I sure know what's in it." She reflected for a moment. "It's not a private vendetta; over the years I've become very professional about it."

"I couldn't believe you when you talked about the boy in the airport."

"He was innocent, just a scared kid. But there have been others like him who weren't innocent at all."

He frowned. "I think I've got a block against it."

"We've been in a war for almost thirty years now, Dane. It's become a very sophisticated war between a worldwide population that, by and large, likes things the way they are and a much smaller population that sees anarchy as offering them a whole new shake. They're people who are convinced it won't happen unless the present house of cards collapses completely. Now they're digging in for the long haul."

She held out her glass for a refill.

"They're drifting over here, a lot of them as illegals, and setting up small businesses and integrating themselves into the community. Every once in a while they mount an operation— usually successfully. If you kept a record of the incidents, you'd know the war is heating up. They happen more often, and they result in larger and larger casualties. And they're winning—look what's happened to the airlines. Indirectly, they're the reason for the bullet train and the cut in the first place."

Nordlund shook his head, still reluctant to believe it. "But the boy at the airport didn't look—"

"Mediterranean? Black hair and olive skin? All-American as apple pie is big in terrorist circles these days. They pick children that look the part to begin with—some of them they even adopt, then they raise them in the country where eventually they'll be used. The children are brought up with a thoroughgoing hatred of the host country. It's sort of the reverse of the Hitler Youth, where the state successfully indoctrinated children so they would report their own parents to the authorities.''

Nordlund grimaced. "That's sending kids into war."

"Not that unusual—in Iran, Khomeini sent ten- and twelve-year-olds to the front lines in the war against Iraq during the 1980s.'' She sipped at her wine, for a moment lost in thought. "We're waiting for terrorists to drop the other shoe, for the day when they decide body counts are as important as media exposure. Western society is vulnerable, Dane. Much more so than an agrarian one of small villages and farms. We can inflict small casualties; they can inflict huge ones.''

"I liked the boy," Nordlund mused. "I couldn't stand the idea that somebody might shoot him—even if he were guilty.''

"Understandable. You wanted children, and Diana couldn't give them to you." It was her turn to look apologetic. "Both of you were rather loud in Andy's the other night.''

"You're right—and I guess we were. It happens when you argue with somebody you were married to for years." And then he was surprised that it hadn't occurred to him before. "You ever been married, Cyd?''

"Once.''

"What happened?''

"It fell apart after the first year. Nice guy, actually. We were just two different people.''

Nordlund wasn't sure how to phrase it. "You never met anybody since?''

"I haven't yet." She smiled. "Once I almost did. Harry Richards. We were pretty close for a year, then decided to leave it at good friends." She put her hands on his. "What about you? You must have been madly in love with Diana at one time.

He had thought on the plane that she was exceptionally easy to talk to, and she was proving it all over again.

"I met Diana at a Beaux Arts New Year's Dance. The chemistry of pure sex—plus she knew how to listen and say the right things at the right time. She worked at it. She knew art, and she knew literature, and she let me know she liked them as much as I did." He laughed. "I don't think Diana ever read a book in her life. She got it all out of Cliff Notes. When she found out I was a baseball fan, in two weeks she knew more about the game than I did. The senator hired a coach from the local high school to tutor her.''

Cyd started to giggle. ''You were a good catch—sorry, I couldn't help that.''

''I guess I was.'' When he looked back on it, it had its funny aspects. But it still hurt. ''The senator checked me out with the university and the professional societies I had joined— and, of course, with all the engineering firms I had worked for. My family had a name—back to the Revolution and all that— but it didn't have any money. DeFolge didn't care. He told me he wanted to 'reinvigorate the bloodline.' ''

His face hardened with the memory.

''I felt like a goddamned Arabian stud.''

They were very close together on the couch by then, and his arm had slipped around her shoulders almost by itself. When he had finished talking, she twisted slightly and kissed him, and his arms tightened around her. Then he had slipped his hands beneath her light wool sweater and was cupping her breasts.

She had set him up for seduction right from the beginning, he thought.

God bless her.

CHAPTER 20

He had been waiting for this opportunity. In the past, he had considered the possibility of tampering with the helicopter, but it was always on the pad within eyesight of the pilot or one of the security guards. Besides, a lot of people used the 'copter; he couldn't be sure who would be passengers on the craft when it failed. The limousine now presented an opportunity he hadn't expected.

The car had been deserted for the last hour, crouched like a huge black beetle in the executive parking area. The men he wanted were working late—they had been working late most of the week, desperately trying to do what they had always relied on Henry Leaver to do for them. The chauffeur was restless and had gone to the small canteen that was kept open for the highballers and the office staff who worked the evening shifts. He could see the chauffeur through the lighted windows, a large, brown man with massive hands and flattened nose, sipping coffee and flirting with the occasional secretary or property clerk who came in for coffee and a sandwich.

In between flirtations he talked to the two security agents who had been assigned full time to the limousine's star passengers. They spent most of their time in the canteen, bored and unhappy, drinking coffee and watching the workers pass by outside.

He knew the chauffeur and had no particular love for him. The chauffeur was arrogant and more than once had caused him trouble. The chauffeur was now preoccupied talking to a girl from the engineering division; he no longer went to the windows to check on the limousine.

The opportunity might not come again.

It was late at night and the sky was overcast, so there wasn't even moonlight to reflect off the freezing slush that covered the

(189

lot. He left the shadowed doorway and ambled past the Field Station building toward the parking lot. He had a clipboard in his hand, and if he were stopped, he already had an excuse made up for being there.

It had started to rain again. The drops spattered against his face, and he almost panicked with the feel of water running down his neck. What must it have been like to feel the water rushing into the tunnel and rising to your head and then being totally submerged, fighting to get out, fighting for breath, and seeing your face staring at you through the glass port as you slowly drowned? He had felt guilty . . . oh, God, he had felt guilty watching Brad drown and knowing at the same time that he himself was going to live.

If only he could have traded places. . . .

He bumped into the limousine, and the waters suddenly receded. He was once again standing in a parking lot on a cold and moonless night. He stroked the sleek limousine almost affectionately. He had considered the use of a detonator in the gas tank once more and then decided against it. For one thing, the limousine was parked too close to the Field Station building, and he had no desire to endanger anybody else. Besides, an explosion so near the building could conceivably destroy valuable records and perhaps delay the completion of the tunnel. He didn't want to endanger that—he was, after all, a tunnel man.

He was in luck. The chauffeur had left the limousine unlocked. He placed his clipboard on the ground next to the car, looked around to make sure that he wasn't being observed, and opened the door. He pressed the dash button that released the hood. It sprang open with what sounded like a small explosion. He froze, sure that somebody would come running out of the canteen. But no, he could still see the chauffeur through the windows. His conversation was animated; the girl had become interested in him.

He pulled a pair of snub-nosed insulated pliers and a length of lead fuse wire from his pocket and went around to the hood. The engine block with all its servomechanisms was an electrical jungle, but he had studied shop diagrams of the limousine ear-

(190

*lier and knew what to do. He disconnected the automatic link-
ages so that the limo would respond only to manual control.
The anticollision airbags were triggered by a small device that
sensed rapid deceleration. He bypassed it with a small fuse wire
and then tripped the device.*

*Nothing happened—nothing would happen until the engine
heated sufficiently to melt the fuse wire. At that point, the on-
board gas generator would fill the bags with vaporized freon,
expanding them suddenly in the face of the driver. The limousine would be on the expressway heading north. To lose control
in the middle of traffic—and with the Christmas parties in the
city, there would be traffic—was a sure death sentence.*

"Good-bye, Frank," he murmured. "Good-bye, Senator."

*They were the last two on the list; the books would be closed
then. But . . . maybe not quite. There were the others, the ones
who were helping Kaltmeyer and the senator right now, the ones
responsible however indirectly for the deaths of Esposito and
Felton. It wasn't fair to let them get away scot-free. Would Brad
have forgiven and forgotten?*

Not very likely.

*He closed the hood, picked up the clipboard, and walked
away. Not quite Christmas Eve, but close enough, he thought.
Fifteen years minus two days. Just a day after his birthday, he
thought bitterly. After their birthday.*

But it was going to be a merry Christmas for Brad after all.

CHAPTER 21

Nordlund woke up to the soft music of a classical radio station and squinted over at the bed table. Cyd's girlfriend had set the clock radio for six-thirty. She had been psychic—it was the same time he usually set his. He started to swing his legs out of bed, then pulled them back in. The bed was warm and comfortable, the room chilly. They had played "spoons" during the night, each of them pressed close to the other, and the bed had become a snug little nest. He smelled her hair and sensed her deep, rhythmic breathing. It had been a long night of love and laughter, one of the very few he'd had in his life.

How different from Diana . . . and then he cursed himself for making comparisons once again. But there really weren't any. Diana had the most perfect breasts of any woman he had ever known, as well as the most perfect legs. And that was the problem. Diana was a collection of body parts, while Cyd had been the complete woman, a physical gestalt.

He started to edge out of bed, not wanting to wake her. He had taken one step away when he heard a soft giggle. An arm suddenly clamped around his knees. "Oh, no, you don't!"

It started out as a romp through the blankets and a five-minute tickling session punctuated by smothered bursts of laughter. It finally ended in pulsing waves of sexuality and a sense of overwhelming affection. They lay for a quarter of an hour clinging to each other, not saying a word, Nordlund holding her head against his chest and gently stroking her hair.

Take it slow, he thought. *Take it very, very slow. . . .*

And then they slowly untangled. "How do you want your eggs?" he asked.

She opened one eye. "You know how to make them?"

"A little butter in a frying pan, slip in two eggs without

breaking the yolks, add a tablespoon of water, cover, and steam until the albumen over the yolks has turned white."

"I hate a man who can cook," she grunted. "Your mother should be horsewhipped." Then: "Don't forget the bacon. Wrap three strips in paper towels, plop in the microwave, and give 'em three minutes. They'll come out crisp, no grease. And Maude left a can of orange juice in the freezer. I checked."

He showered and was halfway through the breakfast preparations when she came into the kitchen toweling her hair, wearing a loosely belted bathrobe. She sniffed the coffee and rolled her eyes. "I think I've died and gone to heaven."

"Live alone, and you learn how to cook in a hurry."

"Tell me about it."

Over coffee, she studied him for a long moment. "I probably shouldn't tell you this, but Diana was obviously lying when she said she was disappointed with you in bed."

He felt his face redden. "Ah, Cyd, I generally—"

"—don't talk about it, right. I don't make a habit of it myself. It's just something I thought you should know, in case your ego was hurting." She sipped at her coffee for a moment, her eyes never leaving his face. "In the last analysis, how good anybody is in bed, Dane, depends on how much you like them."

"We never made love in the morning," he mused. "Diana was very . . . ritualistic about sex."

"Morning's probably the best time—it's very natural then, spontaneous." She put down her coffee and walked over to rumple his hair and kiss him on the cheek. "Take it as a compliment, Dane. You're a lot of fun."

He suddenly grinned. "Thanks." He slid the first set of eggs onto a plate and added the bacon from its nest of paper towels in the microwave. "Diana probably has the most male outlook toward sex of any woman I know. I think she equates sex with power." He frowned. "That's something I generally don't—"

"—talk about," Cyd finished.

"Right," he said, faintly embarrassed. He was saved by the ringing of the phone. "Maude?"

"Maybe. She might have left her credit cards behind, something like that." She took the phone off its cradle on the wall. "Maude's not home. This is a friend of hers, Cyd Lederley." She listened for a moment, her smile slowly tilting and sliding off her face.

She handed the phone to him. "Janice. Said she spent half the night trying to track you down."

He took the phone. "Dane here." He listened for a moment, then said in an empty voice, "I'll be there as soon as I can make it."

Cyd was staring at him, curious but wary. "What's happened?"

"Kaltmeyer. And DeFolge. Their limo went out of control on the expressway. Both of them are dead, along with the chauffeur."

She was suddenly very professional.

"Body identification?"

"Not yet. It was a head-on collision at sixty. Gas tank exploded, and all three bodies were burned beyond recognition."

She dumped her breakfast into the garbage and put the plate in the sink. "I'll be right with you." Just before going into the bedroom, she turned and said, "I'm sorry, Dane. I know Kaltmeyer meant a lot to you."

He nodded, his mind blank. He didn't feel much of anything.

But he knew he would later.

The news was all over the Field Station. Most of those he met talked in hushed tones among themselves as he passed by, watching him out of the corner of their eyes. On the second floor, Metcalf stopped him in the hallway. "He was a great old man, Dane."

"Any details on how it happened?"

"Nobody knows. Apparently the airbags suddenly blew up in their faces. The chauffeur swerved into the oncoming lane, and that was it—head-on with a station wagon."

If the airbags had done anything, they had probably prolonged the agony. And then it occurred to him that he would

(194

have to comfort Diana, that the death of her father would be too heavy a blow for her to take alone. Her mother had died in childbirth, and she had no brothers or sisters.

Zumwalt tried to nail him in the bullpen. "I know you're busy, Dane, but that little project you gave me yesterday—it's really serious."

He brushed past. "I'll get to you after a while, Rob. There's too much going on right now."

In his office, Janice had cleared everything off his desk except his phone and his Rolodex and a pad of yellow paper. She was right, as usual, without even suggesting it to him. Phone calls to Washington, condolence calls to Kaltmeyer's sister in Canada—he had been widowed years before—and to Derrick. It would be tough on him; he had no other family. And of course, he'd have to call Diana, though she was probably on her way over.

"I think I want to talk to the police first, Jan, find out as many details as I can—"

She was facing him, turned so that she was looking through the door to the outer office. Her eyes suddenly opened wide, and she stifled a small scream. Outside in the engineers' bullpen, the usual murmur of conversation suddenly stopped. Nordlund whirled.

Kaltmeyer had just walked into the office, followed by DeFolge. Both of them looked pale and haggard.

"I'm not dead yet," Kaltmeyer said with a faint smile. He dropped his coat onto the couch while DeFolge collapsed into the chair by the desk. DeFolge was visibly shaken, his eyes jumpy and frightened in his chubby face. "Get Harry Richards down here, ditto Phillips. We're going to have to go over the plans for tomorrow—if there's going to be a real problem, that's when it will happen. And tomorrow they might not miss."

Nordlund felt tense. Which one of Cyd's theories was correct? Some group? Some psychotic ex-employee?

"What happened?"

Kaltmeyer shook his head. "Nobody knows exactly. Eyewitness accounts say that Matthews was driving the limousine south on the expressway with two passengers—probably the security men that Harris had assigned to us—when the airbags inflated. Matthews fought the wheel and swerved into the oncoming lane. That would have been all she wrote if Alan and I had been in the car. We took the 'copter across the lake to Benton Harbor.'' He suddenly seemed hesitant. ''Wanted to check on Dietz and his team for tomorrow.''

He was lying, Nordlund thought. He and DeFolge had given the security men the slip and flown to Benton Harbor, probably to raid the records there. But right now, it didn't matter.

Moments later, a somber Richards and a frightened Phillips were in his office, along with Metcalf. Kaltmeyer repeated the story of the airbags and the crashed limousine.

''The police said they'll have a positive ID on the bodies late today, but I'm sure they'll find it was Matthews''—he glanced at Richards—''and the two security men.''

''The company will remember their families,'' DeFolge cut in unctuously.

Richards's expression didn't change, and Nordlund wondered if he had known them well. They should never have let Kaltmeyer and DeFolge out of their sight, he thought. Then he realized that if they hadn't, all five might have driven to town in the limousine, and Kaltmeyer and DeFolge would be dead.

''So what do we do about tomorrow?'' Kaltmeyer asked, staring at Richards. ''What're your recommendations?''

''My first recommendation would be to forget the cameras and the celebration. Restrict access strictly to those who work here, hole through, and get on with the tunnel. And cancel the January ceremony.''

''What's your second recommendation?'' Phillips asked, ashen-faced. ''I've spent two years of my goddamned life out here baby-sitting this project, and you want to throw it all out the window because something went wrong with a car. What proof do you have that it wasn't an accident?''

''Coupled with—'' Richards began.

''Coupled with what?'' Phillips interrupted. ''Max Orencho was hiding out in the city sitting on a million dollars, and somebody did him in. Why is everybody surprised? People have been murdered for a minute fraction of that. And Del Styron was sexually obsessed and associated with the wrong people.''

Richards looked amused. ''Henry Leaver was hardly a thief or sexually obsessed.''

''I never knew him,'' Phillips said. He nodded at Kaltmeyer and DeFolge. ''They worked with him all his life; if Leaver had any skeletons in his closet, they'd know. But all the beads don't have to fit on the same string.''

Cyd had said they might be unrelated, Nordlund recalled. But he didn't believe that. Some thread linked them all.

''The Administration expects to see that ceremony on the news,'' Phillips continued, his voice hoarse. ''They want to see the one tomorrow, and for damned certain they want to see the one in January. They're not going to be happy because everybody back here suddenly got paranoid over unrelated events.''

''You're reaching for it, Steve,'' Nordlund cut in. ''They're connected. We just don't know what the connection is.''

''Proof, that's all I'm asking for.'' Phillips struggled to sound reasonable. ''Just a little proof that I can show to Washington and convince them that there's good reason for halting the ceremony tomorrow.''

Kaltmeyer glanced at Richards. ''What's the alternative, Harry?''

''Nobody goes into the tunnel who hasn't been there before besides the TV camera crew and the few guests of those in this room, people you can personally vouch for.''

''What about the caterers?'' Metcalf asked.

Richards made a check on his note pad. ''I said the tunnel. The caterers will be restricted to the station vault where the party will be held.''

Phillips took a deep breath. ''That's fine by me.''

Kaltmeyer nodded. ''Then I guess that's it. Dane?''

''No objections.''

He didn't like it, but the most that he could pin his protests to was a deep feeling of unease. And nobody would buy that.

After the others left, he walked over to the window and stared out at the access shaft. It was a blustery day, and during the night, the temperature had fallen. The slush was frozen solid on the concrete pad now, and before the day was out it'd be snowing again. How long had it been since he had crept out of the bed he and Cyd had shared for the night? It seemed like a week.

But the smell of her and the feel of her was sharp in his memory. If only he could crawl back into that same haven tonight and feel the warmth of Cyd's body close to his. . . .

"Dane?"

Zumwalt had come in and closed the door. "Janice is on a pee break, and I wanted to catch you while you were free."

He had almost forgotten that Rob had wanted to see him.

"What'd you find out?"

"More than I wanted to, believe me. I'm spooked."

"Were you able to make sense out of the tape?"

"Damned near every bit. I even located the machine he taped it on—Moloney had brought in a recorder so he could listen to classical music while he ate his lunch in the stock room."

He spread a sheaf of printouts on the light table. "The actual data from Lammont's soundings remained in the mainframe memory. His program used those soundings to extrapolate the type of strata we could expect to find in between soundings. Here's a profile of the predicted strata"—he unrolled a computer-generated drawing—"along the complete route." He unrolled another drawing right beneath the first. "Here's a profile of the strata we actually found along the same route."

Nordlund studied the two drawings for a good ten minutes. From time to time there was a correlation, but no pattern, no indication of how an error might have been made. He had never compared predicted strata and actual strata for the entire route, and now that he had, he was faced with an unsettling conviction.

"There's no connection," he said at last. "None at all." He looked up at Zumwalt. "What was on the tape?"

Zumwalt was sweating. "Usually when you make a sounding, there's collateral information involved—date and who made it, equipment used, that sort of thing. What Styron did was go through the original sounding data and ask the mainframe for the collateral information for each sounding. Every time he punched in a question, the mainframe replied, NO INFORMATION AVAILABLE. That's what he recorded—his questions and the same answer each time. The subprogram he erased was the retrieval program for the collateral information.''

Nordlund looked back at the drawings. It was inconceivable, there was no connection. . . .

"Don't you see, Dane?" Zumwalt asked, desperate. "Lammont didn't take the soundings at all—he made them up. It was all a guess. Lammont knows the area backward and forward. The Wisconsin Glaciation was even the basis for a textbook he wrote on strata interpolation. He was qualified to make a pretty shrewd guess, but it would always be a conservative guess; there was no room for any surprises.''

"Why would he make them up?" Nordlund asked, puzzled.

Zumwalt fished a much smaller printout from his pocket, unfolded it, and placed it on the table.

"That's Lammont's file from Personnel. Look at the dates. He was hired just before Kaltmeyer/DeFolge bid on the cut. He didn't take the soundings because he didn't have time to take the soundings. They had to have the information immediately for the bid they would make a week later. It was a last-minute bid, so they got Lammont to forge the whole series of soundings—every goddamned one!''

He'd have to let Cyd know as soon as possible, Nordlund thought. It was going to be a federal case now, and they'd want Lammont very badly. The Bureau would find him. If he was still alive.

Zumwalt started rolling up the drawings and the printouts. "What I don't understand is why Styron recorded all of this. Why didn't he just come to you?''

"My guess is he was trying to use it as blackmail, and somebody wouldn't buy.'' Del had never hidden his desire to move to Florida someday. Warm in the winter, scorching in the summer. . . .

"So they murdered him?" Zumwalt's voice was a squeak.

"Somebody did. But I'm not sure it was the same party.''

He walked over to the coffee machine and made two cups of coffee, then brought them back and handed one to Zumwalt, who had to hold it with both hands. Even then he was shaking so badly, the coffee spilled over the sides of the cup.

"They got away with it," Zumwalt choked. "The bastards took a gamble, and they got away with it." Then: "We should do something—go to the police or the FBI or something. We've got the tape that proves the soundings were forged."

Nordlund was hesitant. "I don't think anybody's going to hang them on the program. The government hired Kaltmeyer/DeFolge to do a job. It didn't tell them how to do it. By tomorrow, the program will be history. The government got its tunnel, on time and at the cheapest price. They're not going to hang Kaltmeyer/DeFolge for that."

Zumwalt was over his first shock and growing angry.

"Felton and Esposito—if it hadn't been for the program, they wouldn't have died."

Nordlund remembered what he had told Beardsley. "A case of criminal negligence wouldn't stand up in court. No program could have predicted an isolated pocket of gas."

"Max is dead, Del's dead, and so is old Henry Leaver. *Somebody* murdered them, Dane!"

For just a moment, he considered the unthinkable. It put Frank and the senator under a cloud, but not much of one. They had wanted Max caught, not dead, and Henry had always been too much of a father to both of them; Leaver would never have testified against them. Lammont's program would be an embarrassment, but they would find some way to finesse it. The tunnel was built; whether or not the program had been forged was irrelevant.

"And somebody tried to kill Kaltmeyer and DeFolge. So where does that leave us? They sure as hell weren't plotting their own suicides."

Zumwalt took the tape out of his pocket and dropped it on the table. "So what do I do with this?"

Nordlund picked it up. "I'll turn it over to the FBI, along with a report—I may need your help on it."

"When?"

Nordlund made up his mind.

"When I resign. This afternoon."

He found DeFolge alone in his office on the third floor, file folders of documents stacked on his desk. He looked up as Nordlund walked in.

"You may be chief engineer, Dane, but the least you can do is knock." He smiled when he said it, but there was a note of irritation in his voice. He was jittery, Nordlund thought, off balance.

"When's Frank due back?"

DeFolge shoved the stack of file folders to one side and clasped his hands over his stomach, resigned to having been interrupted.

"He's down in the cut; I don't expect him back for another hour. He and Phillips wanted to check seating arrangements, installation of the podium, that sort of thing." He helped himself to a mint from a small tin on the desk. "Steve told me you turned down a chance to do a little speech-making. You ought to think it over, Dane; it'd be good for your image—network television and all that."

"I won't be there," Nordlund said.

DeFolge looked cautious. "What's eating you today?"

Nordlund dropped an envelope onto his desk. "That's my resignation."

DeFolge picked it up but didn't open it. His voice was gravel. "What's on your mind, Dane?"

Nordlund took the wooden chair by the desk and turned it around, then straddled it, leaning his elbows on the back.

"When did you hire Lammont?"

"Frankly, I don't remember. Personnel would have the dates."

"It was a week before Kaltmeyer/DeFolge submitted bids on the cut."

What was left of DeFolge's affable mask vanished. "What are you driving at, Nordlund?"

"Lammont faked the soundings for the computer program; he never took them. For four years we worked with a program that was pure guesswork."

DeFolge leaned forward, his chubby face suddenly all planes and angles. "Let me tell you something, son. The cut's finished, it's one for the record books. We had an agreement with Lammont long before he went on salary; if he didn't take those soundings and you're all upset about it, talk to him, don't bother me. And if you think the government's going to get its water hot over something that happened four years ago, you've got another guess coming. The tunnel's been dug, and they couldn't care less how it was done."

"A man was murdered when he found out about it," Nordlund said tightly.

For a moment, DeFolge looked shocked, then his eyes narrowed. "You accusing me, Dane? Think twice before you repeat that. I haven't the slightest idea who killed that little sleazeball, and I don't care, but I'll tell you something. It had nothing to do with Kaltmeyer/DeFolge, it had nothing to do with the cut. While we're at it, I don't know who killed Max Orencho, either, but in his case, I certainly would like to know—maybe we could get back some of the money he stole."

His face suddenly looked shadowed.

"Henry Leaver was a friend of mine for thirty years. We went through hell for each other when the company started. All I know about his murder is that whoever killed him tried to get Frank and me the other night, and it was pure chance that they didn't."

He had been like that before the congressional committee, Nordlund thought. Very fast, very aggressive, very evasive.

"My resignation's effective as of right now, Senator."

He stood up to leave, and DeFolge said bitterly, "I've earned better treatment from you than this, Dane."

"For using me? For involving me in your trust?"

DeFolge shook his head. "Not my trust, your trust. I set it up for you and Diana."

"And who's the trustee?"

"My attorney, of course—that's standard, there's nothing illegal about it. The government might ask a few questions about it, but everything's legal and above board; they won't be able to prove a thing. Besides, you're just one of the two trustors. You had nothing to do with the activities of the trust."

"That trust was involved in buying up real estate along the tunnel right-of-way, wasn't it?"

He thought DeFolge hid a smile, and then he had a sudden flash of insight. The government would never nail DeFolge for buying up property along the right-of-way; that was a smokescreen. If DeFolge were vulnerable, it would be because of Lammont and his forged soundings, something the senator had already dismissed.

"Indirectly, yes. The trust made loans to several companies that bought certain options that were later sold to a third party. Those loans were repaid with excellent interest."

DeFolge tried another ingratiating smile, and the effect was almost comic, like a woman wearing a wig who hadn't managed to put it on straight. He took an envelope out of his pocket and pushed it across the desk toward Nordlund.

"I want you to prosper, Dane, I want both you and Diana to prosper. Working on the tunnel is more important to you than your marriage right now, but that won't always be the case."

Nordlund opened the envelope. Inside was a cashier's check for ten thousand dollars.

"What's this for?"

"The trust is empowered to disburse certain funds above the basic capitalization. This is your share of the interest we discussed. I was going to give it to you after the ceremony tomorrow."

Nordlund stared at it. "You love your daughter very much."

"That girl is the most valuable thing in my life. Whatever she's wanted in life, I've tried to get for her."

"Including me?"

"Including you."

Nordlund dropped the check on his desk.

"The canceled check would also be evidence, wouldn't it,

Senator? Proof that we had all been in the same boat together—and enough to keep me in line, right?''

DeFolge changed then, in a way that shocked Nordlund. The air of injured rectitude, of doting father, slipped away. The man sitting behind the desk now was completely relaxed and gave an impression of surprising physical power. His eyes were very bright.

''I really didn't think you would take it, Dane. But it was worth a try.''

Nordlund studied him, curious. ''You would go through all this for Diana?''

''Of course. But you were valuable to me as well—I should say, to the company.'' This time his smile sat comfortably on his fleshy face. ''I don't give a rat's ass about you personally, Dane, but you always offered two for the price of one. You would be good for my daughter, and you would also be good for the company. You were so righteous, you squeaked. Integrity—rock-bottom integrity—is hard to buy, no company can have enough of it. You were an insurance policy, the best and the cheapest I could get. Shit, Dane, during the hearings alone you were worth your weight in gold.''

Nordlund stared at him for a long moment. ''Up yours, Senator.'' He turned and walked out.

DeFolge's gravelly voice followed him. ''You can offer your resignation, Nordlund, but I don't have to accept it. Not until after the ceremonies tomorrow—and you can attend them or not, suit yourself. Once they're over, you've officially resigned.''

He laughed.

''I couldn't care less—and neither will anybody else.''

CHAPTER 22

He was angry, angrier than he had been in years. Who could have predicted that DeFolge would change his plans and that he and Kaltmeyer would take the helicopter to Benton Harbor? He was sorry about the chauffeur, but he had expected to sacrifice him in any event. He hadn't expected the two security guards to ride into the city with him, and he regretted their deaths far more.

Then he had to forget about them. The important thing was that he had failed badly and now he would have to do his planning all over again.

It would have to be at the holing-through ceremony, the day before Christmas Eve. There would be press and TV coverage, and the world would see his final stroke of retribution. It would be dangerous—but it would also be just. How appropriate to die before a crowd of your peers! There would be security men in the station vault, of course; there would be no escape for him. But he would have tracked down and killed the four men responsible for Brad's death.

After that, Brad could rest. And he could go back to Dr. Merrimac's hospital and the treatments that he had escaped from so long ago. But . . . hadn't something happened to Dr. Merrimac? He couldn't remember.

He went downstairs to the basement, which was one huge shop with workbenches on either side stretching the full length of the room. He walked over to the nearest and paused to inspect his options.

There were a number of rifles and pistols scattered across the bench, several of them disassembled on top of templates of the various parts. All of the pieces of metal gleamed with a thin film of oil. He loved weapons. He considered them pieces of *highly sophisticated machinery, each of them designed to do a specific job.*

Which one would best suit his purpose this time?

He fondled a war-surplus .30-caliber Garand. It had a high charge and an impressive penetration power. But it was much too large and too heavy. And the Uzi was out as well; an automatic weapon would be his last choice—he had no desire to endanger innocent bystanders.

He turned to the part of the bench that held several pistols, including a beautiful little Beretta. There was elegance about the Beretta, but he wasn't sure of the range at which he would be firing, and handguns wouldn't have the accuracy he needed unless he was very close to the target.

This would be his last chance, and he had to be sure.

He settled on a classic M-3 carbine that he had purchased at a surplus auction. He would have to be sure of hitting a vital spot because of the low penetrating power of the round. But the weapon could be easily concealed in one of the paper drawing tubes he used to carry sketches into the cut.

He hesitated. Even with the television cameras, the lighting wouldn't be very good. He examined the conventional .30-caliber rounds for the weapon and discarded them, then rummaged in the drawers beneath the workbench until he had located a box of military tracers. The rounds contained a piece of red phosphorus that ignited during flight, tracing a fiery path to the target. They'd be the best for the job. If he missed the first time, they would allow him to correct his aim easily.

He closed his eyes and imagined that last moment when the hot projectiles, trailing their avenging red fire, would rip into the enemy's body. He would have to practice loading; there were two men he wanted to kill. But there would be a moment of panic after the first one, a moment of incredulity when everyone would freeze, not sure of what had happened, unwilling to believe what their eyes told them. It would be time enough.

And after that? He had imagined a possibility where he would conclude his long search for revenge and then escape. But that wasn't likely. Even now, it was only a matter of time before someone would make the connection between him and the pre-

vious murders and track him down. It didn't matter; there wasn't much point in living any longer. The future would be bleak and lonely with only the memory of Brad, and already that was fast fading into an idealized portrait that was a poor substitute for Brad himself.

Once the desire for revenge was satisfied, all that faced him would be years of loneliness and memory.

He made an almost physical effort to push the black mood away, and a moment later he was back in control, his emotions bleak and cold. Whatever the future held, he would deal with it when he came to it.

He placed the carbine in a vise and began the slow, careful calibration of the sight. He would take it out later that evening and test it in the forest preserves.

In the tunnel, there would be no windage correction, of course, but he could afford to be meticulous with this one.

And then he had a nagging thought. There would be security guards in the station vault, checking everybody once again before they were let into the tunnel. But there wouldn't be any at the head of the cut where the ceremonies were. There was no need for them; everybody would have gone through two security checks by then. When the president showed up for the January ceremonies, it would be something else—the Secret Service would be present both in the tunnel and in the vault. But not tomorrow.

He would be the only man with a gun at the head of the cut.

He could kill all the rest of those involved as well.

If the situations were reversed, Brad would.

CHAPTER 23

After he got to the field station at the East Portal, Michael Dietz spent most of the predawn hours going over his checklist for hole-through. When he had finished, it was eight o'clock; he still had plenty of time to get to the head of the cut. Once there, he'd have to supervise backing up the mole and removing the other large pieces of equipment from the area around the face where his men were skinning off the final layers of limestone.

It had been a ticklish job thinning it down without breaking through. They had even drilled tiny holes in the rock face so they could see through to the other side and check their progress. It had been his idea to shove a speaking tube through one of the holes so they could talk to the west team.

Metcalf had called him yesterday to tell him the limerick about Nubo, the Nubian prince. It was classic; he hadn't heard it before and damned near laughed himself sick. Too bad Metcalf wasn't going to be there for hole-through; it would be a real thrill to step through the shattered limestone and offer him a drink.

Troy had told him the whole show would be on television, and that morning he made sure he shaved. He had already called his parents in Lynchburg and told them to be sure and watch the six o'clock news that night. One thing for sure: when they met the crews from the other side, it was going to be one helluva party.

He picked up his backpack and trudged through the snow to the access shaft, shivering in a sudden blast of arctic air. It wasn't fair—just because they were on the wrong side of the lake, they got twice as much snow.

"Mind if I check out your backpack, Mr. Dietz?" The security guard was polite but firm.

The guard post was just inside the small wooden building that sheltered the shaft. Several other workers had set their bags on inspection tables while the guards quickly riffled through them.

"Go right ahead, Charley—but you can't have any."

The guard dug into the pack, then suddenly smiled. "Going to have a party down there when you hole through?"

Dietz grinned and zipped up the pack, then slung it over his shoulders.

"Sure hope to."

At the bottom of the shaft, he made sure the backpack was secure beside him in an electric car, then settled in for the long trip through the tunnel to the rock face at the end of the cut. Even at top speed, it would be close to an hour and a half before he got there. The west team had it easy in that respect; the head of their cut was only four miles from their access shaft. They had been a lot slower in drilling their bores, but then, it had taken them longer to carve out the station vault than anybody had figured on.

He almost fell asleep once, but was startled out of a half-doze when the vibration of the car told him he was bumping over the tracks for the muck train. He jerked awake and heard the noise of the crews working on the tunnel walls in the distance. He waved at the first finishing crews he passed, laughing as they shouted obscenities and gave him the finger. Fifteen minutes later, he parked the little electric car behind the huge silhouette of the mole.

"Sturm! Pauling! Where the hell are you bastards?"

"Right here, Dietz—where the hell you expect?"

He picked up his backpack and circled around the mole. There were only two men at the face, and both of them were shouting at each other in German. Pauling was Swiss, a huge man with red hair and a pocked face whom Sturm constantly teased about his pronunciation. Sturm, who was born in Frankfurt-am-Main, had a soft, literate accent and was proud of it. He was fifty pounds lighter than Pauling, a slender man with a Hapsburg moustache and manners to match.

Dietz had been born in Pittsburgh and his German was strictly what he had acquired growing up in the neighborhood. But Sturm was careful never to comment on *his* accent. The perks of position, he thought.

"Okay, guys, break it up. Let's see the face."

The two men stepped aside, and he ran his hands over the rocky surface. The section they had been thinning was an area only about twenty feet square. The original plan had been to bring the whole face down, but he had talked to Metcalf and they'd decided that too much falling debris could be dangerous. The limestone was very thin now, some sections so porous, he imagined he could see the gleam of light from the other side.

He nodded with satisfaction and stepped back. "Good job. When they pop this one, it's *really* going to pop."

He just hoped that Kaltmeyer and DeFolge were ready to duck a split-second after they swung—otherwise the flying fragments would really cut them up.

Pauling tapped the face with his forefinger. "All the bosses on the other side, they will think they have achieved something very great." He looked disgusted.

"Just as if they put in a full day's work," Sturm added.

"Quit bitching. Let's move the mole back and make some room. The rest of the shift will be coming down for the party in another hour."

Pauling cocked his head. "I hear them now—not too far away."

"You're full of shit, Pauling, you know that?" Dietz said affectionately. "I don't hear a damned thing."

But a few minutes later he did hear the murmur of a dozen or more electric cars, and moments after that he was surrounded by all the members of his shift, as well as men from the other shifts.

"Thought we'd help out so you'll finish on time!" somebody shouted.

Dietz grinned. "I notice all you guys are wearing clean clothes so you'll look good on TV."

It took an hour to shift the mole a hundred yards down the tunnel, police the area of fallen rock, and store all their hand tools in the jockey box.

When they were through, Dietz zipped open his knapsack. "Considering the occasion, I brought a little something."

"What you bring?" Pauling asked, expectantly.

"Our own little party, that's what I brought." Dietz reached into the backpack and pulled out a two-liter bottle of Liebfraumilch. Sturm whistled, and Pauling's eyes lit up.

"You bring a corkscrew?"

"You got no faith, Pauling." Dietz searched his pockets for the corkscrew and pulled out a dozen plastic cups from his backpack. He slapped Pauling's hands away from the bottle. "I brought it, Sturm will pour it, and you'll drink it. Fair enough, right?"

"Hey, what about us?" somebody in the crowd shouted.

Dietz glanced around, counting noses. Jesus, there must be a hundred of them down there. "As far as it will go!" he yelled. "Okay, Sturm, go ahead and open it."

Sturm pulled the cork and poured the wine into the cups and started handing them around. After a minute, Dietz was amazed—everybody seemed to have a cup. The loaves and the fishes, he thought; then he realized that some of the other highballers had had the same idea—they had just been waiting for him to start it.

Dietz raised his glass.

"To the longest damned tunnel in the world—and the people who built it!"

They drank in silence, then Sturm said, "I don't want to dig through limestone like this again. Too damned porous." He waved a hand at a pile of rock fragments and other detritus that marked a small cave-in from the side of the tunnel.

Dietz felt uneasy. Stand-up time wasn't what had been predicted. He'd feel a lot happier when they got the rest of the shields in place and pumped in the concrete.

"Very lucky," Pauling said solemnly, draining his glass and checking the bottle to see if there was any left. "Three in hospital, no deaths."

"They weren't so lucky on the other side," Dietz said, remembering the two men who had been trapped in the pocket of hydrogen sulfide.

"Only scrapes, rock burns, and bruises on this side," Pauling said.

"We're one lucky bunch of high-ballers!" Sturm beamed. He grabbed the bottle from Pauling and poured what was left of the wine into his glass.

"Lucky as hell," Dietz agreed.

CHAPTER 24

It was Moloney who brought in the projection TV set and the screen, and Metcalf who made the arrangements with Briggs to pipe the signal into the Field Station from WBBM's Instant Eye van parked near the access shaft. They moved the desks out of the center of the room and brought in folding chairs, then set up the screen against the partition wall of Nordlund's office.

"You order the champagne, Jan?"

"It's on Dane's balcony. Two cases—that should be enough for you booze hounds."

She was dressed to kill in a gray wool dress and a pink scarf, her gold-framed glasses hanging from a chain around her neck. Her hair was up in a new permanent, and it was obvious she had taken special care with her makeup that morning. Holcthrough was costing her half a month's pay, he thought.

"It'll freeze—"

"It's only been out there ten minutes. You'll also find some sandwiches in a bag on my desk. Ham and Swiss on light rye, pastrami on dark—and I made them myself, so don't complain." She was excited, her eyes sparkling. "Think you can handle everything up here?"

"Not as well as you can, but I'll try."

She smiled self-consciously. "Do I look all right?"

"Absolutely smashing."

She let him hold her coat for her, turning back to him with a suddenly wistful face. "It's been a short four years, hasn't it?"

"You're one of the reasons why they went so fast," he said, half-kidding, half-gallant. Unexpectedly, she stood on her toes and kissed him lightly on the cheek. As she hurried for the door, he called, "You're half an hour early."

"The early bird gets the best seat, Troy. Let me know how I look on TV."

He went back to the bullpen and watched the TV cameraman set his light levels and test his autofocus on the thin rock wall that Kaltmeyer would smash with his sledge. The bullpen was filling with off-duty computer techs, engineers, and most of the office staff: secretaries, filing clerks, and the half-dozen from accounting. Even old Samuel Wilcox was inconspicuous off to the side, nursing a small glass of what Metcalf suspected was bourbon.

"Troy?"

Nordlund was standing just inside the door of Janice's office. Metcalf hurried over. "What's up?" He took a closer look. "Jesus Christ, what's wrong? You look like you lost your best friend."

"Yeah, I did." Nordlund grimaced and waved his hand in a gesture that took in the entire complex. "Another hour or so, it'll all be yours."

Metcalf looked blank. "I don't get it."

"I resigned yesterday. DeFolge wouldn't accept it until after the ceremonies."

Metcalf couldn't believe it. "What happened?"

"Not cut out for company politics, I guess. Tell you about it later. You see Cyd and Nakamura? They were supposed to meet me here."

"They're in your office—probably out on the balcony watching the troops go down the shaft." He didn't know what to say. "You still going to go . . . ?"

Nordlund shrugged. "I wasn't, but I promised Cyd. And I guess the men would be disappointed if I didn't show."

And then he disappeared inside his office, leaving Metcalf staring. What the hell could have gone wrong? Nordlund was no company politician, but he always got along. Maybe the bust-up of his marriage to DeFolge's daughter had finally backfired. What lousy timing.

Would DeFolge even offer him the job? Maybe. He had turned it down once, and DeFolge might be harboring a grudge because he had. And then he wondered, seriously, whether he really wanted it. When he was forty, yes. Even when he was thirty-five. But right now? He wasn't sure. Like a lot of things in life, he had wanted it more when it was unattainable, when it had belonged to somebody else. And he had—though he didn't always like to admit it—a lot to learn. There was no point in having something handed to him prematurely and then falling on his face. The first might be part of his game plan, but the second certainly wasn't.

He wandered back into the bullpen and watched the screen for a moment. The cameraman had chosen an angle that avoided the boarded-up area standing out like a huge patch on the side of the tunnel. Right now the camera was showing a clear view of the podium and the rock wall behind it. Some of the guests had already started to filter in, and Metcalf could make out DeFolge and Kaltmeyer in the front row, along with Derrick, Kaltmeyer's twelve-year-old son.

"Hey, Moloney, give me a hand with the champagne, will you?"

They went into Nordlund's office just as he was coming out with Cyd and Nakamura in tow. Nakamura looked poker-faced as always, but Cyd was frowning, and Metcalf guessed that Dane had told her. Cyd smiled briefly at him and said, "Take care of things, Tiger," and then they were pushing through the crowd toward the outer door.

When he brought the two cases of champagne back in, he was surprised to see Cyd still there, having a hurried conversation with Harry Richards over by the windows. Did Dane know she was also dating Richards? Metcalf wondered. The lady got around, which was probably unfair. Rumor had it that Richards was an old flame from D.C. But he'd make book that Nordlund didn't know.

He almost bumped into Evan Grimsley while he was coming out of Jan's office with the shopping bag full of sandwiches.

"You mind if I watch up here, Mr. Metcalf?"

Grimsley was pale, his eyes slightly sunken in his craggy face; he looked as if he had lost a good ten pounds.

"Hell, no. There's champagne in the bullpen, and Jan made these sandwiches." He frowned. "You could probably watch it down below—they'd let you in, of all people."

Grimsley shook his head. "I don't want to go down there. I keep thinking of Felton and Esposito." He took a breath. "I don't think I want to work in tunnels anymore."

"You'll get over it." Grimsley would probably drift back to the tunnels, if only to escape his Latin and Vietnamese ladies. "And just call me Metcalf—you call me Mister, I think you're talking to somebody else."

Grimsley looked uncertain, then suddenly grinned. "Fuck you, Metcalf."

"That's more like it—I guess," Metcalf mumbled. He could hear the corks starting to pop; Moloney must already be pouring the champagne. God knew they had enough; they might as well start early.

He was halfway through one of the pastrami sandwiches, his eyes glued to the TV screen as the tunnel below gradually filled with people, when somebody behind him whispered in a low voice, "I've got to see you, Troy."

He turned around. Zumwalt.

"It's important."

He sighed, left the sandwich on his chair, and followed Zumwalt into Nordlund's office. "What's up, Rob? We've only got twenty minutes to hole-through, and I don't want to miss any of it."

Zumwalt was nervous, "I don't know what to do, but I've got to tell somebody, and now that Dane's resigned, I guess you're it."

"He tell you?" Christ, once again he was the last one to hear.

Zumwalt read his expression. "I don't think he's told anybody else yet. I was with him yesterday, just before he went up to see DeFolge."

Metcalf was suddenly torn between hearing more and not wanting to miss any of the ceremonies. Maybe Zumwalt could fill him in on some of the details that Nordlund hadn't had time for.

"Can't it wait?"

Even though the room was chilly, Zumwalt's face looked sweaty. "I don't think so, man—I got a wife and baby, and I'm scared shitless."

Metcalf put a hand on his shoulder. "Take it easy. What the hell happened?"

"I think it had something to do with Styron's tape."

"What did?"

"Dane's resignation. I told him what was on the tape and showed him the graphs—"

Metcalf felt the first wave of uneasiness hit him. "What tape?"

"Styron made a tape of part of the computer program, the collateral information on the soundings that Lammont took." Zumwalt sucked in a breath. "Lammont never took the soundings. He forged them. The whole program was made up. For four years now, we've been lucky. Dane said that Del might have been murdered because he was trying to blackmail somebody with the tape."

Jesus, where was Zumwalt getting all of this? "Where's the tape now?"

"Dane said he was going to put it in a safe-deposit box. But I made a duplicate, and I don't know what the hell to do with it. If I keep it, I'm really asking for it. I'm probably asking for it anyway."

Richards, Metcalf thought. Harry would know what to do.

"Okay, okay, Rob, we'll handle it." He glanced at his watch. Fifteen more minutes. "We'll watch hole-through, and then we'll get hold of Harry—"

"There's something else."

Zumwalt's eyes were flicking to the door and back again, and Metcalf walked over and closed it. Where the hell did Jan keep her Valium?

"The hole-through." Zumwalt squeezed out the words like pellets. "This morning I had the computer extrapolate the surrounding strata—not just where we've tunneled, but the area surrounding the tunnel—using the strata we've actually dug through for the soundings instead of Lammont's figures. Then I used a graphics program to draw up a geological profile.''

He looked pale with fear.

''What'd you find out?''

''Take a look.'' Zumwalt tugged him over to the light table, where he had unrolled a huge graphics printout. ''I tried to reach Dane, but he'd already left.'' He switched on the overhead light and ran his finger over an area of the printout. ''This whole section—it's completely nonhomogeneous.'' He gulped another breath. ''It's the area around the head of the cut.''

Metcalf looked at the graphic for a long moment, trying to orient himself. Then he felt his skin tingle. The entire area was porous, an indication that it was probably filled with organic matter, maybe even a peat bed or an embryonic oil field if the layer above were folded dolomite. At least it was an explanation for the pocket of hydrogen sulfide gas that had killed Felton and Esposito.

Then he remembered when Dietz had called him two days before to report a minor cave-in, that part of the tunnel wall on the eastern side of the cut had slumped. But the rest of the tunnel had seemed solid enough, and nobody would have okayed holding up the ceremonies in any event.

''You try to get hold of Lammont?''

Maybe Lammont would have an explanation. . . . And then he knew better. This was no fantasy; Zumwalt wasn't making any of it up. For reasons that only Lammont knew, the bastard had forged the soundings.

''We'll have to map the whole area,'' he said slowly. ''Drive lateral cuts with continuous gas sampling. Where there's hydrogen sulfide, there could be methane or carbon monoxide or even hydrogen cyanide from all that mass of organic material.''

Zumwalt was staring at him as if he were crazy. ''When the hell are you going to do that?''

''Right now. We'll close down—''

But of course he wasn't. In ten minutes, they'd be holing through. The tunnel was completed; it didn't matter anymore.

(218

Except that it did. The area they were in was unstable, and there were probably pockets of gas all around them under high pressure. Boring through the porous strata had further weakened the rock in which the pockets were trapped; some of them could probably blow out at any time.

His head felt foggy. He'd have to close the cut, call down there and get Dane. . . . Only Dane had resigned. Well, talk to Kaltmeyer, then. He'd know what was at stake.

But he was kidding himself, he thought, sweating. Nobody was going to close down anything just because something might happen, sometime.

Maybe.

CHAPTER 25

He went down into the cut early in the morning, during a change of shifts. The security guards didn't question his sealed cardboard tube, which he had carefully labeled to look like a tube full of blueprints. The carbine was heavy, and it took some juggling to pretend the tube carried only papers.

The guards knew him, which helped, and there were no metal detectors. They would have been useless anyway; high-ballers carried too much metal on them to begin with. Down in the station vault, he helped himself to a sandwich from one of the caterer's tables, then went over to the staging area to pick up an electric car. Some of the men from the midnight shift who were leaving were complaining among themselves about how hole-through had been turned into a three-ring circus. That it was a ceremony usually reserved for the high-ballers alone.

Too bad they weren't going to stay. But the incoming shifts would be there, and so would engineers who had worked on different parts of the project. There would be at least two or three hundred in the audience. That would be enough so that in the confusion he might even be able to escape, though he really didn't expect to. But few of those coming on shift had seen him, and most of those leaving would forget he had ever been there.

Unfortunately, Brad wouldn't be there. But in a sense, he was the guest of honor.

With the confusion of the change of shifts, nobody paid him much attention. He took an electric car and drove toward the head of the cut, automatically noting the progress being made. He'd have to tell Nordlund tomorrow—except there wasn't going to be a tomorrow. Not for DeFolge. Not for Kaltmeyer. And maybe not for Nordlund.

When he got to the head of the cut, he nodded at the men streaming off shift. He had been there so often, nobody thought it was unusual that he should be around this early. Nor did anyone seem curious when he slipped through the door in the wooden partition that closed off the cave from the cut itself.

It was dark, and he took out a small flashlight. There it was. A two-inch gap between the sheets of plywood separating the cave from the tunnel; nobody had really cared about the niceties of construction when they'd built it. It was perfect—just wide enough to see through and maneuver the barrel of the carbine. During the past few days, he'd built up a slope of rocks and debris behind the partition so he could lie flat and have a clear, unobstructed view of the podium a hundred or so feet away. He'd actually be firing over the heads of the crowd and down at the podium.

There was no way he could miss.

He climbed up the slope, then sat down on the rocks. He removed the round metal top of the tube and pulled out the carbine. He checked it carefully. Everything was in order. He shoved the magazine loaded with tracers into the weapon and pulled back the bolt, pumping a round into the chamber.

He had a long time to wait. It was three hours until the ceremony began. It was chilly in the cave, and the air seemed strangely constricted. Even when he deliberately filled his lungs as much as he could, it was still somehow unsatisfying. He felt almost as if he were breathing into a paper bag and slowly exhausting his supply of oxygen.

Gases? Not likely—he was excited, he was hyperventilating. Slow it down, slow it down, he had plenty of time. . . .

He lay on the slope of rock, gradually building up his courage. God, he wished Brad were there to compliment him on his plans and how thorough he had been, to bolster his courage. Brad had always been good at that, but then Brad had had more than his share of the most valuable trait a man could have. Courage. He remembered the day Brad—

It came back then, undiminished by the years. The sound of the alarm, the sense of rushing water, the knowledge that Brad was dead. The memories were fresh and vivid, and for the first time in years he wept, the cold tears rolling down his face.

And after that, he dozed.

He woke up when he heard the crowd talking just beyond the plywood partition. It took a minute to work the feeling back into his limbs and fingers. He edged up slightly on the slope and looked out through the chink between the slabs of wood. The usual hubbub of people talking to old friends, being introduced to new ones and finding their seats. Their faces were highlighted by the string of bare bulbs strung across the face of the cut and from two battery-pack power lights on either side of the podium. There were several reporters and a camera crew, and that pleased him.

Then Kaltmeyer stepped up to the podium, and the crowd settled down. The history of tunnels, the brave men who had died—oh yes, let's not forget the brave men who had died—and then he was in the wind-up of his speech.

He shifted slightly on his slope of mud and rock. Kaltmeyer was introducing DeFolge now.

He rose slightly on one knee and brought the carbine up to his shoulder. All in a row, DeFolge and Kaltmeyer and Nordlund and the woman who had come down into the cut when he had been behind the wood partition, working on building the ramp of rocks up to the gap between the plywood sheets. He had watched her all the time she was down there, and she had never known it. She was supposed to be some kind of an accountant, but he knew better than that. She was too sharp, she was interested in too much. . . .

Both DeFolge and Kaltmeyer gripped the sledge with their right hands and raised it over their shoulders, ready to swing. And now the head of the sledge was crashing down toward the thin sheet of rock that separated the east and west portions of the cut.

His finger trembled on the trigger—

CHAPTER 26

Nordlund found Cyd standing on the balcony, her coat wrapped tightly around her, staring at the skyline of Chicago, half-hidden by the blustery snow. She glanced around when he walked up behind her and said, "I loved this city when I was a kid. I went to Amundsen High School, on the North Side, and my whole world extended from Evanston down to Old Town. Everything that was exciting was here, from parties with fraternity boys at Northwestern to Second City and all the jazz joints in Old Town to half a hundred little theater groups—all of them outstanding. People used to talk to me about the Big Apple, and I couldn't see why anybody would want to go there. Everything in the world that mattered was right here."

She shivered and walked back inside. He closed the sliding door behind her. "When do you want to go down, Dane?"

"In about ten minutes. Where's Hideo?"

"Cream and sugar, Mr. Nordlund?" Nakamura was in the alcove, brewing three cups of coffee.

"Both." He turned back to Cyd. "I resigned yesterday afternoon. I wasn't even going to come down today."

"Why didn't you tell me?"

"I had some things I wanted to get straight in my own mind."

She stared at him, thoughtful, then said, "I think I know why. But you tell me."

"A run-in with DeFolge. I found out that all of Lammont's strata soundings had been forged, that his program for predicting the strata we were digging through was as much a fantasy as the Land of Oz. For four years, we were digging blind."

"What did DeFolge say?"

"It didn't seem to bother him. He doesn't think anybody's going to hang him for completing one of the biggest engineering projects on record—and on time. And he's right."

(223

"He tell you that? Now that it's done, everything's just fine?"

He nodded.

"Then I'm afraid he's wrong," she said quietly. "He may have brought in a difficult project on time, but he certainly didn't bring it in under budget. The cost overruns on the cut have been enormous. If what you say is true and DeFolge knew about it, then both he and Lammont are guilty of defrauding the government. I don't think the Administration will be very happy about that—the opposition certainly won't." She frowned. "How'd you find out?"

"Styron's tape—" And then he broke off. "I'm sorry, Cyd, I should have told you right from the start."

"So tell me now."

He told her about the tape he'd found when they had been at Styron's apartment and Zumwalt's success in deciphering the contents, then his meeting with DeFolge and the senator's attempts to bribe him.

Cyd laughed. "If DeFolge admired your integrity so much, he should have known you weren't for sale for ten thousand— that's an insult."

"I got the impression it was a down payment."

"Depending on how much flack the senator ran into with the Administration, I suppose. I doubt very much it had anything to do with you and Diana." She frowned. "You think Styron was trying to blackmail somebody with the tape?"

"That would be my guess."

"Has anybody managed to find Lammont?"

He stared at her, his mouth half-open. It had been too obvious; it had been there for him to look at all the time. The most logical person for Del to blackmail would have been Lammont.

"Why would Lammont have done it?"

"The only person who can tell you that is Lammont. He may have done it on his own, for reasons only he knows. Or perhaps DeFolge and Kaltmeyer and Max and Henry Leaver knew about it. Lammont is the one person who would link them all, including Del."

"In which case, we might have a murderer on our hands."
His skin suddenly felt clammy.

"If the forged soundings came out, Kaltmeyer/DeFolge might
survive, but Lammont and Associates certainly wouldn't. Lammont might have been afraid the others would talk to save their
own skins. And Del was a dead man the moment he approached
him."

"If there's a single link between them," he said slowly.
"But that may not be true, either."

"It'll do until a better theory comes along. I think we'd
better check with Harry and see if Lammont showed up down
below."

She picked up her purse from his desk, then paused to take
out half a dozen four-by-five photographs. "These just came
back from the police lab. They're all the latent prints—including yours."

Most of them were mere smudges with an occasional bit of
detail. He stopped at one of them, pointing to a section of it.
"What's this?" In the upper right of the photograph was something that looked vaguely like a lightning bolt.

She glanced at it. "Probably a crease in the plastic film they
spray on the print to lift it after they develop it."

He handed the photographs back to her. "Have fun."

"You realize you and Zumwalt might be in some danger?"
she said, worried.

"And Kaltmeyer and DeFolge still are." He shook his head.
"It doesn't smell right, Cyd. If DeFolge hadn't known about it,
he would have been upset because he had paid a fortune for a
strata computer program that he never really got. If he had known
about it, he would have been upset because then Lammont would
qualify as our murderer—he's certainly smart enough to see that
possibility. But he wasn't shook up, and I don't think he's a
good enough actor to hide it if he were."

She shrugged. "It's like a ball of knotted string, Dane—
you keep pulling at loose ends until something works free."

"We must leave or we will be late," Nakamura said,
sounding apologetic. He'd had enough time to brew a gallon of

coffee but had stayed in the alcove, leaving them what privacy he could.

Nordlund and Nakamura shivered in the cold outside for a few moments while Cyd talked to Richards. Then the three of them hurried across the snow-swept concrete pad to the access shaft. Going down in the cage, Nakamura offered each of them a container of coffee.

Nordlund took a sip and his eyebrows shot up. Perfect.

"How'd you do it?"

"It is quite simple. You heat the water reservoir until you cannot hold your hand on it any longer than five seconds—precisely. Then you inhale the aroma of the fresh-ground coffee, adjusting the mixture until your nose detects the same degree of moisture that you might obtain from a moderate steam bath. Three minutes, and your coffee is done."

"That's hardly scientific," Nordlund objected.

Nakamura nodded. "True, but the brewing of coffee has always been an art, not a science."

"The instruction book—"

"Instruction books are written for the export trade. Overseas they expect—ah—scientific directions."

Nordlund stared, suddenly suspicious.

"How come you know so much about that machine?"

Nakamura looked smug. "My company, Nippon Engineering, makes it."

They were late. The converted muck train had already left with its load of guests, and there was only one electric car remaining.

"This will be tight." Nakamura sat on the far right, making himself as small as possible, then Nordlund helped Cyd climb in. He squeezed in beside her.

Cyd laughed. "I thought you were going to ride on my lap."

"Not in one of these, not for four miles." He guided it into the center of the tunnel. There was more of a sense of nostalgia to the trip than he thought there would be; every hundred yards he remembered a problem that had come up and what he'd done to solve it.

"You will not be staying after the ceremony today?" Nakamura shouted at him.

"Who told you?"

"Mr. DeFolge." Pause. "I did not believe everything he said."

"I wouldn't, if I were you."

Nordlund lapsed into silence, staring at the walls, then he heard the noise of a crowd up ahead. He slowed the car, swung out to avoid the mole, and parked in the area marked off for the electric cars. There was quite a crowd, he thought—maybe three hundred people, most of them engineers and high-ballers who had worked on the cut, plus a number of tunnel engineers from all over the country.

Kaltmeyer was waiting for them and pushed Nakamura and Cyd ahead. "You're in the first row, Hideo. The seats are marked. Glad you could be with us, Miss Lederley."

And then to Nordlund, in a low voice: "You're a goddamned fool, Dane. I don't know if I can bail you out of this one or not."

"Nothing personal, Frank, but don't bother trying."

They pushed their way through the crowd to the low wooden steps of the temporary speaker's platform. There were a number of people already seated—DeFolge and Diana, Cyd, Derrick, Phillips, and Swede and Hartman as representatives of the crews.

DeFolge shook hands with Nakamura. His expression was stony when he glanced at Nordlund.

"Diana," Nordlund said, "I'd like you to meet Cyd Lederley."

Diana nodded politely. "I've already met Mrs. Lederley." Cyd smiled, cool and observant. Nordlund thought that he would skip the party afterward. Diana would see to it that neither he nor Cyd enjoyed themselves—though chances were against that in any event.

"Hi, Dane." Derrick was excited and happy.

"How's it going, Derrick?" He turned to Swede. "You bring the sledge?"

Swede shifted slightly so Dane could see the shiny sledge

behind his chair. It was decorated with streamers of red, white, and blue bunting. "She's a pretty one—had it nickel-plated."

Lynch showed up with two clear plastic raincoats, which he handed to Swede. For DeFolge and Kaltmeyer, Nordlund thought, when they swung the sledge. Two more high-ballers were squatting by several portable battery-pack lanterns, adjusting the beams to serve as fill for the lights strung along the overhead arch. Other lanterns flanked the platform, providing side fill along with the lights from the television camera crew.

Then Kaltmeyer walked behind the podium and tapped on the microphone several times until he heard his tapping over the loudspeakers. "Ladies and gentlemen, will you take your seats? We'd like to time this for eleven."

Out front, the crowd quieted down while those milling about in back found their seats. Nordlund inspected the crowd for faces he knew, nodding slightly when he made eye contact. He spotted Janice in the first row and winked, catching a broad smile in return. He'd have to tell her later how pretty she looked in her yellow hard hat.

Behind the microphone, Kaltmeyer was just starting to warm up.

"Traditionally, the holing-through of a great tunnel such as this is a private matter for the crews. We felt this was too significant an event in the history of the nation not to allow for honored guests from the Field Station itself and other tunnel projects around the world. And by inviting members of both the press and television, we've given an opportunity to participate to people all over the globe."

Kaltmeyer paused, and there was an enthusiastic wave of applause from the audience. He then went on—in rare form for a man who didn't like public speaking, Nordlund thought—reviewing the struggles in creating and funding the project, elaborating on what the tunnel and the bullet train would mean to the economy of the country.

Nordlund noticed Phillips, who had been looking tense and preoccupied up until then, suddenly relax.

Kaltmeyer had moved into a detailed discussion of the benefits the bullet train might eventually involve when he saw

DeFolge tapping his watch. Nordlund glanced at his own. Two minutes before the hour.

"We're fortunate in having with us the man whose vision helped carry this great project through from its birth in the Congress to hole-through today, and who has remained true to the dream as it matured. Ladies and gentlemen, Senator Alan De-Folge."

Less applause this time as DeFolge, smiling, stepped up to the podium. He made a few comments of thanks for being invited to what was supposed to be a high-ballers' party, gave a quick "V for Victory" sign, and then Lynch climbed onto the platform to help him and Kaltmeyer into the plastic raincoats. Swede handed the nickel-plated sledge to Kaltmeyer.

DeFolge leaned toward the microphone.

"This is a new birth, a joining of the east and west for a great step into the future."

He and Kaltmeyer walked over to the rocky face of the cut, gripped the sledge in their right hands, swung it over their shoulders, and brought it down against the thin limestone wall.

Chunks of limestone spalled away from the surface, and the next moment, a huge section of the wall dissolved into fragments and rained down on the tunnel floor.

Nordlund had just put his arm around Cyd's shoulders to shield her from the billowing dust when he heard a shot. A thin line of red fire sliced the dust-filled air at the right side of the platform, and Kaltmeyer suddenly grunted and staggered back.

Somebody screamed, and the guests in the front row of seats stood up, uncertain of what had happened.

"Down!" Nordlund shouted. "Everybody down!"

He jumped from his chair and ran up to Kaltmeyer, sitting in bewilderment on the wooden platform, holding his side. Bright-red blood was oozing out between his fingers. Out front, the television cameraman had focused on the stricken Kaltmeyer. The cameraman was the only one still standing in front of the podium.

"Frank, how do you feel?"

"Don't know," Kaltmeyer gasped. And then: "Christ, it hurts."

Nordlund glanced frantically around, trying to find the source of the shot. In the next instant, another bright streak of red raced for the platform. It came from the boarded-up area in front of the cave. A split-second later, the sound of the shot echoed off the tunnel walls.

Nordlund never figured out which came next—the wave of intense heat that swept over him or the explosion that threw him and Kaltmeyer violently to the floor of the tunnel.

CHAPTER 27

Dietz glanced at his watch.

"Okay, you guys, they'll be holing through in two minutes. Pauling, Sturm, get up here."

The two Germans hefted their massive sledge hammers and stepped up to the raw face of the cut. The other high-ballers moved a couple of paces back into the tunnel. Somebody yelled, "You're going to break the cameras, Paulie!" and everybody laughed. The cut was choked with workers now, some of them hanging on to vantage points on the mole. Others stood on top of jockey boxes so they could get a good view of the stone curtain between them and the western side of the cut.

Dietz spoke into the sound-powered phones he had rigged between the cuts. "You there, Swede?"

"Hear you loud and clear, Mike."

"Okay, we're all set over here, just waiting for your signal."

"Stand by," Swede said. Dietz could imagine what was going on on the other side of the wall: the reporters, the TV crews, the platform with Kaltmeyer and the senator giving speeches—thank God, he was spared those—the couple of hundred engineers and high-ballers applauding on cue. . . .

"Mike, you're in the way," Sturm complained.

Dietz moved back, paying out the wire to the phone. A few yards down the tunnel was a service alcove that had been cut into the shield opposite the small landslide area. He climbed into it. When they smashed the wall, there'd be a helluva lot of dust flying about, and maybe the alcove would spare him some of that.

"Hey, Dietz, you dry?"

One of the high-ballers handed up a bottle. He grabbed it

and took a gulp, concentrating on Swede's running commentary from the other side.

"Jesus, Dietz, I didn't say you could keep it."

He gave the bottle back. Maybe the alcove wasn't such a good idea—it was warm from the curing gunnite pumped into the shield that morning, and the heat was making him sleepy.

"I'm starting the countdown!" Swede said suddenly.

"Look alive!" Dietz yelled. "Five seconds!"

Sturm and Pauling raised their sledges, and the men suddenly quieted down. Dietz repeated Swede's countdown. "Five! Four! Three! Two! One! *Now!*"

Pauling and Sturm swung and struck the stone wall simultaneously. After that, Dietz felt as if he were living in a film being shown in slow motion. A ragged hole appeared in the thin area of the curtain wall; then the entire wall began to crumble. Rock dust puffed out toward the high-ballers who scrambled a little farther back into the tunnel.

Odd.

Dietz thought he heard a rifle shot. The limestone just above where the wall had crumbled spattered stone chips in all directions. He was still looking at it when there was a second report.

Then a red nightmare blossomed in the tunnel.

His ears seemed to implode from the force of a violent explosion. There was a tremendous ringing sound, and then he couldn't hear anything at all. Overhead, behind the shield in which he crouched, tons of limestone shifted and cracked, raining white dust over the high-ballers. The uncured shield itself groaned and started to bow under the unexpected load.

Men were running past him, their mouths open as they screamed, although he couldn't hear a thing. Then a second explosion blew out a section of tunnel at what had been the face of the cut. A great smoky flame belched out from some source beyond the wall.

He could see Pauling screaming, even though he couldn't hear him. Pauling had started to run after the others, his feet churning through the shattered rock and dust on the tunnel floor. Sturm was transfixed, still holding his sledge, paralyzed with fear. A wall of smoky fire suddenly engulfed him, and all Dietz could see was the shadow of a man dancing in the reddish glare and then collapsing onto the tunnel floor.

Pauling passed him but hadn't gotten more than a few feet when he was caught up in a ball of dirty flame that roared through the tunnel. It rolled over Pauling, wrapping him in a blanket of agony.

Oh God, Dietz thought, *if I could only hear him scream!*

Then a part of the shield above him gave way, and a loose mass of stone tumbled into the tunnel, falling over the alcove. Dietz's hearing returned with a rush, accompanied by a loud ringing in his ears. Now he could hear the rumble of stone and the shifting of the layers of rock above him.

And the screams of hundreds of dying men.

Then the screams died away, and there was only the roaring sound of the flames and the groaning of the stone layers above. He was trapped in the alcove. For a brief instant, he thought he might be spared. Then the heat began to penetrate. He gasped, trying to find air, and realized too late that he was drawing deadly hot gases into his lungs.

He reeled out of the alcove and took a few steps down the tunnel, stumbling over the huddled bodies that littered the floor. Clumps of smoking charcoal clung to the metal skin of the mole, glowing red in the darkness.

His chest felt as if it were on fire. He kept gasping for air, knowing he was killing himself by doing so. There was a brief moment of pain as the hot gases seared his lungs.

Then he collapsed onto the tunnel floor, thankful that he had only seconds more to live.

CHAPTER 28

For Nordlund, the seconds after the shot seemed to expand to hours. His mind raced, analyzing in a fraction of a second all the variables involved. Someone had shot Kaltmeyer with a tracer bullet. Then there had been another tracer round from the area of the boarded-up cave.

And then, the explosion.

He heard the preliminary *chuff* as the escaping fumes from a gas pocket caught fire, the ominous sound before a combustion makes the transition from deflagration to detonation, from rapid burning to explosion, in microseconds. He knew, as the heat wave from the explosion enveloped him, that the explosion was in the eastern side of the cut, the area where Dietz and his crew had been awaiting hole-through.

He fell onto the rough planking of the speaker's platform, doing his best to pull Kaltmeyer down without handling him too roughly. From the far side of the tunnel, on the other side of what had been the rock curtain between the two cuts, he heard a terrifying barrage of screams, then sudden silence. The epicenter of the explosion must have been a few dozen yards past the platform; the fireball from it had roared down the eastern half of the tunnel.

Dietz's men had been caught in the middle of the explosion. There was little hope that any of them survived.

God, how many men had been on the other side?

As he hit the flooring and did his best to shield Kaltmeyer's body, part of him was convinced that nothing would protect them or anybody else at this point. Diana, Cyd, Derrick, Nakamura, Swede—gone, all gone. He was dimly aware of bodies tumbling around him, either knocked off their feet by the explosion and the resulting wave of heat or else diving to the tunnel floor for the same protection he was seeking.

He shouted, "Cyd? Diana?"

If they answered, he couldn't sort out their cries from those of the others. The air was filled with boiling dust, hot enough that he took as few breaths as possible and kept them shallow. Small rock particles spattered down on his back, then suddenly became larger, some of them painfully so. The rain of limestone from the arch overhead became a deluge, pelting his body with heavy chunks. He raised his head to try to see through the dust-filled air.

The limestone from the unsupported roof of the tunnel was spalling away. To his right and rear, fissures opened and widened as he watched. Suddenly, a whole section of the arch peeled away. He quickly turned Kaltmeyer's face to the tunnel floor and hid his own beneath his arm. The rock above made grinding noises and shuddered, and more shards of stone pelted down. The tunnel floor vibrated as masses of rock fell on it, throwing up dense clouds of limestone dust.

"Oh, Christ!" somebody was screaming. "Oh, Jesus! Jesus!"

And another voice: "Oh, God, somebody help me!"

"Cyd!" he shouted. And again: "Cyd!"

He thought he heard somebody cry, "Dane!" but it was hard to tell among the babble of voices. He twisted and looked behind him, in the direction of the access shaft and the West Portal. A huge white-and-yellow mass of stone blocked part of the passageway behind him. Some of the tunnel wall by the cave had collapsed, and the sheets of plywood they had used to board it up were burning.

Nordlund listened, trying to sort out the sound of further rock movement from the screams and moans around him. Nothing. He started to get up, thinking that now they had a chance to evacuate the area before more falling debris blocked the passageway.

Then the second explosion blew away any hopes he had of getting out.

Later, he realized the collapse of a portion of the overhead arch had opened a channel to another methane pocket and the gas had flooded the rear of the passageway. It had boiled along just below the tunnel arch, its flow deflected from the immediate area around him by the limestone baffles that had collapsed across the passage. Just behind, it combined with the air from the ventilators and formed a deadly mixture, lacking only a spark to set it off. But there had been the taping equipment used by the television crews, filled with sparking motors and relays.

The gas-air mixture caught and raced to detonation.

The explosion was ear-shattering. Nordlund heard Diana cry out before he threw himself down. Shattered chunks of limestone, whole layers isolated by entrapped organic matter, tumbled down ahead of him, blocking the passageway to the station vault and the access shaft. He heard the grinding roar of other layers shattering and spilling into the breach. Rock debris rained over him once again.

This is it, he thought. *Nobody's going to survive this one.*

Another wave of heat washed over him, but there was no searing touch of flame, no more chunks of stone crashing nearby.

He heard the grinding of the limestone strata, but the sound seemed more distant now. He listened to the crying and screams of those around him and wondered how many of the crowd had gotten out alive. Those who could must have run for it after the first detonation.

But those he knew and those he loved had been too close to the head of the cut. Cyd and Diana, Derrick, Nakamura and Swede, some of the other high-ballers . . . and Kaltmeyer and DeFolge.

The favored few who had been given seats up front.

They were all dead, he thought. None of them could possibly have lived through the two explosions.

For Cal Briggs, the scene was one right out of Dante's *Inferno*.

The first explosion rocked the tunnel, showering debris down on the spectators. A fiftyish man, dressed in a blue suit and black tie, leaped to his feet, his eyes glazed with panic, and dropped almost immediately as a large chunk of limestone grazed the side of his head.

Briggs cursed his inability to forget a face. Harcourt, a minor official from the Office of Transportation. Nice guy, a vet of the Jordanian war, a wife and three teenage kids. . . .

An older woman in a knee-length leather coat, starting to get out of her chair on the right-hand edge of the crowd, was seized by an invisible hand and hurled at the shield that had just been installed against the far wall.

Agatha Summers, a recording secretary with the Bureau of Mines, Briggs recalled. She lay motionless where the explosion had thrown her.

The other spectators were stunned by the shock wave, then were stumbling over each other, racing back up the tunnel as more debris fell from the arch, raising a dense cloud of white dust. Moore, his cameraman, had lost his hard hat but held his ground, taping as much as he could of the carnage around him. A Pulitzer Prize was a year away, but Briggs wondered if Moore would ever live to collect it.

He watched in wonderment as Anson Kirk, the replacement for the retiring Mike Wallace on CBS's venerable "60 Minutes," raced fifty yards up the tunnel.

The rain of fragments gradually ceased, and the rocks stopped their groaning. The tunnel was quiet except for the screams of the frightened and the dying. Briggs turned and saw that the major collapse had half-sealed the tunnel behind him. But with the exception of minor debris dribbling from the ceiling, the worst was over. He watched as Moore reached mechanically into his pocket for a lens cloth and wiped the dust carefully from his camera, then continued taping the scene around him.

"Hey, Charley, if you want to go—"

Moore turned to film Nordlund and the fallen Kaltmeyer on the shattered speaker's platform. It was a wonder they were alive, Briggs thought, that anybody that close to the explosion was still alive.

"Another minute, Cal."

Briggs pulled out a pad and pencil to jot down some notes, then said, "Shit!" and stuffed them back into his pocket. No way he was going to forget the scene around him. He bent down and started lifting chunks of rock off people. He felt the pulse of one husky high-baller staring open-eyed at eternity, then let his arm drop and went on to the next. He felt a peculiar thrill, coupled with a sense of detachment. To be on the scene taping

(237

actual pictures of the disaster and the subsequent rescue when it came . . . my God, how lucky could you get.

He knelt by the side of a moaning woman and started to lift her head so she would be more comfortable. He drew away a hand that was covered with blood and wiped it on his trousers. "Somebody will be here soon, miss." But would it be soon enough for her? he wondered. She looked as if she were twenty years old, probably a clerk for the tunnel company.

Strange how life turned out. . . . He had been a television reporter in Jordan during the Shia uprisings and had gained a reputation for daring by going into the middle of a firefight for pictures and a story. He had expected his record to boost his career on returning to the United States.

It would have, too, if he hadn't offended the network brass. He had been younger then and very full of himself, unwilling to take shit from anybody. And they hadn't been willing to take any from him. So they had farmed him out to one of the owned-and-operated stations doing local assignment work like today's story.

Only today's story wasn't exactly local.

He looked up from the young woman just in time to see Hal Jeffries of the *Tribune* pause forty yards up the tunnel, debating whether it was safe to return. Jeffries nervously approached the debris that half-blocked the tunnel, edged around it, and walked back into the area where the ceremonies had been held. The fat little man should never have been assigned to the story, Briggs thought. The Restaurant of the Week was more his style.

There were moans coming from beneath several tumbled chairs a few feet away. Briggs hurried over and started pulling the chairs off the man trapped beneath.

He was totally unprepared for the second explosion.

The blast was nearer this time, tearing huge chunks of rock from the overhead arch and hurling them downward. One fragment hit his left leg, and he sank to his knees, cursing. Somebody screamed thirty yards away, and he glanced up to see a smoky red fireball rolling toward Moore.

The cameraman turned to run, but the fireball wrapped around him like a red cocoon. Moore threw his arms wide and for just a moment was outlined in the flames, his long black hair standing straight up and burning like a torch. The camera mounted on his shoulder harness burst open and half-inch tape spilled out, crisping and flaring as it draped itself over his shoulders and arms.

There would be only the first wave of pain, Briggs knew; the flames would scar away the nerve endings before they could transmit any signals to the brain. Moore died standing up, a blackened stick man that finally fell and broke to pieces on the tunnel floor.

Briggs turned to run then, racing past a frightened Jeffries, who stared at the oncoming fireball, unable to move, as fascinated by the flame as a bird by a snake. Then Jeffries finally turned and ran after him. Briggs was frightened now, his sense of detachment gone, fear pumping energy into his legs. Even then, he didn't seriously consider that he might not make it. He felt growing heat on the back of his neck and heard a sudden scream close by.

Jeffries. The fat little man was silhouetted by the ball of flame behind him, and then the outlines of the silhouette were blurred as the fireball swallowed him. Jeffries kept running even as he burned to death.

The fireball was darker now, cooler looking, but it still rolled inexorably forward. Briggs realized with sudden terror that he couldn't outrun it. He spotted a service niche in one of the wall shields and dove for it, pulling himself up into the tiny space, his body automatically curling into a tight little knot.

He shifted so he could watch the fireball, which was visibly growing darker and slowing as it approached. How long since the explosion? he wondered. Three seconds? Four? Then the fireball was opposite his small niche, sucking the air from his lungs. He tried to breathe and drew in a chestful of scorching gases. He screamed but made no sound; the hot gases had seared his vocal cords.

The edge of the cooling fireball touched his body, and his clothing began to smoke. He felt intense heat on his face and then no pain at all. Abruptly, there was no sight, no sound, no feeling. *I'm dying,* he thought, and had a sudden mental image of a burning village in Jordan, so long ago.

Around him, the polyester of the wall shield bubbled away from the fiberglass sheets and slowly turned brown.

André DuBois, the young French Canadian just promoted to section head on the day shift, heard the first explosion as he and a crew were doing some finish work on the concrete walls of the station vault. The day had been easy duty, made even easier because the caterers were setting up for the celebration after hole-through and nobody seemed to mind if you swiped a sandwich or an occasional boiled shrimp. He had tried to switch shifts with somebody so he could watch Kaltmeyer shatter the last bit of rock between the cuts, but nobody wanted to change. He had even offered a hundred bucks, but no takers.

Well, at least he'd be around for the party, and maybe Deborah, the young woman in accounting, would agree to help him improve his English. He'd asked her before, but she always ended up giggling for reasons he never understood. Maybe he should forget all about the English lessons and just come right out with it—tell her that everything she'd heard about French Canadians was true, and offer to improve her sex life.

Or maybe make it an even exchange. He frowned. She'd be getting the best of the bargain, but what the hell. . . .

He was eating another boiled shrimp when Bailey called him over, scratching his head.

"How do I smooth it, DuBois? I keep getting little balls of cement on top."

He inspected the area around one of the supports for a gigantic magnetic ring, and started cursing.

"Don' you know notting, Bailey? Use more watair, man."

He showed Bailey how to do it, then went back to the caterers' table and swiped a pastry. They had set out hundreds on little paper plates; they'd never miss one.

One of the caterers' assistants, a young red-haired man, spotted him and grinned, and DuBois grinned back, not bothering to hide the cake. *What a 'andsome fellow you are, Du-Bois, everybody love you. . . .* He crammed the rest of the cake into his mouth and winked.

It was then that he heard what sounded like a dull thud down at the far end of the tunnel. He turned and listened, crumbs of cake still hanging on his lips. No alarm Klaxon, maybe nothing. He started walking back to see how Bailey was doing, and then he realized what he had heard.

He stopped. Explosion. There were no gas alarms because the explosion had probably torn out the wiring. But there would be fires—

"Fire in ze 'ole!" he shouted. "Fire in ze 'ole!"

He hit a nearby manual fire alarm and heard the Klaxons wail at the top of the access shaft.

"Bailey! Reynolds! Buchser! Get mask, follow me!"

There was a locker by the cages, and he raced over to it, yanked open the door, passed out the masks, and grabbed a first-aid kit. Not more than a minute had passed since he had heard the explosion. He ran to the marked-off area for electric cars, hit the accelerator of one, and jumped in as it started up. He didn't bother checking to see if the other men were following.

Fifty yards into the tunnel, he felt a sudden pulse of air against his face. The pressure wave from a second explosion. Another hundred yards, and he was riding into a warm breeze. The fire must be at the tunnel face. Gases, everybody had known there were gas pockets. Carbon monoxide, hydrogen sulfide, ammonia . . . He didn't know English very well, but he knew the names of all the gases and what they could do. He slipped on the mask.

He pushed the little electric car for all the speed he could get out of it, then suddenly caught his breath. Up ahead, the electricity had shut off, and he was riding into a pitch-black hole where the only lights were the fireflies.

Only they weren't fireflies, they were the headlights of other cars coming toward him. Moments later, they were passing him. Some of them held three and four people, their faces white with fear, their clothing torn and scorched. There were cars where only the drivers seemed alive, the people next to them wide-eyed and moaning, huge burns on their faces, their eyebrows seared away.

And then, far down the tunnel, he heard screams and shouts. The muck train rattled past, loaded with the frightened living and the motionless dead. There would be a jam-up at the access shaft. There were five cages and maybe three hundred people scared to death, all of them wanting to get the hell out of there as soon as possible. . . .

He was getting closer. The tunnel was crowded with people running for the shaft and crying for help. It was smoky now and difficult to see; the headlight of the little car didn't penetrate very far. But he was almost to the face. The air was hot, the tunnel floor was burned and scorched, and lumps of what had once been people lay motionless all around him. He felt as if he had driven into a burial crypt. Farther down the tunnel, the blackness gave way to a dull red, and he guessed that up ahead something was still burning. He didn't go any farther.

He stopped the car, shivering despite the heat. There could be more pockets of gas in the area. And the rock around him was still shifting, moaning as it sought to find a new balance. He held his breath and listened for anybody who might still be alive. A scraping sound. Somebody was crawling along the side of the tunnel. He drove the car over, its headlight splashing against the tunnel wall. Chris, one of the high-ballers.

DuBois grabbed his first-aid kit and ran over. *"Chrees, Chrees, don' move—eet's DuBois!"*

"Not much you can do, Frenchy," Chris murmured.

DuBois didn't answer. It was hard to see, the headlight was too high, but Chris had lost a lot of blood from a torn leg. He fumbled around in the kit and found a compression bandage and tightened it above the gashes in the leg. That would help some. And then the emergency syringe with morphine. If any junkie had—

They hadn't.

"Zis vill hurt a little, I'm no good wiz ze needle." He gave the injection in the arm, then waited a few moments, glancing up in alarm once when the rock overhead shrieked and some dust sifted down.

"Have to go—right now!"

He helped Chris up and got him into the car, then started back up the tunnel, praying desperately that no more gas pockets would rupture and that the tons of rock above him would stay put.

He would have missed her completely, except he swerved to avoid the tracks for the muck train and the headlight picked her up, crumpled behind a jockey box. At first he wasn't even sure the woman was alive until he stopped the car and heard her sobbing.

He ran over with the kit, afraid for a moment that the scratches on her arms might indicate deeper gashes or broken bones. But there was no pool of blood, and her legs were folded beneath her as if she had suddenly sat on them; they weren't sprawled out at funny angles.

Her face was turned away from him, and her hair was so matted with white rock dust that he wasn't sure whether she was young or old.

"Where does eet hurt, ladee?"

"I can't run any farther," she sobbed. "And Judy—" She broke off, tears streaming down her face.

She wasn't hurt, DuBois thought, only frightened. He put his arm around her shoulders to help her up, and she turned toward him.

His eyes widened in shocked surprise.

Deborah.

He slipped his arms around her waist. *"Chérie, chérie!"* He told her how glad he was that he had found her, how desperately glad that she hadn't been hurt—and then his words slowed to a halt as she stared blankly back, not understanding. It was a moment before he realized he was babbling at her in French.

"You goin' to be all right, Debbee."

He helped her to her feet and half-carried her to the car. She had wrapped her arms tightly around him and buried her face in his shoulder. He grinned in the darkness.

When she recovered in a day or two, maybe he'd try again for the English lessons.

Then there was another rumble from the arch overhead, and powdered rock sifted down the back of his neck. He cursed and bent low, goosing the little car for all it was worth, his eyes intent on the slowly growing circle of light that was the station vault and safety.

CHAPTER 29

Strange party, Metcalf thought. Most of those in the bullpen were having a great time, but there was an odd undercurrent of unease. The tunnel was complete, hole-through would occur in a few minutes. A lot of those watching the screen would extend the party into an all-night drunk, and he might as well join them. Even if Lammont had forged the soundings, nobody was going to do anything about them right now.

He looked over at Zumwalt, who shrugged his shoulders. He still looked worried. *And so am I,* Metcalf thought. Once the ceremonies were over, he'd have to get hold of Kaltmeyer and try to talk him into closing down the cut, then make additional test borings to check for gas pockets. Would Kaltmeyer go for it? He doubted it. Certainly DeFolge wouldn't.

He glanced around the room. Great party—half the people in the bullpen were already high on champagne, and he knew some of them had smuggled in bottles of liquor.

But like himself and Zumwalt, not everybody was excited about hole-through. Grimsley was sitting in the first row of chairs before the screen, hunched forward, arms on knees, concentrating on the images in front of the thin curtain of rock. He was probably thinking that this was what Felton and Esposito had given their lives for and wondering if it had been worth it.

There were others not in the mood for celebrating, either. Harry Richards sat off by himself, casually eating a sandwich and drinking a can of soda. Harry had a reputation for putting it away down at Jimmy's, but he never drank on duty, and any time he spent at the Field Station was duty time. Right now, something was bothering Richards; he looked preoccupied.

And old Samuel Wilcox, sitting in a corner by himself clutching his tumbler of bourbon, looked as if he were a mile away. Probably wondering if he should ask for indictments against

Kaltmeyer/DeFolge and who should be named. There'd be a lot of bad publicity when he announced it, and Nordlund's resignation wouldn't help any.

On the other hand, there were Moloney and Tisch and Pinelli and a dozen women from Accounting and the secretarial pool, half of them already high. Whatever was bothering Richards and Grimsley certainly wasn't bothering any of them.

And Neal Youngblood, the inspector from the Bureau of Mines who had just wandered in, looked as if he were up for a party. For the first few days around the cut, he had been Mr. Grim, but today he looked relaxed and at ease. Maybe because it was all over and he could go back to D.C. in a day or two. He could be a funny man when he decided to party, Metcalf thought. The betting was that he had been a high-baller sometime in the past—at least he spoke the language.

"Jesus Christ, how long's the old man going to ramble on?" Moloney looked impatient. He probably had a date to meet half a dozen other engineers at Jimmy's and celebrate.

"He's waiting for Moses to show up and part the rock," Pinelli said. Mark Pinelli was a young high-baller, a five-foot-five-inch little Hercules with a chip on his shoulder as big as his biceps. A bad guy to go drinking with—Pinelli inevitably picked a fight with the biggest man in the bar and just as inevitably left with a set of loose teeth and a blackened eye. Pinelli's only real handicap in life was his inability to concede that a good big man could usually whip a good little man.

But still, next to Dietz, he got along with Pinelli the best.

"Is it true the old man made Nordlund resign?" Moloney was looking over at him.

He gave a diplomatic shrug. "Got me."

It was Herb Tisch, the gas technician, a veteran of God knew how many hole-throughs, who raised his plastic tumbler and shouted at him, "Toast, toast!"

He didn't want to, but they egged him on, and he finally stood up and raised his own glass.

"To old tunnels and new tunnels, but most of all, to through tunnels!"

"Hear, hear!" Moloney cackled.

On the big screen, Kaltmeyer finally finished talking. De-Folge stepped up and said a few words, and then he and Kaltmeyer, both dressed in plastic raincoats, stood back and swung at the rocky curtain. It shattered, spraying them with rocky splinters. The wall collapsed so quickly that Metcalf suspected somebody had hit it at about the same height and at the same time on the other side.

Then Pinelli hollered, "Hey!"

On the screen, Kaltmeyer had abruptly sat down, clutching his side. At first, Metcalf thought he had been standing too close, that a rock splinter had caught him in the side.

But what the hell had been the red streak across the screen?

Now the camera zoomed in on Kaltmeyer, and Metcalf could see the growing splotch of red on his right side, spreading out beneath the plastic raincoat.

"Jesus Christ!" Moloney said to the suddenly quiet room. "He's been shot! What the hell's going on?"

Metcalf felt growing alarm and glanced around for Richards. He wasn't there—probably in Janice's office calling down to the tunnel to find out just what had happened.

"My God, look!" Moloney again, angry because something was going wrong with the celebration.

Four miles away, four hundred feet below the surface, Nordlund had jumped onto the platform to help the stricken Kaltmeyer. Another streak of red slashed across the screen. The focus was so tight that Metcalf could see chips fly off the tunnel wall where it hit.

Suddenly the camera went crazy, and for a moment he was looking at the tunnel arch, where huge sections of rock were peeling away. The entire scene now started to gray out, and moments later he couldn't see anything at all. *Rock dust,* he thought, numb. Then the cameraman wiped the lens, and he had a clear view of a sea of tumbled chairs with people climbing over them and each other as they streamed past, running away from the face of the cut.

A number of people weren't moving at all. Metcalf noticed Nordlund was now lying over the stricken Kaltmeyer. He couldn't tell whether either of them was alive or dead.

(247

All of those in the bullpen were standing up now, hypnotized by the picture on the screen, the image momentarily more important than the event itself. It was Zumwalt who shouted: "Explosion! It's a goddamned explosion!"

A split-second later, the Klaxon in the compound started bleating.

Metcalf ran for the door; he'd have to get down there. Zumwalt was suddenly standing in his way, his face pale and strained.

"Where the hell you going, Troy?"

He tried to push past. "What are you talking about? I've got to get down there!"

Zumwalt looked close to panic. "Who the hell's in charge up here? They're all down there, Troy, we don't even know if any of them are alive. Who's gonna run things up here?"

It took a second for it to sink in. Zumwalt was right. Nordlund, Kaltmeyer, and DeFolge were all down in the tunnel. There wasn't anybody else; he was the old man of the cut now, by default if for no other reason.

He went on automatic then, pushing back into the room and roaring, "Shut up!" until everybody suddenly quieted down. They stared at him, waiting. Each of them had been assigned roles to play in disaster drills, but this was reality, not a drill.

"Tisch, I want continuous reports on the gas monitors in the cut. Pinelli, you're in charge of Supply. When the rescue crews go into the tunnel, make sure they go down with two masks, one for themselves and one for any of the victims who might need it. Moloney, call the city's disaster center—we need all the ambulances and medical people they've got! Zumwalt—"

And then, behind him in the bullpen, Grimsley said in a hushed voice, "Oh, sweet Jesus!"

Metcalf turned just in time to see the camera go wild again. *Another explosion,* he thought, sick. Then there was a frightening shot of a huge ball of flame heading straight for the camera, like something out of an old Spielberg movie. For a fraction of a second they were looking at a terrifying close-up of the fireball, then the screen abruptly went black as the flames swept over the cameraman.

"They're gone," somebody said in a flat voice.

Metcalf shook himself out of his trance.

"Let's go, goddamnit! People are dying down there! Youngblood"—he pointed at the ashen-faced Bureau of Mines man—"call Great Lakes Naval Station and see if they can helicopter in some rescue teams and hospital corpsmen. Tell them we need everything they've got for burn victims, including every off-duty doctor on station."

His heart was beating in time to the blaring of the Klaxon outside, his mind speeding. He spotted a pale young woman from Accounting standing in a corner, still clutching the remains of a sandwich.

"Liz, get hold of the other women in the building and see the switchboard operator; I want a telephone bank operating as soon as possible. Once word gets out, a thousand relatives will be calling for information." Then to Sam Wilcox, looking confused and lonely in the corner: "We'll need your team as well, Mr. Wilcox."

Wilcox looked grateful and started for the door, then hesitated. "If you hear anything about Mrs. Lederley—"

Metcalf nodded. "As soon as I hear." He hadn't really thought about who might be among the dead and the dying. He couldn't afford to think about it now.

Then he realized he was alone in the bullpen except for Grimsley. Outside, he could hear the shouts of people running across the compound between the station and the access shaft, while over everything was the raucous sound of the Klaxon. It was a bitterly cold day out, and sound carried well—you could probably hear the Klaxon in downtown Chicago. He went into Janice's office and used her phone to dial the police and the fire department, losing a valuable thirty seconds identifying himself to the police. The fire department was already on its way—they had a direct alarm hook-up.

"Mr. Metcalf, anything I—"

Grimsley was standing in the doorway, hard hat in hand. He looked lost.

"Find Richards and tell him I want to see him. Then stick

around after that—I'm going to need you." Grimsley would do all right once he shook off his daze; he knew as much about the tunnel as any man working on it.

After Grimsley left, Metcalf tried to relax for a few moments but discovered he couldn't. It was as if he had a check-off list in his head and was constantly reviewing everything that had happened, or that he thought had happened, and trying to cover all the eventualities. If somebody had asked him right then, he could have drawn a detailed map of Navy Pier and the Field Station and the tunnel itself from the East Portal to the West, not missing a single gas alarm or jockey box—

The thought that had been submerged in the back of his mind suddenly surfaced.

Dietz. Oh, Jesus Christ. . . .

He grabbed the phone and dialed the East Portal. The frightened voice that answered had no information. The Klaxons had gone off there as well, and rescue crews complete with masks were now down in the tunnel. But it was a good forty miles to the head of the cut, and it would be at least fifty minutes until they heard back. Yes, they'd tried the comm line, but it wasn't working. And then, most ominous of all, they were short-handed on rescue crews because so many men had gone down into the cut for the celebration.

"Troy?"

Richards had walked in, looking upset and nervous.

Metcalf put down the phone; he felt stunned. Dietz and his men—but he couldn't think about them right now.

"Harry, we're going to need a squad of security guards down in the station vault—there're only five cages, and they're going to be swamped. Injured and women first, you know the drill. And we'll need an identification check-off system as they come up so we'll know who's still down there. If any of the caterers are still in the vault, get them out of there. And have one of the girls in the phone bank start contacting off-duty security men to report back here as soon as possible."

Richards nodded. "The security men are already down there, the caterers are out. I'll set up a check-off system both in the vault and up here."

"You need a backup team at the front gates? I've called the police—they can supplement your men to keep out any sight-seers."

"Nobody's going to get in unless they swim out here. What about the press?"

It was the last thing in the world he wanted to deal with, but he was going to have to, if only to stop the rumors that would spread.

"Pool reporter setup. We can't have hundreds of them roaming around out here. No access to the vault or the tunnel."

Richards started to leave, then hung back for a moment. "I don't know what the situation is at the East Portal, what teams they'll be sending in or if they'll be able to get as far as the hole-through area. But if they do and they find out anything about . . . Cyd, you'll let me know, right?"

The man was hurting and trying not to show it, and Metcalf felt a sudden surge of sympathy for him. "Sure, Harry. And keep me informed on who comes up on this side, Cyd or Dane or anybody."

Just as Richards got to the door, he added, "I think the FBI ought to start looking for Lammont. We're going to need him back here badly. And once this thing is over with, I'm going to kill him."

"Cyd already talked to me about Lammont." He hesitated, toying with his hard hat for a moment. "If anything's happened to Cyd," he said quietly, "you won't have to worry about Lammont."

After Richards left, Metcalf wandered into Nordlund's office, found a cup of cold coffee on his desk and took a sip, then stepped outside onto the little balcony. In the distance, he could hear the wail of the first ambulance sirens, crisp and clear in the winter air.

I finally got your job, Dane. But I wish to Christ I hadn't.

For the first time since he had seen Kaltmeyer fall on the screen, he allowed himself to think of Cyd and Kaltmeyer and Dane and Derrick and Swede and—

Jesus, it was as if everybody he knew in the world were down in the cut. But there wasn't much more he could do at

(251

the moment. Now would come the long wait as they brought up the injured and the dying and finally those who were still alive.

That was something else that would have to be done. He needed a system for notifying the next of kin, a system for handling the crowds of relatives and friends who would gather outside the gates of the Navy Pier, waiting for some kind of word.

He walked back into the bullpen, where the screen was now showing the confusion in the compound outside. He had hoped by some miracle that the camera in the cut had come back on and Kaltmeyer was just stepping through the shattered curtain of rock to shake hands with Dietz on the other side.

Then Grimsley was saying something to him and holding out a phone.

The East Portal.

He listened a moment, then said numbly, "Keep me informed." He handed back the phone, unable to say anything more.

Grimsley stared. "What the hell happened?"

"Total wipeout," Metcalf said in a choked voice. "Nobody's come out of the tunnel. They don't think anybody outran the first fireball. Three shifts and half the office staff, a total of three hundred and five. Probably all dead."

Grimsley turned blindly away.

Three hundred and five people dead, and that wasn't counting those who had perished in the fireball or had been crushed by the cave-in on their side of the cut.

He had spent four years of his life working on the longest tunnel in the world, hoping that someday he would be in charge.

What he was in charge of was the worst tunnel disaster in history.

CHAPTER 30

It was pitch-black, and Nordlund wondered crazily if he had died. He held his breath, listening hard in the darkness. There was the slight moaning and creaking of the rocks above—and somebody breathing close by. He reached out with his hands and touched what felt like a sheet of crumpled plastic. Kaltmeyer. He was still alive.

"Frank?"

There was a mumbled answer, and Nordlund groped his way off the raised wooden platform and felt desperately around the floor of the tunnel for one of the battery lanterns used as fill for the television lights. He found one, turned it on. Nothing. There were other sounds of movement around him now. He spent a moment more of frantic scrabbling before he found another lantern. He switched it on, and the beam of light splashed against the tunnel walls. He breathed a not-too-silent prayer of relief. The tunnel was still filled with dust, but he could see people moving through the murk. Then somebody else found a lantern and turned it on.

Nakamura. Thank God. They stared at each other for a moment. Nakamura silently nodded, then flashed the lantern around, searching for others. More figures were moving in the dust-filled gloom now, too stunned even to sob. Derrick uncurled from the ball he had rolled into and turned to help Diana next to him.

Nordlund hurried over to her. "You all right?"

"I . . . think so." She was shaken up, biting her lip to keep from showing it. He knew she was automatically running an inventory—no broken bones, no cuts, no concussion. She glanced down and brushed some of the dust from her skirt, then gave it up. As long as he had known her, she had never really cried, and he doubted that she would now.

"Derrick?"

"I . . . think I'm all right."

Swede climbed out from under some tumbled chairs, then helped a frightened-looking Lynch. The slender high-baller's eyes were wide open and terrified. His worst fears had come true; there had been a cave-in, and he was trapped. To be inside Lynch's head right now was to be in hell, Nordlund thought.

There was a groan from behind a section of fallen rock. DeFolge was on the other side, a gash in his head, his hair bloody and matted. For a moment he had difficulty bringing Nordlund into focus. When he succeeded, he pointed to his bloodied head. "How the hell bad is it?"

Nordlund knelt and separated the strands of hair. DeFolge winced but didn't say anything.

"Scalp wound, nothing serious."

"Diana all right?"

"She's fine—a little shook up."

A grunt. "Don't lie to me, Nordlund."

"She's right over there—see for yourself."

Where the hell is Cyd? He beamed his lantern around the first row, where she had been sitting. Nobody was moving. Maybe—blessed thought—she had managed to get out. He walked over to search the row, moving aside the chairs and the rocks and gingerly turning over bodies one by one.

The first one he recognized was Hartman. There wasn't a mark on his face, and it wasn't until Nordlund went to help him up that he realized a shard of rock had severed Hartman's backbone. He let the body sag gently back to the floor and went slowly down the row. Some people had gotten out; there were coats and purses that didn't belong to the bodies nearby.

Cyd was the fifth in the row. There was a bruise on her temple, and he thought, *Oh, Jesus, no,* and knelt by her side, wanting desperately to take her in his arms and at the same time afraid to move her. Then he noticed the slight pulsing of a vein in her neck. He slapped her gently.

"Cyd? Cyd!"

Her eyes fluttered, then focused. She drew in a deep breath, and Nordlund helped her into a chair. She stared at him for a long moment, then sighed with relief. "So we both made it."

"Yeah. Most of those in this row didn't."

"Who?"

He named those he had found whom she knew, and she closed her eyes for a moment. "How many survived?"

"Don't know yet." He raised his voice. "Let's look around, folks—see if we've got company."

It was grisly business, how grisly he didn't realize until he had been at it five minutes. After another ten, everybody met back by the wooden speaker's platform. There was nobody else left alive in the area.

"Are we safe for a while, Dane—or is this just a brief respite?" There was a trace of bitchiness in Diana's voice; her standard defense, he thought.

"I think we're safe for right now."

He flashed the light around the tunnel again, taking a more professional look. Fifteen feet into the other side of the cut was a jumbled mass of rock where the ceiling had collapsed. He wondered if any of Dietz's men had gotten out alive; it didn't seem possible any of them had. He spotted a small section of torn fiberglass jutting out from the top of the rock mass and guessed that a still-curing shield had collapsed under the weight of the rocks above.

It was a similar story a hundred feet behind him. The curing shield just past the mouth of the cave had blistered badly before it gave way, dumping tons of earth and rock into the tunnel. Somehow, even though it didn't have a proper shield, the area around the face of the cut had survived, despite extensive shifting of the roof.

Kaltmeyer suddenly started to groan, and Nordlund knelt down to help.

"Let's have a look, Frank."

The others gathered around while he took out a pocket knife and cut away the plastic raincoat. The side of Kaltmeyer's suitcoat was soaked with blood, and Nordlund carefully sawed at the fabric, doing the same with the bloody shirt and undershirt beneath. The wound was bleeding profusely, but it was a steady flow; the bullet had missed the arteries.

"Is he going to be all right?" Derrick's lip was trembling.

(255

"Don't worry, your dad's going to make it."

He tore away a clean part of the undershirt and used it to sop up the blood so he could see the wound better.

Kaltmeyer grimaced. "Hurts like hell."

"I bet."

The wound was a jagged one. With the red phosphorous melting as the tracer bullet traveled, the round would have wobbled or even tumbled, producing a jagged entry and an even larger exit.

"Got to move you a little, Frank."

"Ricky okay?"

"He's fine."

He shifted Kaltmeyer's body and found a second wound higher up on his back. The wound was tattered and bloody, but the round had exited cleanly without breaking any ribs.

"Swede, we need your shirt. Have to make up a bandage."

Swede took off his shirt and handed it over. Before Nordlund could start tearing it into strips, Cyd knelt beside him and said, "Let me help you with that." She handed him a large, pressed handkerchief to serve as a compress and used the pocket knife to slit the shirt into three-inch strips.

She wrapped the homemade bandage tightly around Kaltmeyer's waist. "Give me your overcoat, Dane, he's going into shock." Kaltmeyer looked gray, and tiny tremors had started to shake his body. Nordlund handed over his coat, and Cyd tucked it loosely around Kaltmeyer, then elevated his feet. "That's about all we can do for the moment," she murmured.

Lynch suddenly said, "He's going to die."

Derrick paled, and Swede turned angrily on Lynch. "Shut your face, Lynch, or I'll shut it for you."

"Keep it cool!" Nordlund ordered. He glanced up and noticed DeFolge watching, a faint smile playing around his fleshy lips, and he suddenly had an almost overwhelming desire to beat the bastard to the tunnel floor. Senator Alan DeFolge was as much responsible for the disaster as Murray Lammont, maybe more. Nordlund knew, as surely as if DeFolge had told him, that whatever Lammont had done, he had done because De-

Folge had wanted him to do it, had paid him to do it. Kaltmeyer/DeFolge had won a last-minute bid for the cut because of Lammont's forged soundings. He suspected their profits had been enormous. But how many hundreds of people had died because of those soundings?

Then he realized DeFolge had read every single thought as it flickered through his mind. The senator still wore his smile, but now it was cast in stone. With that one brief glance, they had become deadly enemies.

"Mr. Nordlund."

Nakamura was standing near the edge of the cave-in that blocked their return to the station vault and the access shaft. Nordlund hurried over. The rock debris was fairly fine and banked in a steep drift. He reached up and tested the position of several pieces of stone at the top of the landslide. The pile suddenly wobbled and threatened to slide downward. Nordlund jumped back.

Nakamura shook his head. "Too much haste, Mr. Nordlund," he warned. He motioned slightly with his hand, holding it near a small gap in the pile of debris. It was a purposefully slight movement, and Nordlund realized Nakamura didn't want the others to see it.

He edged closer to the gap, pretending he was inspecting the stability of the pile, and placed his own hand near it. There was a stream of air coming through the gap, which explained why the tunnel was warm—the air was burning hot. And when he listened carefully, he could hear a distant roaring, like that of a huge welding torch.

The gas pocket just beyond was blazing out of control.

When they walked back to the little group around the platform, Cyd asked, "What happened, Dane?"

"Methane explosion," he said bitterly, staring at DeFolge. "There's probably an extensive bed of peat or perhaps a primitive oil field not too far away. The area is riddled with pockets of trapped gas. We must have been between two large ones."

"How can you tell?" Swede asked.

(257

"Because there are signs of fire both east and west of this part of the tunnel. The first pocket was in Dietz's section. It flashed over and ignited a pocket behind us. Fortunately the pockets didn't join, or we'd have been barbecued, too. Sheer dumb luck."

Diana glanced around. "I would hardly call this lucky."

"Why didn't we know about the gas pockets?" There was an angry edge to Swede's voice.

"I'm not the guy to ask, Swede."

DeFolge shot Nordlund a murderous look, then his face smoothed and he shook his head in sorrow. "We hired the best firm possible to take the soundings, they made continuous test bores. Believe me, there'll be a full investigation once we get out of here."

Swede stared at DeFolge. "There better be."

Lynch walked over to the steep slope of rocky debris between their chamber and the tunnel that led to the access shaft. "We'll have to dig our way out," he said nervously. He started to climb the pile, ready to start shifting rock from the top down.

"Get away from there, Lynch!" Nordlund shouted.

Lynch climbed back down, a small landslide of broken rock trailing after him.

Diana looked upset. "What's wrong with trying to dig our way out?"

He couldn't keep it from them; probably never should have tried.

"My guess is that the cave-in in Dietz's section is too extensive—don't count on getting out that way. Just beyond the pile of rocks behind us is a methane fire that's probably being fed by air from the ventilator shafts. But the same rocks that have us trapped are also acting as insulation against the heat."

"What you're trying to say, Dane, is that there's no way out, right?" The acid in Diana's voice let everybody know that Nordlund was obviously to blame.

"We're going to need air," Lynch said, white-faced. "We'll die if we don't get air."

Nordlund forced himself to be patient. "We're getting air

from somewhere, my guess is the cave system. If they can cap the ventilation shafts or reverse the fans, they can probably extinguish the fire. And there's always the chance that the pocket of gas may simply deplete itself.''

Nakamura had been staring at the tunnel arch. "The rocks overhead are unstable, Mr. Nordlund. The vibrations involved in reversing the fans could be hazardous to us.''

There was a long silence while everybody glanced nervously at the roof of the tunnel.

Nordlund nodded. "I think we should camp out in the cave. The rock formation there is probably more stable than out here.''

"That's a dumb idea, Nordlund, '' DeFolge said, irritated. "If there were another cave-in, we could be sealed up in there, where nobody would think to look for us. Of course, you could always call them up and tell them we're here.''

He should have thought of it. The comm line that had been strung from the head of the cut back to the Field Station used armored cable. DeFolge was right—there was a chance it had survived.

The phone box itself was covered by part of the landslide. He carefully dug it out while the others watched in silence, then opened up the box and took out the phone. He jiggled the cradle, waited a moment, then tried again. Dead. Somewhere in the tunnel falling rock had probably severed the cable.

"So what do we do now?'' Lynch demanded, his voice thinned by hysteria. "You're the boss, tell us what to do now!''

"Make yourselves comfortable. We're going to be here awhile. But sooner or later, somebody will find us.''

"We'll starve before then,'' Lynch said, sullen.

There was a sudden groan from the tunnel roof, and white grit sifted down from overhead.

"I'm moving into the cave,'' Nordlund said.

"Go ahead.'' DeFolge was defiant. "If there's a cave-in, you'll be trapped in there.''

"If there's a cave-in out here,'' Nordlund said, "you'll be buried beneath tons of rock.''

They were splitting into three groups. Diana and Lynch drew

close to DeFolge, while Nakamura, Swede, and Cyd edged nearer to him. Derrick stayed by Kaltmeyer, who had drifted into unconsciousness.

"Suit yourself." Nordlund took one of the battery lanterns and ducked through the remains of the plywood partition that had once sealed off the cave from the tunnel. The others followed.

"I don't suppose anybody brought along any chocolate bars," Cyd said. "They always do in movies."

For the first time since the cave-in, Nordlund smiled.

"We might do better than that."

He went back into the tunnel, to the jockey box just a few feet down from the cave. He broke the lock and lifted the lid. High-ballers kept their hand tools in the box, and six of them had also stored their lunches there. Two brown paper bags were filled with sandwiches, and there were four lunch buckets with Thermos containers of coffee that he would bet was still warm.

He loaded up and stepped back into the cave, ignoring DeFolge and the others still in the tunnel. He pawed through one of the buckets, then tossed a candy bar and a thick sandwich to Cyd.

"There's your chocolate bar and what I'm pretty sure is a ham on rye. No more complaints, y'hear?"

He hadn't gotten through half of the first sandwich when Diana, DeFolge, and Lynch edged past the burned partition.

"I don't suppose you'd care to share and share alike," Diana said, trying to keep it light.

Nordlund doled out the sandwiches, ignoring the malevolent look from DeFolge. "I saved them for you." He wrapped the last half of his sandwich in its plastic bag and dropped it in his pocket. "Better ration them—there aren't any more where they came from."

He took the last two and walked back to the wooden platform where Derrick sat by his father.

"One for you and one for Frank."

Derrick turned away. "I'm not hungry."

"You're going to need your strength," Nordlund said gently. "Your father's going to have to rely on you."

"He's feverish," Derrick said.

Nordlund felt Kaltmeyer's forehead. He wasn't burning up, not yet, but it wouldn't be long before he would be.

"I think we ought to move him into the cave, Derrick. He'll be safer there."

Derrick hesitated. Some more grit sifting down from overhead made up his mind for him. "I guess you're right." Then, worried: "When are they going to dig us out?"

"Soon," Nordlund said. "Pretty soon."

Later, when he was alone in one corner of the cave with Cyd, she asked, "Do you really believe that, Dane? That they'll be digging us out pretty soon?"

"The truth?"

Her face stiffened. "Of course."

He hesitated, then figured that of all the people there, he could be the most honest with her.

"I don't think they know we're still alive."

CHAPTER 31

He had been closer to the explosion than the men on the plat-form, and the blast had dazed him for minutes. He was partially shielded by the small ramp in the cave, but the backlash of flame from the explosion had singed most of the hair from his head. Immediately afterward, his face had felt puckered and dry, and now it was beginning to pain him fiercely. He gingerly touched his right cheek; the pain was excruciating. He turned on his hand flash, being careful to shield the beam. In the dim glow he could see that the hair on his right hand had been singed away and the hand itself was a deep red.

How badly his hand had been burned, he didn't know. But he was sure he could continue to use the carbine.

He was quite angry now. He'd had a clean shot; DeFolge should have gone down with the first round. The movement of the two men when they swung the sledge had suddenly changed their positions, and he'd hit Kaltmeyer first. Kaltmeyer was on his list—but he'd desperately wanted DeFolge.

Through a gap in the plywood partition, he watched the small band of survivors as they discussed what to do next. He swore quietly to himself. He had failed. Perhaps DeFolge would die in another cave-in, but it would not be the same. He had sworn to kill the man with his own hands, and now he had failed.

He watched as Nordlund tested the main pile of debris that blocked the passage. The debris shifted dangerously, and Nord-lund stepped back. He frowned as Nordlund gestured and pointed at the tunnel arch. They were all trapped in this center section, and there was a strong chance that a further shift in the rock above or another methane explosion would bring the overhead down on them.

Nordlund was not stupid. He would quickly decide that there was only one relatively safe place for them to be.

He crept off his homemade ramp and moved silently back into the rear of the cave. He sat behind an outcropping of rock to rest. His lungs hurt, and he felt weak, much too weak. Then he assured himself it would pass. For a moment, he wondered if he could still use the carbine. He had touched off a pocket of methane with his tracers, and he might do the same if he used it again. He decided to wait until the men at the Field Station had put out the fire he sensed was roaring just beyond the landslide. To wait until the ventilators had cleared out any trace of gas. It would be safe to use the carbine then.

After all, it wasn't as if anybody were going anyplace.

His face was still burning, and he could feel a swelling and several large blisters. Second degree burns, he thought, though he couldn't tell how extensive. But he could stand the pain. He had been injured far worse than this in the past and survived.

First DeFolge, he thought. Then Kaltmeyer. And then . . . the others? Oh, yes. The others. Of course. Vengeance is mine, saith the Lord. . . . But it would have to begin with DeFolge. Then the others would follow. One by one. Even the smallest. Brad would have done it.

He froze. Somebody had entered the cave. He slunk farther back, watched as the others entered, then turned and slipped into the next cave behind the main one.

It wasn't until he had sat down, his back to the rocky wall, that he realized he'd left the box of tracers behind. The first chance he had, he'd have to go back and get it. But that would be no problem.

God wouldn't have allowed him to get this far, only to let him fail at the last minute.

CHAPTER 32

Metcalf stood on the small balcony outside Nordlund's office, ignoring the snow that drifted lazily down from the overcast sky. It was bitterly cold, but he didn't feel it except for the bite in his lungs when he took a deep breath. Below him, in the compound, victims were being shuttled to the dozen or so ambulances, while half a dozen men in silvered, flame-retardant clothing and respirator-equipped hoods waited to go down to the station vault. Security guards were on hand, checking off the names of victims as they came up in the cages. Nearby, a detachment of firemen waited for the authority to enter the tunnel.

There were a few dozen high-ballers wandering around as well, wanting to be helpful and generally getting in the way. He hated to do it, but he'd have to get Richards's security guards to clear them out. It wouldn't be easy—their friends were down below.

Lights were on in the nearby instrumentation shack where Tisch was reading the data from the continuous-sampling gas detectors in the forward part of the cut. The last word was that the gas concentration was attenuating and the temperature near the region of the cave-in slowly declining. It would be good news for Chief Osmond, who had been wanting to send his men down there for the last half-hour.

Who was it who had almost gotten up to the fire itself? DuBois? Word was that he had brought out Chris Laverty, a high-baller, and Deborah Stuart from Accounting.

He shivered and went back inside. Youngblood and Richards had just walked in, judging from the snow on their coats. Grimsley and Zumwalt looked as if they had been waiting a while.

He nodded to Richards and said wearily, "What're the numbers?"

"Fifty-eight confirmed dead, but that will go higher. More than two hundred have either been checked into hospitals or are down in the station vault awaiting processing." He hesitated. "I'm afraid some of them can't be moved, at least for a day or so. We should be able to move them then, one way or the other."

"The missing?"

"According to our own check-in records, thirty-two people are still missing." A slight hooding of the eyes was the only indication of his own personal concern for Cyd Lederley. "They're presumed dead."

"East Portal?"

"Total's still the same, fewer missing, more dead."

He turned to Youngblood. "What about the Navy?"

"Four burn teams just arrived, plus enough corpsmen and equipment to handle the people who . . . have to stay down in the station vault, at least for now."

That would take some of the load off the local hospitals and medical personnel. He pitied the authorities in Benton Harbor and the surrounding towns in Michigan. The numbers there were even worse than they were here, and the facilities didn't even come close to handling the load. They were having to fly victims to burn units in Grand Rapids and Detroit.

"Grimsley, you've been down there." He didn't add, *against his orders*. "What's the situation in the tunnel itself?"

Grimsley was soot-stained and his face looked as if it had a light burn; he'd gone far closer to the head of the cut than he should have, Metcalf thought. But then, there had been no way of keeping him out of the tunnel.

Grimsley looked self-conscious. "There were two explosions. I think the first one occurred twenty feet east of hole-through and ripped up maybe two hundred yards of tunnel going toward the East Portal. The reports are it took down most of the shields and a good part of the tunnel arch in the area."

Nobody got out except those who had been in the tunnel going toward the celebration and who for one reason or another had been late, Metcalf thought. The explosion had occurred before they got there. They probably wouldn't make it early to work for the rest of their lives.

"There was another explosion and fire west of the face," Grimsley continued. "Not quite as bad, and not involving as long a stretch of the tunnel. The explosion and the fireball traveled toward the West Portal." He shivered. "Pinnelli went down with me, you can ask him for a report later—he's down below getting some burn salve for his face." He caught Metcalf's expression and added quickly, "Nothing really serious."

Metcalf motioned him over to the light table, where Zumwalt had laid out a diagram of the tunnel system.

"Show me the location of the explosions."

They gathered around the table, and Grimsley pointed to the explosion centers and the directions of the subsequent fireballs and tunnel destruction. Metcalf laid his hand on the drawing.

"Could anybody have survived in between the two gas explosions?"

Grimsley shook his head. "I wouldn't bet on it."

"I would." Metcalf tried not to sound desperate. "They were right between, they were right by the face of the cut." He turned to Zumwalt. "Rob, what's your opinion? You know the strata down there, you've got a pretty good idea what the force of the explosions might have been."

Zumwalt avoided Metcalf's eyes. "Jesus, Troy, what do you want me to say? I don't see how anybody could have survived in between the explosions, I just don't see how. . ."

Nobody wanted to tell him the truth, Metcalf thought—that nobody could have lived through it. Maybe it was something psychological, but he couldn't buy the idea that Nordlund was dead. Or Kaltmeyer or DeFolge or any of the rest of them. They had been too much of his life for far too long; he couldn't believe they were gone, as quickly and as easily as wiping numbers off a blackboard.

"I've got to go down there," he said.

If nobody else could convince him, maybe he'd have to convince himself.

He slipped into his coat and hurried down to the compound, stopping first at the instrumentation shack, where a pale-faced Tisch was jotting down figures from the thermopyles and the continuous-sampling gas detectors.

"How safe, Herb?"

Tisch glanced up from his notebook. "We're getting there. The temperatures are down, and there's been a sharp decline in methane and hydrocarbons. Don't know whether the methane's down because the ventilators are diluting it or simply that the pocket is exhausting itself. But there's still a fire near the face of the cut."

"Will I need a mask?"

Tisch looked surprised. "You going down?" Metcalf nodded. "Yeah, I'd take one along—better safe than sorry." He put down his clipboard and held out his hand. "Good luck."

"I'll be back in an hour or so." Then: "How about the firemen? Okay for them?"

"Sure, send them down. Masks and Airpaks, and tell them to be careful about using their pulldown tools—if they start messing around with some of those burned wall shields, they could end up burying themselves."

Outside the shack, he hurried over to Chief Osmond and the crews waiting by their trucks.

"You can send your men down now. But there's still danger of cave-ins, so tell them to be careful." He frowned. "How the hell are you going to fight it?"

Osmond was a bulky, professional type who looked as if he'd spent a lifetime fighting cork fires in cold storage warehouses.

"With everything I've got—with explosives, if I have to."

Metcalf looked grim. "Tell me that, and I won't let you go near the cut, Chief. That's a methane fire down there; use explosives, and you'll open up another gas pocket and sacrifice all your men and some of mine."

"You going to let it burn itself out?" Osmond protested.

"If I have to. The ventilators are diluting the gas to the point where it may extinguish itself. After that, we'll try to get any survivors out past the cave-in area."

"You're so sure there're survivors?"

"I don't know. This is a freak double cave-in—they may be trapped in the middle."

Osmond was suddenly less sure of himself.

(267

"What're the chances for another cave-in?"

"Damned good. The wall shields were never meant to withstand fire—heat degrades both the polyester-fiberglass shells and the gunnite. Maybe the whole tunnel will collapse before this is over."

"And if you're lucky?"

"Then we'll dig out anybody who's trapped beyond the cave-in area."

A cage was just rising to the top of the access shaft with two men in silver flameproof suits, along with a woman in a paisley dress and two men in smoke-stained business suits, one of whom was coughing violently and leaning against the side of the cage.

"Medic!" Metcalf yelled. Several corpsmen hurried over to help the men and the woman into waiting ambulances. Metcalf stopped a member of the rescue crew.

"How is it down there?"

The man took off his hood. Thomas Buchser, one of the high-ballers.

"Smoky—there's still a fire in the forward area near the face."

"Any more people?"

"Yeah, they're still coming out—mostly walking wounded. There're probably some still alive farther back in the tunnel, but I don't know how far. You want us to go back?"

Another cage came up and corpsmen swirled about it.

"*—broken arm, some smoke inhalation—*"

"*—needs a respirator—*"

"*—morphine over here! On the double—*"

"How many times you been down, Buchser?"

"Pyott and me have made maybe half a dozen trips." His voice sounded harsh and strained.

"Take a break—there are other crews who can go."

Grimsley and Zumwalt followed him as he hurried over to one of the cages. Just before he reached it, a voice shouted, "Get a shot of him!"

Somebody was aiming a television camera at him, and the next moment a microphone was thrust in his face. "Shelly

Leonard, *Chicago Chronicle*—I've heard the explosion resulted from an accumulation of methane in a pocket off the main tunnel."

Metcalf was curt. "You the pool reporter?"

"Pool reporters are down below. You care to comment on the cause of the explosion, Mr. Metcalf?"

"You're unauthorized, Leonard. Get off the station."

"It's a free country, Mr. Metcalf—you *are* Metcalf, aren't you?" He was intense, aggressive—and he was taking up valuable time. Metcalf wanted to slug him but knew he'd have to be diplomatic. Leonard read his expression and grinned. "Care to comment, Mr. Metcalf?"

Reluctantly. "Yes, our gas samplers indicate there was a methane pocket."

The camera was on Leonard now, and he raised his eyebrows in mock surprise.

"You didn't have any warning of the methane build-up?"

"Not on this side. I can't answer for the eastern leg—they have their own instrumentation."

"What set off the explosion?" There was an undertone to Leonard's voice that Metcalf didn't like.

"We're investigating that."

"I understand somebody fired a shot."

Leonard was out for The Big Story.

"I said we're investigating." He tried to sidestep, but Leonard edged in front of him. The camera was on the reporter again.

"The public has a right to know, Mr. Metcalf. It's paying your salary—"

Grimsley stepped in. "You want me to get rid of this turkey?"

Leonard ducked around Grimsley, waving his microphone at Metcalf.

"Don't you have detection methods sensitive enough to map out such gas pockets and determine if they're a hazard?"

"I didn't conduct the soundings," Metcalf said bitterly. He wanted desperately to get down into the tunnel. "I only work with the results. I can't comment on the soundings or their validity."

(269

He tried to push past the reporter, but Leonard blocked his way again, his voice coming out in little puffs of vapor.

"Can't, Mr. Metcalf—or won't?"

Another time, another place, he might have suffered Leonard. But he had been through too much, and there was too much more to come. He no longer cared what anybody thought, and the nice thing about not caring was that he didn't have to stop to think about what he did next.

He hit Leonard with everything he had, and the reporter went down without a sound. The cameraman casually tilted the camera and took in Leonard lying flat on the trampled snow.

"Can you take care of him?" Metcalf rubbed his bruised knuckles. "I don't want to assign a corpsman. They've got more important things to do."

The cameraman nodded. "No problem. You'll be hearing from us, by the way."

"Contact the company lawyer." Metcalf hurried for the access shaft.

"We'll take up a collection back in the newsroom!" the cameraman shouted. "For you!"

"Didn't think you had it in you," Grimsley said, visibly impressed.

"Surprised me, too," Metcalf murmured, immensely satisfied with himself. Then they were in a cage plunging down the access shaft.

Another twenty minutes or so, and maybe he'd know whether Nordlund was alive or dead.

The station vault was chaos. The caterers' tables had been pushed over to one side; half the sandwiches and the little cakes and shrimp were lying in smelly piles on the vault floor. At the far end was a makeshift hospital, with the wounded lying on cots and covered with blankets, a number of them with IVs taped to their arms. A few feet away were serried ranks of dead in body bags. They'd be taken out once the wounded had been evacuated. There was no hurry for the dead.

Closer, by the cages, security guards were taking down the names of everybody going up the shaft, checking them against

(270

the list of guests who had come down just a few hours before. One of the guards was going through the pockets of the dead searching for ID, while another was sifting through the contents of a stack of purses, also searching.

The muck train came out of the tunnel, loaded with rescue crews and a number of bodies. Metcalf forced himself to walk over and look at them as the bodies were handed down. A number of high-ballers whom he knew, but no Dane or Cyd or Kaltmeyer or DeFolge or Derrick.

He walked over to Scott Morgan, the head of the crew. "How's the air in there?"

"Stinks, but it's breathable." Morgan took off his hard hat and wiped the sweat from his face. "You got to expect that—considering. A number of guys back there were really cooked." He looked as if he were going to be sick.

"Anybody left alive?"

"A few walkers. We'll pick them up next time in." He waved at the bodies still being carried off the train. "Thought we'd bring these poor bastards out first. Who knows, we might've goofed—maybe some of them are still breathing. If you get them here as soon as possible, they might have a chance."

He frowned at Metcalf, dubious. "It's no picnic in there. We didn't get them all, you know. The ones we skipped aren't very nice to look at."

Metcalf grabbed an electric car, and Grimsley climbed in beside him. They were about half a mile into the tunnel when Grimsley said, "Slow down. Somebody's walking this way."

Metcalf slowed, then made out the figure of a man limping toward them. He caught his breath. The man was wearing a suit and looked about Nordlund's height and weight. He stopped the car and ran over to help.

"Dane! Dane?"

The figure shook its head. "He didn't make it," it croaked.

His face was sooty, almost unrecognizable, but there was no mistaking the accent. Phillips.

"Anybody behind you?"

Phillips shook his head, grimacing with sudden pain.

"The moment I heard the first shot, I ran. If somebody was

aiming at anybody official, they wouldn't overlook me. I glanced back at the second shot and saw the explosion. Nobody in the first few rows made it out."

"Tell me what happened at the explosion," Metcalf said. "Try and be as precise as possible."

There was a thread of annoyance in Phillips's voice. The explosion and cave-in hadn't changed the bastard at all.

"What do you mean, 'What happened?' The roof caved in, that's what happened. The rocks came down, and that's all I saw. Everybody trampled over everybody else on the way out. It wouldn't have done any good to stay behind, nothing I could have done to help. I got a couple hundred feet down the tunnel, and there was another explosion." He shuddered. "I didn't look back."

Just as well he didn't, Metcalf thought. "How's your leg?"

"I don't know. Think it's bruised, that's all."

"Climb in—we'll take you back."

They took Phillips back to the station vault, then turned the car around and started out again. After a mile a frowning Grimsley said, "I think we ought to let the rescue crews take care of the walkers. Otherwise, we'll never get to the face of the cut."

Metcalf's first impulse was to protest, then he nodded. "Right."

Another half a mile.

"He mentioned a shot," Grimsley said. "I'd forgotten."

"So has everybody."

He'd have to talk to Richards about it when he got back. About who could have been down here, who would have wanted to shoot Kaltmeyer. For the first time, it occurred to him that it was probably the shot that shattered the thin wall between the tunnel and the methane pocket and ignited it.

They passed a dozen more walkers but didn't stop. The air in the tunnel now had a disagreeable, scorched smell. It took him a moment to identify it, and when he did, he almost gagged. Once on the freeway, he'd been present when a cattle car and a gasoline truck had collided. The smell was very similar.

The signs of fire were everywhere now, the wall shields sooty and scorched. The heat had been sufficient to partially decompose the gunnite, and the shields where they met at the tunnel arch were badly bowed. He'd have to get crews down here with titanium bracing to shore them up. Then they passed the huge shadow of the mole, and a moment later the car's headlight picked out the slope of the cave-in. They had gone farther into the tunnel than anybody else, and the air was hot and stuffy. He knew better than to touch the metal skin of the mole, but there was no fire—thank God for that.

He stopped the electric car, and they walked over to the debris slope. It was unstable and decidedly hot to the touch. He wondered if a fire was roaring on the other side, then decided it wasn't. Tisch had said the temperatures were close to normal.

There was a sudden groan from the rocks overhead, and they froze, too petrified to move.

"I think we ought to get out of here," Grimsley said nervously. "I don't know what the hell we can do."

"You're right. We can't do anything right now."

He turned the car around and the headlight flashed over a patch of gray fabric caught beneath the debris of the slide. Metcalf stared, then ran over and started digging frantically around the rocks, ignoring Grimsley's shouts that he would bring the entire roof down on them.

Janice.

He remembered she'd been dressed to kill in a gray wool dress and a pink scarf. That was the only way he knew that the crumpled, bloody body half-hidden beneath the debris was hers. The dress and the scarf and the shattered gold-framed glasses still attached to the silver chain she wore around her neck.

The tears had been a long time coming, but now he couldn't hold them back.

CHAPTER 33

None of them were doing very well, Nordlund thought. The fires were out, and the air was turning chilly. Cyd and Diana and Derrick hadn't spent any time below, and he doubted that DeFolge was very familiar with tunnels or caves. Certainly none of them had ever spent hours sitting in the cold and clammy dark. They had turned the lanterns on low to save batteries, and now the cave and tunnel were populated only by shadows.

Lynch was coming unglued, Diana seemed distant, and an increasingly nervous DeFolge sat apart from the rest of them, occasionally walking over to a barely conscious Kaltmeyer to whisper to him. He seemed at once friendly to, and annoyed with, Kaltmeyer. Nordlund couldn't put the two attitudes together, finally concluding that DeFolge wanted desperately to discuss something and was frustrated and angry that Kaltmeyer couldn't reply.

Cyd held her watch closer to the lantern so she could read the time.

"It's been five hours, Dane. I know they'll dig us out, but I can't help but wonder."

"I've got great faith in Metcalf," Nordlund said. But he kept thinking of all the times they had disagreed about a project and all the times Metcalf had used poor judgment.

"Dane?" Derrick had been sitting by Kaltmeyer and now looked up, concerned. Diana put her hand on his shoulder, but he shook her off. "It's Dad. Could you take a look?"

Nordlund and Cyd hurried over. Nakamura had contributed his overcoat along with Nordlund's to help him keep warm and Kaltmeyer's skin was now far less gray. The fine tremors had faded. He was conscious and trying to talk. Nordlund leaned closer. The only word he could make out was *water*.

"He's dehydrated," Diana said sharply.

(274

The earlier attack of shock-induced perspiration had probably done it, Nordlund thought. But there wasn't any water, and the Thermos containers of coffee had long since been emptied.

He shrugged his shoulders, helpless, then remembered when Dietz had called the day before and said they would be having a party on the eastern side of the cut after hole-through. He took one of the battery lanterns and started for the tunnel. "I'll be right back."

It wasn't much of a chance, but you never knew. He stepped up onto the wooden speaker's platform and climbed over the shattered rock into the eastern half of the cut. There had been a landslide, but it was a good thirty feet from the site of hole-through to where the debris fan started.

He sniffed. Something funny about the air. And then he knew what it was and shivered—the stink of death. He flashed the beam from the lantern around the tunnel. The pocket of gas had exploded just past the curtain of rock, and the fire had flared from there on back. There were dozens of huddled bodies on the tunnel floor just before the start of the landslide, and he guessed the landslide itself covered hundreds more.

He took a hurried look. Some had obviously died of asphyxiation; others had been burned beyond recognition. One of them had died while drinking a can of beer, and Nordlund had a sudden surge of hope. They'd been celebrating like Dietz had said they would.

He walked up to the edge of the debris fan and searched the walls with the lantern, finally spotting a small side bore, one of many intended to connect with the service tunnel. If he were going to be lucky, that's probably where the lightning would strike.

He was luckier than he had hoped. Set far back in the small tunnel were some cans of beer. He fished out the first one and swore. It had exploded from the heat.

The cans behind it were in better shape. Five cans of warm beer, probably saved because the liquid from the exploding can in front had cooled them enough so that they hadn't suffered the same fate.

He pulled out the cans, then hurried back to the cave. Diana looked up in surprise and he said, "Beer—it was all I could find."

"It will have to do. At least it'll put some sugar into his system. Raise his head—but be careful!" Her voice was sharp, and he felt sudden anger. They were all under a lot of stress; Diana wasn't the only one. He glanced over at Cyd, who shook her head, warning him to be silent. Apparently Kaltmeyer had become Diana's project. To have a "project" had always been her alternative to dealing with life's problems.

He popped open one of the cans and gave it to her, then lifted Kaltmeyer's head. Kaltmeyer groaned and partially opened his eyes when Diana moistened his lips with the beer. He drank a third of the can before he raised a hand to wave it away.

"Ricky?" he whispered.

Derrick moved closer. "Right here, Dad."

Kaltmeyer looked at Nordlund. "What happened, Dane?"

"Gas explosions, two of them. They dropped a lot of the tunnel roof before and after us."

"There shouldn't . . . be any gas pockets around the tunnel site."

But he looked away when he said it, and Nordlund felt a sudden pang. DeFolge and Lammont weren't the only villains in the disaster.

"He's tired," Diana said, moving in to protect him. "He can't answer any questions right now."

"I wasn't asking any, I was answering some," Nordlund said, angry. There were several hundred people in the tunnel who would have loved to ask a question or two.

If they had been able to.

He took one of the lanterns and walked over to sit with his back against the wall of the cave with Cyd and Nakamura.

"She's very possessive of him," Cyd said in a soft voice.

"She's always been possessive of the men in her life," Nordlund said, and was sorry the moment he said it. The past made no difference now; the marriage was dead and buried.

"I do not think it has anything to do with being possessive," Nakamura said slowly. "She is full of . . . contradictions. She loves the boy, but I am not sure she loves the man."

Nordlund glanced back to see Diana, silhouetted by the lantern, leaning over Kaltmeyer, stroking his head and listening to him breathe. Derrick was crouched nearby, his eyes intent on his father's face. A strange sort of family tableau, he thought.

"She likes him well enough; Kaltmeyer's her godfather."

He reached down and flipped the switch on the battery lantern so its beam faded again to a soft yellow. He reached into his pocket. "The last chocolate bar," he said, handing it to Cyd. "You can divide it up when the time comes."

"Too late, I'll eat it myself." She meant it as a joke, but it fell flat, and there was a long moment of silence. Nordlund was unpleasantly aware of the stillness of the cave, the slight musty odor of damp rock and earth, and somewhere in the cave system behind them, the small, sharp, staccato sounds of drops of water hitting stone.

"You ever been trapped underground before?" Cyd asked in a quiet voice. "Either of you?"

Nordlund shook his head. Nakamura said, "I was once. It was a long time ago, and the tunnel was a relatively small one on Hokkaido. We were buried alive for something like twenty hours. I became very fatalistic after that. But I firmly believe I shall die in bed."

"All high-ballers think that," Nordlund said.

"I think perhaps they are looking for a kind of rebirth underground. What you might call a return to the womb." Nakamura smiled in the gloom. "I have come to believe my wife when she insists that a family spirit watches over me."

"He must have been looking the other way at hole-through," Nordlund said.

Nakamura shook his head in protest.

"We have been lucky. By all rights, we should have perished in the first few moments. The collapse of the roof undoubtedly shielded us from the violence of the second explosion. Nor were we consumed in the fire. The gods must really love us to have worked so hard against the odds."

(277

There was a sound behind them, and Nordlund turned to see Swede come back into the cave. He had been baby-sitting Lynch out in the tunnel; the young high-baller had taken DeFolge's words to heart and insisted on remaining in the cut, afraid he'd be overlooked by the rescue party if he were trapped in the cave. The fact that DeFolge had later sought shelter there didn't seem to make any difference.

"There's something you ought to see, Dane."

Nordlund followed him out. Swede walked over to the landslide and held his hand at the bottom. Nordlund crouched beside him.

"Feel the air currents?" Swede asked.

Nordlund moistened his hand and ran it along the loose edge of the debris. Then he pulled a pack of matches from his pocket, lit one, and held it along the edge. The flame flickered, bending sharply toward the pile. The air flow was now away from the chamber.

"They've reversed the ventilators. The fire must be out. That means they'll be digging us out soon."

Swede crossed himself, and Nordlund looked surprised. "I didn't know you were religious."

"I wasn't," Swede said.

Before going back into the cave, Nordlund walked over to take a look at Lynch, who was lying on his back and breathing heavily.

"How're you feeling, Lynch?"

"It's hard to breathe," Lynch gasped.

"It's probably an anxiety attack and you're hyperventilating. Try holding your hands over your nose and breathing through your nostrils—get a lot of carbon dioxide into your system."

But it *was* stuffy in the tunnel, despite the air flow from the cave. He felt uneasy. It could be a carbon dioxide build-up from the same source as the methane, which meant they'd have to get more air in there as soon as possible.

But that was impossible. Nobody even knew they were there.

When he reentered the cave, DeFolge said nervously, "Dane, let's talk for a moment."

Nordlund walked over and crouched down beside him. "I don't think we have that much to talk about, Senator."

Strangely, DeFolge was sweating. "You've got me pegged as the villain, Dane, but you're not thinking. I'm trapped down here just like you. Why the hell would I endanger my own life? Or Diana's? If I had thought the tunnel was unsafe, why would I even have come down here? Both Frank and I were taken in by Lammont—he had the best reputation in the business, and believe me, he charged the corporation a handsome fee."

"Lammont did whatever you told him to do; you were paying him. It wasn't the other way around."

In the light of the battery lantern, DeFolge looked strained and haggard.

"If there's another landslide, I'll be buried right along with you. If there's another fire down here, I'll burn right along with you. What more do you want, Dane—blood?"

"There's been enough of that shed already—and all of it innocent."

"I've made mistakes," DeFolge said, his eyes luminous in the gloom. "I tried to buy you. But long before then, I gave you the most valuable thing in my life—my daughter. You can claim that I bought you for her, but that's a two-way street, it's just as valid the other way around. Think about it for a moment, Dane. You haven't always been right in your judgments. What if this time you're wrong?"

Nordlund didn't answer but turned and walked back to Cyd, now sitting on a little ramp of rocks that led up to where the partition had been. Nakamura had gone into the tunnel, probably to check on the same flow of air that Swede had shown him.

"What'd he say?" Cyd asked, curious.

"What you might expect. That I was making a big mistake, that I had him pegged all wrong."

"He almost convinced you, didn't he?"

"You underestimate me, Cyd."

She was silent for a moment, then said quietly, "Sometimes I don't give people enough credit, Dane."

He reached out and squeezed her hand. "I'm naïve, but not that naïve."

It was getting colder, he thought; the rocks they were sitting on felt clammy. Without the fire raging on the other side of the landslide, it was to be expected. But a few hours of falling temperature, and they would all be in bad shape. And it wouldn't be long before the bodies they had stacked at the far end of the tunnel and those in the eastern side of the cut became a psychological problem, if nothing else. The dead made poor company, a constant reminder of what might happen to them. Lynch wouldn't be able to take that for long and, he guessed, neither would Diana or Derrick.

"What do you think of the senator, Cyd?"

"Right now?"

"Yeah."

She shrugged. "I think he's got a galloping case of claustrophobia and it's all he can do to keep from screaming. For a longer view, I think he's very dangerous. There are hundreds of people dead, and somebody will have to pay for it. His friends on Capitol Hill can't help the senator now."

He thought about it for a moment, then asked, "What about Diana?"

"Don't ask me, Dane. She's still your wife—and I don't really know just how . . . separated you are."

She was right, of course. Diana couldn't give him a family; Diana had made an art of hurting him. But there had never been the finality of divorce, and until there was, she would always have a hold on him.

"Tell me anyway. I won't hold it against you."

She sighed. "I'm not so sure of that." After a moment: "I think she's very frightened of something, too. But it's not the same thing the senator's frightened of. And I don't think it has anything to do with you."

Off-the-cuff opinions were like Tarot card readings and probably no more reliable.

"I better check on Swede and Lynch."

"I'll come along." She scrambled off the ramp, then knelt to pick something up. "You dropped your lighter."

He stopped, the hair on the back of his neck rising slightly. "What lighter?"

"The one you left back there on the rocks," she said.

"I don't use one." He held up the lantern to see it.

"It's not mine," she said, puzzled. She looked back at the little ramp of rocks. "But nobody else was over there."

He walked back and flashed the light from the battery lantern over the rocks they had been sitting on. Some of them looked wet, and he touched his hand to one, then held it closer to the light. Cyd gasped. There was a bright smear of red on his palm. They had been sitting in small pools of blood.

He shifted the beam to the ground and picked up a trail of large wet splotches that led off into the chain of smaller caves.

He had forgotten about the man who had shot Kaltmeyer, the man who had built the little ramp of rocks so he could lie on it and sight through the plywood partition with his rifle. He must have been injured in the explosion, and when they came into the cave, he'd fled into the caverns just beyond, still carrying his rifle.

Max Orencho had been electrocuted in his own bathtub, Henry Leaver had been burned alive in his car, Styron had been shot, and DeFolge's car had been sabotaged so both DeFolge and Kaltmeyer would have been killed in an accident on the expressway.

Cyd's theory about a group of terrorists murdering the men most responsible for the cut hadn't proved very realistic after all. It wasn't a group, it was just one man.

Nordlund felt his heart suddenly lurch.

Not only had they been trapped underground, they had been trapped along with a madman.

CHAPTER 34

Progress was slow but steady—and grim, Metcalf thought. In addition to the rescue teams digging at the head of the cave-in, there was a team of Navy corpsmen standing by to zip up the dead in body bags and take them back to the station vault for identification.

Battery-powered lanterns were still the only source of light, but electricians were rigging temporary power lines and had trucked in half a dozen huge floods. A team of high-ballers had brought small portable shields up to the wall of debris as protection for the teams clearing away the rock and the spoil. They were moved forward as the men tunneled deeper into the debris.

Metcalf glanced at Tisch standing next to him, intent on the dials of a portable gas detector. With his graying hair and long horseface, Tisch always reminded him of a friendly undertaker. His nervousness was catching.

"How's the air?"

"All right—so far, at least. A slight rise in methane." He glanced around the tunnel, as if he could smell where the gas was coming from. "There's a slow leak from someplace, but it doesn't seem to be serious."

Behind him, Metcalf heard the clatter of the muck train as it pulled up to the debris fan. Pinelli jumped off the lead car, and Grimsley climbed down after him.

"I've got just what the doctor ordered, Troy—Ziegler rigged it up in the shop." Pinelli pulled a length of one-inch pipe off the train and handed it over to him.

He looked at it dubiously. "Is this going to be big enough?"

"Plenty big for air." Pinelli waved at the stack of pipe behind him. "I brought fifteen sections, each one a yard long. They screw together." He demonstrated with another length of pipe. He was obviously very proud of it. "There's a cutter that fits on the end, and it can bore through loose rock; the whole stretch of pipe is rotated through a series of step-down gears. It may not work with all fifteen sections, but I'd bet money it'll work with eight or ten."

Metcalf handed the pipe to Grimsley. "What about it, Evan? Will it work?"

Grimsley looked as if he had reservations but nodded. "If Pinelli thinks it'll work, it'll probably work. I figure it's sort of like a power drill."

"Naw, you don't have the picture at all," Pinelli said in disgust. "It's more like a Roto-Rooter." He fingered the end of the pipe, pointing out the drilling head of carborundum and tungsten. "Should cut through most rock like a knife cutting through cheese. Once it bores into a cave or whatever, compressed air will pop off the cutter and you can pump through air or water for anybody who's trapped."

Metcalf pointed at the debris pile. "Okay, let's see it work."

Pinelli positioned the drive motor on the tunnel floor, outside the small shield where the rescue teams were digging. "It'll take a few minutes. We'll have to bolt the motor to the concrete."

Twenty minutes later, he had secured the motor to the tunnel floor. Then he connected the first section of pipe to the rotating fixture on the motor and added a yard-long extension. Grimsley was right, Metcalf thought; it looked more like a horizontal drill press than anything else.

Pinelli positioned the head of the pipe at the base of the debris wall. He started the gasoline motor and eased the starting lever forward as the pipe slowly rotated. The cutting end began chewing into the debris. The vibrations shook down a small amount of rock from the overhead. Metcalf glanced up in alarm, then relaxed when it stopped.

Half an hour later, two sections of pipe had disappeared under the debris. Pinelli disengaged the gear train to add another section.

It would work, Metcalf thought. The unknown factor was

how many sections of pipe would be needed, and was there really a pocket between the two cave-ins to begin with?

By the end of the second hour, they had cut at least twelve feet into the pile of debris. Pinelli added still another section of pipe and winked at Metcalf. "Piece of cake."

Metcalf nodded his approval and walked over to Tisch, huddled over his instruments. "How's the air holding up?" He was almost afraid to ask.

"The methane's up a few parts per million, but I don't think it's anything to worry about." He sounded uncertain, the note of unease in his voice even more pronounced.

Metcalf looked over Tisch's shoulder, so intent on reading the dials and interpreting the figures for himself that he wasn't aware of the electric car that had driven up until he heard Phillips's voice in his ear.

"Glad to see you're moving right along, Troy."

Phillips and Youngblood had come down together. The Bureau of Mines man walked over to inspect the titanium piping they were using for shoring. He nodded once at Metcalf but stayed over by the work area.

Phillips had washed and was now wearing a clean suit; he must have kept a spare in the office. He didn't look any the worse for wear except for a deceptively sleepy air about the eyes and, surprisingly, a slight stagger when he walked. He probably had a shot too many to bolster his courage before coming back to the tunnel, Metcalf thought, then changed his mind in favor of twenty milligrams of Valium—it was more Phillips's style.

Phillips smiled. "You making good progress, Troy?"

It was the smile that did it. Metcalf was immediately on guard.

"Not too bad. It will take perhaps three days to clear the debris—provided there are no more explosions or cave-ins and depending on the conditions we find farther in."

"Three days." Phillips looked thoughtful. "If we used the mole, we could get through the debris quicker than that, couldn't we?"

Metcalf had trouble hiding his annoyance.

"Sure, we could use the mole, Steve—and half an hour later we could start digging it out, too. I'd make book that the rest of the tunnel would collapse around it."

Phillips nodded, as if he had asked a question to which he already knew the answer but wondered if Metcalf knew it, too. He walked over and looked at the piping slowly drilling its way through the bottom of the debris fan.

"You're going as fast as you can, right?"

Metcalf nodded. "That's right."

Phillips touched the piping with his foot. "What's this for?"

"Pump in air. For survivors."

"Survivors." Phillips studied the piping for a moment, then looked up at Metcalf in feigned wonder. "That's irrational, Troy. There were no survivors—I know. I was the last one out, remember? Or damned close to it."

Metcalf fought to control his temper.

"We have reason to believe there was a pocket between the two explosions. If a pocket exists, then there may have been survivors who are trapped in it."

" 'If,' " Phillips mimicked. " 'May have been.' How about some proof?" He stepped so close, Metcalf could smell his mouthwash. "You're afraid to go too fast in clearing the debris for fear of bringing down the rest of the tunnel on any survivors, right? That's commendable, but the fact is we know who is dead, and we know who was wounded, and we know who survived. Those who are missing are dead. I've contacted outside authorities, and to a man they tell me there's no way anybody could have lived that close to the explosions."

He kicked at the pipe, and Metcalf almost hit him then and there.

"I think you ought to pull this out, and I think you ought to push your men as hard as you can."

"I don't think I ought to do any of that, Phillips." Metcalf fought to keep his voice even.

Phillips showed his teeth in a bleak smile. "You misunderstand me, Metcalf. I'm not asking you, I'm telling you. Washington has assured me I have complete authority."

There was no way Dane would have "handled" Phillips in

a situation like this, Metcalf thought. He would have taken a chance and hit him where he was weakest. And where Phillips was always weakest was in the assumptions he made about his own authority.

He looked over at Youngblood, standing a discreet distance away. Phillips had brought along his replacement.

"You're the heir apparent, Neal—I think you ought to be in on this." Youngblood walked over, a look of faint embarrassment on his face. Metcalf pointed his thumb at Phillips. "I imagine you talked to Washington, too. Is your understanding the same as his?" Phillips went white, and Metcalf knew he had guessed right.

Youngblood tried to hide his half-smile. "My understanding is that Mr. Phillips is authorized to replace you but not without cause."

"In your opinion, has he cause?"

Youngblood hesitated, glanced at the furious Phillips, and shook his head. "So far you've done exactly what I would have done."

Metcalf smiled at Phillips.

"Get the hell out of my tunnel, Steve. You're holding up progress." He turned back to the rotating length of piping, watching Phillips out of the corner of his eye as he stalked back to the car.

He had won the first round. But the moment he fucked up, he'd be out and Youngblood would be in charge. And neither Youngblood nor anybody else shared his faith that somehow Nordlund and the others had survived.

The floodlights lit up the face of the slide so brightly, it almost hurt Metcalf's eyes to look at it. They had pushed thirty feet of piping through the base of the debris, and now the air compressor was making soft muttering sounds as it delivered a steady flow of air through the pipe to the pocket beyond the wall of debris.

If there was a pocket. He had calculated the total distance from the start of the debris fan to where the pocket between the explosions had to be if it existed at all. Then he had gambled,

(286

stopping the drilling motor and blowing the cutter off the end of the pipe. There was no resistance; at least they had hit a void. Now either he was pumping air into a chamber holding some survivors or he was air-conditioning a crypt.

Phillips and Youngblood had returned and were watching from the tunnel wall. Youngblood talked to him from time to time, but Phillips stayed well out of harm's way, looking sour and disapproving.

During the last hour, more crews had moved in with additional titanium bracing for the damaged wall shields and a comm team had strung a sound-powered telephone line back to the Field Station. If he wanted them, Tisch could now telephone the instrumentation shack to get the latest gas level readings.

Pinelli was supervising a pick-and-axe brigade beneath the shield, and every few minutes Metcalf's heart would skip a beat when a spatter of rocks and dirt cascaded down from the overhead and hit the shield.

Grimsley drifted over to watch. He was nervous and sweaty, and finally Metcalf said, "What's eating you?"

Grimsley glanced up at the arch, then back to the rescue crews, now fifteen feet into the debris pile. "We tunneled through the strongest part of it the first time. What's up there now is just waiting to come down."

"We'll be okay once we replace the wall shields." Metcalf said it with assurance he didn't feel.

Underneath the small protective shield, the rescue crews were digging around two huge slabs of limestone that blocked the cut. Pinelli examined the slabs, then ran over to Metcalf. "We'll have to drill through these and take them out in sections."

"What about a jackhammer?"

Pinelli glanced up at the ceiling and shook his head. "Too risky—it's slower this way, but we'll live longer." He looked haggard, and Metcalf guessed that constant worry about the thousands of tons of groaning rock above his head had worn his nerves thin.

After Pinelli returned to the dig, Metcalf nudged Grimsley and said, "Have them turn one of those floods so it shines directly on the overhead." A moment later, he was staring up at the outer surface of the wall shield. It was smoky in color, and there were areas where the polyester had charred and bubbled.

Grimsley pointed to one section of the shield. "It's starting to buckle." A thin rain of particles suddenly spalled away from the ceiling and fell to the tunnel floor. Metcalf picked up one of the pieces. It was a blackened piece of fiberglass.

He turned and shouted to Pinelli, "The gunnite in that shield is half-powdered from the heat, Mark. We'll need more buttressing."

Pinelli threw him a mock salute. "You got it, boss."

The two slabs were the main holdup. There couldn't be that much more debris to dig through to get to the chamber in between the two explosions. But once he got through, would anybody still be alive?

He walked over and inspected the contents of one of the muck cars. Chunks of limestone, layered with organic matter. The stone cleaved easily along the thin lines of dark organic stuff. No wonder the men were making fast progress in removing the slabs. But it also meant the rock above them was exceptionally weak and porous.

He sniffed the air, then said, "Where's Tisch?"

Grimsley pointed. "In the corner, taking a leak. I'll get him for you."

Tisch came over and checked the portable gas detector, then called up to the instrumentation shack. When he hung up, he looked worried.

Metcalf could feel the sweat trickle down the back of his neck. "Is it really bad?"

"Not yet, but it's getting there. The methane's apparently oozing in from a side pocket."

All he wanted was enough time to get Nordlund and any other survivors out. "Give me a safety margin, Herb. When we hit it, we'll shut down all the gasoline motors and electrical equipment until we can flush it out—"

There was a shout and a rumble. Men suddenly bolted from under the portable shield, followed by a thick cloud of boiling dust. Metcalf tensed, ready to run. Then the sound of falling rock diminished, and moments later the tunnel was quiet again except for the mutter of the air compressor.

Pinelli appeared at the mouth of the small protective shield, completely gray from his hard hat to his workshoes.

"What the hell happened?" Metcalf yelled.

Pinelli walked over; rivers of sweat were carving thin channels in the dust that covered his face.

"The rocks shifted when we took out that last slab. We lost a good foot of progress."

He reached up to brush some of the grit off his forehead when a sudden rain of fiberglass fragments thudded down on his hard hat. One of the workmen pointed up and shouted, his words lost in the rumble from overhead.

Metcalf glanced up to where the floodlight still shone on the curved arch of the wall shield. A whole section of the shield was bowing, and the bow grew, even as he watched.

He yelled at Pinelli, "Get everybody out! Out!'

More and more material rained down from the overhead. Metcalf recognized the gritty green-gray particles of gunnite that had decomposed under the heat of the original explosion and fire. The crews were streaming past him now, and he finally turned and ran. Ten yards up the tunnel, he heard a loud ripping sound.

He spun around just in time to see a huge section of the wall shield separate and slowly collapse. Two men, caught in front of the small dig, disappeared from sight as the huge piece of shield struck the forward debris wall. The edge of it swept away the air compressor and hit Pinelli's ventilation pipe full on.

Metcalf turned and raced in the direction of the access shaft. Behind him, the earth and limestone strata overhead shrieked and groaned as tons of earth and rock plunged into the section of the tunnel he had just left.

A hundred yards farther back toward the access shaft, Metcalf paused and leaned against the side of the tunnel, his chest heaving. Pinelli and Grimsley sank to their knees on the tunnel floor.

(289

The wall shields here had been in place for several weeks and were relatively safe.

A boiling cloud of rock dust made it difficult to breathe and also hid the end of the cut. The floodlights had been swept away, but Grimsley turned on a battery lantern and several others followed. Pinelli got to his feet, shaking his head. "That whole last section slumped down like it was made of butter."

"Beardsley was right," Grimsley panted. "Give me cast iron any day."

He had lost the gamble, Metcalf thought dully. He had failed Nordlund and any others who might be trapped with him. But maybe he had been kidding himself all along. Maybe Phillips was right and they were all dead. And now two more had been added to the total.

"Evan, take a roll call. I'll need to know the names of those who didn't make it."

Grimsley came back a moment later. "Pyott and Benson. Some of the guys said they were up on the debris slope, right at the forward edge of the shield."

Metcalf looked back down the tunnel. "We have to check the damage."

"I'll go," Pinelli offered. "Moloney will go with me."

"Check it out and come right back. If you hear anything start to shift—anything at all—get the hell out of there."

"You don't have to tell me twice," Pinelli murmured.

Tisch walked over with the portable gas sampler and set it on the tunnel floor. He shook his head. "It's not good, Troy. Take a look."

Metcalf crouched down beside him. Tisch turned on the sampler, and the read-out windows lit up, brilliant squares of light in the dusty gloom. Metcalf watched as the numbers sped past, flickered back and forth, and finally settled down.

"Methane," Tisch said.

"Rate of increase?"

"Too high."

Metcalf stared at the haze into which Pinelli and Moloney had disappeared. "They'll be coming back in a minute."

"When they do, we better clear out," Tisch warned.

Metcalf nodded. "You're right. Start getting the rest of them out now."

He was standing alone by the battery when Phillips and Youngblood walked up.

"You're relieved, Metcalf!" Phillips said in a shrill voice. "As of right now! When you come up, I'll have the papers ready."

Youngblood said, "I'm sorry, Troy," and Metcalf guessed he had tried to argue with Phillips, that he had told Phillips that what had happened would have happened no matter who was in charge. But Phillips now had his grounds, and there was no way he could fight them.

Grimsley started to protest, but Metcalf held up his hand. "Save it, Evan—but thanks." He turned back to Youngblood, ignoring Phillips. "Pinelli and some men are checking out the damage. They'll be right back. I'll ride out with them."

A minute later, three figures appeared in the murk. Pinelli looked discouraged. "It's pretty nasty back there. Tons of stuff fell in, and the whole area is unstable. It'll take weeks to get through that mess."

"We'll get through it quicker than that," Phillips said bravely.

Pinelli stared at him, then spat on the floor. "Sure we will." He looked up at Metcalf. "You can smell the methane. I think this last cave-in opened another pocket, and my guess is that it's a big one."

Tisch switched on the sampler again, watching the delta indicator, the meter that showed the rate of increase. Metcalf guessed he would have given anything for a continuous monitor right then.

"Figure twenty minutes before it's explosive."

Metcalf turned to the crews who had crowded around him, waiting for a decision on what to do next.

"That's it! Cut all the motors and any other electrical equipment! Everybody back to the shaft!"

Youngblood touched him lightly on the shoulder. "We can all take the muck train back, Troy—save the walking."

Metcalf stared at him. The muck train. The long metal rails that ran beneath the cave-in and almost right up to the thin rock curtain that DeFolge and Kaltmeyer had smashed. The rails cut right into the pocket between the explosions.

He jerked away from Youngblood, grabbed a rock hammer from Pinelli's leather tool belt, and ran to the nearest rail. He hit it three times, waited a moment, then hit it three more times.

"Have you gone crazy, Metcalf?" Phillips was staring at him. Only Youngblood guessed what he was up to and ran over to the rail and put his ear next to it.

Metcalf held his breath.

It seemed like hours, but it was only a few seconds before they heard an answering three taps, loud and clear in the darkened tunnel.

CHAPTER 35

His right hand was very swollen now, though there were no signs of blistering. Not yet. His face, which had throbbed so painfully an hour or so ago, now felt numb. He knew he had been burned, but how badly he wasn't certain. If it were really serious, surely he'd be feeling far more pain. He could feel the skin of his face starting to pucker, and he was certain that some of it was blistered but convinced it wasn't that serious.

The rock beneath him was cold and damp, and he could feel it draining the heat from his body. He turned on his flashlight, shielding it so only a small glow escaped from one end, and looked around. There had been very little water seepage since this cavern had been carved out by some ancient stream. The ceiling glistened with solidified limestone from the earlier water flow, but there were no signs of further build-up, not even embryonic stalagmites or stalactites.

He felt around for the carbine in the darkness and pulled it closer to him. He could imagine what the others felt like in the main cavern, especially the civilians, being trapped below ground. To most high-ballers, it was the ultimate nightmare. But he had long ago made peace with himself about the hazards of his profession.

He remembered the stories his father—their father—told of working in the Lötschberg Tunnel in the Swiss Alps. How the rock within the tunnel had been under enormous pressure for aeons from the mountains all around it, and when the high-ballers had cut into it, the rock had lost its solidity and flowed like putty. . . .

It was getting hard to stay awake now. He felt enormously tired. Finally he lowered his head onto his arms and was asleep almost instantly. He was back in his father's home now—before the orphanage, when his parents were still alive, and they lived in a huge house on the corner in Forest Park, Illinois. It had been another world then, with a Gypsy family living across the street. The patriarch of the family made a living wrestling at carnivals with a trained bear. He remembered he had been good friends with the son, who had gone on to the University of Chicago and become a famous mathematician. . . .

When it was cold, the middle of winter, and he and Brad were very young, they had shared a bed in the unheated attic. The attachment had started then and had grown as they got older. When Christmas came, they would lie awake upstairs in the attic and listen to the sounds downstairs of closet doors being opened and gifts being taken out of their hiding places and arranged beneath the tree. The gifts he and Brad gave each other started taking on added significance.

He rolled in his sleep, and his head hit a rock. He woke to excruciating pain. He was still in a dream state, though this time it was a different dream. For a moment, he was back again in that other tunnel as the Klaxon sounded, and he was rushing forward, throwing himself through the airlock door. He dreamed once more of vainly trying to open the second door as the wall of water approached. The whole river now roared into the tunnel, and he relived that last terrible moment once again, looking through the glass at the doomed men and seeing that dear, now-dead face drift past his agonized stare.

He woke again, bathed in sweat, biting his lips to keep from screaming. He touched his face, trying to wipe away the perspiration. But his face felt hot and dry. He brushed his fingers across his forehead, then brought his hand down and rubbed his fingers together. They were sticky with moisture.

He gulped a breath of air and sat up in sudden alarm. An oppressive pressure was developing in his chest. He took another breath, then realized he wasn't getting enough oxygen. He sniffed suspiciously. The air had a faint, musty odor with a touch of corruption.

Gas, *he thought, and pulled himself painfully to his feet. He walked farther back into the cavern, noting without surprise that the floor of the cave was slowly rising. A few yards more, and he was above the level of the gas; there was no longer the feeling of constriction within his chest.*

He sat down on the cave floor behind a mass of rock that must have fallen from the roof decades before. He figured he had walked a good hundred yards back from the main cave. He wondered when the trapped group would start to move. It had to be soon, or they would succumb to the gas. He silently prayed that this wouldn't happen, enraged at the thought that the gas might cheat him of his final satisfaction.

He picked up the carbine and pumped a round into the chamber, wincing at the pain in his hand. Sooner or later, either the gas or a cave-in would drive the group in the main cave into this one, or perhaps into the one just beyond. But they would have to pass by him, and he would have his chance.

And then he remembered. He only had the one round; he had left the box of tracers in the main cave.

He'd have to go back and get it, and soon, before the gas got too bad.

CHAPTER 36

They had been trapped for thirteen hours, Nordlund thought, glancing at his watch. It was almost one o'clock, Monday morning. Christmas Eve. And there was actually something to be grateful for. Kaltmeyer was better, though DeFolge was still pale and sweating, constantly glancing at the rocks overhead. The others were holding up fairly well.

With the exception of Lynch. The man's deterioration had shocked him. Most of them had managed to doze off for a while, but Lynch had never closed his eyes nor left the base of the debris wall. Occasionally he would dig at the debris, and rock fragments would tumble down the slope. Then Lynch would retreat with a whimper and eye the barrier with a hurt look on his face.

"We ought to do something about him." Swede looked concerned.

"Like what? He's not causing any trouble. We couldn't do much anyway. Restrain him, that's about it."

Lynch watched them while they talked, his eyes wide and staring. Suddenly he scrabbled at the barrier, shouting, "They're coming, I can hear them!"

Nordlund hurried over and crouched down, listening. There was the occasional mutter from the groaning rocks above, but that was all. They were undoubtedly digging out the bodies trapped beneath the debris, but the sounds were masked by the noises from the limestone overhead or muffled by the dust that had sifted down into the tunnel.

He left Lynch in Swede's care and walked back into the cave.

As he entered, Kaltmeyer whispered, "Dane." He was sitting up, leaning on one elbow. Diana was in a corner talking in low tones with DeFolge, while Derrick had curled up a few feet

(296

away and gone to sleep, using a flat piece of rock for a pillow. Nordlund noticed with a sudden pang that Diana had draped her coat over his shoulders.

"Dane," Kaltmeyer called again. Nordlund couldn't tell whether he was whispering because he didn't want to wake Derrick or because his voice was weak. He walked over and sat down beside him. In the soft light from the lantern, Kaltmeyer looked remarkably improved; his skin color was good, and his eyes were alert.

"We had no idea this would happen," Kaltmeyer wheezed. It was an apology to the world.

Nordlund hesitated, then said, "Don't talk about it now. You can worry about it when we get out of here."

"I'll worry about it for the rest of my life."

Nordlund didn't say anything. Kaltmeyer wanted to talk, and the least he could do was listen.

"Alan and I started out together," Kaltmeyer continued in his thin voice. "We both worked for the same company. I was a supervisor, and Alan was the head accountant. I wanted a business of my own, and Alan had a good head for figures, plus family money." He chuckled softly in the gloom. "You don't run across that combination very often."

He was quiet for a long moment, thinking of the past. Nordlund guessed he thought he was going to die and was talking because he wanted some sort of validation for his life. He prompted Kaltmeyer noncommittally: "It couldn't have been easy."

"Getting the jobs was the tough part," Kaltmeyer whispered. "Making money on them was the easy part. With Alan . . . we couldn't miss. I'd worry, but we'd make it anyway." He was quiet again, then: "Sometimes we bid too low. We had to make it up on the job."

"Shaved costs?" The temptation to question Kaltmeyer was overwhelming.

A reluctant nod. "Shaved costs, shaved maintenance, bought old equipment, patched up what should have been thrown out. We weren't the only ones who did it, but we were the best at it."

Or the worst, Nordlund thought.

Kaltmeyer was getting restless. "We had accidents," he blurted. "But everybody has accidents, Dane, even the best of them."

"You always got along with Alan?"

"He wheeled and dealed. And I compromised. And then one day I . . . discovered I had nothing left to compromise."

"You should have broken up the partnership."

Kaltmeyer turned his face to the wall. "You're an innocent, Dane. That's what I've always liked about you."

"He's tired," Diana suddenly said in his ear. "Can't you see that? He needs some sleep."

Kaltmeyer looked up. "I don't need any sleep." He closed his eyes for a moment in contradiction, then opened them wide. "Always had high hopes for you, Diana. Hoped Dane would be your salvation."

DeFolge walked over, and Kaltmeyer winked at him. "Hi, partner. Looks like this is one we didn't pull off."

"You're talking too much, Frank," DeFolge said in a heavy voice.

"Don't worry." Kaltmeyer's chuckle turned into a thin wheeze. "Old Sam Wilcox is five miles away, Alan. And if we're ever dug out of here, we can always deny everything. Besides, Alan, what's the sense in having been a pirate all your life if you can't tell somebody you've been a pirate before you die?"

"You were talking about my daughter," DeFolge accused.

"The lovely Diana," Kaltmeyer sighed, closing his eyes again. Nordlund guessed that he really wanted to sleep now. "She *is* lovely, Alan, that's the one thing we never argued about. The good Lord knows we argued about everything else."

"You went along," DeFolge shouted, his face orange with anger in the yellow light from the lantern. "You cashed the checks. You weren't too proud to take the money!"

"I was poor once. I was afraid of staying poor."

DeFolge bent over him. "And I made you rich, remember?"

Kaltmeyer turned his face away. "You made me ashamed," he whispered.

Swede appeared in the entrance to the cave. He looked at Nordlund, ignoring the others. "Anything wrong, Dane? I heard some shouting."

DeFolge swore and stalked back to his corner of the cave. Diana followed him.

Nordlund shook his head. "Nothing's wrong. How's Lynch?"

Swede frowned. "I think I'm hearing something, too."

Back in the tunnel, Lynch crouched at the debris wall, his eyes intent on its base, like a cat at a mousehole. Nordlund walked over to the slope of rubble and listened carefully. This time he heard it—a distant, rasping sound.

"What the hell is it?" Swede asked.

Little landslides of rock were rolling down the face of the debris pile now as the scraping sounds grew louder.

"I think they're trying to force through a ventilation pipe."

The others had come out of the cave and gathered around Lynch. Several small rocks at the very bottom suddenly popped away from the base, and the first inch of a slowly rotating pipe appeared. A few minutes later something like a foot of pipe extended from under the pile.

Lynch grabbed for it and Nordlund yanked him back. "You'll cut yourself, Lynch—there's a drill head on the end of the pipe." The rotating tip suddenly blew off and ricocheted around the tunnel.

Swede ducked and swore. "They're trying to kill us, for God's sakes."

Then all of them were aware of the stream of cool air coming from the end of the pipe. Lynch promptly fell in front of it, his lungs working to suck in the fresh air.

"Get him the hell away from there!" DeFolge shouted.

"Screw you," Lynch mumbled. He took a stranglehold on the pipe.

Nordlund held up his hand.

"Listen."

It was the faint sound of shovels and pickaxes on the other side. Diana was the first one to shout, and then the others joined in. When they finally stopped, Nordlund shook his head, smiling. "They can't hear us—the noise on the other side is too much."

"It will not be much longer, I think," Nakamura said.

Nordlund added, "An hour or two more, and we should be out of here."

They carried Kaltmeyer into the tunnel and propped him up with his back to the tunnel wall. Then they sat on the dusty speaker's platform, waiting, trying to make small talk.

Lynch still clung to the pipe, and DeFolge paced nervously back and forth in front of the wall of rubble. Nordlund knew exactly what he was thinking. Once they were out, there would be a congressional investigation and DeFolge would have to testify. There would be obvious conflict-of-interest charges; after that, charges of corruption and mismanagement. And sooner or later a criminal trial.

Once DeFolge stopped pacing, looked directly at him, and said, "I've got friends, Nordlund. Powerful ones. Don't forget that."

"Is he always going to be like that?" Derrick asked. He was staring at Lynch, sprawled on the floor with both hands wrapped around the ventilation pipe, afraid to let go.

"I don't know, Derrick," Nordlund said. "Once we get out, we'll get him all the help we can."

He had seen men like Lynch after a cave-in once before. All of them had been badly shaken, but some had had their psyches shattered. He suspected they lived the rest of their lives in constant terror of confined spaces, whether the spaces were automobiles or elevators or simply small rooms—any one of them would bring back the horror of being trapped under tons of earth.

Derrick shivered. "I think he's scary."

"He's no danger," Nordlund said.

Nakamura looked curious. "Do you think he might be?"

"I think he might be if we tried to get him away from the pipe."

(300

Then Swede frowned and said, "Listen." Nordlund cocked his head. The sounds of digging from the other side had stopped. Diana looked directly at Nordlund, and once again her tone of voice was accusatory. "What's happening now?"

"Probably shoring up the section they just dug through."

"They wouldn't use explosives, would they?"

Swede looked disgusted. "That would bring down the whole damned tunnel."

Nordlund stared at Lynch and the pipe, thinking that something was basically wrong. Metcalf had made a mistake, he thought slowly. He had gambled; he didn't know whether they were alive or dead. He should have tried communicating through the pipe before hooking it up to the air pump. It had been a natural error in judgment—but errors in judgment could kill them.

For the first time, he wished somebody other than Metcalf were in charge.

There had been little landslides all the time they had been sitting there. Now there was a deep grinding sound, and a large mass of stone started to slide down the pile of rubble. Without thinking, Nordlund grabbed Lynch and yanked him away from the pipe. Rocks rolled down the twenty-foot slope, thudding onto the tunnel floor where Lynch had been a moment before. The tumbling rocks stopped, and he let Lynch go. The man whimpered and crawled back to the pipe.

Nordlund took the lantern and directed its beam at the ceiling. "Okay, folks, back to the cave. When they dig through what's left out there, it may weaken the ceiling, and we could be in trouble."

He hurried over to Kaltmeyer. "Feel strong enough to walk, Frank?"

Kaltmeyer looked pale. "I can make it if I can lean on you and Ricky."

Nordlund helped him up. "Let's try it." They had just gotten Kaltmeyer back inside the cave when there was an ominous rumbling.

"Everybody inside—let's go!"

Swede flashed his lantern at the tunnel arch, and Nordlund

(301

saw cracks spreading like those on a frozen pond in winter. He ran back to the cave mouth. "Lynch, get the hell in here!"

Lynch had the pipe in a death grip, ignoring the rocks crashing down around him. Swede yanked Nordlund back inside the cave just as a loud clang rang off the tunnel walls. Nordlund glanced back. Lynch had disappeared. So had the ventilation pipe.

After the rumbling died, he stepped back into the tunnel. Once again, they had been spared; the tunnel collapse had occurred on the other side of the pile of debris. But Lynch had vanished. He thought for a moment that Lynch might somehow have made it into the eastern half of the cut when Swede glanced over his shoulder and his eyes widened. "My God."

Something on the other side of the debris pile had struck the ventilation pipe with tremendous force. It had shot forward and pinned Lynch to the far wall of the tunnel, like a butterfly in a collector's box.

Nakamura and Cyd had followed him out into the tunnel. She saw the body and stared at it without expression. He couldn't tell whether she was shocked or not. It was his first real indication of what her life with the Bureau must have been like.

"We're really trapped now, aren't we?"

"It'll take more time for them to dig us out," he said slowly.

"Days?"

"Probably," he said. Then he added harshly, "Help Diana with Kaltmeyer and the boy; Swede and I will have to get Lynch down."

They carried the body into the eastern half of the cut and left it there. There was no point in trying to bury it; none of the others had been.

Merry Christmas, he thought bitterly. They wouldn't be dug out until the New Year, and that would be much too late.

They were about to reenter the cave when Swede tensed and said, "Listen."

He heard it then, loud and clear. Three heavy clangs on one of the muck train rails.

For a moment he was frozen with shock, then he grabbed a rock and struck the rail three times.

Almost immediately, there were another three taps in return.

The outside world finally knew they were alive.

Derrick was the only one who knew Morse code, but Diana didn't want to let him return to the tunnel.

"Listen to the rocks, Dane—you can hear them groaning overhead. He's risking his life going back out there. That ceiling could come down any minute."

"You're sounding like a mother," he accused.

"And you think it's a little late," she said sarcastically.

He wouldn't argue; none of them could afford the time. "We have to let them know who's here, Diana. The moment I hear a rumble, we'll run for it."

Derrick cut the argument short by ducking under her arm and running over to the rails. Nordlund followed, flashing the lantern at the overhead and guessing that they had, at best, a few minutes.

"Give them the first three letters of everybody's name, Derrick—that's probably all we're going to have time for."

Derrick took a rock and methodically banged out the code on the rail. Nordlund watched the rocks overhead for any sudden shift. On the last name, dust started to silt down from the arch, and he could see the cracks widen.

"Last letter and that's it—run for it!"

Derrick finished and dashed back to the cave. Nordlund ran over to the jockey box, keeping an eye on the overhead. He had meant to look earlier for anything they might be able to use if they were going to be trapped for a while. He yanked it open and grabbed a leather tool belt. Just before he let the lid drop, he seized a coil of triple-stranded communication wire. If he could. . . .

Then the rocks started falling from the ceiling, and he dove for the cave opening.

"Everybody down, cover your heads!" Behind him, huge slabs of limestone fell onto the tunnel floor, and rock dust boiled into the cave. It took minutes to quiet down, and when he finally looked up, he realized there would be no way out through the tunnel itself. The cave opening was completely choked by the limestone slabs and smaller debris.

Behind him, Cyd said, "At least they know we're here."

He didn't have the heart to tell her that everybody on the surface would assume they had died in this last cave-in.

And now there was no way to tell them they were wrong.

CHAPTER 37

It was eight o'clock the morning of Christmas Eve, and all over the city, people were showing up for a frantic half-day's work and the final push for last-minute presents. But it was a damned poor Christmas Eve for Nordlund and the others, Metcalf thought. It had been twenty hours since they had been trapped below without food or water.

He glanced around at the others in the office. "We know there are eight people down there—Dane, Cyd Lederley, Derrick, DeFolge, Diana DeFolge, Swede, Kaltmeyer, and Hideo Nakamura. We know that for a fact. I'm not the only one who heard the taps on the rail—"

"We all heard them, Troy," Phillips interrupted. "What we don't know is whether or not they're alive now. There's not much chance they survived that last cave-in."

"I don't agree," Metcalf said in a tight voice.

"I'll miss them as much as anybody, Troy. At the same time, we have to be realistic." Phillips shrugged. "Have their relatives been notified?"

"The Red Cross offered to contact them," Tisch said.

"Very kind of them." Phillips leaned back in his chair and examined his fingernails. "How bad was the cave-in, Troy?"

"We sent two men with respirators down to check it out. It looks like the cave-in blocked most of the cut under the last shield and probably a good part of the tunnel beyond the debris from the initial explosion."

Phillips nodded. "That would be the part of the tunnel where Dane and the others were trapped, is that correct?"

"That's right."

"You think Nordlund's party got to the cave in time?"

"I'm betting on it."

(305

Phillips made a small tent of his fingers and leaned his chin on it. "And what are the chances of getting them out?"

"We'll have to wait until the gas dissipates. A single spark right now could detonate the whole tunnel if the methane concentration is high enough."

"And if gas weren't a problem?"

"Tricky. We can't use the mole—that kind of debris is like butter for an automatic digging machine, but we don't know how unstable the stuff is above the roof of the tunnel. It might just keep coming down."

"And we'd need more shields, right?"

"We'd have to fabricate at least three or four new ones." Metcalf paused, hating the questions Phillips was asking. "With curing time, it would take four to five days."

"How long before we could reasonably expect to reach them, then?"

Metcalf fought to keep the despair out of his voice. "Say a week—ten days at the outside."

Phillips leaned back in his chair. "Sorry, Troy—just trying to make a point."

"I know the point," Metcalf said bitterly. "I just don't agree with it." He turned to Tisch. "What are the gas levels?"

"We've been sampling at the ventilator shafts. There's a steady build-up of methane with an appreciable amount of carbon monoxide. We may be getting false readings, though, since carbon monoxide is lighter than air and would rise in the shafts."

"Carbon dioxide?"

"Some—it's heavier than air. We're also getting increasingly high levels of hydrogen sulfide."

"What about in the cave?"

Tisch hedged, not meeting his eyes. "Probably lots of carbon dioxide, maybe even methane and hydrogen sulfide. Basically, the area has all the characteristics of a small primitive oil field."

"Dangerous levels?"

Tisch looked unhappy. "I don't know, Troy. Probably. We never installed any monitors in the cave, so I have no record of gas levels in there at any time. Even if we had installed them, the cabling wouldn't have survived this last cave-in."

Metcalf walked over to the coffee machine to brew himself a cup of coffee and gain some time. Maybe Phillips was right in hinting there wasn't any hope. Maybe the real problem was that he didn't want to face reality.

Youngblood waited until he was behind his desk again, then said sympathetically, "You really think they found shelter in the cave, Troy?"

"Yes." He ticked the points off on his fingers. "We know that they're down there. And we know that they were near the cave and that Nordlund was familiar with it. It's a safe assumption that they would have sought shelter there the moment the cave-in began." He looked at Phillips. "We have no proof at all that they're dead—with the emphasis on *proof,* Steve."

"We don't know that they're alive, either," Phillips said patiently. He could afford to be patient now.

Zumwalt said, "There's no way of communicating with them. Not anymore."

Metcalf glanced at Youngblood. "You think the cave collapsed, too?"

Youngblood hesitated. "No, I think it probably survived. It was a natural construction, far more stable than the tunnel itself."

"If they got to the cave," Metcalf said desperately, "then there's reason for hope. There has to be another way out—the same way the two kids and the Indian got in."

Nobody would meet his eyes. Phillips studied his fingers and said, "The entrance to that cave was probably paved over decades ago. Ten to one a shopping mall is sitting on it now."

Metcalf snapped the pencil he had been holding. His voice was brittle.

"Alive or dead, Neal? What's your opinion?"

Youngblood hesitated for a moment, then: "Professional opinion? Dead."

"Tisch?"

Tisch's long face looked sadder than usual. "Face it, Troy,

they're goners. If the cave-in didn't get them, the truth is the gas levels are probably high enough to have killed them by now."

"Rob?"

Zumwalt was sweaty with indecision. "I don't know, Troy. I don't want to—" He took a breath. "I have to vote with Tisch. Dead."

"Steve?"

Phillips's face was expressionless. "It doesn't matter what any of us think, Troy. Let's assume they're alive, that they're sitting in the cave right now, hale and hearty, waiting to be rescued. Doesn't matter. They've got no food, they've got no water, and the air is going bad. The only thing that's debatable is how soon before they can no longer breathe it. Most important, we've got no way of getting them out."

He slammed his hand onto the coffee table in front of him. "It doesn't matter whether they're dead or alive, they're trapped down there! We can't talk to them—and we can't get to them! Can't you see that, Troy? There's no possible way we can get them out!"

He stood up, the conference over.

"That's it, Troy, I'm sorry."

Which meant that clearing the tunnel would be their first priority. Rescuing Dane and the others would be second.

The storm front blew in at noon, bringing gusting, frigid winds and the first few flakes of what the radio weatherman warned would be the monster blizzard of the season. Metcalf stood on the balcony in his shirtsleeves, staring blindly out at the access shaft and not caring very much whether he froze to death or not. He had been standing there for almost ten minutes, feeling as frustrated as a rat in a maze. There should be something he could do—but there wasn't. Not a damned thing.

"You'll catch pneumonia out here, Troy."

He turned. "Yeah, you're right, Harry. So what?"

Richards grinned. "So I got somebody I want you to meet. The Bureau tracked him down in the Upper Peninsula, near Escanaba. He claims he was fishing. Hardly the season for it, though."

Metcalf stepped back inside. The man facing him was tall and thin, with a thick moustache streaked with gray. He was carrying his coat over one arm and had just finished lighting his pipe. He looked very professorial, a living monument to dignity and reserve.

Murray Lammont.

Metcalf closed the sliding door behind him and motioned both Lammont and Richards to take a seat.

"We've missed you, Mr. Lammont." His voice was heavy with sarcasm.

Lammont glanced around for a rack on which to hang his coat, then sat carefully down in the chair.

"There aren't many telephones in the Upper Peninsula, and frankly, since I wanted to get away from it all, I didn't listen to the radio much. Otherwise, I would have been back here as soon as possible. I told the agents that."

"You were fishing?" Metcalf asked. "It doesn't seem like the best time of year for it."

Lammont looked faintly amused. "For ice–fishing, it's the only time of year."

Metcalf didn't say anything for a moment, wondering what Lammont would volunteer. Lammont simply waited, expectant, and Metcalf realized the man would wait him out, answering any questions that were asked but offering no other information at all. If he pressed him too much, he would probably call for his lawyer. It was a wonder he hadn't already.

"Coffee, Mr. Lammont?"

A brief flicker of surprise that vanished almost as soon as it appeared. It wasn't a question he had expected. "That's very kind of you; cream and sugar if you have it."

Metcalf brewed two cups. When he came back, he didn't sit down but leaned against his desk, forcing Lammont to look up at him.

He shot a quick glance at Richards, standing behind Lammont, who drew an O with his finger. Nobody had told Lammont anything.

"Del Styron's dead, Mr. Lammont. Shot while he was in his apartment."

(309

Lammont paused with his cup halfway to his mouth, for a moment very close to being flustered. Something else he hadn't expected—something major. Metcalf guessed he was frantically trying to see the connection between Styron's death and the tunnel disaster.

"I'm sorry to hear that. But I don't see how—"

"I used to talk to Del quite often about you. He considered the two of you very close professionally. I'm assuming you knew him as well in a personal sense. If you have any idea who his other friends and visitors were—"

Lammont put down his cup of coffee and shook his head. "Oh, no, we were never personal friends. Our association was strictly professional."

"You were much closer professionally than personally, then?"

"Yes, of course, much closer. I never approved of—"

"His personal life wasn't involved." Lammont stuttered to a stop. "He was murdered in an argument about a tape of your program. The police ruled out any personal entanglements."

Lammont stared. His forehead was shiny.

"I really didn't know him that well pro—"

Metcalf frowned, tapping his fingers against the desk. "But you just said you did. Which would stand to reason, of course. He was the head geologist here. It's logical you and he would have been close." He paused. "In a professional sense."

Lammont looked rattled.

"I think I should call—"

"Your lawyer?" Metcalf looked surprised. "Why? Nobody's accused you of anything, Mr. Lammont."

Lammont hastily changed his mind. "No, of course not. If there's anything I can tell you—"

"About the program? I know you'll be glad to tell us." Metcalf smiled down at Lammont. "We appreciate that." He took a sip of coffee. "What none of us understood is why anybody would kill Del for a copy of your program."

Lammont started to pull himself together. "I have no idea, though I always had the impression that his personal life was such—"

"You're a sanctimonious son of a bitch, aren't you?" Metcalf said, still smiling. "I told you his personal life didn't play a part."

Lammont looked uncertain again. The smile and the words gave conflicting clues.

Metcalf let his smile fade. "We analyzed the tape and checked back in the records. We couldn't find any collateral data for the soundings you took, the soundings on which you based your program."

Lammont stared up at him, his mouth open. They had been talking about the murder of Del Styron, and now, somehow, they were talking about the soundings. From a position of easy denial, he was suddenly deeply involved.

"We did a check, comparing your soundings with what we've actually found for the past four years. There was no correlation, none at all."

"There must—"

"—be some mistake?" Metcalf's voice was harsh and accusing now. "I don't think so. What I do think is that a man who sold as expensive a program as you did to Kaltmeyer/DeFolge, based on soundings you never made, might have good reason to murder the person who discovered that. The government will be interested from a criminal standpoint. I know Frank Kaltmeyer and Senator DeFolge intend to press civil charges, for fraud if nothing else."

Lammont shot up then, scattering his cup and saucer over the carpet, his face red with anger. "They knew—"

"—all the time, didn't they?" He stared at Lammont for a long moment, his face just inches away from the geologist's. Then: "Sit the hell down, Lammont, before I lose my temper completely."

Lammont sat down, his face pale. Metcalf put his cup on the desk and pulled over a chair.

"You're in deep shit, Lammont; what I don't understand is why you aren't smart enough to realize it. I don't think you shot Del Styron, but that leaves more than six hundred people dead or missing, counting both the eastern and the western cuts.

(311

They're dead because we never knew for sure what sort of strata we were digging through. I'd like to know why.''

Lammont tried once more to bluff it out. He leaned back in his chair, detached and arrogant. ''You're not the judge, and you're not the jury, Metcalf—I don't have to answer your questions.'' He reached for the phone. ''If you'll pardon me, I have a call—''

Metcalf ripped the phone from his fingers and threw it across the room without moving from in front of the desk.

''You're right, Lammont, I'm not a judge, and I'm not a jury, and I'm also not a cop, so I don't have to read you your rights or let you make any phone calls. But I'll tell you what I will do. In the compound outside are three hundred high-ballers and relatives of high-ballers who lost a friend or a son or a husband because of your program. I'll tell them you're here, and then I'll stop in the canteen and have a sandwich. By the time I get back, there won't be enough of you left to cremate with a match. You think I won't do it, just try me.''

Lammont read his face and crumpled. ''There wasn't enough time,'' he muttered.

''Kaltmeyer/DeFolge submitted their bid at the last minute. And you were hired at the last minute. There was no way you could have made those soundings, was there?''

Lammont shook his head in agreement. ''No,'' he whispered.

Metcalf stared at him, puzzled.

''Why did you do it?''

Lammont took a ragged breath.

''I used to teach in a small college in Wisconsin. I wanted out. I wasn't the Mr. Chips type. I had set up my own company, and I was running out of money. Then I heard Kaltmeyer/DeFolge had wanted to bid on a job but they were too late, they didn't have the time to take the soundings. I offered to fake them—my idea, not theirs. If anything happened, I would take the fall.''

''And this time?''

''Their idea. Alan wanted to bid on the tunnel early, but he

(312

didn't have the financing. When he finally got it, it was too late. He was willing to gamble that what had worked so many years ago would work again. He asked me to do it. I wouldn't, so he threatened to leak what I had done on that first job. It was history, but it would have ruined my company. And me.''

"So you invented the data for the soundings and based your program on them.''

Lammont nodded. "The geology of the area is well known; I knew I would be right most of the time. The chances of a really serious glitch were . . . slim.''

There was something that was being left out, Metcalf thought.

"You didn't know anything about the explosions and cave-ins here?''

Lammont shook his head. "I swear to God.''

Metcalf glanced up at Richards, who nodded. In his opinion, Lammont was telling the truth.

"How did Kaltmeyer/DeFolge think they could get away with it?'' On impulse, he added, "The first time.''

"I took the soundings after the fact. They substituted the data as they went along.''

Metcalf stared. He almost had it.

"Why didn't they do that this time?'' Not everything in a corporation was decided by a board of directors, he thought. Sooner or later, one man had to make a decision.

"It was too big a project, too many people were involved. Somebody would have figured it out. So they went ahead and took the risk.''

Metcalf studied Lammont in silence. He wasn't dealing with a corrupt DeFolge or a ruthless Kaltmeyer. He was dealing with a man who had agonized over his decision and now undoubtedly felt his share of guilt. Probably always had. And if he had—

He knew the answer even before he asked the question.

"And after they won the contract, you went ahead and took the soundings they should have had to begin with. You covered your ass, just like you did that first time. Only this time, they were afraid to use them. Right?''

A silent nod.

"Do you have copies of the original data?"

Lammont looked surprised. "Of course."

"Soundings of the entire area?"

Another nod.

He was home free, Metcalf thought.

"And you could take them and make a detailed map, using system graphics?"

Lammont frowned, not knowing what he was driving at. "I already have."

"Do you remember anything about the cave down below?"

"I remember there was one. Actually a small cave system, heading in toward shore."

An idea was beginning to take shape in Metcalf's mind.

"At what depth?"

Lammont was slowly regaining his composure. He frowned, thinking. "I'm not sure. I'd have to refer to the map. As I recall, it was variable, from several hundred feet below the lake bottom to perhaps three or four."

Metcalf glanced up at Richards. "Take him to his office and bring him back with the map. As soon as you can."

Richards followed him out onto the balcony, nodding at Lammont still inside. "He won't go anyplace—he's afraid to walk through the compound without me." He shook his head in admiration. "I didn't think you could break him."

Metcalf shrugged. "Irishmen are born actors, Harry. Besides, he had a guilty conscience—he probably wanted to talk." He stared moodily out at the small pier, jutting into the lake from the island. Then he realized what he was staring at and started doing calculations in his head. He felt a suddenly growing optimism. Jesus, it might just work. . . .

"What's ugly, made of concrete, and might save eight lives, Harry?" Richards looked blank. Metcalf said, "Tell you later. Just bring Lammont back with the map as soon as possible."

They could do it, he was sure they could do it.

If there were a way of finding out if Dane and the others were still alive. If there were a way of finding out their exact location in the cave system—if they were in it at all. And if somehow there were a way of talking to them.

That was the first half of the problem, the part to which he had no answers.

But now he knew how to solve the last half of the problem. With a little luck. . . .

CHAPTER 38

They were beginning to crack, Nordlund thought. Conversation had died hours before, except for an occasional short question and equally short answer. The groaning of the rocks overhead had diminished but never completely disappeared, and everybody jumped when there was an occasional sharp squeal. The battery lanterns had been turned as low as possible, so the cave was gloomy in the center and black around the wall areas. All of them were huddled together in the middle now, even De-Folge. He was jumpy and sweating, his eyes flashing to the ceiling every time there was a rumble.

Cyd had found a pack of cards in her tote bag and was playing solitaire—nobody had the concentration for a game of gin or poker.

"How much longer?" Swede asked.

Nordlund shook his head. "I don't know, Swede. There's a few more tons for them to dig through out there; it won't be easy."

Cyd shuffled the cards, not looking up. "Just how bad is it?"

"Metcalf and his men know we're here. They'll find a way to get through to us. In the meantime, the cave is apparently stable, and we have to breathe. They should be able to get a pipe through to us in a day or so, and then they can pump in food and water."

"You are being somewhat optimistic, am I correct?" Nakamura said.

"Maybe," Nordlund said curtly. "It's better than running around telling everybody we're going to die." He shivered in the chill. "Sorry, Hideo, that wasn't fair."

Nakamura shrugged. "You are under a great strain as leader. But I have always tried to make a realistic estimate of perils and act on them with full knowledge. I do not think it helpful to base actions on delusions.''

"He's got a point,'' Cyd said, amused. "So what do we do now, leader?''

"Wait, hope, and pray. There's not much else.'' He looked over at her. "You've borne up pretty well.''

She thumbed the cards in her hand, then laid them down. "Actually, Dane, I'm scared to death, and if it would help to run in circles, scream, and shout, I'd be more than willing to try it. Ask me again in a few hours, and I may not need much incentive.''

She leaned back and closed her eyes. Swede gathered up the cards and started to deal himself a hand, then gave up and turned toward the cave mouth. Nordlund couldn't tell what he was thinking, though occasionally Swede looked at DeFolge with murder in his eyes.

It all depended on Metcalf now. Somehow, the little Irishman was going to have to figure a way to get them out.

He sat there for five minutes, then glanced at Cyd and realized to his surprise that she was dozing. Swede's eyelids were drooping, and Nakamura seemed withdrawn into whatever private world he called his own. He stood up quietly and walked over to Derrick and Kaltmeyer. Diana hovered nearby.

"Frightened, Derrick?''

The boy looked up and nodded. "Sure. Aren't you?''

"We'll get out, Ricky,'' Kaltmeyer mumbled. "The worst is over.''

Nordlund wished he could be that sure. "How're you doing, Frank?''

"My side hurts like hell. I guess that's to be expected.''

"Diana?''

She swiped at her forehead, brushing back a strand of blond hair. "I'm fine, Dane. Thanks for taking the time to ask.''

The streak of annoyance in her voice got to him.

"What's eating you, Diana?''

She glanced around the cave and rolled her eyes. "Outside of this, nothing, Dane, nothing at all.'' Then, in a hesitant voice: "She's rather pretty.''

(317

"She's beautiful, Diana. Be generous."

"She can cook, too, I suppose."

"About as well as you could."

She forced a smile.

"The older woman usually isn't the competition."

"Cyd hasn't any competition."

She turned away. "Your tastes have changed," she said in a chilly voice.

"I hope so."

The usual argument with Diana, he thought, but without the usual bite. Ordinarily, she didn't give up that easily. She seemed depressed—understandable. Little warning signals went off then. Both Cyd and Swede were dozing. . . . He glanced at Kaltmeyer, who was breathing much too rapidly and too deeply.

And so was he. He was actually struggling for air. He drew in a deep breath and found it oddly unsatisfying. And there was a faint, musty odor to the air, the smell of something oily.

Derrick noticed the action and sniffed the air himself. "It's not very strong, but it sure smells rotten."

Nordlund tested the air again. Under the musty, oily smell was the odor of rotten eggs, faint but discernible. He turned to Swede.

"You smell something?"

Swede pulled the air slowly in through his nostrils, seeming to swallow it as he inhaled. "Gas. I think it's building."

He walked over to the choked entranceway to the cave, kneeling and sniffing at the openings between the slabs of fallen stone. He hurried back.

"It's stronger out there, much stronger. I think the collapse of the tunnel opened another gas pocket, and it's draining into the cave."

Nordlund raised his voice. "On your feet everybody, we've got to move farther back into the cave."

DeFolge scrambled to his feet.

"A few hours ago, you told us we were trapped in here with a madman, that he was somewhere behind us in the cave system. Now you tell us we have to leave here. He won't be behind us then—he'll be ahead of us, and we'll be walking right into his arms!''

"We haven't any choice, Senator—there's a gas build-up in here. Haven't you noticed how much more difficult it is to breathe?''

DeFolge sounded jittery. "You're out of your mind. We're comfortable here. They'll get another tube through to us eventually. Then they'll try talking to us, and if we're not here to answer back, they'll think we're dead.''

"That's the breaks. If we stay here, we're dead for sure.''

"I'm not leaving,'' DeFolge growled.

"Suit yourself, Senator. Swede, grab the lights.''

They started moving slowly through the cavern, Swede bringing up the rear with a lantern and Derrick and Nakamura helping Kaltmeyer. The floor became rougher, with more stone debris scattered around. Once Cyd yelped with pain, then cursed like a trooper.

They were climbing a rather steep incline when he heard a shout. He turned to see Swede shining the lantern at DeFolge, scrambling up the incline behind them.

"You son of a bitch, you took all the lights. You knew I couldn't stay behind without them!''

"Our survival depends on them, Senator. We've got two lanterns and a flashlight; I couldn't leave half a lantern behind.''

"If we ever get out of here alive, you'll never work again!''

It was Swede who growled, "Shut up, DeFolge.''

They had struggled up another thirty yards of incline when Diana caught up with him. "You're not being very kind to my father.''

"There's not much reason to.''

"You can at least suspend hostilities until we get out of here.''

"I did a body count back in the tunnel—a hundred and six. And there's probably twice that buried beneath the rocks.''

"And you blame my father?''

"That's right.''

"That's a rush to judgment, isn't it? Whatever happened to people being innocent until they're proven guilty?''

(319

He could imagine her eyes flashing in the darkness.

"I'm not a court of law, Diana. It's too much to ask me to be impartial. I knew most of those who died. And I know the company better than you do."

She turned without comment and stumbled back to her father. She had never left DeFolge, he thought bitterly. Not even for marriage. She never would leave him.

They were coming into a small cave where they could rest for a moment. The air was still foul, though not quite as bad. And he wanted time to think about what they were going to do next.

He couldn't afford to forget that somewhere up ahead a madman was waiting for them.

"Dane." There was urgency in Cyd's voice, and Nordlund hurried over to where she was kneeling by Kaltmeyer. "He's starting to bleed again. I think the compress has probably slipped. With all this exertion, it was just a matter of time."

He untied the bandages and gently lifted the bloody compress. The wound in front was oozing blood and looked inflamed. The wound in back was covered with a thick clot; there seemed to be no seepage.

"I'm afraid it's my fault," Nakamura said. "He was a heavy load, and I could not give him the support he needed. He insisted he could make it alone, and occasionally I let him try."

"Don't blame yourself because a madman shot him, Hideo." He inspected the wound again. "I'll need some more cloth for another compress."

Cyd leaned down and used his pocket knife to rip away the bottom of her skirt. Diana, standing nearby, said, "If you need more cloth, Dane, just ask."

"About the same amount again. It's going to take a lot."

He fashioned a pad from Cyd's skirt and pressed it over the wound, then used the cloth Diana handed him to make a pressure bandage that encircled the shoulder. It would last for a while, but if help didn't arrive soon, Kaltmeyer would gradually bleed to death.

"I can walk if I have someone to lean on," Kaltmeyer said, his voice sharp with pain.

Nordlund nodded. "Sure, Frank." Then to Swede: "Carry him if you have to. Hideo, help Swede as much as you can. Derrick can handle the lantern."

Swede helped Kaltmeyer to his feet. "No problem—you're a lightweight, boss."

"Tell my doctors that," Kaltmeyer said painfully.

Nordlund looked at him, doubtful. "Sure you can make it?"

"It hurts like hell," Kaltmeyer gasped, "but I'll make it."

Another ten feet up, and they'd be high enough so the air would be relatively pure, Nordlund thought. After that, they'd have to stay alive until the main tunnel was cleared. When Metcalf and his crews didn't find their bodies, they'd investigate the caves.

There was a rustle, and he jerked around to see DeFolge close behind him. "I meant that, Nordlund. You'll never work again."

"I don't think you'll be in a position to hire or fire anybody, Senator."

"You think I'll go to jail, Dane? I haven't done a goddamned thing. Anybody who says I did is going to have to prove it."

"Don't kid yourself, Senator," Nordlund said in a low voice. "Lammont and Kaltmeyer aren't going to sacrifice themselves for you. They'll sing to save their own necks."

"Don't forget the trust, Dane—your skirts aren't exactly clean." And then, in a fadeaway voice as he began to fall behind: "Someday you'll need a powerful friend. I helped Frank, I helped Murray—I could have helped you."

"The kiss of death," Nordlund muttered. "No thanks."

He stopped to take a breath, and Cyd caught up with him.

"Daddy-in-law getting to you?"

"That son of a bitch would buy and sell his own mother."

"It's probably just occurring to him how much trouble he's in." She paused. "If he were anyplace else but here, he'd be dangerous."

They started walking again. At one point, Nordlund flashed his light to one side of the cave when he thought he heard something. The next moment his left foot stepped into nothingness, and he clutched frantically at the wall to his right, dropping the lantern. He watched as it tumbled into a fissure at his feet, lighting up the rocky walls as it fell. It was a good fifty feet down, a clean drop; there was no way he could climb down and get it.

"Derrick, bring over your lantern."

The boy was beside him in a moment, and he flashed the light across the chasm. The other side was six feet away, relatively flat but rocky enough for a good grip. They could stay on this side, but they'd be a lot safer on the other; the cave system tilted steeply upward there—it would put them well above the gas level.

The others crowded up behind him. Derrick raised the lantern so they could see the fissure better. Nordlund backed up a few paces, took a breath, ran, and leaped over the small ravine. It was a short jump and an easy landing.

"Cyd, think you can make it?"

She took off her shoes and ran forward and leaped. He caught her. Another easy jump. Diana hesitated a moment, then made a frantic running jump. She made it, then almost fell backward. Cyd grabbed her arm and pulled her up. Derrick made the jump easily, flying into Nordlund's arms.

Swede was the last over, leaving DeFolge and Nakamura on the other side with Kaltmeyer, helpless, between them.

"Mr. Kaltmeyer will be a problem," Nakamura said slowly. "He cannot possibly make it across."

Nordlund felt for the coil of communication wire he had taken from the jockey box. It was fairly heavy three-stranded wire with thick plastic shielding. He threw one end to Nakamura and DeFolge.

"Tie it around Frank's waist and loop it over his good shoulder. Leave yourself about ten feet to hang on to." He waited while they did it, then said, "Swede, I'll need your weight to hold my legs." He lay on his stomach and inched forward over the fissure. "Hideo, Senator, take up all the slack on the wire—

(322

not too taut, but be ready to put your weight into it if I start to lose him.''

He felt Swede's weight on his legs and inched farther out.

''Okay, swing him out over the side, but don't let him go. Frank, keep your legs as stiff as possible.''

Kaltmeyer gasped as he extended his rigid legs over the edge. DeFolge and Nakamura held on to his trunk. Nordlund slid over the edge up to his navel.

''Steady!'' He edged a little farther out.

''That's about the limit,'' Swede warned. ''You're starting to slip.''

Nordlund wrapped his arms around Kaltmeyer's knees.

''I've got him,'' he grunted. Part of Kaltmeyer's weight was being carried by the wire rope, held now by DeFolge while Nakamura still held on to Kaltmeyer's shoulders. Kaltmeyer's knees bent, and Nakamura let go of his shoulders. Nordlund could feel all of Kaltmeyer's weight on his arms now while the man hung head down in the abyss.

''Grab the wire, Hideo! Lift him up!''

He began to inch backward with Swede's help. The muscles at the base of his spine strained with the weight.

Suddenly Kaltmeyer grunted with pain and twisted. His legs started to pull free of Nordlund's grasp.

''Grab that rope, goddamnit!''

Both Nakamura and DeFolge took up the small amount of slack, and Kaltmeyer's shoulders lifted. Nordlund shifted so he could grab at the wire rope around Kaltmeyer's good shoulder.

He had almost touched it when Kaltmeyer started sliding off the ledge. On the other side, Nakamura threw all his weight backward on the thin cable. DeFolge lost his grip, and Kaltmeyer's body suddenly dropped. Kaltmeyer's legs were over the abyss now. Nordlund grabbed for an ankle; Kaltmeyer slipped still farther. Then suddenly Nordlund was holding a shoe, and Kaltmeyer hung in the abyss, suspended only by the rope.

On the other side, DeFolge had fallen backward against the cave wall and the wire rope was running through Nakamura's hands.

Nordlund leaped for the wire rope on his side, now held by Swede and the two women. Kaltmeyer dangled in the fissure, now supported only by the wire that Nordlund and Swede and the women were holding.

"Act as anchor. I'll try to pull him up."

Nordlund stood on the ledge and started hoisting Kaltmeyer up, then noticed with horror that Kaltmeyer's body was getting no closer, that the loops of smooth plastic-covered wire were slowly slipping past one another.

Kaltmeyer glanced up once and said, "Ricky—" Then the end of the wire had slipped through the last of the various knots, and he plunged to the bottom. Nordlund heard him strike the walls twice before his body hit bottom. At no time during the fall did Kaltmeyer cry out.

"Sweet Jesus," Swede said softly.

Nordlund pulled back from the ledge, stunned, still clutching the precious wire rope. Behind him, Derrick was sobbing.

On the other side of the chasm, Nakamura said, "Why did you do that?" The little man, his face dark and accusing, was facing DeFolge.

"I lost my grip," DeFolge panted.

Nakamura shook his head. "I do not believe that."

DeFolge reddened. "Are you saying I let go deliberately?"

"I am quite sure of it," Nakamura said.

CHAPTER 39

He had been keeping as far ahead of the little group of survivors as possible. He could hear their voices behind him as they struggled through the caverns, Nordlund occasionally giving orders. He could even see the yellow beams of their lanterns and envied them. His own flashlight had started to weaken, and now he used it as sparingly as possible, depending more on touch than sight to guide his progress.

He had turned the flashlight off and was feeling his way along the path when he nearly fell into the chasm that cut across the rocky floor. His foot slipped on the edge, and he very nearly lost his balance, surviving only because he threw himself backward. It was all he could do to keep from screaming with the pain. His face ached and throbbed, and he had scraped his injured hand on the stone floor.

He had dropped the flashlight and wasted a valuable two or three minutes scrambling around on the cave floor, searching for it. The people behind him were getting closer. He found the light and turned it on, carefully cupping his hands around the beam to keep anybody from seeing it. The crevice wasn't particularly broad. He stepped back and played the light over the edges and into the chasm itself, trying to keep all the details in his mind. Then he left the carbine in a niche in the rocky wall, took a deep breath, and ran a measured four steps before leaping into space. He sprawled on the other side, his face sliding along the stony floor.

Once again he almost screamed with pain. He lay there, moaning softly, realizing now that he was more badly burned than he had thought. Then he heard the voices coming closer. He couldn't travel faster than they could; he would have to hide and then follow them. He looked around frantically, saw a small opening between two rocks, and crawled into it.

(325

He was feeling nauseous now, and physically weak. He un-buttoned his shirt down to his navel and sat against the stone wall, letting drops of moisture from the ceiling fall onto his bare belly. He reached down and rubbed the water against his skin. Strange how thick and sticky it felt. . . . Then he thought of the water from the East River, how cold it must have been. He could almost feel it creeping up his chest and flooding into his lungs.

He watched as Nordlund jumped across the small ravine, the others following. It wasn't a particularly dangerous jump, but one of the women almost didn't make it. He watched with curiosity as they tried to get the wounded Kaltmeyer across, and he wondered what they were using for rope. They were trying to get him across by sheer brute force. Nordlund was risking his own life by edging out over the ravine. DeFolge, he noted with wry amusement, was handling the rope on the far side. The fox had been put in charge of the chicken coop. He knew what would happen even before it happened. Kaltmeyer would never live to testify against DeFolge.

And then DeFolge let go of the rope, and the wounded Kalt-meyer dropped to the bottom of the crevice. DeFolge had cheated him of Kaltmeyer, he thought, blind with rage. He thought then that when he shot DeFolge, he would not shoot to kill. Not at first.

It was almost like a violent dream now. He would have to follow them before they got too far ahead. He reached for his carbine, then cursed violently to himself. He had left it on the other side. He moved back a few paces, once again jumped the ravine, and quickly found the carbine where he had left it. The others had walked right by and never noticed it.

Then he hesitated. His anger at Kaltmeyer being killed had flooded his system with adrenaline, and he was now very wide awake. He felt far stronger than he had a few moments before. He remembered now. He needed the box of tracer cartridges.

He turned and loped back in the direction he had come, back to the original cave just outside the tunnel.

CHAPTER 40

Metcalf slept on the office sofa for an hour, then put on his flight jacket and left the office for the compound, trudging through the freezing slush toward the access shaft. The compound was largely clear of ambulances, though several were standing by to take the dead as they were brought up.

The Christmas rush was over, he thought cynically. All the survivors had left for home or the hospital, and the little infirmary in the station vault had gradually emptied as the injured either improved to the point where they could be moved or died from their injuries.

Phillips was just coming out of the shaft, and he hurried over, flapping his arms around himself to warm up, his breath coming out in little clouds of vapor. He looked enthusiastic, Metcalf thought—always a bad sign.

"They're making great progress, Troy—another week, and we should be able to truck in new wall shields. Have to push the January dedication ceremonies back by a few days, but that's still close enough."

"Any word on Dane or the others?"

Phillips blinked, and Metcalf realized he had already written them off as martyrs to progress. A week from now they'd have the disagreeable task of going in and bringing out the bodies, but Phillips wouldn't worry about it until then.

"No, there's nothing new, Troy. No reason why there should be—or could be, to be more accurate." He realized he sounded callous and tried to make up for it. "Dane and I had our differences, but I think we respected each other, and over the years I had gotten to know Frank Kaltmeyer pretty well. And of course, the loss of Senator DeFolge is a tragedy for the country at large. I'll miss them all, and my heart goes out to the families."

Metcalf watched the flicker of emotions parade across Phillips's face as he tried to sort out the one that would be most appropriate. Phillips finally settled for sorrowful-but-determined-to-complete-the-project. Metcalf wanted to throw up.

"Come off it, Steve. You don't have to fake it for me." He poked Phillips in the ribs, man to man. "You don't really give a rat's ass, do you? Do the job, bull it through, collect your brownie points from Washington, and when it's all over, go back home to Georgetown and reminisce about all the strange people you met out here." He started walking away. "Keep up the good work, Steve, your country's proud of you."

"That's uncalled for," Phillips shouted to his back.

"It was called for a long time ago, Steve." He didn't care whether Phillips heard him or not.

He was halfway across the compound when he spotted Shelly Leonard filming background material around the instrumentation shack. Why the hell had Richards let him back in, or did Leonard have unsuspected pull someplace? He'd have to throw the bastard out himself. The reporter saw him coming and edged closer to his cameraman for protection.

Metcalf suddenly grinned to himself. Why not? If Dane were here, he'd do the same thing.

"Sorry about yesterday, Shelly. You can appreciate the pressure I was under. Really sorry. I follow your show, it's one of the best."

Leonard frowned in suspicion. "You'll hear from my lawyer, Metcalf." But there wasn't much force in it; he was too curious.

"Sorry to hear that, Shelly. I was going to make a slot for you among the pool reporters." The cameraman snickered, and Metcalf thought, in a pig's eye, I am. What he was going to do was give Leonard a very special assignment.

Leonard relented but was still a little uncertain. "Yeah, I have bad days, too, I guess."

Why didn't he just hit him and get it over with? Metcalf thought. But there was always the chance of killing two birds with one stone. He forced a smile. "Right." He glanced around the compound. "Confidentially, Shel?"

(328

Leonard followed his eyes. "What's up?" he whispered.

"The real story isn't down there, Shel, it's up here. What you should really do is an in-depth interview with Steve Phillips—his efforts to rescue the personnel trapped down below. He'd be good on camera, and he's full of great quotes. Ask him about all the latest attempts to rescue Dane Nordlund and the others. Scratch him right, he'll be glad to talk. The disaster's over with; the big story's in the rescue attempt." He paused. "Just don't mention my name. I'm sure he'd like to think it's his own idea."

Leonard nodded, already seeing a five-minute slot on the network news. And it was a story that would play for a week. He hurried away, not bothering to say thanks. The cameraman trailed after him like the tail of a kite.

Metcalf watched him go, sober-faced. It was more than a gag. Leonard was persistent, and it wouldn't take long to flatter Phillips into an interview. Steve would put his foot in it, saying it was too bad but rescue attempts wouldn't be cost effective and so on. Leonard was obnoxious but no dummy; he'd play the interview for outrage. At the very least, it would keep Phillips out of his hair. At the most, it would launch a public campaign to redouble the rescue efforts.

Either way, he'd be ahead of the game.

Down in the cut, he took an electric car to the head of the debris pile and watched while teams of high-ballers worked with picks and shovels to clear away the slabs of limestone and fragments of rock. Tisch wasn't around, so he figured that, at least for the moment, gas represented no threat.

He stared at the mountain of rubble, once again reviewing everything he knew about the tunnel and the cave. Damn, there had to be something he'd overlooked. . . . Lammont would be returning with the map of the area, including the cave system, and maybe that would lead to something.

"Something wrong, Troy?"

Zumwalt had pulled up next to him.

"Nothing's wrong, Rob—just thinking about Dane."

Zumwalt looked away. "Yeah."

It's not that he didn't feel anything, Metcalf thought; it was just that there was nothing to say.

They watched in silence as the men filled the cars of the muck train with debris, then suddenly stopped and gathered around something they had discovered beneath the pile of rocks. One of the men waved to a waiting group of corpsmen, who trotted over with a stretcher and a body bag for another badly burned corpse.

"It's a great cut," Zumwalt said. "The biggest in the world."

"Dane was very proud of it," Metcalf said bleakly.

Zumwalt nodded in commiseration, then tried to change the subject. "I wonder what the professor found."

"Professor?"

"Yeah, Professor Coleman—the guy from Northwestern who was digging around in the cave. He spent almost a week down here."

He had forgotten about the professor, Metcalf thought.

"I guess he picked up all the bones and left." But that wouldn't have taken more than half a day or so. "What the hell else did he do down there, Rob? He could have picked up the bones in an afternoon."

"Explore the caves, I suppose. Look for more bones and artifacts, that sort of thing."

The professor had kept himself busy, Metcalf thought, dismissing it. Then his mind edged back to it again. Nobody had complained about the professor tying up the comm line; in fact, he couldn't remember the professor ever using it. All out calls would have been patched through the switchboard, and with hole-through coming up, the switchboard had been worked to capacity. Somebody would have complained if Coleman had tied up the line—or even been on it.

And with the professor exploring an unknown cave system, you would think he would have taken along some sort of radio to communicate with his assistants back at home base. After all, what if he got lost? So if Professor Coleman had used some sort of radio, what the hell kind had it been?

Maybe it was nothing at all, but Professor Coleman and his

work in the cave had been the only thing he hadn't considered. And Dane Nordlund and friends were now trapped in the same cave system.

An hour later, he was back in his office brewing a cup of coffee for a skinny graduate student named Gil Genovese who was all elbows and Adam's apple and cynical enthusiasm. At first Metcalf thought Genovese was barely seventeen. His hair was jet black and full, his face unlined, with high spots of color on the cheeks. On closer inspection, Metcalf noted the lines under his eyes and the rugged look to his hands. Make it mid-twenties, he thought.

"Professor Coleman would have come down, but he's out of town for the holidays," Genovese explained. He sat on the edge of his chair, his eyes constantly glancing at the balcony and the noises of the compound that came in through the doors. History was being made at the Field Station, and Gil Genovese was there.

"What was the professor doing in the cave system?" Metcalf asked casually. "I know he spent about a week down there. Doesn't seem like the skeletons of the two children and the Indian warranted that much time."

Genovese looked self-conscious. "In one sense no, but we wanted to search for additional artifacts, particularly Indian artifacts—pottery and that sort of thing. Professor Coleman also thought the caves might have been used for storage, maybe even as a sort of armory. We found a number of bows and clubs stashed in one of the side caves."

"Wasn't that dangerous, wandering around an unexplored cave system like that? Wasn't there a danger of getting lost?"

He wasn't sure what he was driving at himself.

Genovese shrugged. "It's not that big a cave system. Besides, we had battery lanterns, and the professor had a little radio transmitter we used for communicating with the team in the central cavern."

"Radio?" Metcalf frowned. "Underground?"

Genovese looked surprised. "It's no problem."

"I'm not that up on electronics," Metcalf said slowly.

Genovese was suddenly self-important. He had come down thinking he could learn something, and now he was teaching something. "Actually, the rig is a small audio tranceiver, modulated at about three thousand cycles. The fidelity's about equal to that of a telephone."

"You can broadcast and receive through rock?" Metcalf felt the same surge of excitement that he had felt when he started to suspect that Lammont had made real soundings as backup.

Genovese cleared his throat. The cortical pause for a teaching assistant, Metcalf thought. After all these years, he still recognized it.

"You can go through hundreds of yards of rock provided there's no ferrous component—iron ore, for example, acts as a pretty good shield. Skin depth through water is maybe a hundred and fifty meters, say four to five hundred feet. That's fresh water," he added hastily. "Salt water cuts it way down. Actually, at that frequency we're dealing more with the magnetic component of the wave than the electric. In a sense, it's similar to ELF—the extremely long-wave systems the Navy uses to communicate between submarines and shore."

"Wouldn't it take a lot of power?"

Genovese shrugged. "Not that much. A dozen D cells. Of course, you couldn't hold a really long conversation."

Loose ends, Metcalf thought. Bits and pieces, and nothing he could really put together. Lammont could provide a map showing the cave system. Coleman had gear that could be used for radio receiving and transmitting underground. But it was still a case of if-we-had-some-ham-we'd-have-ham-and-eggs-if-we-had-some-eggs.

"Actually, I'm glad you called me," Genovese said. "As soon as the tunnel's clear, I'd like to go back to the cave and get the rigs."

Metcalf put his coffee cup on his desk; his hand was shaking. "You left them down there?" he said politely.

Genovese was uneasy. "I hope it was okay. We got the two we used in the tunnel itself for relaying messages from the cave to the station vault. The two we used in the cave system we stashed behind a couple of rocks just inside the entrance so they wouldn't be in anybody's way. We were going to pick them up after your hole-through ceremonies, and then all hell broke loose and I figured you guys had your own problems, ours could wait."

"You wouldn't happen to have another unit back at the department, would you?"

Genovese looked blank. "I just told you—the two from the tunnel. We bought four from the supply house so we could always equip two teams out in the field."

But there was no indication that Nordlund knew about them, Metcalf thought, beginning to burn with frustration. Even if Dane had known about them and tried to use them, he had probably abandoned them when he didn't get any response.

"They're behind the rocks at the right as you go in," Genovese continued. "They're easy to spot. They've got a loop antenna a foot in diameter, maybe twenty-five turns—"

"Did your team ever work with anybody from here, Gil? Maybe help you set up, show you around, anything like that?"

"Yeah, several guys." Genovese thought for a moment. "One of the women had a crush on this one guy—big blond guy, maybe early twenties. I think they called him Swede."

Genovese had suddenly sprouted wings and a halo. Metcalf clapped him on the back and quickly sketched in the situation.

"I want you to bring back the two rigs and set up a watch, day and night, just outside the area where the tunnel collapsed. Okay?"

Genovese disappeared on the double, and Metcalf started pacing the floor. Maybe Swede had been so concerned with simply staying alive down there he had forgotten about them. Maybe he had never known what they were to begin with, though Swede had always been too curious for his own good and had probably asked.

But it would take just the right question from Dane or somebody else to trigger Swede's memory.

Lammont and Richards returned in the middle of the afternoon, and Metcalf called in the other engineers. They gathered around

Zumwalt's computer in the outer office while Lammont loaded a program and waited for it to come up on the office projection screen.

A moment later, they were looking at a section of what Metcalf recognized as a U.S. Coast and Geodetic Survey map. Across the lower part ran a thin double line, representing the tunnel. As they watched, Zumwalt's fingers played over the computer keyboard, and the picture on the screen slowly rotated until they were looking at a cross-sectional view of the lake and the tunnel and the strata around it. Various sections appeared in different colors.

"The colored areas are the discontinuities in the strata, generated from the real data," Lammont said in his best professorial voice. He stepped up to the screen and traced an area under the lake and north of the lines that represented the tunnel. "Here's your phantom oil field."

"Is it really oil?" Metcalf asked.

"Close—in another umpteen million years it will be. But it's enough of one to give all kinds of trouble to a tunneling crew that doesn't know of its existence."

There was sudden silence in the room and a muted hostility that made Lammont flinch.

"What about the cave?" Grimsley asked.

"That's a little trickier. We're limited by the resolution capabilities of the computer, but you can get a good idea of it. The white area represents the cave system."

Onscreen, one tiny section of white in the middle of the picture suddenly expanded and grew a number of branches that feathered and disappeared as their size shrank below the resolution limit of the computer. The main cavern emptied into progressively smaller ones that continued east and north of the line of the tunnel and the ventilator shafts. Some fifteen hundred yards short of the edge of the lake, they vanished completely.

Metcalf pointed at that area on the screen. "What happened?"

"The cave system no longer reaches the shore, or it's too small to be resolved—probably the latter."

"Could you rotate that some more—and zoom in a little?"

(334

Lammont punched at the keys, and the white area indicating the caves grew.

Metcalf put his hand on the screen.

"This area right here—as large as you can get." His hand covered a stretch of cave that passed very close to the bottom of the lake.

The underwater cave expanded again. This time the edges looked fuzzy and indistinct.

"What scale are we looking at? How much lakebed between the cave and the bottom of the lake?"

"Three to four feet."

"And the lake above it?"

"Maybe ten feet or so of water."

They were all staring at him, puzzled. Zumwalt said, "What are you thinking of, Troy?"

"The barge. We could take the barge out, sink a ring of caissons over the area where the rock is thinnest between the cave and the lake bottom, then blow a hole through with shaped charges."

Grimsley slowly shook his head. "Sounds too Mickey Mouse."

Zumwalt looked thoughtful. "No, it could work. With a little luck."

"I don't think so," Tisch objected. "We don't know where Dane and the others are. We don't even know if they're still alive, and if they are, how will we tell them where to go? This is something that would have to be coordinated pretty closely, and that takes communication—which we don't have."

"I'm working on it," Metcalf said grimly.

Phillips said, "Has the barge ever been used before, Troy?" His voice was cool.

"No, it's experimental."

"I see." Phillips stared for a moment longer at the picture on the screen. "I'm afraid it can't be done."

"We'll try," Metcalf insisted.

"No," Phillips said firmly. "We won't."

Metcalf stared at him. Phillips was no longer debating the subject; he was issuing orders.

"Why not?"

"Nobody here is going to try it, and I've got several squads of National Guard troops out there to make sure."

This was a different Phillips from the one he was used to, Metcalf thought, uneasy. This Phillips was very positive and very sure of himself. This Phillips was dead certain he could pick up the phone and Washington would back him all the way.

Phillips leaned forward in his chair, his pale eyes fixed on Metcalf's.

"What if you fail, Troy? What if you blow through the top of the tunnel and your caisson doesn't hold? What happens then is that you'll not only lose any survivors down there, you'll flood the tunnel from the East Portal to the West, from Benton Harbor to Cicero—all sixty miles of it. You'll have sabotaged the cut as effectively as if terrorists had blown it up."

He shook his head.

"Not a chance, Troy. The government won't allow it. Period."

CHAPTER 41

Five o'clock, Christmas Eve. The subways were jammed with people going home from work, the stores were selling what was left on their half-empty shelves. Those who had waited until the last minute were struggling home with trees that wouldn't look at all bad if you put the skimpy side toward the wall.

Up above, it was the standard frantic, festive Christmas Eve, Nordlund thought. For Derrick Kaltmeyer, it had turned out to be the worst Christmas Eve of his life.

A moment before, Diana had tried to talk to him, and he had angrily shaken her off. Not surprising; Diana was the only one there who still talked to DeFolge, and like the others, Derrick blamed DeFolge for Kaltmeyer's death. After Nakamura's accusation, they'd had to pull Derrick away from DeFolge, who had cowered before the boy.

Nordlund walked over to where he sat, huddled against the wall.

"I know it's tough—"

Derrick turned away, facing the wall. He wasn't going to talk to anybody.

Nordlund thought for a moment, then said, "Follow me, Derrick. This is important."

Derrick hesitated, then trailed after him as he walked a few hundred feet back to the edge of the ravine. Rituals, Nordlund thought. The antiquated, outdated rules we live by. But one of the things they were good for was to acknowledge the end of somebody else's life so you could go on living your own—no matter how short it might turn out to be.

He stood a moment in silence, his head bowed, then said, "I think your father would have appreciated a prayer, Derrick."

Derrick stared at the tunnel floor. Finally, in a shaky voice: "Our Father . . ."

(337

When he had finished, Nordlund said, "It's your father's grave, son. Drop something in it that means something to you."

Derrick thought for a moment, then opened his wallet and took out a swimmer's badge. He had been on the seventh-grade swimming team that year, Nordlund remembered, and had won the diving championship. He had been excessively proud of it. So had Kaltmeyer.

Derrick held it over the chasm, then let it drop. A moment later, he wrapped his arms around Nordlund and was sobbing.

"It's okay, Derrick—there's a time for crying."

Nordlund held him for a long minute, then gently pushed him away and found a wadded-up handkerchief to hand him. "That's the most we can do for him right now."

Derrick blew his nose and glanced at the cave where DeFolge was sitting by himself. "I hope they get him," he said in a strangled whisper.

Nordlund had the feeling that with Derrick, the worst was over.

In the cave, Cyd, Swede, and Nakamura were talking in low voices among themselves. Diana was standing by DeFolge, who had sat down, slumped against the cavern wall. He was sweating and staring at the cave walls, holding on to Diana's hand. Diana glanced up when he and Derrick walked in, jerked away from DeFolge, and hurried over.

"Ricky—"

Derrick ignored her. But he didn't push her away when she put a hand on his shoulder.

Cyd glanced at Nordlund and said in a low voice, "I think you're wrong, Dane—she might have made a pretty good mother after all."

"Derrick's the only one she's practiced with. She took over when Kaltmeyer's wife died three years ago."

"She has a knack for it."

He looked over at Derrick and Diana, engaged in a deep conversation. Maybe he had misjudged her. But even if he had, it was much too late. She had been very quiet the last few hours, he thought. Kaltmeyer's death had shaken her up, but he had a feeling something else was bothering her as well.

"Think we'll get out of here, Dane? Honest answer."

He reached over and took Cyd's hand. "It depends on what Metcalf and the others are doing. And eventually food and water will be a problem."

"How long?" Swede asked.

"I figure it'll take them a week. Maybe longer."

Nakamura nodded. "We shall get very thirsty. And hungry."

"It would be nice if we could call out for a pizza and Coke. That's a joke." Cyd made a face. "Forget I said it."

"If the professor hadn't taken his radios with him, maybe we could do it," Swede said.

Professor Coleman, Nordlund thought. Funny man—he'd met him only once, but he'd had a sharp sense of humor. Then: "What radios?"

"He was using them when he was exploring the caves—had a couple set up in the tunnel, too. He took them out just before hole-through."

That's right, Harry Richards had mentioned them, something about Professor Coleman using radio transceivers to explore the caves. He had been mildly curious at the time, then had forgotten about it. But something—

"How many?"

Swede looked surprised by the sudden intensity in his voice. "I helped him set up four—two in the tunnel, two in the cave."

Nordlund sat there with his mouth open, staring at Swede and trying frantically to remember everything that Richards had told him. Harry had reported it when Coleman brought them in. And he had mentioned it when Coleman took them out. But Richards had reported Coleman taking only two radios out—probably the two that Coleman had used for communication in the tunnel itself. The last day they had been damned busy getting ready for hole-through. Ten to one, Coleman had let the two in the cave stay there, with plans to remove them after hole-through.

"What'd they look like, Swede?"

Swede blocked out their size with his hands. "About so

big. They had big loop antennas and worked off flashlight batteries.''

If Coleman had them down there, then they probably could transmit through rock. Why the hell hadn't he stayed awake in his electronics classes so long ago? And probably through water. Hmmm. Fresh water, probably not salt.

"Maybe he left one behind."

"You're reaching for it," Cyd said.

It was strictly a shot in the dark, but it was the only shot they had. The alternatives were to sit there and rot or look for a cave entrance that probably no longer existed.

"Optimism may be an empty package," Nakamura said somberly, "but it costs little to buy it."

Nordlund grabbed the flashlight. "You're in charge, Swede." If he stayed and debated it, he would end up agreeing it was useless even to look. He ran for the ravine. It was one chance in a thousand.

And if he found them, one chance in a million that anybody would be listening.

But it was better than no chance at all.

He jumped the ravine with no difficulty, then stumbled down the rocky trail they had taken from the lower caverns. Once he almost turned his ankle when he slipped on some small rocks along the cavern floor. Another time he paused at a juncture of two caves and wondered desperately which was the right way to go. The only thing that had mattered when they fled the lower cave was to follow the route that ascended the fastest, to leave behind the growing pool of gases. Now he had to determine which route had the steepest rate of descent. The first time he chose wrong and wound up trapped in a rocky cul-de-sac.

He found his way out and once more hurried down the rocky pathway toward the first cave, the original cavern choked off from the tunnel by the roof collapse. He stopped once to catch his breath, realizing with horror that he had no idea how long the air would remain breathable but that with every step he took it was getting less and less so.

He was choking when he finally entered a large cave, shined the beam of the flashlight against the far wall, and recognized the landslide that had choked the cavern entrance. He remembered the small flat-topped rock that had served as a dining table for the lost children's last meal. And the flat stretch of rocky floor nearby was where the Indian warrior had died, hugging his chest with the arrow buried deep inside.

Where would Coleman have put the radios? He flashed the light around the edges of the cave. Nothing. Then he started to walk the perimeter, looking behind rocks that were close to the wall.

He found it behind a rock near the entrance—a small portable transceiver not much larger than a shoebox, with a loop antenna that could be folded and collapsed into a receptacle on top. He hefted it. Maybe fifteen pounds. He turned it over, found a latch for the battery pack, and opened it to make sure there were batteries inside.

Praise God for Coleman and Swede.

He hesitated, then snapped up the antenna and flicked the "on" switch. If they were going to be disappointed, better find out now—

And then he sensed that he wasn't alone in the cave, that somebody was there with him, hiding. He swung the light around, noting the several exits. He started toward one, making the mistake of turning his back to the other. The only warning he had was what sounded like the drop of a small pebble.

He whirled, and a foot caught him in the groin. He tumbled backward, the flashlight flying against the wall. The only light in the cave now was the dull glow of the flashlight beam reflecting off the rock walls.

Another kick, and he managed to grab the foot and twist. Somebody standing over him made animal sounds, then fell on top of him, arms tightening around his waist in a bear hug. The man's breath was foul-smelling.

Nordlund jammed his elbows under the thick arms wrapped around him. The man was silent, a huge, slimy animal that occasionally grunted as it tried to force the air from his lungs.

He strained, twisting in the slippery embrace, then struck upward with his knee. There was a grunt and a scream of pain. The hands slipped upward, found his neck, and tightened.

He fumbled for the man's face and ripped downward with his fingernails. The man screamed and loosened his grip. They rolled across the floor, over something that felt like a sharp rock except that it shattered under their weight. They struck the flashlight, and the beam of light swung crazily across the roof of the cave, then abruptly went out.

He had never known what claustrophobia was until that moment. He shouted and struck out with his feet, hit something soft, heard a whimper and then the sound of his attacker shuffling away toward one of the caves at his rear.

He was alone on the rocky floor, entombed in a limestone crypt hundreds of feet below the rolling surface of Lake Michigan. He started to babble then, terrified of the rocks pressing above him, acutely aware of the tons of limestone groaning overhead. He scrabbled frantically around searching for his flashlight, and when he found it, he almost threw it away thinking it was just a smooth, cylindrical rock.

He felt for the switch, and yellow light leaped out and fanned over the rocks and the pile of rubble at the entranceway. Then he remembered and flashed it down at his feet.

The radio was smashed, the coil of wire that was the antenna crumpled and torn. He had to fight to keep from sobbing, telling himself they were no worse off than they had been an hour ago, before he had come back here.

He paced the perimeter of the cave once again. Maybe Coleman had left some food behind—a partially-eaten sandwich, an apple in a lunch bag that he had tossed away. Anything—

He found the other radio set just a few feet from where he had found the first one. *Oh, God, thank God. . . .*

He picked it up, then knelt by the smashed remains of the first one and pocketed the batteries. He stumbled toward the exit that led back to the little band of survivors he had left an hour before. He was exhausted, his chest burned, and he felt dizzy.

(342

He'd have to hit clean air, and soon, or he would never make it at all.

And all the time he struggled upward, he was sure he heard footsteps behind him.

Swede saw him first. "Jesus Christ, Dane, what the hell happened?"

Nordlund crawled into the cave, the radio pressed to his chest. He set it down, then rolled onto his back and gulped in lungfuls of air. The familiar faces and the glow of the battery lantern almost made it seem like home.

"I got the radio. There were two, but one got smashed in the fight."

"What fight?" Cyd asked, alarmed. "With who?"

"Our maniac friend. Never saw his face. Fought in the dark. Big as hell, sweaty . . ."

Nakamura said, "I am afraid it was not sweat, my friend."

Nordlund looked down at himself in the light from the lantern and almost gagged. Huge smears of sticky blood coated his T-shirt and his pants and his skin. It took him a moment to stop shuddering. He turned to the radio.

"Okay, let's set it up."

He pulled out the antenna, turned the set on, and adjusted the headset over his ears. He spoke into the small microphone, didn't hear anything, then started tapping the mike. After a moment he was rewarded with the amplified sound of his finger striking the plastic cover.

"Hello—"

The first bullet spattered against the rocky wall behind him, a faint red trace in the air marking its flight from the cave entrance by the ravine.

"It's the goddamned sniper!" Swede yelled.

Another tracer raced through the air, close by DeFolge, who screamed and tumbled backward, frantically trying to hide behind a small rock.

Without a word, Swede jumped to his feet and raced in a broken-field run toward the cave entrance and the sniper beyond, the air around him pink with tracers.

Nordlund grabbed for the tote bag that Cyd had carried all through the ceremonies and into the cave. He ripped it open and dumped its contents onto the floor, snatching up her blue-barreled .38.

"Dane, don't—"

"Don't what?" he grunted. He ran toward the entrance, crouching as he ran, the gun and the flashlight thrust ahead of him. Just outside the small cave he saw Swede sprinting toward a figure on the other side of the ravine. Then another tracer split the darkness. Swede gasped with the impact of the shot and crumpled to the floor of the passage. Nordlund fired wildly into the darkness. A tracer cut over his head, and he emptied the .38 at what he figured was the source, then suddenly realized he had exhausted the rounds. Another tracer plucked at the sleeve of his coat, and he froze. The next one wouldn't miss—

Behind him a voice hissed, "Drop the flashlight and roll away!"

He dropped the light and rolled frantically away from it. A tracer ricocheted off the rock where the light had come to a stop. Then, from behind him, three shots were fired in rapid succession. Across the ravine, there was a cry, the sharp noise of metal striking rock, and the shuffling sound of somebody running into the caves beyond.

Nordlund fumbled for the flashlight and leaped the ravine. He ran a few yards and stumbled over something in the pathway. A carbine, and close by, a half-empty box of cartridges. He flashed the light at the sound of running feet ahead of him. Nothing but rock and a dozen darkened nooks and crannies where somebody could be hiding.

He shoved the box of cartridges beneath his T-shirt, clamped the carbine under his arm, and recrossed the ravine. Cyd was still kneeling in the FBI crouch, both hands holding a Beretta. She slowly lowered it, her face grim.

"That was very brave. And very dumb. He was aiming at the light. One more round, and he would have hit you."

He nodded, momentarily irritated. "Yeah, it was dumb." And then in sudden thankfulness: "Thanks for being there. Didn't know you carried a spare."

She smiled slightly. "Leg holster. Damned uncomfortable, let me tell you."

"Swede . . ." Nordlund hurried over to him, motionless on the rocky pathway. His eyes were staring into the darkness, sightless, blood oozing from a massive wound in his chest. Nordlund felt his throat, checking for a pulse.

He walked back into the cave, shrugging helplessly at those waiting. "Swede's dead—"

And then he stopped. From the radio headset near the cavern wall, a tinny voice was saying, "Hello? Hello? Is anybody there?"

CHAPTER 42

Metcalf napped for an hour late in the afternoon, then turned on the television to catch the network news. There was the usual update on the exact whereabouts of Santa Claus and his eight faithful reindeer, now somewhere west of Toronto and south of Calgary, for the benefit of the small-fry watching. And right after that, Shelly Leonard had a short interview with Steven Phillips about the rescue operation, followed by an outraged commentary by Leonard.

He had mousetrapped Phillips, and Steve had walked right into it, sounding like a combination of Simon Legree and Madame Defarge. Metcalf suspected Washington was on the horn to Phillips a split-second after the segment ended. Next year was an election year, and right out of nowhere, Steven Phillips had suddenly become a mountain-size millstone around the neck of the Administration.

It was ten at night when Gil Genovese burst into the office, shouting that he had contacted Nordlund. Metcalf rushed down into the tunnel, where Genovese had set up the small transceiver. He talked briefly with Nordlund and was stunned to hear about both Kaltmeyer and Swede. Then he sketched in the only possible method of rescue, knowing full well that Phillips had expressly forbidden it. But he didn't tell Nordlund that.

By midnight, he had rounded up Richards, Tisch, Zumwalt, Grimsley, and Gil Genovese for a private meeting in Nordlund's office.

It was Richards who wondered aloud why Phillips wasn't there.

"Because I don't trust him, Harry. Because he'll want to play it safe, and we can't afford to play it safe—because six people will die if we play it safe."

Richards was hesitant. "I think I know what you're going

to talk about, Troy, and I don't think I should be here. We don't work for the same people.''

"I thought you'd be interested, Harry. Dane and Cyd and the others are alive.''

Richards sat down, his face suddenly pale.

"How do you know?''

Metcalf nodded at Genovese. "Tell them.''

Genovese filled them in about the radios, pausing when Zumwalt suddenly interrupted to look at Metcalf and say, "You said six. What happened to the others?''

"Both Swede and Kaltmeyer are dead. Swede was shot to death; Dane didn't go into details on Kaltmeyer.''

"Jesus Christ, Swede," Grimsley muttered. "Who the hell shot him?''

"Probably the same sniper who shot Kaltmeyer when we were watching the tube.''

"How are the rest of them?'' Zumwalt asked.

Genovese looked self-conscious. "Mr. Nordlund said everybody else was fine, that the air was breathable but that they were thirsty and hungry.''

Tisch said, "Can you track them?''

Genovese nodded. "We can zero in on their radio signals. The water isn't very deep out there—we shouldn't have any problem. But you'd have to have a boat . . .'' His voice trailed off.

Richards glanced over at Metcalf. He looked uncertain. "What are you planning to do, Troy?''

"Not much of anything before daylight. At dawn, we'll have the barge towed out and sunk over the highest point of the cave system. We'll get a fix on Dane and his party and direct them to where we are. Then we'll blow a hole through the top of the cave and get them out.''

Tisch shook his head. "It won't work, Troy. You heard Phillips—he's got National Guard troops stationed on the barge. You set foot on it, you'll be arrested.''

"I'm not going to set foot on it—not right away. Come morning, Harry"—he nodded at Richards—"is going to have it towed to a safer mooring. The weather's turning bad, and the

(347

company doesn't want to risk having it broken up while tied to the pier; it's too exposed.''

"Looks pretty solid to me,'' Zumwalt said, frowning. "I don't think it's in any danger of breaking up.''

"It's not. But Steve Phillips wouldn't be a good judge of that. Once the barge is out in the lake, we'll have it towed to the spot where the rock skin is thinnest between the lake bottom and the cave system. Then we'll sink the barge, pump out the water from the caisson ring, and blow our way through.''

Tisch still wasn't willing to go along. "There's not enough time, Troy. We'd have to make up charges for the caissons, get that whole rig ready.''

"It's ready now. Dane and I were going to test it after hole-through.''

"It won't work,'' Richards said slowly. "Phillips was right about one thing—you run the risk of flooding the entire tunnel.''

"I don't think so, Harry. We sink the barge and spike the caissons in the muck at the bottom, pump out the water inside the caisson ring, set the shaped charges, and blast through the roof. If for some reason the caisson ring is breached, we set the charges under the water enclosed by the barge itself. At the worst, we might dump thirty thousand gallons into the cave system. But I think the system could handle that without flooding the tunnel.''

"What if the barge itself is breached? That's a mighty big lake out there.''

Metcalf was starting to sweat. "Then we'd have to cork the bottle, Harry. Dump gratings in the hole and fill it up with rocks and sand, make enough of a stopper to hold out the lake until we could seal off the cave system from inside.''

Richards locked eyes with him, and Metcalf hoped he hadn't guessed wrong about Richards. He was the one man Phillips considered reliable. Phillips would believe it if Richards told him the barge had to be towed for safety's sake, and he would accept without questioning if Richards confirmed that he and Grimsley had to make an early-morning helicopter trip to Benton Harbor—though the actual destination would be considerably closer.

(348

"You're taking one helluva gamble, Troy. You could regret it the rest of your life."

"I'd regret it even more if I didn't take it at all. We have a lot to lose, but the people trapped down there have a lot more."

Richards hesitated a long moment, mentally tossing a coin. Then he said, "I think you ought to wait. I think you ought to tell Phillips and try to get his cooperation."

He didn't really mean it, Metcalf thought. He was more than halfway convinced, but he needed one more argument.

"Maybe I could persuade Steve to help, maybe I couldn't. Since we hate each other's guts, I probably couldn't. But Dane and the others don't have the time to wait while we argue about it. They're cold, they're thirsty, they're hungry—and they're being hunted. I don't want to win an argument twelve hours from now, go through the drill, and then find out I was twenty minutes late—that Dane and Cyd had been slaughtered by some madman."

Richards flinched when he mentioned Cyd's name.

"Okay, Troy. Your dice—roll 'em."

They spent the rest of the night going over Lammont's map, pinpointing exactly where the thinnest layer of rock was between the caves and the lake bottom. At four he went into the tunnel with Genovese and talked briefly to Nordlund, asking him to describe the different caves he had already passed through and the choices he had made if there were two or three possible paths. He traced Nordlund's progress on Lammont's map and finally pinpointed it a good four hundred yards from where they would be holing-through the lake bottom and the cavern roof.

The one thing that bothered him was that the map was an approximation. It showed continuity in the cave system but there were also squeeze points where he wasn't sure they could make it through. A long time ago, an Indian warrior and two children had, but there was no way of telling if the rocks had shifted since then.

The last thing he worried about was Steven Phillips, but it was a nagging worry just the same. Phillips might get too curious about moving the barge. Or Phillips might start asking questions about him and Grimsley flying to Benton Harbor in the company helicopter.

Phillips had been born with an insatiable curiosity. The only thing they had going for them was the possibility that Richards could stall him.

At five he lay down on the office couch for half an hour's nap and the next thing he knew, Grimsley was shaking him awake.

"Get your ass in gear, boss, we're behind schedule."

Twenty minutes later, he was out on the helicopter pad with Grimsley, waiting for the company chopper to show up. Genovese had taken the radio and gone ahead with Pinelli on the barge. He shivered in a temperature that had plummeted overnight. The sun had just started to come up, and the city was deathly quiet. It was Christmas day, there wouldn't be any early-morning traffic rush. The air was crystal clear. You could hear the rustle of a newspaper three blocks away.

The chopper settled, and the pilot cut the engine, leaned out, and waved at them.

"All aboard, gentlemen."

They climbed in, and Metcalf handed the pilot a grid map of the lake with an X marking the high point of the cave system. "That's where we're going, Joe."

The pilot glanced at it and handed it back, frowning. "Something's wrong, Troy. I'm cleared for Benton Harbor."

"Destination's been changed," Metcalf said shortly.

A brief look of alarm. "Hey, I don't want to get in any trouble, Troy—"

Metcalf settled back in the jumpseat and buckled in. "Did you watch the news last night?" The pilot nodded. "I want to get them out, Joe."

"Glad you told me. Hang on to your seat, it's going to be bumpy—the weather's closing in."

A moment later, they were airborne.

The sky was clouding up in the northwest, and the wind was whipping up a chop on the surface of the lake below. Sudden gusts of wind buffeted the 'copter, and the pilot had to fight to keep the trim on the aircraft.

Metcalf said, "Can you set down on the barge in this weather?"

"I can unless it starts to blow some more. I don't want to smash this baby against the hull," the pilot shouted.

Suddenly Grimsley shouted, "There she is!"

Metcalf stretched to look out the window. Below, he could see two tugboats towing the lumbering concrete barge, which rolled slowly from side to side and showed a pronounced tendency to veer to the left. It was large—fifty feet by thirty—with thick, double-walled hollow sides cast from reinforced concrete. It was open at the bottom, and when water was let in, the heavy concrete sides would settle deep into the silt at the lake bottom. A frame that stretched across the open hull held the ten-foot ring of caissons, each a foot in diameter, connected by a circular skirt.

It was going to take a lot of luck, Metcalf thought, worried. The theory was that once the barge was seated, gas-generating charges in each caisson would force the lower half along with the skirt deep into the mud at the lake bottom. After they pumped out the water, they'd have a water-free circle ten feet in diameter into which they could sink a ventilator shaft.

The only problem was that everything had been tested on dry land; none of it had been tested in the lake. He was betting the lives of Dane and the others on what he himself had once called a Rube Goldberg contraption.

The 'copter circled lower over the barge and the landing platform at one end. Pinelli and Genovese and the two explosives technicians were waving from the small cabin at the other.

"I won't be able to set down!" the pilot shouted. "The barge is lurching too much! You guys are going to have to jump for it!"

He angled the chopper closer in until it was only two to three feet away from the plunging platform below. Grimsley was the first to slip over the side, sitting on the floor of the 'copter with his feet dangling out the open door, then sliding out when the waves drove the barge upward. He dropped, flattened out to hug the surface of the platform, then scrambled to his feet.

Metcalf was next. He waited until the barge had swooped upward, then shoved himself away from the helicopter. The moment he dropped, he knew he had miscalculated. The barge was rising up but also shifting sideways. He hit the platform, the barge slid down the trough of a wave, and he found himself rolling across the ice-slick platform toward the lake. At the edge, somebody grabbed his jacket collar and hauled him back to safety.

Pinelli let him go and stood with his hands on his hips, looking down at him and laughing. "What's the matter?" he yelled. "Haven't got your sea legs yet?"

"Probably never will," Metcalf grunted. His whole side felt as if it were one big bruise. Pinelli helped him into the cabin, where Grimsley and the technicians had taken shelter. Genovese sat in the corner, huddled over the radio.

"Any further transmissions, Gil?"

Genovese shook his head. "No—haven't sent any, either. Figured we'd get back in touch once this thing settles down."

The barge was beginning to drag on lake-bottom silt. Its progress was slowing in spite of the increased power of the tugs. Metcalf walked out on deck to watch, holding on to an edge of the cabin so he wouldn't slide overboard. The hard scud, driven by the wind, stung his face, and he had to watch through slitted eyes.

The tugs were at full throttle now, but the barge slowed still more, hung up on a sandbar. The cables at the lead end of the barge sang with the strain. At the last minute, just when Metcalf suspected the tug captains were about to cut power, the barge shook itself and tilted to port. There was a dull, scraping sound, and suddenly it was free, wallowing in the shallow water.

Ten minutes later the tugs did cut power, and Metcalf knew they had arrived. He turned and shouted at Grimsley, "You and Pinelli get to the stern—let's sink this sucker!"

He ducked around the edge of the cabin and found the wheel of the inlet valve, then glanced back to see Pinelli doing the same at the far end. He twisted the wheel, then cursed. Frozen shut. He could hammer it open but that was risky—he might end up hammering it closed. He found an oil-soaked rag, tied it around the bottom of the valve, and lit it with his cigarette lighter. He waited until the burning cloth fell away, then twisted the wheel.

At the far end, both Grimsley and Pinelli had put their muscle behind the wheel, and he could see it slowly give. From somewhere beneath him, there was a gurgling sound. He hurried back to the cabin to wait with the others while the hull gradually filled with water.

It seemed like an hour later that he felt the tapered ends of the caissons touch bottom and begin to sink in under the weight of the water-filled hull. The whole barge was groaning now. Metcalf heard a loud mechanical screech and glanced toward the front end. A crack had appeared in the outer hull and ran halfway across the decking that connected it to the inner one.

"She's breaking up!" Grimsley shouted.

Metcalf held his breath, watching the crack. Then he felt a low *thrum* and realized they were on the lake bottom.

"That's it, Grimsley. Signal the tugs to take us off, and tell the technicians to set the caisson charges."

Fifteen minutes later, the men had finished and one of the tugs was rubbing against the wall and bobbing up and down with the waves. Pinelli and Grimsley waited until the side rail of the tug was even with the deck of the barge, then jumped for it. The technicians scrambled over next. Metcalf shivered with the cold and the wet, and wondered if he had enough strength to make it. When the rail swung close, he grabbed it. Pinelli and Grimsley seized his arms and yanked him aboard. The tug immediately started pulling away.

Fifteen minutes later, he'd warmed up a little, helped by a cup of strong coffee. He left the pilot house and went back on deck, where a technician held the detonation transmitter in his hand. They lay to, several hundred yards from the barge.

"You sure this is going to work?" Grimsley asked.

Metcalf shivered. "Hell, no. I'm just hoping that it will."

The technician with the detonator looked at him, and he nodded.

For a moment, the results were anything but spectacular. They could see the smoke as the gas charges in each of the caissons ignited, filling the hollow structures with rapidly expanding gas that drove the lower part of the caisson downward like a powerful piston. The lower section would seat itself and the skirt several feet deep into the muck.

Everything looked fine—

"Oh, Christ!" Pinelli yelled.

Two hundred yards away, one of the upper caissons had broken loose from its mooring and was climbing into space like a rocket at a launching. Metcalf watched it rise nearly fifty feet, tumbling as it went. Then it arched back and hit the surface of the lake with a splash.

Grimsley looked stunned. "You think it ruptured the water barrier?"

Metcalf nodded. "Had to."

Which meant that when they did hole through, they'd be dropping thirty thousand gallons of water on the survivors below. And if the crack in the hull widened any futher, they'd be dropping half the lake as well.

CHAPTER 43

The message was irregular and broken, but Nordlund had no difficulty making out Metcalf's words.

". . . trying to pinpoint your location . . . have Lammont's original data and three-dimensional map of caves . . . go to high point, directions follow . . . we'll blow a hole through lake bottom . . ."

He motioned to Cyd for a pen and paper. She rummaged through her tote bag and handed him several index cards and a pencil, and he started sketching a map. Toward the end, Metcalf's voice started to fade, and he had to ask him to repeat the instructions.

When he signed off, Cyd said, "What's wrong? He sounded very faint toward the end."

"I am very much afraid the power drain is too much. The batteries are wearing out very fast," Nakamura said.

Nordlund sighed. "We're going to have to ration transmissions. We've got a spare set of batteries, but they won't last long, either."

"What about the directions to get out?" Cyd asked.

Nordlund fanned the index cards to show them the rough map he had drawn. "The cave system splits up ahead, and then the two paths apparently come back together. But Metcalf can't tell whether they actually come back together or whether one of them dead-ends just before it meets the other."

"Perhaps we should split up," Nakamura said. "I could take a flashlight and investigate one path while you explore the other. We both know the type of structures down here."

Nordlund shook his head.

"Splitting up isn't a good idea. In the long run, it doesn't save us any time. And there's still a madman out there in the dark. He may not have a weapon now, but he has his hands, and he's stronger than any of us.''

He stood up, looped the wire rope around his shoulders, tightened the leather tool belt around his waist, and picked up the carbine. ''Okay, let's go. Metcalf said the weather was turning bad, that they've got a window of maybe a couple of hours. There's only going to be the one chance.''

Nakamura folded up the antenna and tucked the radio under his arm; Derrick took the lantern to lead the way, and Cyd brought up the rear with the flashlight. Diana, Nordlund noted, had been nervous and quiet the first twenty-four hours they had been trapped. Now she seemed very much Diana—very proud, very self-contained. The real Diana, with less pretense than he could ever remember.

The damp walls of the cave narrowed, the roof and the floor slowly drawing together. There was a small exit where they had to crawl through a narrow passageway. Their only guarantee that it would open into a larger cave was the map Nordlund had drawn from Metcalf's instructions.

''I . . . can't go any farther,'' somebody said in a high, fadeaway voice.

Nordlund turned around in the narrow passageway, shining the lantern behind him. The others were lined up single file. He picked out DeFolge immediately. The senator was sweating so much, he stank.

''It's the only way out, DeFolge.''

''I can't, goddamnit.'' And then DeFolge had turned to the wall and was dragging his fingernails down the rock. ''I've got to get out of here,'' he mumbled. ''I can't stay down here, can't you see that?'' Then he exploded, screaming in panic, *''I've got to get out of here, goddamnit! Out of here! Oh, Jesus, get me out of here!''*

It was Diana who slapped his face and squeezed his arm so hard her fingers almost met in his flesh.

''I'm behind you,'' she said, her voice a whip. ''Now get the hell up there. The boy can do it—so can you.''

Sobbing, DeFolge crept slowly forward.

Nordlund turned away. To see DeFolge humiliated had been a secret wish. Now he had seen it, and the sight sickened him.

They crawled a hundred yards, then the path opened up and split in two. Nordlund didn't hesitate but signaled for them to take the left branch. Another fifty yards going steadily upward, and then he stopped. Directly ahead was a massive slide that blocked the passage from side to side. He threw the carbine to Nakamura, gave the coil of wire rope to Derrick, and retrieved the gun from Cyd's tote bag.

"Wait here, I'll be right back."

He ran back to where the caves had separated, feeling the hair on his neck standing on end with every step, expecting to meet the madman at every turn. He took the other path for about fifty feet, then turned back when the walls gradually sloped together and the cave abruptly ended in a sheet of limestone.

Back in the main cavern, he gave the gun to Cyd and started up the slope, feeling carefully for footholds. Four feet up, he started to slip on a layer of fine, loose debris. He grabbed frantically for an outcropping of stone to halt his slide, then gave up and slid back to the cavern floor in a shower of gravel and rock fragments.

He stood up and dusted off his pants and T shirt.

"You are too heavy," Nakamura said. "Perhaps I should try."

Then Derrick tested the slope with a foot. "That doesn't look too hard."

Cyd glanced down at him. "You think you could make it?"

"That's out of the question," Diana said in a tight voice. "There's no point having him risk his life."

"He wouldn't be risking it," Cyd objected. "And we don't have a choice."

The overprotective mother and the adventurous aunt, Nordlund thought. God in his infinite wisdom confused a lot of boys by giving them one of each.

"It's easy," Derrick insisted.

"I am afraid Mrs. Lederley is right," Nakamura said, "We

have only limited time. And of the two of us, the boy has the better chance.''

They were all looking at him now—Diana with her I'll-never-forgive-you look—waiting for his decision.

''Put the flashlight in your pocket, Derrick, so you can look around at the top of the slope. Search for the best grips. If you start to slide, don't fight it. And if any large rocks start moving, come down as fast as you can.''

It was more than twenty feet to the top. If Derrick fell, Nordlund would never forgive himself.

He flashed the light from the electric lantern over the face of the slope, and Derrick scrambled quickly up it, barely touching the patch of loose rock. Ten feet up, he started to slip. Rock fragments and gravel rolled down the front of the slope. Derrick flattened against the rubble, spreading his legs and arms so he covered as much area as possible.

Nordlund flashed the lantern beam farther up the slope.

''Edge over to your right. There's a flat area with rock sticking out just beneath it.''

Derrick carefully extended his right foot, feeling around for the rock.

''I . . . can't, I'm sliding.''

Nordlund held his breath. ''Come on, Derrick—only a few inches to go.''

On the slope, Derrick was starting to slide still more. He suddenly stood on the moving gravel, pushed violently away from the surface, and leaped to his right. He clawed at the unstable layer of stones beneath him, then his right foot found the flat surface and the rock below it, and he stopped sliding.

''You all right?'' Nordlund called.

''I think so. I skinned my knee, but I'm okay.''

Derrick waited a moment, then began to ease up the slope. There was less small debris now, but the rocks were larger, and if they started to roll, he would be risking a lot more than just a skinned knee. Nordlund held his breath. Derrick was now at the top of the pile of rubble and had taken out the flashlight to look around.

Nordlund said, ''Is there any opening?''

"Yeah—I can get through it, but—"

"But what? What's wrong with it?"

"It's blocked by a slab of stone. I can get around it, but I don't think any of you can."

Nakamura smiled slightly in the dark. "It is an engineering problem. Perhaps I should go up and take a look."

"I'm going to throw up the rope, Derrick," Nordlund shouted. "See if you can secure it up there."

He found a fragment of rock roughly the size of a softball, tied the wire rope around it, then shouted at Derrick, "Catch!"

Twenty feet above, Derrick snagged the wire, then pulled up the rock and wedged it between two slabs of stone.

"I'm coming down."

He half-climbed, half-slid down the face of the rubble, using the wire rope as a stabilizer. When he was safely down, Diana immediately went over to him. She put a hand on his shoulder, and they stood silently for a moment in the lantern light before he pushed her gently away and walked over to help Nakamura buckle on the leather equipment belt.

For a moment, Nordlund couldn't see anything but Diana's hand on Derrick's shoulder. He wished he hadn't seen it at all.

But at least one mystery was solved.

Nakamura climbed up slowly, carving footholds where he needed them, using a screwdriver as a wedge and a hammer to drive it into the soft rock. At the top, he inspected the slabs, then slowly climbed back down.

"A wedge of limestone is blocking the exit above."

It took a moment for Nordlund to dismiss Diana and concentrate on what he was saying.

"Can we push it aside?"

Nakamura shook his head. "I do not think so. But a low-order explosive in the cracks might shatter the stone."

Nordlund grimaced. "Where the hell are we going to get explosives, Hideo?"

"The carbine ammunition—plus the rest of the rounds from the revolver. If we get some cloth scraps, we can make a packet of powder, and I can tamp it into the cracks with more cloth."

(359

"What are you going to use for a fuse?"

"If anybody has some cigarettes, we can use some of the powder wrapped in cigarette paper. It will be a very small fuse, but it might do."

Cyd fished around in her tote bag. "What about some Kleenex?"

Nakamura nodded. "Very useful. Perhaps you can help me break open the bullets and prepare the charge?"

He had to settle it now, Nordlund thought. He wasn't thinking about anything else, and none of them could afford that.

"Go along and help them, Derrick."

Derrick caught the expression on his face, looked from him to Diana, then hurried after Nakamura and Cyd.

Diana tucked her knees under her, then reached over to Cyd's tote bag and found herself some cigarettes and matches. De-Folge sat quietly nearby, watching her with a curiously intent expression.

"Not my brand, but they'll have do do." She lit one and leaned back against the rocky wall, studying Nordlund. "She's really a very handsome woman, Dane. And I'm sure she likes you a lot."

"I don't want to talk about Cyd."

She wouldn't meet his eyes. "You finally noticed I was feeling neglected. I'm flattered."

The old, brittle Diana was back. But he would rather have her bitchy than quiet and withdrawn.

"You've done very well with Derrick."

"I like him—he'll grow up to be a strong man."

"You're partial to strong men," he said sarcastically.

She nodded. "Starting with my father. There aren't many men who can measure up to him. That means you, Dane, but don't feel bad—I never found anybody else who could, either."

"Derrick—"

She looked impatient. "I know what you're going to say, Dane. And please, for once don't be simple. Because I like Derrick doesn't mean I ever wanted half a dozen children of my own. We both know that I was—am—much too selfish for that."

"You're a competitor," he accused.

"Against you? Of course."

"And your father," he added.

She thought about it for a moment. "If I am, I don't do badly."

"Sometimes you do better than he could have done," he said slowly. "He'd be the first to admit it."

She exhaled a stream of cigarette smoke.

"You're trying to say something, Dane, and you're butching the job."

"Were you ever in Del Styron's apartment?" he asked.

"Del never had that kind of money," she laughed, "to say nothing of my own standards of taste." She stubbed out her cigarette on the rocky floor. "What makes you think I ever was?"

He reached over and took her hand, turning it so the scar on her thumb was visible in the lantern light.

"This."

She looked at it for a long moment. "I thought I had gotten rid of all the prints," she said quietly.

"You killed him," Nordlund said.

She never lost her calm.

"Not intentionally."

"How'd it happen?"

"Father told me that Del had called; he had found something wrong with the computer program and was going to blackmail him. He wanted a lot of money."

He remembered then. "That was the night we had the argument at Andy's."

"Sorry about that. Going to see Del was a last-minute decision, and I was running behind schedule. I had to break off the dinner at Andy's, and the only way I could think of was to start an argument and then walk out." She looked amused. "You were never all that bad, Dane."

"Alan sent you to see him?"

"I offered to go. I went there with a hundred thousand dollars in cash. That's what he said he wanted, or he would put Father in jail."

"And you argued."

"When I got there he had changed his mind and wanted a

(361

quarter of a million. I told him we couldn't raise that much. He was drunk and said if we didn't raise it in twenty-four hours, the price would go up to half a million.''

"So you shot him?"

"That's right."

"Just like that?"

"Of course not. He was willing to lower the price if I was willing to be a little friendlier. If you buy sex for as long as Del did, I suppose you eventually wind up believing that anybody's willing to sell it if you offer them enough. There was a gun on his desk, I grabbed it, we struggled, and it went off. Just like in the movies. No jury will convict me, Dane—I was defending my honor. And don't laugh, you know they wouldn't."

"And you cleaned up the apartment afterward."

She grimaced. "Tried to. Apparently I missed some prints."

"And you call me naïve," he said harshly.

She looked startled. "What do you mean?"

"You were set up."

Her cheeks reddened with anger.

"You're going to have to explain that one."

"You volunteered to go only after Alan told you all about Styron's phone call and how much better you could deal with Del than he could."

She shrugged. "He thought I could bargain better."

"And what the hell were you supposed to bargain with?"

She stood on the brink of something then, and without thinking, he pushed her over.

"All your life, you've thought he's done everything for you, Diana. But most of the time it's been the other way around. He sold you to me as part of a package deal—Kaltmeyer was going to retire in a few years, and he needed somebody as ignorant and as self-righteous as I was to front his company. He knew Styron's weaknesses as well as we did and he sent you over as a bargaining chip. Of course you could bargain better than he could—all *he* could offer Styron was money. He figured when push came to shove, you'd give your all to save his neck. And you did, but not the way he figured you would."

(362

He had said more than he intended, and the moment he said it, he regretted it. Something faded in her violet eyes then.

"I'm sorry, Diana."

"I am, too." She said it in an oddly squeaky voice, sounding like a small child who had been badly hurt.

Behind him, Nakamura said, "Dane, can you look at this?"

He walked back to where Nakamura sat on the floor. He and Cyd had made a small bag of silk scraps and had emptied all the powder from the cartridges into it. Sticking out of the bag was the twisted cigarette paper, the near end of which bulged with a load of power.

"It will be a short fuse," Nakamura said, "but I think it will work."

"I'll place it," Nordlund offered.

Nakamura smiled. "I believe in your country the man with the bushiest beard is the one chosen to deliver the presents on Christmas Eve. Next to Derrick, I am the lightest man here. I am the logical one to climb back up and set the fuse."

"Your logic is impeccable, Hideo, I can fault it in only one respect—I'm the man in charge. More important, I know the limestone structures around here better than you do."

He buckled the leather equipment belt around his waist and used a strip of cloth to hang the hand-flash around his neck. Cyd kissed him and said, "Please be careful."

"Always am," he said, and winked at Derrick, who was watching him with a worried look on his face. "Be down in a minute." He raised his voice. "When I shout, everybody take cover."

He tested the wire rope to make sure it was still firmly wedged in the rocks, then started up the slope of rubble. Halfway up, he glanced toward the rear of the cave to see Diana crying in the arms of her father.

He wasn't sure whether he felt guilty about that or not.

CHAPTER 44

He was angry with himself. He had let the man get away when they had fought in the cave, and then when he had followed and found the little group, he had fired too hastily when his target moved within range, and he had missed. He had killed the man who had run after him. He had killed . . . what had they called him? Swede? He had known a Swede once, a big man, a man he had treated like a little brother.

But it wasn't the same man, it couldn't be, he wouldn't let it be. He decided not to think about it.

He teetered on the edge of complete madness then, finally pulling himself back. He'd been justified; another few seconds, and those massive hands would have been at his neck. . . .

He dropped back farther into the cave system, seeking the protection of distance and darkness. His hand ached and throbbed now with an intensity almost too great to bear. He had been hit in the shoulder, but it was superficial. He had dropped the carbine because of his hand. If only his sight had been better, he thought. Now he was weaponless and half-blind.

He paused at one of the cave junctures, aware that he could no longer hear the group. He fumbled in his pocket for his flashlight, then decided against using it. They might see the reflection of the light. He stumbled forward in the dark, feeling his way along the wall with his good hand. He silently prayed he would run into no more crevices; it would be far too easy to plunge into one.

His probing hand told him that he had come to a branch in the tunnel, and he guessed he had passed there earlier, before retracing his steps. He sidled down the left-hand passageway, then paused some fifty feet into it. He had a sense of remembering where he had been down below, but the passageway some-

how felt strange, unused. He took out the small flashlight, cupped his hand over it, and turned it on.

He inhaled sharply. He was in a little cul-de-sac that Indians had used long ago as a storage place for weapons. There were bows with disintegrating strings and quivers of fragile-looking arrows with feathers half-rotted away. . . .

And battle axes.

There was one beauty, four feet long, made of black, polished hardwood and ending in a knob head with triangular blades of obsidian set in opposite sides. He hefted it. The end fit comfortably in his hand, as if it had been made for him. He ran his thumb along one of the blades and smiled when it cut the skin. He could imagine it sinking into flesh and bone.

He had to blink to keep the blood from running into his eyes, and with every step he took the pain in his side was excruciating. He couldn't bear it much longer, he thought.

He knew he wouldn't live to see the outer world. He would die below ground, just as surely as Brad had. But so would all the others.

He hefted the battle axe, turned, and shuffled back the way he had come. Somewhere up ahead he could hear the thrumming of machinery and the shouts of men, and overall, the shriek of the Klaxon.

Blowout! he thought. And Brad was trapped behind the airlock door. But this time he had the battle axe—he could batter down the airlock door and rescue Brad.

He could rescue Brad. . . .

He could . . .

CHAPTER 45

Nordlund followed every footstep that Nakamura had chiseled into the rock, carefully testing it with his toe before he put his full weight on it. It took him about ten minutes to reach the top of the debris pile and make himself comfortable in a small recess. He ducked his head and slipped off the strip of cloth holding the flashlight. There were several large cracks in the slab he was sitting on, one of them two inches wide and tapering down to a thin slit.

He took the small sack of powder and pressed it into the crack, being careful not to apply so much pressure that he'd split the silk and spill the powder or ruin the fuse. He tamped the Kleenex tissues down around the charge, then filled in with strips of cloth wadded on either side. The charge was firmly in the crack now, with only half an inch of fuse showing.

He fumbled in his pocket for matches, turning slightly to shout at those below, "Everybody duck! I'm going to light it!"

He waited a moment while they scattered to the far corners of the cave. One of them took the battery lantern, so he was left in total darkness except for the beam from his hand-flash. He struck a match and brought the flame close to the end of the fuse. The end glowed and held the coal. It would burn slowly until it hit the powder in the lower end; then he would have only seconds.

He pushed out of the recess, grabbed the wire rope, and started down as fast as he could, holding on to the rope while he felt for holds with his feet. Two-thirds of the way down, he glanced up to see sparks shooting into the darkness. The glowing twist of paper had reached the powder in the fuse.

Oh, shit . . .

He let go of the rope and slid the last eight feet, hitting the floor and immediately rolling away from the slope.

A second later, the charge went off. There was a muffled roar, and stones and fragments of rock started raining from the ceiling. He covered his head with his arms and raced for the wall. A heavy piece of limestone struck him on the thigh, and he yelped in pain and fell to his knees. Around him, other rocks shattered on the floor.

There was sudden silence, and then Nakamura and Cyd ran over to him.

"You all right?" Cyd tried to help him up, but his leg gave way and he sat back down on the cavern floor.

"No, I'm not all right—it hurts like hell."

Nakamura knelt down and felt the leg. Nordlund winced. "Jesus!" Nakamura pulled up the trouser leg to look at the skin. Beneath the wool, the skin was bright red and already showing the blue of a bruise.

"Bend it—slowly."

Nordlund tried, grimacing with pain, but the leg bent without any difficulty. Both Nakamura and Cyd helped him to his feet, and he discovered that the leg would support his weight, even though he could move slowly at best.

"You are very lucky, Mr. Nordlund. The skin is not broken, and there is no indication of a break in the bone." There was a faint smile on Nakamura's face. "Bruise easily but heal quickly is what you say, correct?"

"I wouldn't call that easily," Cyd said. For the first time, it sounded as if there were a hint of hysteria in her voice. He reached up and squeezed her hand for reassurance.

"Let's see how we did." He took the lantern and directed the beam upward, against the shattered rock overhead. The air was still dusty from the explosion, but at the top the pile of debris showed a black opening into another cavern twenty feet over their heads.

"Bigger than I expected." He swung the beam sideways and picked up the wire rope, still suspended from the rock wedged tightly at the top. Most of Nakamura's footholds were still intact, though the higher ones were filled with rock dust.

"Let's go up, folks."

Nakamura stopped him. "Last time, your pleasure. This time,

mine." He grabbed the rope and started up before Nordlund could object, pausing every few feet to clear the footholds of dust and fine rock debris. He disappeared through the hole at the top, then reappeared and waved to those below.

"I think it is the cavern we seek."

Derrick went up next, the radio tied to his back with a homemade harness. Cyd and Diana followed, leaving DeFolge and Nordlund to the last.

"You're next, Senator."

DeFolge stared at him through sunken eyes. "You hurt her, Nordlund," he rasped. "You didn't have to."

"I owe her an apology, Senator—you owe her a lot more than that." He pointed at the slope. "Let's go, we're behind schedule."

Once the senator was up, Nordlund followed. At the top, he turned and hauled up the rope, yanking at it to dislodge the rock it was tied to. The cave beyond was the largest of all, long and wide with a high ceiling and a faint feeling of moisture in the air.

"You're on, Derrick. Call topside and get our position."

Derrick shrugged out of the harness and quickly set up the radio. After a minute of trying to operate it, he looked up, panic-stricken, and said, "Something's wrong—it's not working."

Nordlund slipped on the headphones and spoke quickly into the mike. "Troy? Troy, you there?" No answer. He tapped the mike with his finger. Dead. Batteries. . . . He fumbled in his pockets for the replacements but only found seven. He must have lost the others climbing through the caves. He'd have to use five of the old ones and hope he had enough power.

He clicked in the batteries and tried again.

"Troy? You there?"

"Dane! Keep talking, we'll get a fix."

The reception was weak but clear, and a few moments later Troy gave him the location where they would be holing through. When Troy finished, Nordlund took off the headphones and rocked back on his heels for a moment, thinking.

Cyd read the expression on his face.

"Bad news?"

He didn't answer. "Okay, folks, let's go; we'll have to use the wire rope and lash ourselves down. Probably the safest place would be close to where we just came in."

Cyd looked puzzled and suspicious. "Why lash ourselves down, Dane? What's happening?"

They had a right to know the truth, Nordlund thought. It was their lives as well as his.

"The barge gimmick didn't work quite like we'd hoped. When they blow their way through the roof, something like thirty thousand gallons of water are going to drain down here."

They were all very quiet then. It was an outraged DeFolge who said, "What's to prevent the rest of the lake from flooding through?"

"Not much, Senator," Nordlund said softly. "Not much."

Every movement now was painful. The air was filled with rock dust, and he had trouble breathing. More serious was the haze that filled the air, which his flashlight couldn't penetrate, a haze more serious than just the dust. His eyes, he thought. Something was wrong with one of his eyes. He stumbled along the path and after fifty feet reached a wall of debris. He looked up and saw the hole at the top of the slope of rubble that led into another cavern. He had to tilt his head to see out of his good eye, to make out the jagged edges of fresh rock.

That explained the explosion, then. Somehow they had blasted through to the next cavern. Where had they gotten the gunpowder? It was difficult to think, to puzzle it out. And then he was pretty sure he knew how. The powder from the cartridges. They had probably used all of them, which meant the carbine and their guns were useless.

He was the only one who had a weapon.

He staggered over to the debris pile and tried to stumble up it. Several times he grunted in agony as he slid back down. He clutched at the rock spoil with his wounded hand and almost screamed at the pain. He forced himself to be silent—he was stalking them. He finally made it up the pile of rubble by swinging the battle axe ahead of him until the blades caught on an outcropping of rock. Then he pulled himself up.

(369

He rested at the top for a long time. He tried to lick his lips because they were dry and caked from the fluid that oozed from his face. He dozed off and dreamed once again of being in the airlock beneath the river, looking through the port and watching the dead faces float by.

Brad . . .

He jerked awake and crept over the small rise that led into the next cave. He watched as they gathered around the radio, then walked toward him and started tying themselves down with what looked like thin rope. He didn't understand what they were doing but waited patiently until they had finished.

He brought the cool obsidian blade of the battle axe near his lips and kissed it. Then, holding the axe with both hands, he half-slid, half-lumbered down the slope toward the little band of survivors below.

He could see Brad's face just behind the airlock door.

Nordlund fastened the lead end of the wire rope to an outcropping for an anchor. He left a length of the wire for himself, then made sure the others were bound to various outcroppings. When he got to Cyd, he kissed her and said, "See you after the flood, kid."

Derrick was looped together with Diana. Nordlund tightened the knots, then said to Derrick, "Take care of her."

Diana was dull-eyed and distant. She had aged, he thought, but then, they all had.

"I'm sorry about before," he said.

"You've already told me that."

"I mean it."

Something stirred in the depths of her eyes. "What do you want, Dane? Forgiveness? You want to cheer me up? You break an egg, it's broken, that's it."

"I didn't mean to hurt you," he said stiffly.

She looked away. "We've been hurting each other for years."

He glanced at DeFolge, who ignored him as he knotted the end of the rope. Then he turned and limped back to the outcropping he had picked as an anchor and started looping the wire around his waist, making sure the end wouldn't slip free. He

(370

had just finished when he heard something that sounded like footsteps in the cavern they had left half an hour before.

He looked up at the same time Diana started screaming.

Nakamura had been holding the lantern, following Nordlund as he had lashed them down, one after the other. Now he was shining it on Nordlund—and on the cavern and the rubble slope behind him. Nordlund jerked his head around.

The thing shambling toward them was something out of a nightmare. It stood, a vague, manlike shape, clutching an ancient Indian battle axe and swinging it around its head as it staggered toward them. Up close, it was a thing of horror. Shreds of skin hung from its raw, bleeding face, and its eyes were half-blind and out of focus. The hair had been burned from its head and chest, and its trunk and legs were seared black.

Nordlund wasn't sure it recognized any of them. But he recognized it.

"Beardsley!"

The figure shambled toward Diana and DeFolge. Nordlund worked frantically at his waist, trying to loosen the wire. They had no weapons, and they had broken all the shells for the gunpowder; there was nothing but the rocks on the ground.

At the other end of the wire, DeFolge was doing his best to untie himself. Beardsley was close to Diana now, chopping at the air with the axe. She was held fast by the wire rope and couldn't move. DeFolge slipped free and Diana screamed.

"Run!"

DeFolge stumbled a dozen steps away, Beardsley following. The senator scooped up a rock fragment as he ran and suddenly stopped and turned.

Nordlund's last view of them was of Beardsley and DeFolge grappling. The senator was a big man, and desperation had given him strength. Beardsley raised the axe and brought it down just as the cavern shook with the force of an explosion directly overhead. Chunks of limestone and earth fell from the ceiling. A piece of falling rock knocked the lantern from Nakamura's hands, and moments later all of them were coughing in a dusty darkness. Nordlund thought he heard a scream, but it was lost in the roar of falling rock.

(371

Then the rain of debris stopped. In the darkness, Nordlund waited for the deluge of water while a thick silence settled over the cavern. He listened carefully for the noise of struggle, but there was only the sound of Diana sobbing.

Another five minutes, and he knew there would be no sudden rush of water, that Metcalf had failed. He started working again with the knots of wire that held him against the rocky outcropping.

"Cyd? I'll be right there."

From somewhere in the dark he heard her say, "Be careful—he may still be out there."

"Turn on the lantern, Hideo."

A grunt. "I cannot reach it; I am held too tightly."

He had a sudden nightmare of Beardsley finding the lantern, turning it on, and seeing them still tied to the rocks, helpless. Then the slaughter would begin. . . .

He redoubled his efforts and a moment later slipped out of the last loop of the wire. He found a match and lit it, hastily searching the ground for the battery lantern. He found it and switched it on, then swept the cavern with the lantern. There was no sign of Beardsley or DeFolge. He turned and yanked at the loops of wire that bound Cyd and the others to the rocks. The moment he freed Diana, she ran toward an outcropping nearby, the last spot where he had seen Beardsley and DeFolge. He ran after her.

"Oh, God . . ."

Diana looked down at the rocks and started to crumple. Nordlund caught her and glanced down at her feet.

Senator Alan DeFolge was staring vacantly up at the rocky roof overhead. The battle axe was buried deep in his stomach, and the rocks around him were streaked with rivulets of blood, coated now with a thin layer of gray dust.

It took a moment longer to find Beardsley, half-buried beneath the rubble. His chest was bloody and badly crushed; the sternum showed the white of splintered bones.

The others gathered around. Cyd held Diana while she rocked and sobbed. Derrick gaped in morbid fascination at Beardsley but glanced only briefly at DeFolge. Nakamura knelt down to look more closely at Beardsley.

"What must have driven the man? To struggle so hard to take a life . . ."

Nordlund turned away from the bodies and shined the light on the ceiling, searching for any trickle of water that might grow into a stream and then into a torrent. Nothing.

"I'll call and find out what they plan to do now."

Derrick paled and said, "You can't."

"Why not?"

Derrick pointed, and Nordlund followed his finger. Just a few feet from where they had been roped together, the radio lay on the ground, smashed beyond repair by a small boulder that had fallen from the ceiling.

CHAPTER 46

"You tell Nordlund the procedure?" Grimsley asked.

Metcalf nodded. "Yeah. I told him the whole core of the barge was filled with water and there was no way of pumping it out, that they'd have to lash themselves down and be prepared for a dunking."

"Unless the charge opens up the concrete hull," Pinelli said. "Then we'll be dumping all of Lake Michigan on them."

Metcalf shivered and moved back to the lee side of the pilot house. The slight breeze had gotten stronger, and the chill was finally getting to him. Too many days with too little sleep and constant worry about those down below. And a growing conviction that he had been grasping at straws, that the whole barge idea was Mickey Mouse, as Grimsley had once described it.

But if that didn't work, he had no ideas left at all.

"They got the rig set up yet?"

Grimsley nodded. "It's back at the rear—they just finished."

The technicians were working on an aluminum frame five feet in diameter with ten packages of explosives strapped to it.

Metcalf watched for a moment. "Why so big?"

One of the technicians looked up. "That's so we can focus the blast on one spot at the lake bottom."

Metcalf felt dubious. "It'll be tough getting it aboard."

Pinelli shook his head. "We'll use the tug's winch."

Metcalf glanced at his watch. Nordlund and the others had had more than enough time to tie themselves down.

"As soon as you guys are through, let's do it."

He watched as they placed the detonators in each shaped charge, then ran the wires to a timer box the size of a cigarette package taped to a bar at the center.

"You going to ride it over, Pinelli?"

"Yeah—I'm gonna feel like that guy in *Dr. Strangelove.*"

Metcalf pointed to a red metal sleeve on the side of the small box. "That's the arming switch. Don't activate it until just before they lower it into the caisson ring."

The tug edged closer to the barge until it brushed against the hull. The boom swung out, then hesitated over the hull. Pinelli, standing on the cable hook, motioned it over still more until the frame with the explosives was directly over the caisson ring. He signaled the winch operator to lower away. When the frame hit the surface of the water, he reached down and set the arming switch, then motioned the operator to continue lowering. When the wires holding the frame went slack, he signaled stop, slipped the wires off the hook, and rode it back to the tug. He jumped off when he was still two feet away from the deck and ran over to Metcalf.

"How much time we got?"

"Eight minutes. Let's get the hell out of here." Metcalf waved at the captain, and a moment later the tug circled slowly around and stopped two hundred yards away.

It was the longest eight minutes in Metcalf's life.

He had begun to think the timing device had failed when a geyser of water erupted from the center of the sunken barge. Chunks of mud and rock splashed around the barge. He signaled the captain again and they slowly approached the barge. As they neared, Metcalf noted that more cracks had snaked across the barge's concrete hull. They touched, and he and Grimsley jumped onto the hull and peered over the edge to see the effects of the explosive charge.

The caisson ring was shredded, and several loose caissons were bobbing around in the water. But there was no indication of any water draining out a hole in the bottom of the lake.

"We didn't make it," he said slowly. *"Goddamnit, we didn't make it!"*

The wind was getting stronger now, and waves were lapping around the barge. The weather was deteriorating, and whatever he was going to do, he would have to do it soon.

"What happens now?" Grimsley asked.

"We've got a spare frame and charges on board the tug, don't we?"

"Yeah, but . . ." Grimsley shook his head. "The barge won't take it, Troy. Look at the cracks—the next explosion, you'll dump the whole lake down there."

Chances, Metcalf thought. If he didn't try, Dane and the others would die of thirst or starvation before they could clear the tunnel below. The only hope they had was to set another charge and pray to God the barge held together long enough afterward to get the survivors out.

"Tell the technicians to set up the other frame with the charges. We'll try once again. I'll radio below and tell them."

But after trying for ten minutes, he gave up.

"What's wrong?" Pinelli asked.

"I don't know. They're not answering."

"Cave-in?"

Metcalf shook his head. "No, probably their batteries are getting pretty weak. Their last transmissions were starting to fade."

The technicians had set the other charges into the frame, and they had just hooked it up to the tug's winch when Grimsley pointed at the lake and said, "Bad news."

Metcalf looked up. Heading through the choppy waves toward them was a Coast Guard boat. He didn't have to ask to know who was on it, probably with a court order and half a dozen police.

Phillips.

"You're under arrest!" Phillips shouted as soon as he got aboard. "You, too, Grimsley—and you, Pinelli! Goddamnit, you're all under arrest!"

Half a dozen self-conscious Coast Guardsmen with rifles followed Phillips aboard, standing a yard or so behind him. The last to come aboard was Youngblood, looking slightly embarrassed as always.

Metcalf felt a slow surge of anger. "You got the authority, Steve?"

(376

Phillips was completely bundled up in a heavy Navy offi-
cer's coat and wool watch cap, with a thick scarf wrapped around
the lower part of his face. He spat out part of the scarf and
thrust a piece of paper at Metcalf.

"It's right there, damnit—read it and we-we-weep!" He was
stuttering with anger.

Metcalf glanced at the piece of paper, then let it flutter away
in the wind. It had been more and more of a gamble as time
went on, justified less by rational thought than by wishful thinking. If God had wanted to save those below, why the hell was
He making it so difficult?

It was starting to sleet; the drops were cutting his face and
stinging his ears. In half an hour, the tug would be iced over,
and rescue operations would have to be called off. It was do it
now—or not at all.

"Steve, come into the pilot house before you freeze to
death."

He held the cabin door open for Phillips, who stared, then
ducked inside. Metcalf followed, closing the door after him before anybody else could crowd in. The captain looked up and
nodded, then went back to the wheel, trying to hold the tug in
position against the wind and the waves.

"The men have already seen the order," Phillips said stiffly.
"Throwing it away won't help any."

Metcalf nodded. "Yeah, I know." He walked over to the
small cabin hotplate, poured a cup of coffee and held it out to
Phillips. "It's powdered cream, no sugar, I'm afraid."

Phillips took it, suspicious. "I want this tug turned around
and headed back to port, Metcalf." He nodded at the captain.
"You can tell him or I can order him—you choose."

Metcalf poured himself a cup, then leaned back against the
cabin wall, careful to keep the coffee from sloshing out of his
cup as the little tug pitched and rolled beneath him.

"You'll be abandoning all the people down below, Steve."

"Can you prove they're still alive? Can I talk to them?"

"Their radio's out."

Phillips's lips thinned. "Sure it is." He looked a little green.

(377

"Look, Troy, there's no way I can agree to anything that's going to endanger the tunnel."

"What do the papers say?"

"That I'm a villain, of course." Phillips's eyes narrowed. "You had something to do with that, didn't you?"

Metcalf raised his cup in a quasi-toast.

"Here's to both of us newly retired."

Phillips stared. The expression on his face reminded Metcalf of Daffy Duck in the old cartoons, wondering how Bugs Bunny was going to get the better of him next.

"You're newly retired, Troy—I'm not."

"Your replacement's just outside that door, Steve."

Phillips shook his head. "Not mine, yours. You've got it backward."

"Actually, if you stop to think about it, Youngblood is sort of an all-purpose replacement—depending on who's supposed to be replaced." Metcalf looked curious. "Steve, what's your directive from the Administration? What do they want done?"

Phillips puffed up a little. "I've got complete authority; it's my decision."

"And that didn't make you suspicious?"

Phillips hesitated. "Why should it?"

"Because you're the Administration's sacrificial goat, Steve."

"It won't work, Metcalf." But Phillips didn't order the captain to return to port.

Metcalf put his coffee down on the small cabin table that had a rim to keep things from sliding off. He stepped closer to Phillips.

"Figure it out, Steve. The Administration's taking a lot of heat from the media because you're willing to sacrifice half a dozen people for the tunnel. In the Administration's eyes, that's probably the right thing to do. But once it's all over with, they're not going to take the heat—you are. You've got full authority, it was your decision, right? You're politically expendable, Steve."

He waited a moment for it to sink in.

"Let's play it another way. Let's say we hole through to the cave and we end up flooding the tunnel." Phillips now was a pale green. "That was your decision, too. And once the cheers wear off for having saved Dane and the others, somebody's going to submit a bill for a billion dollars to pump out the tunnel so it can be usable. You'll take the blame for that decision, too. That's the one that worries you the most, but believe me, make either of those decisions, and you're a footnote as far as history goes."

Phillips was staring at him, nodding slightly. Metcalf stepped even closer for the clincher, his face only inches away from Phillips's.

"There's a third way, Steve. You blow through the roof, you rescue the survivors, then you immediately fill the hole so there's no danger of flooding it. Whose name is in the headlines then? Who gets all the credit? Who'll be able to go to Washington afterward and get any assignment he wants?"

He stepped back, his eyes never leaving Phillips's.

"There're three ways to go, Steve. That's the only one where you can win."

The cabin was stuffy and hot from the small propane heater, and the tug was now pitching and rolling even more. Metcalf reached into his pocket and casually threw two greasy brown paper bags onto the small table.

"We brought along some sandwiches, Steve, just in case you're hungry. Pinelli picked them, so don't blame me—one's tuna salad, the other's sardines and Bermuda onion."

Metcalf left the cabin then, not looking back.

Outside, he yelled, "Let's go—Pinelli ride the winch over and drop the frame into the bottom of the barge where the caissons were!" He glanced at the clouds rolling in and noted the height of the waves. They couldn't stay out much longer. There was also a chance that Phillips might change his mind. "Set the timer for five minutes—and then pray!"

He looked at the Coast Guardsmen, who were puzzled and uncertain. He motioned with his thumb at the cabin, where the noises inside told him Phillips really wasn't concentrating on the task at hand.

"He changed his mind. We'll be blowing through the cavern roof in a few minutes. Maybe you can help us fill the hole when it's all over with."

He walked to the fantail, pulled his coat tighter around his

(379

neck, and watched as Pinelli rode the winch over and set the timer. The tug started pulling away then, and he muttered a small prayer.

He wondered if those below realized that in trying to save them, he might very well end up killing them.

CHAPTER 47

"What do we do?" Cyd asked.

He had to think like Metcalf, to review all the decisions Troy had made in the year that he had known him and try to figure out what he would do now. Why had he kept Troy on as an engineer? He hadn't gotten along with the crews, he had been abrasive. What had been his assets? There were other engineers just as smart, and there were other engineers who had the common touch when it came to the crews.

The one thing he had always admired about Metcalf was that he never gave up. No matter how dim the chances, he always went the distance.

"They'll try again. Probably as soon as possible."

"Are you sure?" Diana asked bitterly.

He nodded. "Yes, I'm sure."

"It does not depend upon the engineering," Nakamura said slowly. "It depends upon the man."

"We could go back to the main cave," Derrick said. "We could wait there."

Nordlund shook his head, remembering the fight in the cave with Beardsley and how his lungs had burned afterward.

"Can't do it, Derrick. None of us can go back there. We couldn't breathe the air."

"I guess I forgot."

Nordlund looked at him sharply.

"You afraid?"

Derrick shook his head. "No—just tired."

Nordlund froze for a moment, wondering if it might be the rising gas level in the caves. Then he shrugged. What difference did it make? There was only one roll of the dice left in any event.

"Okay, folks, back to your places." He started tying them down again with the wire rope. At first he thought of tying Derrick close by Cyd and Nakamura, then decided that Diana needed somebody near her. And over the last two days, the dependence had become mutual. Derrick needed her as much as she needed him.

"You going to be all right, Diana?"

"Don't worry about me, Dane."

He picked up on the emptiness in her voice and squeezed her shoulder.

"Everything will be fine."

"Trite to the very end, right, Dane?" she said bitterly. "I've lost Alan, I've lost you, and I'm losing Derrick. Nothing's going to be fine, ever again."

The tears started to leak down her face, and he looked away. He didn't want to see her break, and he knew she didn't want him to see her. Even to the very last, they couldn't be emotionally honest with each other.

He checked the rope around her waist. She had torn strips of cloth and had used them as well as her belt to secure herself to the line. More strips of cloth held Derrick. A few feet behind her was the now-collapsed debris wall that had separated this cave from the lower one. If a lot of water came down, the presence of the wall might help them.

He finished checking Derrick and glanced again at Diana. "Watch out for him, okay?"

She nodded, and Derrick added, "I'll take care of her."

"I know you will."

He walked back to where Cyd stood against one side of an outcropping. He tied her tightly to it, then glanced down at her pale face.

"You okay, kid?"

She forced a smile. "What are the odds, Dane? The truth."

He shook his head. "Sometimes it doesn't pay to figure the odds, Cyd. Sometimes you have to go on faith."

"This is one of those times, isn't it?"

He shrugged. "We've made it so far."

"I like you," she said. "A lot."

He kissed her lightly and said, "I love you."

She forced a smile. "That, too."

"You all right, Hideo?"

Nakamura nodded. "Remind me tomorrow to show you how to operate the coffee machine—the scientific way, for the export market."

"You're on."

He took the battery lantern and put it high up in a niche in the wall. If they survived, they would have light. He tied himself down close to Cyd, checking his leather equipment belt to make sure the wire cutters were still there. They might have to get untied in a hurry—enough of a hurry where it might be easier to cut the wire rather than try to untie it.

He raised his voice. "Hold on as best you can. If someone breaks loose, we'll try to get to them."

"May good fortune be with all of us," Nakamura added. It almost sounded like a benediction.

Nordlund stared at his watch. It might be a few minutes. It might be half an hour. It might be never—

The explosion took him by surprise. The cavern shook, and rock once again thundered down from the ceiling. A moment later, from the other end of the cavern, came the sound of churning water tumbling over rocks. It was a low, distant sound at first, then it mounted in volume and fury. In the dim light from the lantern, he could see a rivulet of water racing down the center of the cave. Then the icy water was lapping at his feet, quickly spreading the full width of the cave to become a raging river.

Now the lake was pouring into the cave, and a wall of water was rushing toward them. He took a deep breath and had just reached for Cyd's hand when the water struck. His body was slammed back against the stone, and he lost his footing. He fought to regain it, turned his face, and leaned into the flood. He could feel Cyd's hand clutching at him, and he grabbed it, terrified that she had been torn free of the rock. His face and chest were battered by the water, the air driven from his lungs.

He inhaled a ragged breath that was half air and half water and broke into a fit of violent coughing.

"Help, Dane!"

Somebody was calling for help, but he couldn't make out who it was. He blinked the water out of his eyes and saw Diana's arms stretched out in the yellowish light from the lantern. The sudden deluge had torn Derrick away from the rocks. He was hanging on to the rope, fighting to pull himself back. His body was almost horizontal, the torrent of water dragging it toward the ragged debris wall.

Nordlund fought to free himself, to find a handhold so he could struggle over to the boy. Then Diana had torn loose and was moving hand over hand along the rope, reaching out for Derrick. He clutched frantically at her, and she caught his hand and pulled him to the rope, looping a belt around his waist and the plastic line. It was her own belt—her major tie to safety.

The deluge was starting to slacken, and Nordlund shook the water out of his eyes and tried another breath. Oh, God, thank God—both of them were going to be safe.

Then the debris wall gave way, and the water rushed through the opening down to the lower caverns. Nordlund could see the current tear at Diana's body, and he saw her lose her footing. One hand was wrenched from the rope and then the other. The raging waters tossed her to the surface, where she tried desperately to swim, then scooped her up, tumbling her toward the breached wall at the rear of the cave. She hit the edge of the ruptured wall and her scream cut off in midnote.

A moment later she disappeared, swept away by the racing waters as they plunged into the lower caverns.

Then the level of the water abruptly started dropping, but it was still nearly two feet deep when Nordlund let go of the rope.

"Derrick! Derrick!"

"I'm over here!"

Nordlund spotted him by one end of the debris wall. The belt hadn't held, and he had almost been swept over along with Diana.

"Cyd? Hideo?"

They both checked in, and he hastily fumbled out the wire cutters and cut the rope that bound them. The current was swift but manageable, and he struggled over to where Derrick was still holding on to a rock. "Time to leave, Derrick."

He seized Derrick with one hand and pulled him to the center of the cave, then grabbed Cyd with the other. He struggled against the water toward the gaping hole at the far end, through which poured both water and the gray light of a winter's day. It was the first natural light he had seen in seventy-two hours.

Moments later they were beneath the hole, looking up through the drizzling stream of lake water and pelting sleet. Then he heard somebody shout, and a bosun's chair was being lowered through the opening. Metcalf was riding in it; he jumped into the chill water when it was still only halfway down.

Nordlund splashed forward. "God, Troy—"

"Kiss you later, Dane, we've got to leave right now—the barge is breaking up! Cyd, Hideo, into the chair—Derrick, sit on their laps."

He boosted them in, then looped his arm around part of the canvas chair. "Dane, grab the other side—"

The drizzling stream of water through the hole suddenly became a flood that almost swept them away. Nordlund guessed that part of the hull of the barge had collapsed. He had a glimpse of Cyd, Derrick and Nakamura jammed together in the chair, water cascading over their heads. Then the chair started to rise. He struggled frantically toward it. He missed his hold on the canvas, then lost his footing completely as the water tore at him and started to carry him back into the cavern.

He struck out with both arms, and somebody grabbed his wrist in a death grip; he locked his own hand around the arm above. It was like being pulled through a waterfall the long way. The chill water tore away his shoes and socks, and then he was rising into a gray, cloudy sky with icy sleet drumming against his chest and face. A few feet below him, a small whirlpool had formed over the hole, then started to choke up with broken concrete from the barge. A tug was moving in, its deck covered with rock and gravel and iron grillwork.

Metcalf had thought of everything, even plugging up the hole afterward.

"Hey, Dane!"

He glanced up as the winch swung them toward the deck of another tug. Metcalf was holding on to his wrist with a grip like iron. He was grinning.

"Merry fucking Christmas!"

CHAPTER 48

"You must always use filtered water," Nakamura explained, "and fill it to *there*." He pointed. "For brewing time, add one minute per cup. Temperature is a constant—do not move the dial once you set it."

"And that's all there is to it?" Nordlund asked.

Nakamura smiled. "Not quite. If there is a burnt taste to the coffee, you hit the machine *here*." He struck the front panel with his fist, still smiling. "There is a relay that sometimes sticks." He shrugged. "The penalty of having a reputation is that foreigners think you can do no wrong. Actually your Mr. Coffee does a quite adequate job."

He walked over to the couch and sat down, then sipped at his coffee and frowned. "Strange—but no matter. You have recovered?"

It had been a week since their rescue. He had spent four nights at his own apartment sleeping the sleep of the dead, and the next three at Cyd's, where they had shared everything, including their nightmares.

"Yeah, I'm okay." He said it without enthusiasm, but it would be awhile before he was okay—if he ever was.

"I feel guilty," Nakamura said.

"What about?"

"I am stealing a man of yours."

"I don't understand," Nordlund said politely.

"Your Mr. Metcalf. We hope to bid on the western leg of the project. We are confident we will get it. We believe Mr. Metcalf has the necessary experience, and he has also shown the capacity to grow and the ability to function during an emergency. Rare qualities in one so young."

Nordlund stared at Nakamura, stunned. It had never been

(387

discussed with him, though Nakamura had once hinted . . . it didn't matter what Nakamura hinted.

"He accepted?"

Nakamura nodded. "After some persuasion." He frowned. "You do not seem pleased."

Nordlund's smile was forced. "No, I'm delighted. Troy's a good man, I wish him the very best." For just a moment, he remembered what Kaltmeyer had once said about Troy's loyalty. And then he dismissed it—he really did wish Troy the best, and it wouldn't be sour grapes when he told him so.

"We would have offered it to you," Nakamura said. "But we thought you would want to finish the cut, that you would want to complete what Mr. Kaltmeyer had started."

"Of course," Nordlund said. "You're absolutely right. I couldn't have left right now in any event."

He thought that Nakamura would say something polite and then leave but the little man didn't. He had settled back to nurse his coffee.

"You have not asked us how we persuaded Mr. Metcalf."

There was a trace of a smile playing around Nakamura's lips, and for a moment Nordlund wondered if he was going to rub it in with details of Troy's salary and perks.

"I'm sure your offer was very generous."

Nakamura was grinning now. "I am teasing you. It is unkind of me. There was only one inducement—we convinced him that he would actually be working for you."

Now Nordlund really didn't understand.

"The entire project has long been too expensive for your government alone. After the first of the year, we are scheduled to hold discussions with the Administration. If they are successful—and they will be—the project will come under the joint sponsorship of both governments. I am assured that Nippon Engineering will then assume the assets and debts of Kaltmeyer/DeFolge."

Nakamura stood up and held out his hand. "We would like you as chief engineer—of the entire project." His grin grew broader. "I believe that is an offer you cannot refuse."

(388

Nordlund shook his hand, speechless. Nakamura picked up his hat and coat and walked to the door, then paused.

"Your coffee machine is what you call an orange. I will have the factory send you a new one."

As soon as Nakamura had left, Metcalf slipped in. He glanced around for a moment, his face somber.

Nordlund's own smile faded. "I was going to congratulate you, but you look like you just lost your best friend."

"We both did, Dane. It's not the same around here without Janice."

Nordlund raised his cup of coffee. "Neither of us will ever forget her."

Metcalf sat down. "Hideo told you?"

"Yeah—it couldn't happen to a bigger pain in the ass."

"I try. You hear about Phillips?"

Nordlund looked curious. "Not from Phillips—he never told me anything."

"He was called back to Washington."

"Serves the bastard right."

Metcalf grinned. "Where the hell you been the last week, Dane?—don't tell me. Our boy Steve was interviewed on "20/20," he made this week's cover of *Time,* and I think somebody said he's been offered a book contract."

Nordlund stared. The little snivelling son of a bitch . . .

"You're kidding."

Metcalf shook his head. "Cross my heart. He's Washington's fair-haired boy. He's now special advisor to the president for transportation."

"So what? In a year nobody will remember him."

Metcalf shook his head, confident. "You wanna bet? Phillips has staying power, believe me."

Nordlund yawned. He couldn't get enough sleep these days, though the evenings with Cyd hadn't been very restful in some respects.

"Make yourself some coffee, Troy. Make me some, too." He walked to the sliding doors that opened out onto the balcony and cracked them so some fresh air could get in. It was warm outside, the warmest it had been in a month. The sun had finally come out, heating the air and turning the little islands of snow that remained into heaps of glitter.

He watched the activity on the compound for a moment, then turned back to Metcalf.

"Troy, wasn't there a moment when you wanted to write us off? It was a long shot right from the start, and it just got longer and longer."

"I never even thought of giving up," Metcalf said slowly. "How do you give up on your friends?"

"You used your head in getting us out."

Metcalf smiled. "It wasn't hard. I just kept thinking, 'What would Dane do?' "

"Ah—thanks." He felt embarrassed. "When do you leave?"

"In about a month. Incidentally, I'll be stealing two of your men." Like Nakamura, Metcalf looked uneasy.

"Who?"

"Grimsley and Pinelli." Metcalf shook his head, remembering. "I couldn't live without them. Pinelli is a born high-baller, and without Grimsley, I'd probably get a swelled head."

Once Metcalf had left, Nordlund sank back on the couch, lost in thought. The little Irishman with the gift of gab. Cyd had once told him he could learn a lot from Troy, and she had been right. Maybe not so much in engineering. But in a lot of other ways.

Cyd was gently shaking him. "Time to wake up, Dane. We'll be late for our reservations at Andy's."

He blinked and struggled upright on the couch, trying to shake the sleep out of his eyes.

"How long have I been out?"

"Three hours." She laid her fingers on his lips when he started to protest. "Nobody wanted to bother you. Besides, it was a dull day—and you needed your sleep."

"Anybody call?"

"Nobody important. Except Derrick."

She was dressed in the same dark blue cashmere suit she'd been wearing at Washington National Airport. She looked sensational, and he immediately wondered if he could cut the evening short at Andy's.

"What'd he want?"

"He just wanted to remind you that you've got a date for the Blackhawks game tomorrow." She frowned. "What's going to happen to Derrick? His mother died three years ago, and I understand there are no close relatives."

"He's got an aunt on the North Side, but she's too old to take care of him. I've already talked with her about assuming custody." He hurried into his explanation for why, wondering if she would understand. "It wouldn't be for that long—he's twelve years old now. Six more, and he'll be eighteen and ready to leave home anyway. Go off to college, that sort of thing."

She nodded in approval. "You'll be good for him. And he'll be good for you." She looked down at her hands. "I'm sorry about Diana, I really am."

"What can I say, Cyd? So am I. We were married for four years, but I never really got to know her. Maybe she didn't know herself."

She took a folded sheet of paper from her purse.

"We checked out Beardsley, just to make sure he was alone, that he hadn't teamed up with some organization."

He shivered, remembering the huge bleeding man in the cave below, swinging his battle axe about his head as he lumbered toward them.

Cyd glanced at her notes.

"Arthur and Brad Gentry. Twin brothers; their mother died when they were three, the father was killed in an automobile accident when they were nine. They were raised in an orphanage until they were both eighteen. At nine, it's difficult to find couples willing to adopt children. As twins, they were close, and that made them even closer—I suspect they were lovers. It's poetic, but psychically I suppose you could say they shared the same soul."

She paused a moment, then turned the page.

(391

"They both worked on a tunnel under the East River that DeFolge's first company built. They were at odds with DeFolge management; DeFolge and company were buying old equipment and not maintaining it properly. One Christmas there was a blowout, and Beardsley watched his twin brother drown." She looked up, thoughtful. "It must have been like watching himself drown."

"And Beardsley swore vengeance."

"Apparently. He spent some time in an institution, murdering a doctor when he escaped. He'd sworn to kill the four men he considered most responsible—DeFolge, Kaltmeyer, Leaver, and Orencho."

"He got them all," Nordlund said. Then: "You'd think somebody would have recognized him."

She shook her head. "Not really. He'd put on a lot of weight in twenty years, probably worked at changing his voice, and of course he had changed his name. Most important of all, he was out of context—the blowout had been a long time ago and half-way across the country. And he probably avoided the others as much as possible, working the midnight shift, that sort of thing."

She glanced at her watch. "Up and at 'em. Put on your shoes, and let's get out of here."

He reached for her hand and pulled her down onto the couch.

"What are we going to do about you, Cyd?"

She ran her hands through his hair. "What's your complaint? I'm here when you want me."

"I want you full time. And besides, you're going back to Washington."

"It's not that far away," she said.

He shook his head. "I don't do well on weekend commutes."

"Marriage?" she asked.

"We could try. Derrick would like that."

"When do you need to know?"

He drew her close and kissed her. "Tomorrow morning will be fine."

She pushed him gently away. "I'll think about it. Put on your shoes and get your coat. I'll start the car." At the door,

(392

she stopped to look back. "Odds are fifty-fifty—you've got to convince me."

He watched her as she left, then wriggled into his shoes and picked up his coat, glancing back into an office that now was filled with ghosts. Frank and Diana and Swede and Janice . . .

He shivered and closed the door after him. He had a whole night to make Cyd change her mind.

He grinned. He couldn't lose.